# TATTOO

# TATTOO

## ANTHONY BRITTO

*To Buddy.*

*Best wishes*
*Anthony Britto*
*11-11-97*

ST. MARTIN'S PRESS
NEW YORK

Design by *Bryanna Millis*

Library of Congress Cataloging-in-Publication Data

Britto, Anthony.
    Tattoo / Anthony Britto.
      p.  cm.
    "A Thomas Dunne book."
    ISBN 0-312-15220-5
    I. Title.
PS3552.R4972T38    1997
813'.54—dc21                            96-45540
                                                   CIP

First Edition: June 1997

10  9  8  7  6  5  4  3  2  1

# Acknowledgments

A first book is a Herculean project under any circumstances, particularly when trying to keep up with the demands of a medical practice, and I would like to extend my deepest gratitude to the following people for helping to make this one possible.

I have always loved to write, but it was Brother O'Malley, thirty years ago and on the other side of the world, who first showed me that my words could give pleasure to others. And all the members of the Writers' Club of Whittier, who helped me get out of first gear with the simple question "Where's the plot?" But most of all it was Heather, through whose patience and understanding I had free rein to indulge my fantasies.

Also Jeffrey Heintz, for his technical expertise; Serita Stevens, for her good judgment; and Nickolae Gerstner, without whose encouragement this manuscript might well have ended up in the basement next to my abstract paintings. And finally, Ruth Cavin, who rescued me from an endless cycle of query letters by opening the door.

# TATTOO

I EASED THE ALFA ROMEO CONVERTIBLE through the stream of water pouring down the access ramp into the alley, urged on by the curt message that had logged in on my pager just fifteen minutes earlier. "Call Dr. Varta in ER" was all it said.

It had the desired effect. A call to the emergency room always got my adrenaline pumping. No matter what they said over the phone, I never quite knew what to expect. A plastic surgeon on the emergency panel can be summoned for a variety of problems, and in eight years of taking call I had learned to reserve judgment. Sometimes a thirty-minute time-out to fix a cut on the chin will turn into a five-hour marathon looking for a severed facial nerve. Sometimes a potential all-nighter to replace an amputated finger will have to be aborted because the parts are damaged beyond repair. I would find out what this one was about soon enough.

Right then, I was more concerned about avoiding submerged obstacles, outrunning sucking mud slides, and watching the road ahead for emerging sinkholes. Those jealous Midwesterners, thinking Californians have nothing better to do than bask in the sun and warm sea breezes all year round, have no idea of the immense natural dangers we in Los Angeles face during the rains. What I needed at that moment was one of those bayou river pilots who worked the Mississippi Delta, someone to help me navigate the last hundred yards to the parking lot.

Memorial Hospital was an architectural nightmare. The property meandered southward from an impressive two-story frontage on Greenfield Boulevard, through an irregular hodgepodge of buildings, to the employee lot in back. The original five acres had been bequeathed by a lumber baron in the fifties, an unused parcel next to his mill on the commercial side of town. Additional land had been purchased piecemeal, interspersed among the neighboring warehouses. The physical plant had been added to over the years as funds became available, with wings, extensions, and freestanding clinics placed wherever they would fit. It was a project in a constant state of flux. As soon as one stage of construction was over, another would be conceived. Not just a place of healing, it seemed to play a side role as supporter of the local building industry. Patients would pull into the main entrance, then suddenly slow down, faced by a maze of signs and decisions. Frantically coping with directions scribbled on prescription blanks, they would weave right and left, looking for any available parking space—perhaps wondering if they might make it to their destination still alive.

The three-day rainstorm just made things worse. Debris had washed into the large drainage grates in the pavement, barely big enough to cope with the runoff from these sudden storms. I took a shortcut past Rehab and turned left at the clinics, narrowly avoiding a hesitant Ford sedan with a broken windshield wiper. There were two spaces vacant in the lot next to the emergency room, one marked BLOOD DELIVERIES ONLY and the other CLERGY. Not wishing to tempt fate, I chose the former.

The automatic doors to Emergency swung open as I hurried in. They were as busy as I'd ever seen. All ten cubicles were full, and there were patients waiting on gurneys near the front desk. Paramedics, lab technicians, and nurses scurried to and fro, while patients and their families huddled in groups, fixing every passing white coat with an anxious glare, like hungry diners waiting to be served. If I'd had a cart, I might have done a fair trade selling hot dogs and sodas.

"Hi, Dr. Lloyd. You got here fast!" It was Gail Prystupp, the charge nurse on the evening shift.

"I was in my car when I took the call. What's the crowd for? We giving away freebies today?"

"It's the rain. Does this every time." She came closer and looked me over. "I like your hair long. You should leave it that way."

I flicked the dark curls off my forehead in a self-conscious reflex. "It's just wet. Been a while since I had time for a haircut. What's this case they want me for?"

She shrugged. "A head-on collision down in the warehouse district. Two cars involved. They brought one here and he's pretty bad. He's in the trauma booth now. Dr. Varta's in there with him. He'll fill you in on all the details. All I know is they've called Dr. Bernardo to fix his leg. And you, of course. I have Anna Morales working with you." With that, she shooed me out of her space so she could get on with business.

The trauma booth was the largest cubicle in the emergency room. The heavy curtain around it was meant in part to maintain privacy, but partly also to conceal the cold brutality of the resuscitation process from inquisitive eyes. The sight of a mangled, bloody human figure lying prostrate on a stretcher might have seemed ghoulish enough to the casual onlooker, but even the morbidly curious could grow weak at the knees once we started poking long silvery needles into soft flesh, pushing rubber tubes into every orifice, and generally pounding, pulling, and zapping the chest with electric paddles in order to bring the body back to life.

The curtain was only halfway drawn now, to make room for a portable X-ray machine that stood a few yards from the gurney. Nurse Anna Morales stooped over the patient, working the blood pump with her left hand and adjusting the intravenous tubing with her right. She would watch the viscous liquid drip down into the tubing for a few seconds, then shift her gaze nervously to the blood-pressure monitor on the wall, then back again to the tubing, and her left hand would pump more desperately.

Mike Varta, trauma surgeon and team captain, was leaning against the supply closet, scratching his neck. His blue surgeon's cap fit snugly on the crown of his head, and, with bushy eyebrows drawn together in concentration, the muscles on his forehead stood out in bas-relief.

"Hey!" he said, pushing away from the wall as he saw me coming. "Do we have a tall, dark, and handsome plastic surgeon? Heck. Two out of three ain't bad. Gareth, hope we didn't pull you away from anything important."

I grinned. "I did have a date with Meg Ryan . . . but I canceled. She *was* disappointed."

He smiled back. "No shit. And I suppose your audience with the Pope will have to wait as well."

"Uh-uh. Not even the Pope could give me absolution for what I wanted to do to Meg Ryan. What have we got here?"

"A goddamn mess, Gareth, that's what we got. Paramedics brought him in about a half hour ago. Two cars playing rhino-rocket with each other. As far as we know, our man was sitting in the back without his seat belt and got smacked up against the windshield. They found him with his head on the dashboard and his feet still in the rear, his buddies in the front both dead at the scene. The ones in the other car got taken to St. Elsewhere. They figured this one needed real help and brought him here."

He paused and turned to the monitors. "How's the blood pressure, Anna?"

"Eighty over forty." She interrupted her pumping to adjust the flow of oxygen in the nasal cannula. "It's up a bit now, but we've sent for two more units of blood. I'm worried about his breathing. It seems labored and the oximeter's down to ninety."

"Let's get ready to intubate," Mike said. "And have that chest tube ready!"

He turned to me and scratched the back of his head again. "Something going on in his chest. I can't hear a thing in the left lung. He's got at least one broken rib up there, probably more. We took some portable films and I'm waiting for the results. The left femur's fractured; Gil Bernardo's on his way in to take care of that. Tell me what you want to do with his face. We can get some more films once he's stable."

Mike Varta had the nervous habit of thinking out loud, a quality that made him ideal as the team leader. Nurses and technicians need to be prepared so they know what to do next. But the one thing he left unsaid was the worst prognosis—that the young man could have a hole in his lung from the jagged edge of the broken rib. Or in his heart. He could be drowning in his own blood.

The weight of this knowledge was the rightful domain of the doctor in charge, and Mike bided his time, holding back until he was certain. Leaning against the closet door, he pondered his next move, absentmindedly curling imaginary hairs on the back of his neck. He must have picked up the habit when he was younger. Now, even with the paper surgeon's cap he wore for cover, it was plain that he didn't have a single hair left to curl. The top of his head was as smooth as an egg.

I pulled on a pair of gloves, leaning closer to examine the man on the gurney. I was struck by the acrid stench of half-digested rum. It took a minute to get used to. His short, curly black hair was matted with blood. There was no question that his face was a mess. Dried blood was everywhere. His forehead had been pulled forward from the hairline to expose the cranium, and the left eye was half covered with the bloodied tissue. His lips were torn in several places, and two front teeth were missing. There were smaller cuts and scrapes all over his face and chin. Bits of glass were scattered in the open wounds.

He might have been in his late teens, or just past twenty. Lean and wiry. His chest heaved with each gasp for more oxygen, the ribs pushing outward with the effort. Occasionally, his muscular arms would flex and twitch, as if fighting some invisible demon for his life. The tanned skin on his right shoulder bore a tattoo of a marijuana leaf. His abdomen and groin were covered with a sheet, but the left leg was exposed, swollen and bruised at the thigh, strapped in a box splint.

"How's the belly, Mike? Anything there?"

"Soft as a limp dick."

In this case that was good news—no internal bleeding in the abdomen.

"Dr. Varta, we're down to eighty on the oximeter," Anna declared, her tone sharp with urgency. "Do you want the crash cart?"

Mike pushed away from the closet door. In a sudden, fluid motion he was at the gurney.

"Let's get that chest tube in now."

Anna wheeled the instrument tray over. With smooth, unhurried movements, Mike steadied the left side of the patient's chest and made his cut with the scalpel blade, well away from the heart. The young man's body twitched, and Anna struggled to restrain him. I lent a hand, watching Mike select a shiny steel trocar and ease the tip through his incision, pushing a hole between two of the lower ribs. Quickly, he inserted a large plastic tube into the left pleural space. Dark red blood came gushing out. We watched the digital readout of the oximeter in silence, as the heaving in the patient's chest slowed to normal, and the little red numbers on the face of the machine went up to ninety-eight. Slowly, his pressure crept back to normal.

He was coming back to life.

"X RAY'S BACK," ANNA PROCLAIMED, RE-
turning to her blood pump.

"You keep that up, Anna. And give him one
more unit after that." Mike went over to the desk to
read the films. I followed to look over his shoulder.

"There it is," Mike said. "Three fractured ribs on
the left and the chest full of blood. Cardiac silhouette looks
normal, though, and I don't see any air bubbles. That chest
tube should do the trick."

He returned to the patient's side while I stayed to
read the rest of the films. There were no fractures in the
neck, which meant we could move the patient without worrying about damaging his spinal cord.

"What's in store for him tonight?" a voice behind
me asked.

I turned to see Gil Bernardo, the orthopedic surgeon on call, and briefed him on the events as I knew them.
He glanced at the X ray of the left thigh, clearly showing a
break at midshaft.

"I need to fix his face, Gil," I said, watching for his
reaction. When a critical patient needs more than one surgeon, there is always the question of who goes next. I
thought the face had priority over the broken leg, and I was
hoping I wouldn't have to resort to anything so dreary as
pushing my weight around.

"Sounds as if it will take all night," Gil said. "The

fractured femur can wait until morning. I'll leave him in traction and let you get on with it."

I was relieved. Mike came over to join us and we arranged to get a CAT scan of the head so I would know if there were any broken cranial bones before I started. Gil Bernardo busied himself setting traction to the man's leg, leaving the weights for the nurses to hang later, when the patient was safely upstairs. I rechecked the face and eyes to make sure I hadn't missed any major damage. I had to get used to the smell all over again.

"I guess he's had a few Cuba libres tonight," I remarked to Mike.

"No shit, Gareth. I'd say he's had a few other toxic substances as well. The drug screen is still pending. Did you get a load of his tattoo?"

"The marijuana leaf? Yes. You don't think it's just for show?"

"I don't think he's trying to tell us he's a Democrat, if that's what you mean. I'd say he's inhaled a few times, probably passed one around right before he launched into the windshield. We're not going to know what he has on board until the drug screen gets back. I wonder how Anesthesia will react to putting him under. I guess you're going to want him asleep for this."

The technician arrived to take the patient to the scanner, Gil Bernardo left to dictate his consultation report, and I dialed the scheduling desk at the operating room to see if they were busy. I was in luck. They were just getting started on an appendix but would be done within an hour, nothing pending after that. I briefed them on our case to make sure they'd be ready.

Mike and I grabbed some coffee and headed for the door. "Reminds me," he said, thumping me on the back as we walked toward the lounge. "Do you know what's the last thing that goes through a bug's mind when it smacks up on your windshield?"

"Tell me."

"His asshole!"

I'd been half a block from home when the beeper had gone off. The rain had put me in a lazy mood, and I'd been looking forward to a quiet evening—a bowl of spaghetti alla carbonara, perhaps a glass of Brunello, and a rerun of *Mystery* on public television. I wasn't even on first call. But when they put me through to the emergency room, and Mike had asked if I was available, there was only one thing I could say.

I liked working with Mike Varta. Mike and I looked out for each other. He gave me work when he could, and I returned the favor. After eight years in private practice as a plastic surgeon, I was still running to the emergency room two or three times a week—a little short on my long-range goal for hitting the big time. I had hoped to be able to scale back on emergencies and book a lot of face-lifts and nose jobs, the lifeblood of a lucrative practice, thereby returning some order and a few riches to my life. But it turned out Greenfield wasn't that kind of place.

The monied old guard in our town were more preoccupied with escaping the clutches of the Grim Reaper than with avoiding the kneading fingers of Father Time. They would fuss and pore over serum cholesterol levels, worry about arterial and bowel blockages, and throw themselves down on my surgical table with reckless abandon for a suspicious freckle or a malignant, hair-bearing mole, whereas nips and tucks were relegated to the Beverly Hills crowd, few of whom graced the quiet streets of Greenfield. Exploding silicone breast implants might have been a hot topic at backyard barbecues, but such concepts as liposculpture and the laser-assisted buttock lift were better left to wild guests on *Geraldo*, *Oprah*, or *Jerry Springer*, being considered vaguely tribal rituals, on a par with scarification or the piercing of body parts for ornament. For the most part, I contented myself with the reconstructive side of plastic surgery, the more accepted notion of "fixing up poor old Lloyd/Loretta, after his/her terrible misfortune/bloody stupidity." I was busy enough, in this unassuming way, and was glad of it. Times had changed, and some of my surgical colleagues weren't doing as well.

Of course, there were some who were making fortunes riding high on the current wave of interest in cosmetic surgery. Jack Ehrenberger, for instance. That is, until someone shot him.

In spite of the crime all around me, I had never before personally known anybody who was shot. I had witnessed the results of violence firsthand, treated victims of it in the emergency room. I had heard stories that could make your hair curl, seen strong men cry out in pain, and watched young lovers fall apart, their dreams shattered by the cruelty of a moment's rage. All these things happened to other people. As a physician, I was insulated from fear, keeping its cold hand away from my heart.

All that had changed the past Monday. Somebody had shot Jack Ehrenberger. Just as he was leaving his safe little office and getting into his safe little car, heading, no doubt, for his safe little fortress, somebody mowed him down. Right there on the pavement. I had found out on the eleven o'clock news.

My cocoon had collapsed that day. Layers of insulation had peeled away, and I had plummeted to earth, cradle and all. I was no longer an outsider, but an interested party to a murder. What haunted me was not that I'd known and worked with Jack, patted him on the back, sat down in the comfort of his inner office and sipped scotch with him. It was Elaine.

Elaine was Jack's wife. And, until recently, my lover. That was all. Nothing more significant than that. Once it was over, I could see it clearly. For about six months we met once a week . . . to make love and indulge in each other's company. An affair. As far as I knew, we had done a good job of keeping it a secret. Nobody knew for sure, although my friend Peter Heering probably suspected. Actually, I was glad it was over. I felt as though I could sweep it under the rug and pretend it never happened. It was something I wasn't especially proud of.

Now that Jack had been killed, all that would change. Somebody would comb through his past looking for likely suspects. My tryst with Elaine was bound to be the first place they'd look. Things were going to get messy, and I hated that. Unless they figured he was another victim of gang violence and closed the case. It could happen.

For the rest of the week I had rooted through columns of newsprint, frantically switching stations on the car radio by day, glueing myself to the television by night, eager to hear more about the crime. But for all I had learned, nothing satisfied. On Wednesday there was a quotation from Detective Kenneth Akimoro of the Beverly Hills Police Department. An investigation was under way, but they had no leads, either to motive or to the identity of the killer. The detective hadn't ruled out the possibility that the drive-by shooting was a gang initiation, with Ehrenberger being a "purely random victim."

The "why" didn't bother me, it was the "who" that I was worried about. Not even so much "who did it," but "whom did they suspect." Anybody but me, I hoped. I was just beginning to hit my stride after ten years in Greenfield, and at this stage of my career I couldn't afford to be dragged into anything as sordid as a murder investigation.

It had been a long road. I had finished medical school back home in Cardiff, Wales, with a respectable but not outstanding record. Then my father died, the modicum of influence he wielded went with him, and I lost all hope of gaining a coveted plastic surgery training post. I didn't want to stay in Cardiff anymore. I wanted to hide, to lose my memories somewhere far away from the coal dust. I answered an ad in the *Lancet*, the British medical journal, and went to Rome for six months to do medical research.

It was in Rome that I met my wife, Rafaella: lean, tanned body, hazel eyes, and a smile as fresh and promising as a dish of gelato smothered in almond liqueur. She was intoxicating at first, although as time passed she had taken on more of the qualities of a hangover. I extended my contract another six months, basking in the warm glow of the Italian sun and the power of passion, but it also became apparent that without a degree in a foreign land my opportunities were limited. They were just using me for my English, and when the project was over I was out of a job.

The rewards of my first move were still fresh in my mind; the lessons learned made it easier to pick up roots again. I applied for immigration to the USA, sponsored by my father's younger brother, Uncle David. In order for Rafaella to accompany me, we were married in a quick ceremony at the British consulate. We arrived in Los Angeles on New Year's Eve. It was a glorious sunny day.

With a lot of persistence and a little bit of luck, I finally found the position I was looking for. Someone at the University of Southern California's Department of Plastic Surgery had decided that my application sparkled enough to catch his attention. Later, we settled in Greenfield, some twenty miles from the heart of downtown. I'd been trying to carve a niche for myself in private practice ever since.

Mike Varta and I had that in common. Mike had trained in Mexico, after applying to fourteen medical schools across the United States without any luck. We had both started at Greenfield Memorial Hospital about the same time, casting ourselves into the sea of medicine like two ships without navigators. We knew how to practice the healing arts but understood nothing of the business of health care. We had thought it would be plain sailing, and nothing was further from the truth.

In California, specialists in private practice were becoming anachronisms. Managed care had taken over, and their admitted goal was to slash the cost of insurance by limiting the number of consultants a patient could see.

They were cutting down on reimbursement, denying services that were formerly allowed. They were streamlining the cost of medical care. In the new order of medicine the general practitioner ruled, and specialists were fighting for insured patients, stabbing one another in the back for a place in the breadline. In order to stay in the game, we had to get our names on as many insurance panels as possible. In order to do that, we had to agree to cut our prices to whatever lowball bid they waved under our noses. Many of my colleagues had fled, picked up and moved to the Midwest or the South, where things were rumored to be easier. I had come close to it myself.

It was the divorce that stopped me. Actually, it was Jillian and Emma. My two daughters were transforming before my eyes, growing up much too fast. Watching this change, sharing their growth, trying to give them some direction from lessons of my past was not a chore. It was one of my greatest pleasures. I could not bear to move away and leave it all to Rafaella.

And so I stayed and coped with health maintenance organizations, and gatekeepers, and presurgical authorization forms. There was something else that made it all worthwhile—the force of the scalpel and the suture. The power to cure. This was the most exhilarating, the most absorbing, and the most rewarding thrill of all. When face-to-face with a patient who needs your help, only one thing fills the mind—the complexity of the job at hand, and the best way to solve it. Every earthly distraction fades away, and the only problems are the ones that stand in the way of the result. It is only later, sitting in your office after hours with your ledger, trying to meet payroll, faced with a pile of bills laying on your desk, that you start to think about the money. How much is your time worth?

"What's the deal on this guy, Mike?" I asked, sitting in front of the lounge television. "He have any identification on him?"

"Tons. He had a driver's license and a bunch of credit cards. Even an insurance card."

"Really? That's a switch. I didn't think he'd be insured."

"Don't get your hopes up, Gareth. I didn't say he was insured. All the ID was in someone else's name—probably stolen. We could tell it wasn't his from the photo on the driver's license."

"Nothing in his own name?"

"There was a Social Security card with a second name, Juan Rodriguez or something like that. But even those can be faked, so we don't have much to go by. Far as we know, he's a John Doe."

"No family come to claim him? No one buzzing around with questions?"

"Nope. No one as yet. And the other two guys in the car aren't talking." He laughed at his own joke. "I think the sheriff's working on it, though. They're trying to trace the plates."

We got word that the CAT scan was ready, and it was time to get back to work. I examined the special films carefully but didn't see any fractures or signs of internal bleeding. After three units of transfused blood, the patient had stabilized. The chest-tube drainage slowed to a trickle, and his blood pressure and breathing were now normal. Mike cleared him for surgery, and we wheeled the patient into the operating room about thirty minutes later. Mike wouldn't be needed for the repair I was planning, but he agreed to wait around in case something in the chest went sour.

Just as I suspected, Al Crowe from Anesthesia was less than thrilled to see us.

"Not another one with a full stomach. And I thought I was done after that appendix. You want me to load him up with an antibiotic?"

"Already done, Al," I said.

"And loaded up with everything else as well. Take a

look at his drug screen. If I was selling half that stuff, I wouldn't need to pass gas for a living."

"But you're a dedicated gas-passer, Al."

He ignored my comment. "Good thing he's young and strong as a bull. My God, he stinks. Couldn't you find someone better-looking for this hour of the night? Jeez, how in hell am I supposed to put a tube down his throat with that blinding stench?"

"I'm the one who has to look down his mouth for the surgery, Al. You can sit back and read your magazine. What does the centerfold look like this month?"

"She's a sizzler." He held up the magazine for our inspection. "You want me to tape her up here for inspiration?"

"Better not. I might get too inspired and do a breast implant instead."

The operation went without a hitch. I removed several glass splinters from the patient's face and cleaned him up, sewing the pieces back where they belonged. It took two hours. Halfway through, I sent word to Mike that everything was fine and he was no longer needed.

With the patient safely in recovery, I finished the paperwork and returned to the dressing room. I changed back to my street clothes in front of the mirror, taking my time. I was proud of my permanent Southern California tan, but the sun had its drawbacks. Fortunately, I noticed no new spider veins, moles, or signs of basal cell carcinoma. I tried to put out of mind that in less than two weeks I'd turn forty.

My beeper went off. There was a phone by the lockers.

"We have your wife on the line, sir. She'd like to talk to you."

Two years divorced, and they were still calling her my wife. Maybe they had a new operator, or was Rafaella still introducing herself that way?

"Ex-wife," I hissed.

"Pardon, sir?"

"She's my ex-wife."

"Oh. I'm sorry, sir. Do you want me to say you're unavailable?"

"No. Just put her through. . . . Rafaella?"

There was a pause.

"Gareth. Gareth, it's me, Elaine."

"Elaine!" Damn! Much too soon for us to be talking. It was only Monday that her husband had been murdered.

"You were expecting Rafaella? I told them I was your wife. I know they log these calls and I don't want anybody to know we spoke tonight."

"Elaine, you shouldn't have called. I thought at least you'd wait a couple of weeks. Jesus, you know they must be investigating." Was she out of her mind?

"Gareth, I have to speak to you."

"Look, Elaine, I'm really sorry about Jack."

"Why haven't you tried to reach me? Don't say you're that paranoid."

"Yeah? Well, I am."

"Gareth, we have to talk."

"Why? This doesn't change anything."

"You don't know what they've been asking me. I have to see you, Gareth. Can we meet somewhere?"

"What? They've been questioning you? This is not a good idea, Elaine."

"Don't give me a hard time. How about Sunday? Our restaurant?"

"I don't think so, Elaine." I could see her sitting by the phone, coolly sipping a chardonnay and planning our next date, only three days after someone had blown her husband away.

"Seven o'clock. Say you'll be there."

"It's not going to look good." Why hadn't I just said no? She never took it for an answer, anyway.

"Come on, Gareth. Say it. Please! You'll be there?"

"I'll be there." I hated myself.

"Good. Seven on Sunday."

She hung up. I didn't think it was good at all, but I had three days to call her back and cancel. I would have to make a few inquiries, see how the wind was blowing.

On the way back to my car I had to pass through Emergency. Things had slowed somewhat, the pace less frantic, and three gurneys were actually empty.

"How'd it go, Dr. Lloyd?"

I turned to see Gail Prystupp, clipboard under her arm.

"Fine, Gail. He's in recovery now. He'll be ready for Dr. Bernardo in the morning."

"There's a cop here who wants to talk to you," she said. "I didn't know you were finished. I was about to call surgery when you walked by."

A cop. They certainly worked fast. Did they have my exchange tapped? I had only just gotten off the line to Elaine.

With my pulse racing, I followed Gail to the front desk, where a young police officer was talking to the desk clerk. He had friendly blue eyes and a broad smile, and introduced himself as Officer Hank Reinholdt from the local precinct.

"Doctor, are you taking care of the perpetrator they brought in at five-forty?" he asked. "The one from Chestnut and West Lane?"

I relaxed. "I'm not sure about a perpetrator. I've just finished operating on an accident victim."

"And you're the attending physician?"

"One of them. Dr. Mike Varta is the trauma surgeon in charge. And Dr. Gil Bernardo is the orthopedist."

"What's his condition, Doctor?"

"Fair but stable, I suppose. Have you found out who he is yet? Any family?"

"We don't know that, but the car was stolen. When will we be able to talk to him?"

"He'll be out of the recovery room in about an hour. I'm not sure how soon he'll be ready to talk, though; he was pretty drunk. Blood alcohol point one eight. I might need to designate a driver just for inhaling his fumes."

The officer smiled. "You've no objection to me talking to him, then."

"None. He'll be in intensive care all night. You can check with the nurses. They'll let you know as soon as he's coherent."

"What about his face? I understand he's pretty banged up."

"He was. I've got him wrapped."

"If you don't mind, Doc, how soon can the bandages be removed? We'd like to ID him."

"How urgent is it?"

"We think he's a known drug dealer. If he's our man, there's a warrant out for his arrest. We need to make a photo identification."

"I see. The nurses can take his bandages off anytime you're ready. I just need to call and let them know that I don't mind."

"Would you do that, Dr. Lloyd?"

"Sure."

I dialed the ICU and made the arrangements.

"Is he recognizable?" Officer Reinholdt persisted. "I mean, he's not going to look like some Frankenstein or anything, is he?"

"Not that bad, just swollen and a little bruised. There are stitches all over his forehead, but you can still make out the features. What I mean is, people who are familiar with him should have no trouble, but if you're working from a photograph, you may need a nice, clear shot."

"Well, thank you, Doctor. We sure appreciate your help."

I headed for the automatic doors.

"Just one more thing, Dr. Lloyd," he said. "Is he in any condition to leave tonight?"

"You want to transfer him out?"

"I'm talking break out . . . escape."

"Oh! I doubt it. He's got a chest tube and a broken femur. They'd have to disconnect him from the suction and wheel him out in a gurney. There's no way he could just walk out of here."

"Right. That's what I wanted to hear. Thanks again, Doc."

When I reached my car there was a card on the windshield, soggy with rain but the print still visible:

*This is a warning. You are illegally parked. Your vehicle number has been placed on file. If you are in violation again, your car will be ticketed and towed.*

WHEN I GOT HOME IT WAS ALMOST ELEVEN and I didn't feel much like cooking. I zapped a frozen pizza and turned on the television, just in time for the news. I poured a shot of Laphroaig into a snifter and settled down on the sofa to watch, scooping mouthfuls of soggy dough smothered in tomato sauce, wishing I'd taken the time to use the oven instead of the microwave. Thank heaven for the scotch.

They started with the recent rainstorm that had paralyzed the city, snarling traffic and causing mud slides everywhere. There were several live stories from reporters on the scene, all decked out in the latest rain gear—yellow oil slickers, and khaki trench coats fresh off the rack from Abercrombie & Fitch—looking like mannequins in the glare of the videocam lights. There were interviews with motorists on how it felt to be stuck in the mud. I longed for the entertaining break of a commercial.

I held the glass up to my nose and inhaled. I took a sip . . . switched channels. Another little girl missing, went for a walk and never came back. Police were searching a nearby park. I shuddered . . . switched channels again. Michael Jackson was making history once more—doing something or other to his skin. I didn't wait to find out. I switched back to more coverage of rain and turned the sound down. Sometimes watching the news was like reading headlines in the glossy scandal rags while waiting in line at the supermarket. If I'd been caught doing that, I might have been ashamed. I remembered the comprehensive nightly coverage they had back in Italy.

"*Ècco*, Luigi, this is what we in America call news."

They were elegant, those two newscasters in the little glass window, he wearing Hickey-Freeman, and she in Donna Karan. And so eloquent, tossing little anecdotes into the airwaves, like a couple of performing seals.

"Here's another little story we heard today."

Together they probably made a million dollars a year. Didn't they have some sort of obligation to the public?

I raised the snifter again, rolled the golden liquor around my tongue, studying the peat and savoring the malt before letting it slip smoothly down. I thought of Jack Ehrenberger, who had broken out a bottle of Johnny Walker Blue the last time I'd seen him. I wondered if he was thirsty now.

Jack didn't wear Hickey-Freeman; he was Armani to the core. It was roughly two months ago when I had visited him, after the feature article in *Los Angeles* magazine. I had gone with Peter Heering. Peter was an associate professor of plastic surgery at University Hospital and a close friend of mine over the years. We had both been intrigued by the magazine photographs of Jack's new setup and had decided to see for ourselves, pretending we were there to discuss some surgical technique.

It had turned out we didn't need an excuse. Jack was happy to show it off. He had choreographed us through the suite with practiced pride, beaming as he led the way from room to room, pointing out every architectural detail and nuance, taking two steps for every one of ours. Peter and I were waltzed from lobby to storage, through five thousand square feet of Louis XV reproductions—Jack's little "palace of beauty." This was not like any medical office I'd seen, more like some high roller's suite at Caesars Palace: green, white, and black marble from Italy, chintz and lace everywhere you looked. I was awed, struck by the heresy of all that opulence and at the same time by the inspiration of his vision.

For an instant, as he stood caught in freeze-frame against the background of his own creation, I had a glimpse of Jack through Elaine's eyes. He had looked almost handsome, his chest puffed out, strutting around like a bantam cock on a victory walk, the shimmering green silk fabric of his Armani suit rolling off his shoulders and down his back, glistening in the subdued halogen lighting like so much well-preened plumage. This had to be it, I imagined, the reason she couldn't bring herself to leave, the reason she kept going back to him, as if shackled by some invisible bungee cord. It had to be more than just money.

No question, Jack could make money better than anybody else I knew. Green was his favorite color. His overhead must have been fifty thousand a month. Elaine probably cost him just as much again, with her taste in jewelry, fine clothes, and the trips to Paris. That was a lot of cash for one surgeon to pull in a year. Most of it had come from the movie trade. Jack had started out doing implants for the hookers on Sunset and worked his way up from there. He got his lucky break when one of his soap opera queens mentioned his name on a daytime talk show. He had never looked back. By the time the article came out in *Los Angeles* magazine, he had made a reputation as the slickest salesman in the annals of surgery. Whoring his wares from his high-priced penthouse office, he would book two procedures for every patient who walked in: the one they came to ask about, and the extra one he talked them into. His ads in the glossies were polished and glib. If there was some new gimmick buzzing around the daytime-TV circuit, Jack would enroll in a weekend course and proclaim himself an expert by the end of the month.

He was good with his hands, I had to admit. You don't get as far as he did on hot air alone. And he had done us all a favor, in a way. His hype had created a market for our services, and the demand helped increase business for the lot of us. It had been no surprise that most of my colleagues talked about him with disdain behind his back, all the while trying to emulate him.

But who would try to kill him? Who could hate him so much to take him down in his own parking lot? I wondered if Jack believed in the hereafter. I remembered the joke he told Peter and me back in his office that day, about a lawyer and the Pope getting to heaven at the same time. Jack had loved lawyer jokes—he'd been sued enough times.

Suddenly I put the glass down. The TV had my full attention. There it was, a photograph of Jack in the background. I turned the sound up.

"Funeral services for Dr. Jack Ehrenberger, plastic surgeon to the stars, will be held tomorrow afternoon. Ehrenberger was killed Monday outside his Wilshire Boulevard office."

The photograph was of a good-looking man in his forties with thick dark hair. It was his standard publicity shot, the same one he had used in all his brochures and press releases for the past ten years. A more recent one might have shown the hair a shade grayer and thinner, the jaw a little slacker, and the rings under his eyelids more pronounced. That was how I remembered him.

"Police are still interviewing witnesses, but so far no arrests have been made. And now we take you to Beverly Hills, where our reporter has some comments from the local businessmen."

They cut to a coffee shop, where a man in a T-shirt was smiling at a microphone thrust under his nose.

"How does it feel to have something like this happen right here in your own neighborhood?" a voice asked.

"Well," the man replied, carefully selecting the words he would relay to several million viewers. "It's, like, really scary, you know."

I turned the set off, hoping for their sake that war hadn't broken out somewhere in the world.

Sliding the phone closer, I dialed Peter Heering's number. Peter was close to the political pulse of the Los Angeles Society of Plastic Surgeons, and I was close enough to Peter that I could count on him to tell me if there were any palpitations circulating through the community, especially in the form of rumors about me. Besides, the cemetery was unfamiliar, and I needed directions to the funeral.

I knew Peter would be awake, but I had the uneasy feeling I should have called in the afternoon, when he was in the office and alone. My luck being what it was, Cindy answered the phone.

"Hello, Gareth," she started out, in that cooing tone I knew too well. She had something to say, and I knew I wouldn't be talking to Peter until she was through. Worse, she'd be listening to every response he made to me.

"You coming to Jack's funeral tomorrow?" she asked sweetly.

"I don't know. It's going to rain, and I haven't made up my mind."

"Well, you should, Gareth. Everybody from the university will be there, and they'll expect you there, too."

"I was hoping they wouldn't."

"Well, they will. He was a plastic surgeon after all, and we have to stick together and show support. Anyway, there may be some TV coverage, and I'm sure you can use the publicity. Don't you want your patients to see you on the news?"

"You know me better than that, Cindy."

"I don't understand you, Gareth. I've heard all your arguments against publicity, but you can't go on thinking that way forever. When you're practicing out in Greenfield, you need all the help you can get. I know about your problem with cash flow. Rafaella tells me the alimony and child support checks are coming later and later."

She could be as subtle as a hippopotamus.

"Cindy, can I talk to Peter now?"

"I'm sorry, Gareth, but you know I'm only thinking of those two lovely girls of yours."

"Thank you, Cindy. I'm sure it has nothing to do with Rafaella."

"No, it doesn't. I'll get Peter for you. *Peter!*" she yelled down the other end. "Peter, it's Gareth Lloyd on the phone."

There was a pause. "He'll be here in a minute, Gareth. He's in the kitchen. Anyway, do you know I was there when it happened?"

"When what happened?" I took another sip and considered switching on David Letterman, turning the volume up so she could hear it back in Westwood.

"When Jack was shot. It was the most horrible thing. Rafaella and I were sitting in that new outdoor café across from his office building . . . you know, the one that just opened next to the nursery. I was raving about this new pasta dish. Oh, it was fabulous—these weird mushrooms, and sun-dried tomatoes, and just the right amount of garlic."

"You were with Rafaella?"

"We always have dinner together Monday nights. Anyway, the waiter, he was sort of young and muscular, real nice-looking. He was standing there asking us how we liked the pasta, really getting into it with Rafaella."

An involuntary muscle somewhere in the back of my neck twitched at this news.

"I started to look across the street and I saw a man pointing a gun out of his car window. I was so shocked. It was a long, black, ugly thing."

"You saw the killer?" She had my attention now.

"He was right there in front of me in this little blue car."

I was fairly on the edge of my seat. "Did you tell anybody?"

"Sure. I gave a statement to the police. I was their star witness."

Their star witness! I couldn't believe it. Here I was, looking to the media for more news, and Cindy had been right there on the corner with Rafaella. I felt a surge of relief. Their testimony would get me off the hook. Why hadn't Rafaella called me about it? Surely she would want to brag a little.

"I haven't heard a word of this from Rafaella."

"Oh no?" Cindy needled the question down the phone, implying surprise that I didn't chat with my ex-wife more frequently. "Well, she was a little mad that she missed the killer. She was too busy talking to the waiter."

"I'll bet. So what kind of man was he?"

"The waiter? He had a nice tan, long hair—"

"No, not the waiter . . . the killer."

"Oh, him. Well, I can't exactly describe his face. He had this hat drawn down low, like that Aussie hat you bought. You know, the one we kept teasing you about."

"Was he white? Was he a gangbanger? You can tell me more than that, Cindy."

"He was white, I think."

"You think? You saw him, didn't you? Was he a kid? Did he look like a hit man? Maybe he looked like an angry patient." I smiled to myself.

"Gareth, you don't believe me, do you? I can tell you're making fun of me. Well, I'd know him if I saw him again. I'd remember his nose."

"His nose! What was that like?"

"Straight, with a little round tip. Something like yours."

"Thanks. I suppose you told that to the police."

"Everything. It took over an hour. And they believed every word."

I could see it now, the police composite of the killer, and all they had on the paper was my hat and my nose. "What else did you see?"

"Well, I looked over to the parking lot, where someone was screaming, and I saw Jack's Rolls-Royce. You know, I've always wondered what it's like to ride in one of those, they seem so . . . so decadent. Jack was standing with the door open, about to get in. I said to Rafaella, 'It's Jack Ehrenberger, the plastic surgeon. I think he's been shot.' As she turned around he started to collapse. He fell against the seat, then rolled down to the pavement. It was horrible. I could see the blood starting to come out of him. I mean, on his suit it looked like wet stains, but on his white shirt it was red."

"Hello, Gareth," Peter's voice came on the line. "You coming tomorrow?"

"Hi, Peter. I suppose I ought to."

"You do what you think best, Gareth."

"Can you give me directions?"

"Well, I'll say good night," Cindy's voice interrupted. "See you tomorrow, Gareth."

It was a command. I heard a click, but Peter remained on his line to give me the directions. When he was done, I asked if Cindy was still listening.

"She's joined me in the kitchen."

"Can she hear my questions?"

There was a pause. "No."

"Peter, have there been any rumors about Jack's death?"

"There's lots of speculation. I'll tell you about it tomorrow."

"Peter, are they saying anything about me and Elaine?"

"Not that I've heard."

"And you'd tell me if you heard, wouldn't you, buddy?"

He didn't answer directly. "Is there something I should know?"

"You know how people talk. Don't believe all the gossip you hear. I just want to know what I'll be facing if I show up tomorrow."

"I don't have a clue. The only way you'll find out is to show up."

"Thanks, Peter. That's a great help. I guess I'll see you tomorrow."

I hung up and lifted the glass back to my lips.

MY TOES WERE DAMP, THE LEATHER around the soles of my thin Italian loafers soaked through. I was standing on a small grassy mound some twenty yards from the gravesite, watching the funeral proceedings. Peter Heering was on my left, his arms around Cindy's waist.

The rain was relentless, and little puddles were scattered around the uneven ground, some hidden under a thick carpet of new grass. A crowd of about four hundred mourners were spread in clusters around us, standing on the drier patches as much as they could, and shifting slowly as the puddles spread. The subdued black and white tones of their clothing contrasted sharply with the gaudy umbrellas and raincoats, the whole canvas of colors tied together with a backdrop of lush, wet green.

A rabbi was droning on in prayer, but I couldn't see him over the umbrellas and could hardly hear him over the rain. I picked out a few surgeons I hadn't seen in months and a few more I hadn't seen in years. Cindy whispered that she recognized a couple of soap opera stars and thought they were Jack's patients. There were only two camera crews. Every now and then one would pan over the crowd, but for the most part their interest was centered on the widow.

Mine was, too. I had chosen our vantage point deliberately. There was a gap ahead where a deep pool of water threatened to float the socks off anyone who strayed into our line of sight, and I had a clear view of Elaine standing at the grave. She stood tall, head erect, five feet six inches of unruffled pride. She seemed to be absorbed in something, perhaps the rabbi's words, paying no attention to the distractions of the camera crews or the weather. She resembled less a woman in mourning than one at peace with herself, as if any rumor aimed at her would simply bounce back, reflecting more shame on the person who dared doubt her grief than on its intended target. Her chestnut hair was held snugly in back with a black velvet bow, and the simple black dress she wore showed her slender figure to full advantage. Even her umbrella did not detract from the elegance. Around her neck glistened a line of white pearls. I pulled my umbrella low, to cover my face. I bent my head to look at my wet shoes and felt my socks squelch.

I didn't like funerals. In all the years through medical school, residency, and private practice, death was no stranger. But I shied away from funerals, especially after the last one.

I remembered it now with a chill, as the water soaked through to my toes on the rain-drenched mound. Seventeen years ago, in Cardiff, Wales, on the other side of the world. I could still feel those cold north winds blowing as if it were yesterday, gusting so hard we had to tie the wreaths down. The wind had cut like sharp ice on my face, burning my cheeks, while I stood and watched them lower my giant of a father into the smallest hole in all of South Wales. A father so much larger than life that I hardly had a chance to know him.

My father was big in many ways, but the ones I remembered most were not physical. He knew what he wanted from life, he knew what was good for his family, and he never wavered or changed his mind about anything. I couldn't argue with him; he wouldn't hear of it. He never conversed, he lectured. He had a panoramic vision of the future, but he never took the time with me to paint it clearly, and when he died it was as if the road had suddenly faded away.

I remembered the image of a gray Welsh sky as I watched the sheen on the polished mahogany box become slowly clouded with lumps of soil. I remembered the collieries with their black coal dust, which got him in the end.

I was suddenly aware that the rabbi had stopped, the casket had been lowered, and a low rumble of movement had taken the crowd. People were getting ready to pay their last respects and throw clumps of dirt on Jack's coffin. Actually it was mud, and there was nothing new in that. People were doing it to Jack while he was still alive.

Peter said something over the sound of the rain.

"I'm sorry, Peter. I didn't catch that."

"It's not important." He shook his head. "I was just remarking about Jed Neifosh. You remember him?"

"No. Who's Jed Neifosh?"

"He was a plastic surgeon in Houston, on the board with me three years ago. This funeral reminded me of him."

"I don't pay much attention to who's on the board. Why does this remind you of him?"

"Oh, similar story, in a way. Poor bastard was shot one evening while he and his wife were waiting in line at a movie theater. Happened last year, maybe six months back. It was a really brazen killing, more like an assassination. It made all the Texas papers. They never did catch the guy. There was a rumor it was some kind of underworld connection, but I had my doubts. He didn't seem that deep. Sort of a nice guy, really."

"Always happens to the nice guys," I remarked. "Except in *this* case," I added, sotto voce.

Peter gave me a hard look. The crowd began to disperse. I stepped back to get out of the way and almost trod on the toes of a young woman. I had noticed her before, the way any man notices an attractive blonde nearby, but I had forgotten she was there. She sidestepped quickly to avoid me, and the leather knapsack she was carrying fell to the ground. I muttered an apology and bent down to pick it up.

"Excuse me," she said. "I'm sorry, I guess I was standing too close behind you."

"Entirely my fault." I smiled and handed her the bag.

She returned the smile with a wonderful pair of full lips: not too wide, not too thin. I was mesmerized by hazel eyes, tinted green. She had a pretty face, vibrant, mysterious, with a straight, proud nose, framed by thick blond hair combed back down to her collar.

"Are you . . . planning to let go?" she asked, looking down and laughing.

I followed her gaze. A ring on her outstretched hand caught my eye. It was unusual, a silver skull and crossbones with two glistening emerald eyes. Appropriate for a funeral, although she probably wore it all the time.

"I'm so sorry." I released my grip on the knapsack. "I can't think what . . . "

But she was gone.

"Will you be going up to the house with the family?" Peter was asking me.

"No," I said, looking at the crowds gathering around Elaine. "I think I'll head home, beat the traffic."

"Same here. Cindy and I are going to the theater tonight. I'd better go up and pay my respects to the widow first. You coming?"

"I don't think so, Peter. I'm not up to it."

He looked at me sympathetically. "Well, good-bye, then, Gareth. And don't be a stranger. We'll have you over for dinner sometime soon. Promise."

Not likely, I thought. Not for another setup with one of Cindy's friends. My feelings toward Peter's wife had polarized since my divorce, perhaps because she was still in thick with Rafaella. The few evenings we had spent together were painfully polite and stilted, and she kept inviting one or another of her most boring single friends. I wondered if they had been selected by Rafaella herself; it was as if they were both getting back at me, and I wondered if they would gab to each other about it on the phone all the next morning.

I made my good-byes and headed for the parking lot.

Saturday morning the weatherman promised a beautiful day. I was up at six. Not that it was my habit; to me, six in the morning might as well have been the middle of the night, especially on a Saturday. But I had to drive my older daughter to San Juan Capistrano.

Jillian was thirteen, and in eighth grade. Next year she would be ready for high school. My younger one, Emma, was only ten, still safely tucked in childhood, but Jillian had reached the age at which hormones were beginning to rage, and mind and body were being transformed into a discordant, rebellious entity—one that Rafaella found too difficult to handle. Had I lived with them, I would have had enough trouble controlling her myself. We had decided she'd be better off in a boarding school.

I discussed it with her first, of course. I told Jillian that she might be safer in a more peaceful, countrified setting. She disagreed, arguing that although teenage violence in some of our neighboring cities was escalating, Greenfield wasn't exactly a hotbed of gang warfare. I tried suggesting that it would do her good to mingle with a more affluent class of people. This was not well received at all. Jillian was quite happy in her present circle of friends, thank you, and she had no desire to be pitched into a den of snobs. Finally, I reminded her that the local schools were sadly overburdened, understaffed, and mired in mediocrity, and could hardly be expected to adequately educate anyone, except in football, cheerleading, and other rites of passage. I considered this the clincher, although it met with mixed reaction.

One of the first steps to admission was to take the SSAT, offered conveniently on-site at the school we preferred: the Acoma School in San Juan Capistrano, about an hour and a half away. We were due there promptly at eight-thirty.

I pulled up at Rafaella's doorstep at six-thirty. I should say my old doorstep. She got the house, of course.

After three days of rain I was looking forward to the drive down the coast road and had dropped the ragtop on the Alfa in anticipation.

"No way, Dad. I'm not going to arrive for the test with my hair all over the place."

Like mother, like daughter. Never argue with a woman when she's talking about her hair.

We put the top back up and headed south to the Santa Ana freeway. There wasn't much traffic at that hour on Saturday, and we made good time.

"What if I don't do well, Dad?" Jillian broke the silence.

I told her not to worry, we would still love her anyway, no matter how she did. I reassured her that the test didn't count for everything; her grades and past record were good and would bear equal weight.

"Did you go over the mock test last night?"

"Yeah, Dad. That was easy. These questions will be different."

"I know that. But at least you got used to the format." I tried to give her a few tips on how to deal with multiple-choice exams, casting back years to my own experience. She finally settled down to listen to her favorite radio program.

My mind stayed with my own thoughts for a while as I kept a steady pace in the moderate traffic. The air was clear after the rain, the sun already high in the east, threatening to burn off the few remaining cumulus clouds over the hills. It looked as if the day would turn out just as the weatherman had promised.

My schedule was open, with no patients to see in the hospital that morning. The John Doe from two nights ago was safely tucked away in the jail ward at University Hospital, transferred to the jurisdiction of the Los Angeles Police Department. As Mike Varta put it, after I sewed up his face he had passed his screen test and they wanted him for a starring role in the county lockup. He turned out to be one Fernando Rojas, wanted for some reason or other beyond mere car theft. The police had waited until Gil Bernardo was through putting a rod in his broken femur before carting him away. His follow-up care would be in the charge of residents at University Hospital. I was relieved he was gone, and hoped I'd never see him again, but I told Mike to put my name and phone number on the transfer sheet, just in case the county residents had any question about what I'd done. I wondered if I could safely bill the LAPD for his surgery. Patients treated while under arrest were covered by the county; not the best reimbursement in the world but better than nothing. The cops had the power to turn him into an insured patient just by slapping the cuffs on him, but retro-billing was a gray zone, and we would have to call for authorization. Likely they would turn it down.

I thought of Elaine, and I wondered how I would handle myself when we met on Sunday. The best course would be to cancel the date, but something made me hold back. It was the most eerie coincidence that while I was saying a final good-bye to her last Monday, her husband was being murdered. I didn't particularly want to think about that anymore.

I tried to concentrate on the day ahead. I was looking forward to touring the Acoma School, wondering how it would compare with my own school back in Wales. Having researched the subject for weeks, I had picked one of the best schools in the region, and the tuition reflected it. I wondered how I would cope, on top of alimony and child support. Still, I firmly believed I was doing the right thing. If there was only one gift I could give my children before they went out in the world, I wanted it to be the best education that I could afford; and in the face of all the money I would be spending on tuition over the next fifteen years or so, this would be just a fraction more. I would just have to lift a lot more faces to pay for it all.

We were about forty-five minutes into our trip when I started to get a little concerned about the sky-blue Ford Taurus. I had noticed him on my tail soon after we got on the freeway. He played tag with me at first and I didn't think much of it; actually, I was glad of the company at the speed I was going. I didn't want to be the only target if we came across the highway patrol. By the time we passed Disneyland I was getting a little wary of the game and decided to let him go by.

I slipped into the slow lane. He stayed on my tail and I didn't like that. I waited for a fast-moving line of cars to come up on my left, and then cut in quick, irritating some kid in a pickup truck, who flashed me the finger. I sneaked a glance to see if Jillian was looking and flashed him one back. I didn't like pickups, never trusted them, figured half of them were out to kill you, one way or another. I endured his glares and gestures for a couple of miles, keeping constant vigil on the rearview mirror.

It seemed as if my ploy had worked: The blue Ford stayed well behind. I finally moved over, in front of a large semitrailer. Five minutes later the blue car was right behind me. By now I was starting to worry. Maybe it was the color. Cindy had said the car she saw when Jack was killed was blue.

We passed the connector from the San Diego freeway at El Toro, and traffic started to thicken as we joined the weekend beach crowd. I was relieved to see it. I thought I could lose the blue Ford now.

The disc jockey on the radio began to talk about some girl he had met at a Hollywood party. He was getting a little crude.

"Must you listen to this station?" I asked Jillian, annoyed.

"Why, Dad? I like this music. Why are you driving so fast, anyway?"

"I'm not driving fast. It's just a long way. And it's not the music I'm worried about."

"Then what is it, Dad? I thought you liked this station."

"I used to like this station. Not anymore. I don't think his jokes are for thirteen-year-olds."

"Don't be silly, Dad. I've heard it all before."

She was quiet for a moment.

"Dad! You're driving like a crazy man."

She was right. Three sudden lane changes, three stupefied motorists honking and waving their middle fingers at me, and the blue Taurus was still following behind. I realized if I kept it up, I would soon attract the attention of the highway patrol. I slowed down, trying to rein in my imagination before it lost control. It wouldn't do to spend the rest of my life suspicious of every blue Ford sedan just because Jack's killer had been driving one. My exit was coming up soon and the guy would probably whizz right by, on his way to San Diego, or maybe Mexico.

He didn't. When I took the exit for the Ortega Highway, he stayed two cars behind. He didn't head west to the beach, either; he kept with me in the left turn lane. I tried to make him out in my rearview—red baseball cap and sunglasses were all I could tell. What about the nose? Cindy had said it looked like mine from across the street. That narrowed it down to about a million suspects.

I was aware of breathing faster. I had to try and

calm down or Jillian would become alarmed. This whole affair was getting too far-fetched. Why would someone who might have killed Jack Ehrenberger now be after me? I didn't think we had anything in common.

Except Elaine!

Elaine was the wild thread that connected us, or used to connect us—this guy in the blue car may not have known I'd broken the tie. Could he be some fanatic secret admirer who was trying to eliminate the competition? Jack Ehrenberger was dead. Was I next?

Now I was truly scared, and it wasn't only for my sake. Jillian was in the car. Would a crazed assassin spare the life of an innocent thirteen-year-old girl? I couldn't count on it. We went under the overpass and through an intersection. Soon we would be on open road, heading for the hills. I had to think fast.

There was a mini-mall on the right, with a big supermarket and a drugstore—plenty of parked cars. I snapped the steering clockwise. The Alfa roared up the parking aisle and launched itself off a speed bump. I scared the life out of a little old lady with a shopping cart. I scared Jillian as well.

"What are you doing, Dad?"

"I just remembered something I forgot to buy."

"What? This is too weird!"

Something told me she wasn't going for it. I figured she'd be better off with the truth.

"I think we're being followed."

"Yeah, sure." She turned around. "By who? Are you making this up?"

"A little blue car."

"That one behind the Slug-Bug?"

I sneaked a look. A red Volkswagen Beetle had slowed him down at the speed bump.

"Yeah. Him."

"Are you sure? He's staring at us. Look! Now he's trying to get around the Slug-Bug. Quick, Dad, turn here."

I did, two quick rights. Every getaway car needs a copilot. I was two lanes from the blue car, going the opposite way.

"Damn!" Somebody was backing up ahead, maneuvering out of a tight spot. I stepped on the brakes.

"You've got to do something, Dad. He's moving fast now."

There was an empty space on my left; a tight squeeze, but a clear shot through to the next lane. I went for it. I heard the crunch of metal on metal, a tinkle of broken glass.

"I think you got his side mirror, Dad."

"Probably never used it anyway." I raced back up toward the store.

"He's stuck behind the same car you were."

"Let's hope he can't fit through the same space."

"I can't see him anymore, Dad."

Opportunity knocked—a delivery truck unloading bottled water. Using the truck for cover, I headed for the back of the store. Nothing there but Dumpsters and packing crates. I went the whole length of the mall down the back alley and returned to the Ortega Highway one block west of where we'd been. Tires squealed as I took the turn, but I didn't care who was watching. I aimed for the hills and floored it.

Just before we went past the first rise, I looked hard in my rearview. I was relieved not to see the blue car.

THE HILLS WERE ARID AND FORSAKEN, LEFT to chaparral and an occasional manzanita bush—the western border of the Cleveland National Forest. The Alfa twisted through the curves, in and out of shallow, rocky canyons. We climbed slowly.

"Why was that guy following us?" Jillian asked over the sound of the engine.

"I don't know, honey."

"Then why were you avoiding him?"

"I don't like being followed."

"Oh! It was cool running away from him, Dad."

She fell silent. If Rafaella had been that understanding, we might have still been married.

The radio began to drift and finally sputtered with static. I turned it off. We climbed over a small rise, and the panorama opened up to a great, sweeping valley. Most of it was open meadow, but there were clusters of eucalyptus, and oak and pine along the hills. At the far end was a group of buildings. Looking right, we saw a glimpse of blue ocean in the distance.

"There's the school. It's beautiful, Dad."

Indeed it was. We followed a redwood fence to a trellised archway over a large grate, and went down the driveway, flanked by more redwood on either side. Several horses were grazing behind the fence. The gravel lot at the end of the drive was full. A small crowd had gathered on the open lawn before the main building, a large Gothic structure with arched windows and finished in gray stone. Ivy covered most of the facade, snaking its way up to the eaves. Beyond lay the rest of the complex, less impressive but just as pretty: whitewashed stucco, balconies lined with clematis and hibiscus, and roofs of Spanish tile.

The crowd was an equal mixture of parents and their teenage kids, casually dressed but with enough designer labels evident to make Jillian forget her nervousness and remember instead all her past misgivings.

"They look like a bunch of nerds, Dad."

"Go get 'em, Sissy." I used the name Emma, her younger sister, always used. She allowed me a kiss for luck. I stole a hug instead and watched her trudge toward the auditorium.

I had mixed feelings as I joined the rest of the parents for a tour of the school. It was exciting to see my little girl about to start a new phase in her life, and sad to see her go.

We split into groups for a tour of the premises. Sarah was the tour guide for my group. We shuffled behind her, past classrooms and labs, around the library, the dining room, the student lounges. Through a typical dorm room, the photography lab, and the gym. She saved the best for last.

The school was founded on the site of an old sanitarium, where eighty years earlier patients with tuberculosis had come to recuperate. As a means of therapy, they had started a small commercial pottery. The potters were long gone, but the trustees had funded a small museum in homage to their memory, and it was rumored to hold one of the best collections on the history of ceramic art in the region.

I had a passion for art pottery. Over the years, I had acquired a small collection, housed in a Mission-style bookcase in my living room. I even had an old piece made at the school, a little brown jug with purple flowers in a slip glaze. The design was simple and functional, thrown by some patient perhaps only just learning to use the wheel, but it was beautiful nevertheless. You could see the pride and dedication glowing in it, bearing up strong even after seventy-five years of use.

Sarah led us to a small adobe building, partly hidden by the stables. Taking a key from her pocket, she unlocked a heavy wooden door. My eyes widened as I saw the old kilns, the wheels, the brushes, and the vats of glaze. I could almost smell the moist red clay waiting to be kneaded by wiry fingers. I lost track of time for a while, then became aware that Sarah was waiting for me so she could lock up.

We made our way back to the main building and I had a reassuring conversation with her about life as a boarder. There were thirty minutes left to the end of the test. I thanked Sarah for her time and decided to wait for Jillian on the front lawn, in plain view of the students as they exited the auditorium. Whistling a tune, I walked back to the Alfa to fetch the novel I'd brought to read.

The parking lot was shaded by a line of tall oaks that also served to screen the cars from the front of the school. My good mood was soon shattered by the sight of a sky-blue Ford Taurus in the first row. It seemed to glare out at me from the line of sober Mercedes and BMW's all around it. The crunch of my footsteps on the gravel took on the same eerie dimension as the echo of footsteps in a dark and deserted underground city lot. I began to glance over my shoulder.

There was no one else in sight. Fortunately, I would hear anyone approaching long before they ever got close. But that wouldn't help if they had a gun.

My pager went off, jolting me. I shut the vibrating machine off and took my car key out, ready. When I reached the car I unlocked the door and was in the driver's seat in one fluid motion. I locked the door behind me, acutely aware that when it came to defense, the ragtop was no better than tissue paper. I scanned my surroundings again, trying to assure myself that I was in no need of protection. Nevertheless, when I turned the ignition to activate the car phone, I decided to start the engine and leave it running. Just in case.

I called my exchange. There was a message from a Detective Kenneth Akimoro of the Beverly Hills police. The name sounded familiar. With a heavy heart I told them to put me through.

"Dr. Lloyd, I'm with the Beverly Hills Police Department. I'm investigating the murder of Dr. Jack Ehrenberger. I understand you knew him?"

It was reassuring to be talking to a policeman, even as I surveyed the parking lot around me for the man who might have followed me. "Yes, I did know him."

"We need some help with our investigation, Dr. Lloyd," he said. His voice was clipped, fairly deep, and not a trace of accent. "There are some questions you might be able to help us with. Can you come back to headquarters and give a statement?"

"What kind of questions?"

"Routine. It shouldn't take very long."

Suddenly, I felt uneasy talking to him. It was as if my imaginary stalker was no longer somewhere around me in the parking lot, but had magically transported himself through the air waves and was haunting the device I held against my ear. "You want me to come to Beverly Hills?"

"That's right."

"Now?"

"The sooner the better. We'd like to close this case as soon as possible."

"You think I can help you close the case?"

There was a pause. "I think you could help us a great deal, Dr. Lloyd."

"I see. Will I need a lawyer?"

"Not really. I just want to take a statement, that's all."

"What if I refuse?" I was testing him, waiting for the response.

"Is there something you're afraid of, Doctor?"

"No. You haven't been following me, have you?" The words were out of my mouth before I realized.

"Why do you think that?"

"Nothing. It's just . . . a blue car. I must have panicked."

"Someone's been following you in a blue car? What make? Did you get the number?"

"No, I didn't." Perhaps I *had* just imagined the whole thing. "I'm sure it was nothing. Look, Detective, it's inconvenient for me this afternoon. There's something else I need to do."

"How soon can you be here?" he asked.

I mulled it over. There was no way out without raising suspicion. "This evening okay?"

"We'll be waiting for you."

JILLIAN CHATTERED ALL THE WAY HOME, the tension pouring out of her now that the test was over. She talked of the exam—she had found it hard. She'd made a new friend, a girl her age from Laguna Niguel. She asked about the summer; would we be going on vacation?

I was not very responsive, restricting my comments to monosyllabic grunts. I wondered who had been driving the blue Ford. Had he somehow followed me all the way up to the school? Perhaps not. It was a fairly common car, after all, and I hadn't seen anyone suspicious in the parking lot—or tailing me in the school. I looked around. There didn't seem to be any blue Fords around me on the freeway as I drove back home.

I thought about my upcoming interview with the Beverly Hills police. I would have to go; I had no choice. Perhaps it was for the best. An opportunity to explain my innocence and get them off my tail.

I passed a large billboard on the side of the freeway. A model in a skimpy bathing suit posed seductively. BODY BEAUTIFUL, it said. The message offered plastic surgery as the answer to life's basic problems. There was a phone number with an 800 prefix. I recognized the surgeon; it was one to whom I had lost a couple of potential patients over the last few months. They had been sucked in by the message and serenaded by the hype. I thought of Jack Ehrenberger, and I wondered if somewhere there was a plastic surgeon mad enough to take out a contract on his competition. The Beverly Hills police must have been wondering the same thing about me.

Normally, I would let Jillian off in the driveway and wait until she was inside the house before I sped off. This time I walked up to the door with her and rang the bell myself. I had to talk to Rafaella.

Emma opened it. "Hi, Daddy," she said cheerfully.

"Hi, lovely." I gave my little ten-year-old a hug. "You know you should never open the door by yourself. It's not safe."

"But Mom's right here, Daddy."

Rafaella stepped out from her hiding place. She was wearing a beige and brown outfit, something a lot snappier than I was used to seeing her in. Now that I wasn't around to appreciate it, her taste was improving.

"Hello, Gareth," she said.

"Hi. You look nice today." I regretted my answer as soon as I gave it.

Rafaella flushed perceptibly and stood a little taller. Jillian rushed up to her mother to give news of the test.

I ruffled Emma's hair. "What have you been up to this morning?" I asked.

"Nothing. Are we going with you today?"

"No, not today. I've got something to do." I knelt down and rubbed her tummy where it tickled. I loved doing it; she always went limp in a paroxysm of chuckles.

"Tell you what," I said. "I'll come back tomorrow afternoon and take you out somewhere. Just you and me. We'll go someplace Sissy doesn't like to go."

Divide and conquer—a child-rearing tactic I had learned more from Rafaella's Roman ancestors than from Dr. Spock. There was an instantaneous whine from Jillian, and a yelp of glee from Emma. The two began talking at once.

"Where are we going to go?" Emma demanded.

"I want to go, too," Jillian whined.

"We just spent half a day together. Now it's Emma's turn."

"It's not fair," Jillian said. "You just took me to a school. I never get to go anywhere exciting."

"You don't like horseback riding, anyway," I said. "I think it's fair, and that's that. Run along now, you two. I want to speak to your mother alone."

Jillian sullenly trudged toward the family room. She must have figured Mum and Dad were about to have another fight. Emma pranced after her singing, "We're going horseback riding," and dodged a swing from Jillian just before they disappeared.

"Do you think she passed the test?" Rafaella asked when they had gone.

"I'm sure she did." I noticed she was wearing a new perfume. Maybe she had a new boyfriend to go with it. Perhaps a muscular waiter from Wilshire Boulevard. Her auburn hair fell straight to her shoulders, framing her round, tanned face.

Once, I would have seen the sparkle in her eyes— chestnut eyes, framed by long lashes. Now, I noticed the furrows in her forehead, above those thick, bushy eyebrows that seemed to grow wild.

"Well," she said. "What have I done now?"

"Did I say you did something?"

"You said you wanted to talk to me."

"Oh! You never told me that you were with Cindy the night Jack Ehrenberger was murdered."

"So!"

"So I thought you might have mentioned it."

"Why?" She stepped up to the door and grasped the knob firmly, as if ready to slam it shut the minute I strayed back over the threshold.

"Because . . . Well, it's not everyday that someone witnesses a murder."

"I didn't witness it. Cindy did." She looked at me with cold eyes, a blank expression on her face. "I thought you had something to say to me. Was that it?"

"I was just wondering . . . " It was difficult trying to find the words I wanted. "I wondered if Cindy had said anything to you."

"What about?" She tossed her head. "I can't believe this, Gareth. Do you have something to say to me? Because if you don't, I have things to do. I can't wait here all day."

I hated the way this was turning out. It seemed as though we couldn't even have a simple discussion anymore.

"I've been asked to go and talk to the police. They want me to tell them everything I know about Jack."

"Then you'll have to tell them all about Elaine." She smiled petulantly.

"You know about her?"

"What I want to know, Gareth"—there was a fire in her eyes—"were you fucking her while we were still together?"

"Rafaella!" I was shocked. "Keep your voice down. The kids will hear."

"They probably know, too. They're not dumb."

"No. I didn't know her then." I gave her a sour look and kept a wary eye on the door, lest she decided to swing it like a weapon.

"I suppose if you knew her, you would have."

"Yeah, right. Like I was jumping a new one every week."

"Maybe you were."

"Rafaella, there's no need for melodrama."

"Melodrama, is it? Gareth, did you have anything to do with Jack's death?"

She was doing it again, pushing my buttons, whether it made sense or not. I tried to remain calm.

"Rafaella, that's pretty low. You know me better than that."

"I don't know you anymore, Gareth." Her face was

inches away from mine. "But I know that woman. She has you exactly where she wants you. And I'll tell you something else . . . she's capable of things you wouldn't even dream of."

She closed her mouth so tight there was a white rim around her lips. Her eyes bored into me. For a moment I thought that merely by instinct she had accessed a truth that was beyond all my analysis.

WHEN I FINALLY GOT BACK HOME, IT WAS just after one. Detective Akimoro may have wanted me to go to Beverly Hills and give a statement, but I had other plans for the afternoon. He would just have to wait. Malbone's of Pasadena held their antique auction every Saturday, and I never missed one of them unless I was in surgery. Antiques were my relaxation. Malbone's was my way of unwinding for the week, and Akimoro was not going to deprive me of that.

I went upstairs and put on a fresh T-shirt, a faded pair of blue jeans, and my hiking boots. I selected my old denim jacket, deliberately kept unwashed for these flea-market forays. My lucky outfit, Rafaella had called it. I thought of it more as my disguise. I retrieved the small eight-power lens I kept in the top drawer of my desk and headed for the door.

I started the car and punched the radio preset button, switching from Jillian's station to one of mine. Eric Clapton playing the blues. I rocked my head to the rhythm of "Goin' Away Baby" as I headed down the freeway to Pasadena. My eyes stayed glued to the rearview, but I saw no sign of a blue Ford Taurus.

I pulled into the back parking lot of the old warehouse north of Colorado Street and climbed the short flight of stairs beside the loading dock. The sound of the auctioneer's amplified voice was like a pacemaker kicking in—a shot of adrenaline!

Malbone's of Pasadena had been holding a weekly sale every Saturday at twelve for over half a century. They had become an institution in the Los Angeles antique circuit, making their name as a dealer's auction, a clearinghouse for large estates of medium value. I put their staying power down to volume rather than quality. If you found something of real historical interest at Malbone's, it probably slipped in by mistake. All the rare and high-end antiques, anything of unusual provenance, would be shipped by consignors to Butterfield's in Los Angeles, or even back East to Sotheby's or Christie's. At Malbone's, nothing was cataloged, and all the lots were sold with the age-old caveat—let the buyer beware. They would rip through hundreds of items every Saturday, working their warehouse from one end to the other until it was picked clean. Prices were right if you knew what you were doing. Even if you didn't, and ended up with a ringer—if your fabulous Meissen figurine turned out to be made in Hong Kong— you could put it back in the auction next week and someone else would buy it. That was the beauty of Malbone's.

I went there to learn, to study the marks, to feel the finish and admire the craftmanship—to serve my apprenticeship in the study of antiques. There was no school like it. I could pick up and handle everything in the room without having some dealer breathe down my back. Every once in a while I got lucky. I would find some gem, outbid the dealers, and take it home to a coveted place in my display cabinet. My collection was one of the few things I had salvaged from the divorce; Rafaella had wanted nothing to do with old pots and vases. I was getting to the point where there was hardly room for any more. Yet I was drawn to Malbone's each Saturday, eager to see if there was one more jewel there for me to take home.

Today the dealers were out in force, thick as thieves, milling about on the warehouse floor. Sunday was flea-market day, and they were anxious to restock their shelves. The good weather would bring Angelenos and tourists flocking to the Rose Bowl on Sunday, and a hand-cut piece of crystal, or a tin toy with its paint still intact, might fetch two to four times its auction price. Cash in the pocket.

I felt comfortable in my denim disguise. I didn't care to flaunt my occupation in their presence. The dealers would have expected a plastic surgeon to be one of their Sunday customers, buying their handpicked goods at full premium, not competing with them at Malbone's, where they were trying to make a living.

Wisps of cigarette smoke drifted upward from sundry groups of people on the warehouse floor, as if the nervous tension made them smolder in anticipation. The white trails spiraled lazily toward the high ceiling, drifting in and out of bright rays of sunlight piercing the skylights. The stale smell mingled with the musty odor from decades of dust and grime, coating each item with a veneer of authenticity. Nobody cleaned anything before putting it on display; it would mar the illusion. A heavy crust of scum was worth money at Malbone's.

I wormed my way to the front. Halfway there, I bumped into Rocco Gambella.

Rocco was deeply tanned, about thirty pounds overweight and proud of it, judging by the tight burgundy shirt and low-slung jeans, which were tucked into a pair of shiny black cowboy boots. He had thick black hair to match, slicked into a ponytail down to his neck. The bright turquoise and sterling Navajo watchband made a striking contrast to his bronzed, hairy forearms.

"Hey, Rocco! Anything good today?" I asked.

"Nothing real tasty for me. But there's a shipment of rugs everybody's buzzing about."

"Persian? The real thing?"

"Yup. And some of the older ones may be worth looking at, going by the number of rug riders they got slinking around here." Rocco hitched his thumbs into his waistband, the movement uncovering a large, shiny Navajo belt buckle to match the watch. I caught the garlic on his breath.

Rugs, Persian or Pakistani, didn't hold much with Rocco. He was strictly an art man. There wasn't a lot about nineteenth-century American painting he didn't know. Not that you could guess from looking at him, but rumor had it in the past five years he had made a small fortune picking up unrecognized works for next to nothing and shipping them over to collectors back East. Some of the money could have gone up his nose, but someone told me he had three kids from a previous marriage, and child support must have taken the rest.

I looked around. There did seem to be more than the usual quota of Middle Eastern types wandering about, spitting at one another in Farsi and in Arabic, hawking their throats and their wares, discussing the merits of weft and weave. They would bid for the rugs, then huddle and do their swaps, holding an auction within the auction, until, by the end of the day, a rug may have been bought and sold a dozen times without ever leaving the warehouse.

I shrugged. "I think I'll pass. I'm only interested in the pottery, anyway. See you later, Rocco. I'm going to have a look around."

The auction preview was my treasure hunt. I would scan the tables and display cabinets, looking for the right combination of shape, color, and texture that would set off the internal alarm. I didn't know what I was looking for, but I would recognize it when I saw it.

I started on my quest through tables and shelves loaded with paraphernalia, cutting through groups of people and dodging obstacles in my way. I whipped out my eight-power lens and put it through its paces, observing utensils for signs of wear, checking marks to see if they were authentic to the piece, and, in general, having a wonderful time. For an hour, I was lost in the musty past, forgetting all about Akimoro, Jack Ehrenberger, Fernando

Rojas, Elaine, alimony, child support, tax collectors, insurance companies, and lawyers.

I found some early Meiji period Imari, thrown in with a cluster of dusty Hong Kong dinnerware. And a Clarice Cliff teapot hidden behind a stack of copper pans—pity about the missing lid. There was a Wedgwood majolica jug, with the mark so faint that it might easily be missed. In fact, somebody picked it up after I did and remarked that it was Italian, which gave me the resolve to watch for it as it came up. I loved the "sleepers"—items that were not faddish enough for their value to be recognized by the crowd.

I was on my return sweep to the podium when I noticed a group of dolls and little porcelain figurines dressed in period costumes. One in particular caught my eye, a Japanese girl doll in a flowered robe, holding a parasol. About six inches high, she had an exquisitely painted face, simple but radiant, and delicate hands, floating, as if caught in the middle of an aria from *Madame Butterfly*. I picked her up for a closer look. She was made of baked clay, hand-painted under a delicate glaze. She wore a kimono of silk with gold brocade, in the style of a geisha girl, hand-stitched and finished to minute detail: a jewel among the rest, a custom-made doll that would have been highly prized at a collector's show. Carefully, I replaced her on the shelf and moved into the hub of activity around the podium.

I waited patiently as Easton, the auctioneer, worked his magic, earning his wages as he hammered and cajoled bids out of the seasoned crowd. The Wedgwood jug came up. He wasn't going to let it slide.

"What am I bid for this lovely piece of Wedgwood majolica?" he said, drowning my hopes. Announce it to the world, won't you, Easton. It went for three hundred and fifty. Not for me at that price.

I waited for the geisha doll. It wasn't the kind of

thing I actively sought, but I found it so charming I was curious to see what it would bring. Rocco came up by my side while I passed the time.

"You getting anything today?" he asked.

"Not yet. How about you?"

"Just some etchings so far. There's an oil coming up."

I nodded. Five minutes went by. Rocco seemed to have the same philosophy as I did about auctions: Too much conversation and you could miss a sleeper.

"So what kind of pottery do you collect?" he finally asked, making no attempt to bid on his painting.

"Art pottery." Most times, this proclamation would have been met with an embarrassing silence, as people tried to figure out what that meant. Rocco understood.

"You should talk to the captain. He knows all about Rookwood and Weller and that stuff. Flies one of them big airliners for Southwest. Deals pottery, too. Got a little booth in Sherman Oaks, in one of them antique malls. Puts his stuff in a showcase, locks it up, and he's gone. They do all the work for him; show it when someone's interested, take the money, figure the tax, credit cards, you name it. End of the month they give him a check for what's been sold, minus ten percent for their trouble."

"Ten percent. That's not bad, really."

"No, it ain't, when you figure he can be gone out of town on his regular job and his stuff is still making money for him. Lots of guys do it that way. Beats hanging around all day waiting for a sale, especially when you have a lot of smalls. Some people can come around and keep you talking for hours on a ten-dollar sale. Waste of time, if you ask me."

"Sounds good, Rocco, but I'm not selling."

"No? Well . . . I don't mean to pry . . . but you some kind of doctor or something?" He fidgeted, as if flustered by a breach of his own code of etiquette. "I mean, that's just what folks say around here," he added, by way of explanation.

"Yes, I am."

"Well . . . Doc. Mind if I ask you a personal question?"

"Go ahead."

"Do you know anything about the prostrate? I was just wondering how that works."

I resisted a smile at his pronunciation. I hadn't figured him for being that old. "It's not exactly my field. I'm a plastic surgeon."

"Oh! A plastic surgeon. No kidding. Well, I guess you don't know much about prostrate cancer, then."

I wasn't too current on the subject, but I tried to explain what I remembered as tactfully as possible, not knowing if I'd be unduly alarming him with the information. I had to cut it short when I saw the geisha doll being carried to the podium.

"Excuse me, Rocco, I just want to see how this one goes."

The other figures went first, at hammer prices varying from thirty to sixty dollars. They were too run-of-the-mill to create any excitement. I suspected Easton knew the value of the geisha doll when I saw him hold it back for last.

"Now change your sights," he said, holding up the little doll. "We have a beautiful little geisha girl, a handmade collector's item. I don't know how it got in with the others but it's for sale. Who'll start me off at two hundred? No? A hundred anywhere? How about fifty?"

Someone obliged, and the bidding moved up rapidly. My pulse began to race. It was the thrill of knowing that I could lay claim to the piece by the simple effort of raising the bid. And yet that effortless little wave of the hand took on the weight of a complex maneuver, and my fingers were locked to my side with indecision.

Did I really need it? How high was I prepared to go?

I had to think fast, or watch it slip through my grasp. Better if I didn't think at all. I went for the gut feeling, jumping in with a wave of my hand and staying with it up through two hundred and fifty. The bidding seemed to be faltering, and I thought Easton might hammer it down at any second, maybe even to me. Not so. Perhaps it had gone farther than he had first anticipated, having started at fifty, but now he was going to play it out—milk it as far as he could. "Come on now," he said. "This is the real thing, folks. Fifteen hundred retail. Do I hear two seventy-five?"

My hand was starting to feel quite heavy.

"Two seventy-five in back," I heard him say.

I kept my arm raised.

"Three hundred to the man in front."

That was me. Three hundred to me. My mind switched on again. Did I really want a geisha doll at three hundred dollars?

"Do I have three twenty-five? Anywhere?"

He was about to hammer it down to me. The gavel descended halfway to the podium, then suddenly switched direction as he pointed it to the back of the room. "Three twenty-five in back," he said, holding his gavel high again. "It's the lady's bid."

Now he was looking directly at me. "Do I have three-fifty, sir? Three-fifty to you."

I looked down. My hand was stuck to my side once more; it didn't seem to want to move. I raised my eyes to Easton and shook my head.

"No! Thank you for bidding. Sold for three twenty-five to the lady." He squinted through the smoke. "Your number, miss? Five-o-nine," he called to the record keeper.

Coming down from my adrenaline rush, I heard a buzz of conversation start up. I hadn't realized that we'd been the cause of some general excitement. It seemed as if everybody had followed the bidding. Perhaps it was because they thought we went too high. Or maybe the piece itself had warranted it.

Rocco slapped me on the shoulder. "Rocking and rolling on that one, weren't you?"

I grinned outwardly, although regret was setting in. "Maybe I should have gone for it?" I mused.

"Looks to me you did. She outbid you, that's all."

I nodded. He was right about that. "Who is she, Rocco?"

He shrugged. "Never seen her before. Cute little number in a black dress. She's back there by the coffee machine."

I looked over at the coffee dispenser. She was easy to spot, a shapely figure in a black minidress. She stood out in the crowd as surely as that geisha doll among the porcelain figurines. Her back was to me and I couldn't see her face, but the view I had was interesting enough. A shock of straight blond hair capped her slim neck; I could almost see the vertebrae stand out as she tossed her head in conversation. The black knit fabric of her dress clung to her back, all the way down to her thighs. Beneath the hem a pair of slim legs descended to the floor.

She was talking to a young man, late twenties, with a closely cropped head. He looked like a young Marine on leave, out of uniform and slightly disheveled. He was wearing a black leather jacket, jeans, and black leather boots. I felt his eyes boring in my direction, and something about his expression made me uneasy.

"GOT TO CUT OUT," ROCCO SAID, PATTING me on the back. "Sure appreciate the medical information, Doc. If I can ever do anything for you, don't hesitate. Maybe you'd like to buy some paintings sometime." He handed me his card.

I thanked him. ROCCO GAMBELLA. ART DEALER TO THE TRADE, the card said. There was an address in Riverside, a phone number, and a fax number. I stuck it in the top pocket of my denim jacket and watched him go.

It was four o'clock. The auction would continue for another hour at least, but I realized it was time I went down to the Beverly Hills police station and had my talk with Detective Akimoro. It couldn't be that hard, just answering a few questions about Jack Ehrenberger. And what if he did ask me about Elaine? Sooner or later he was bound to find out. In an oblique sort of way, I was actually glad that he wanted to talk to me.

Last Monday, after my meeting with Elaine, I had returned home with mixed emotions. I'd told her I didn't want to see her anymore and had closed another chapter in my life. Physically Elaine was a pinup of the perfect woman, from the tanned smoothness of her body to the polished elegance of her ways. But emotionally she was a wasteland—the soul had been cored out of her. I had enjoyed getting to know her, but the challenge was short-lived, and once I'd taken my fill of the physical I found myself wanting more. Only there was no more.

I thought that taken at a leisurely pace, one evening a week, we could go on forever. But we were playing the game with too much intensity; words became superfluous. There were evenings when we hardly spoke at all. In the end, it was this lack of dialogue that did us in. Intercourse without discourse.

As for her husband, I never had any guilt at what I was doing to Jack—in my mind I had already tried and sentenced him for other crimes against humanity. But I was stunned when I returned home that Monday night and heard the news of his death. I knew, because of the circumstances, that there would be an inquiry, and I knew that my role would sooner or later be public. I had expected to hear the knock on the door every day for the past week, and I was relieved that it had finally occurred. I looked forward to the catharsis of getting it off my chest.

I was about to head for the door when I saw Easton holding up an object that drew my attention. It was a blue and beige vase, with painted chrysanthemums in a palette of pastel colors. I had missed it in the preview, but I knew instantly what it was. A Weller Hudson vase, a coveted piece of art pottery that was right up my alley.

He started his preamble. "A nice arts and crafts vase. No maker's mark, but it's signed by the artist on the side."

My feet stopped in their tracks. An unmarked Weller Hudson was not as desirable as a clearly branded sample, but that would mean most people would not know what it was, and the bidding could go low. Yet the signature meant that it could be researched, provenanced, and dated without too much effort.

I snagged it for only sixty dollars. Ecstatic with myself, I ambled over to the cashier's booth to pay up.

The blonde was there, too. Alone, the young Marine type nowhere in sight. She was laying crisp new

Franklins on the counter. I was intrigued by the hundred-dollar bills.

I watched her as she counted out the money. Slender hands, smooth and sinewy with pearly rose nail varnish. I caught my breath. On the left fourth finger was a ring—a silver skull and crossbones with two glistening emerald eyes. The same one I had seen at Jack's funeral. How many rings like that one could there be? And how many blondes were wearing them?

She turned around. It was the same girl. She smiled at me—a wide, playful smile, that same enchanting pair of lips. Hazel eyes. Rose lipstick.

I paid for my vase and hurried over to the lockup room to collect. I made it my business to be standing next to her as they handed her the geisha doll.

"Nice buy," I said.

"Excuse me?" She turned to see who it was and smiled at me again. She was twice as pretty as she'd been the day before, and for some reason getting prettier by the minute. Her skin looked smooth and pale, and she wore an amused look. Not amused at me, but at life, as if she was having a wonderful day.

"Beautiful piece you've got there." "Body" is what I meant.

"Oh! Yes, it is. Aren't you the guy who was bidding against me?"

I nodded. We stood facing each other. There was a brief silence. Not knowing quite what to say next, I handed the clerk my receipt for the vase and waited for him to find it.

"You look familiar," she said. "Have I seen you before?"

I shrugged. "Maybe in a past life," I said. "A hundred years ago. I think we were married."

She was taken aback at first, then she laughed out loud. I liked her sense of humor already.

My vase arrived and I made a show of checking the finish for flaws. It's always a risk buying something at auction without carefully examining it first. Happily, there were no defects.

"That's a beautiful vase," she said.

"It's my passion. Art pottery."

"Is it? Mine, too. That's a Weller Hudson, isn't it?"

I nodded, impressed. We stood in silence again, like two old lovers reunited by chance and not knowing where to begin. It was not an uncomfortable feeling.

I noticed we were in the way of others trying to collect their lots and took her by the arm, moving her over to one side. She didn't flinch from my touch. I wondered again about the young man I had seen with her.

"Are you some kind of astrologer or psychic?" she asked.

"No way. I'm a regular, down-to-earth type. Why?"

"Why did you say we were married in a past life?"

"Oh, that was just a joke. Wishful thinking, I guess."

Her cheeks flushed slightly. "I guess," she repeated. "We seem to have the same taste in antiques."

"We were also both at the same funeral yesterday."

Her face changed. "Are you a cop?" she demanded.

"No. I'm not a cop."

"Then why are you following me?"

"I'm not following you, believe me. I was just there because I knew him."

"Was he a friend of yours?"

"Not really. A colleague."

She relaxed.

"I was the one you bumped into at the end. Remember? You dropped your bag."

"Oh, yes. That's right." She looked deeply at me. "That was you, wasn't it?"

"That was me. And why were you there?"

"Oh, same reason."

"A friend of yours?"

"No, not a friend. A patient. I was a patient of his."

I looked pointedly at her chest. Those breasts had obviously not seen benefit of the knife.

She flushed once more. "None of your goddamn business." Then she calmed. "I changed my mind. Canceled the operation."

I was relieved. The crisis seemed to be over. The smile had returned, and I might be back in the running. I stood there, relishing the feeling for a moment. I had cleared the first hurdle, but the race wasn't won.

"Well, I'm afraid I have to go now," she said.

"I was hoping . . . "

She waited for me to finish.

" . . . that we could go somewhere and have a coffee together."

"I can't."

"We could talk about our collections."

"I'm sorry. I have somewhere to go."

"Or about our past life together." I was grabbing at straws, thinking she might have a present life with that Marine after all.

"Maybe some other time," she said.

"When?"

"I don't know. It's hard for me to say."

"You have a boyfriend?"

"No." She denied it quickly.

"You're married, then?"

She laughed. "No. Not that."

"May I have your number?"

"I think it would be hard for you to reach me."

"Oh?"

"I'm sort of between addresses right now."

The excuse seemed flimsy.

"Maybe I'll see you here next Saturday," she said, this time as if she meant it.

"I'll be here."

We faced each other in silence again, she clutching her treasure, and I mine.

"Before you go," I said, "can you tell me your name?"

"Miranda. Miranda Pelton. What's yours?"

"Gareth Lloyd."

"Gareth. That's a nice name."

"I knew you'd like it. I like yours, too. See you next Saturday, then, Miranda."

She nodded and turned to leave. I watched her as she picked her way through the throng of people, concentrating my gaze on the back of her dress and the play of light off the pale skin on those two lovely legs. When she had crossed the threshold of the warehouse door and was past the crowds and into the bright sun of the parking lot, I noticed that there was another figure keeping step with her. It was the young man with the short haircut.

CHAPTER 10

THE BEVERLY HILLS CIVIC CENTER WASN'T hard to find, with its dome of blue mosaic and gold cupola dominating the skyline. I parked and walked up endless concrete ramps lined with ornate wrought iron, winding around the huge white octopus of a building, until I found the police headquarters. I was shown into a small room on the second floor, somewhere deep within its entrails, and told to wait, presumably for the assault of its various digestive enzymes.

One of the enzymes, in the form of a muscular young man with close-cropped red hair and a freckled face, entered and took a seat across from me. He wore a dark suit over a white shirt, bulging at the arms and chest. A few pale hairs peeked from above the rim of his undershirt, just visible at the open collar. He looked young enough to be an intern at the county hospital, and just as impulsive. Steroids, I thought. He busied himself with loading a fresh cassette into the tape recorder on the table.

He introduced himself and told me we were waiting for Detective Akimoro. They had called him at home and he was on his way. I imagined the man in a long silky robe sitting hunched on the floor of his dining room when the call came, shoeless, and scooping a bowl of soupy noodles into his mouth. I hoped he wouldn't be too upset at my late arrival.

The room we were in was obviously furnished for one purpose alone. There were no windows, and the paneled walls were bare, except for a mirror that took up most of the wall in front of me. A central table with six chairs around it occupied most of the floor space. Except for the tape recorder, a cumbersome, industrial-strength model of some age, the room was devoid of accoutrements. The bleakness of it all made me uncomfortable, and I toyed with the idea of donating some ornament for those stark walls, something suitable to the occasion: perhaps a collection of thumb screws, or a display of rubber hoses.

The rigid, steel-frame chair beneath me did not help. It pushed my back forward into the table, the way my grandfather used to whenever we visited him for Sunday dinner back in Caerleon. "Sit up straight at the table, Boyo," he would say. "Dinner is a formal occasion in this house." Just as it had back then, the prodding in the small of my back intensified my aversion to being there.

I peered at the mirror, wondering who was gathered on the other side, waiting for my little recording session to start. Who was calling the tune? They had probably already interviewed Elaine. She would be the first to give a statement. They must have known of our little affair by now. Why else would they have sent for me? Surely all they wanted was to confirm the story they had learned from her. But what was all this show with the tape recorder? What could Elaine have told them? Did they suspect me for the murderer? I desperately wanted to tell my story and clear my name, but my version was not going to leave me blameless. I was still an adulterer.

In the mirror, I noticed anxious lines on the dour face that glared back at me. Forty years old next week. Elaine had liked my face. I wondered what Miranda Pelton thought of it. Maybe she preferred the young Marine, the muscular type; perhaps somebody more like my companion sitting by the tape recorder?

An Asian man in a blue blazer and gray slacks stepped into the room and introduced himself as Detective Akimoro. He was taller than I expected, of medium weight and build, with a thick head of cropped gray bristles to match the color of his pants. His hairline came down low on his forehead, where two deep furrows seemed permanently etched. A wisp of gray mustache balanced on his upper lip. He had a round face, and the skin over his cheekbones was stretched to a rosy shine, which gave the effect of a circus clown and added to the sinister irony of the situation.

I watched him solemnly take a seat across from me next to the young policeman. His crisp white collar framed a perfect Windsor knot on his striped silk tie. He made me feel quite self-conscious in my jeans and jacket, as if I were already guilty of something. A cat burglar, caught with crowbar and pliers.

"Thank you for coming, Dr. Lloyd."

He had a formal but pleasant voice.

They started the tape. He told me I had the right to have a lawyer present. I said it wasn't necessary. He explained that the procedure was a routine part of his investigation, that he might have to ask me some questions which would make me uneasy, but that I should try to answer all of them as truthfully as possible, because I would have to sign the transcript when it was typed. I told him I understood.

He began by asking me for biographic details. He proceeded to my relationship with Jack, "the deceased." He went into some depth about the last time I saw him, and my feelings toward him. This was the easy part, no different from depositions I had given to lawyers before, sometimes even getting paid for it. I bounced back the answers with confidence. Soon, he was in the murky waters of my relationship with Elaine.

"How well did you know Mrs. Ehrenberger?"

"Quite well," I answered.

"I see. Were you having an affair with her?"

"I was."

"And how did that start?"

*She took off her clothes, and I took off mine.*

"It started about six months ago," I said. "She volunteered to raise funds for a charity ball given by University Hospital. It was called 'Face of the Future,' a benefit for cleft lip patients in Central America. I was the coordinator for our district in Greenfield. We spent a lot of time together. She was lonely, I was divorced. You know how these things go."

"What I want to know, Dr. Lloyd, is where they lead." He paused, licking the edge of his mustache with the tip of his tongue. Were those bristles really tipped with gray, or was it salt crystals left over from his soup?

"How often did you meet?" he went on.

"Once a week."

"Where?"

"At the Bel Age Hotel."

"Never at her house?"

"She liked the Bel Age."

"When was the last time you saw her?"

"Monday."

"The day he was shot?"

"Yes."

"Was that the day you usually met?"

"Yes."

"Tell me what you did that Monday."

The questions came swiftly, as if they had been rehearsed, reinforcing my suspicions that he already knew the answers. His manner was inscrutable and he showed no hint of judgment at any of my responses.

"We met about five o'clock. I picked her up on Wilshire Boulevard—"

"Was that your usual procedure?" he interrupted.

"Yes. She would go to Jack's office Monday afternoons. She ran a cosmetic clinic there for special patients, people with burn scars and blemishes. She taught them how to use makeup for cover. She knew about that stuff.

She would usually get away by five and spend the rest of the evening with me."

I saw Akimoro lean stiffly to one side, as if he had eaten too many beans and was trying to relieve himself of gas pains, but then he put his left hand in his pocket and extracted something from it. Something small enough to remain completely concealed in his fist. He began to clench and unclench his fingers, making an annoying, grinding sound.

"And how did she excuse these absences from her husband?" he asked.

"I don't think she had to. Monday nights he would go to the spa. Then I think he usually went to a sports bar. To have dinner, a few drinks, hang out with his buddies—whatever. I know she always got home before he did. Maybe he was out whoring, I'm not sure. It was her night off, and it was his night off."

He got his exercise, and she got hers. Some marriages work out that way. I became aware that I needed some exercise myself; the chair was getting quite uncomfortable. I shifted in my seat.

"Let's go back to Monday," Akimoro said. "You picked her up at five. What then?"

"We drove up Beverly Drive, to the park by the reservoir."

"Why didn't you go to the Bel Age?"

"I wanted to talk. I'd been trying to break it off with her for the past three weeks."

"I see. And you couldn't talk at the Bel Age?"

"I suppose we could. But the bed got in the way."

He registered a smile. A small one, but I caught it.

"And what did you do when you got to the reservoir?"

"We parked. And then we talked. We must have talked for about an hour. Then I drove her home."

"Did you stop anywhere?"

"No."

"You're sure of that?"

"Yes. I'm sure."

"And when you were parked at the reservoir did anybody see you? Somebody walking their dog? A jogger? A child playing? Anybody?"

"I don't think so."

"So. You are her alibi, and she is yours."

"I guess that's the way it is."

"I see," he said.

I waited for the tongue to make another appearance. It didn't. The grinding sound from his left hand continued unabated.

"Are you comfortable, Dr. Lloyd? Can I get you anything? Coffee? A glass of water?"

"No, thanks."

Actually, I could have used a cigarette. After twelve years of quitting, I figured I had one coming. I wanted to blow the smoke in his face. I wished he would stop crunching whatever it was in his fist.

"Did you see her again after Monday?" he asked.

"No."

"Do you plan to see her again?"

"No."

I was glad I wasn't hooked up to a lie detector; it would have screamed. I wondered if he knew about the phone call. He might have had her phone tapped.

"Did she talk to you since Monday?"

He must know. Perhaps it wasn't even a phone bug. Elaine might have told him when she went through this process herself. I wondered how her transcript read.

"Yes," I replied softly. "She called me yesterday."

"And what did she want?"

"To meet. Tomorrow night. To talk."

"Talk about what?"

"I don't know. She didn't say."

"And you didn't agree?"

"I . . . Yes, I did."

In the harsh light of the room, the mirror reflected the color in my cheeks.

"I see."

He paused, opening his fingers and tilting his left palm into the table. A pair of ivory dice rolled out and spun to a stop in front of him. He studied the seven they registered for a moment, then swept them back into his hand.

"What did the two of you talk about at the reservoir?" he asked.

"The future. Leaving each other. It was time for us to split up."

"That took the whole hour?" His words registered disbelief, but his face was stolid.

"It wasn't easy. Actually, it took three weeks." Like giving up smoking.

"Did the two of you ever discuss what things would be like if Dr. Ehrenberger was out of the way?"

"We never discussed killing him, if that's what you mean."

"Oh?" He ground the dice louder. "Did you want her to leave him?"

*I dreamed about it. Long, fanciful daydreams.*

"No."

"She never talked about it?"

"We realized it wouldn't work out. That was one of the reasons I decided to break it up."

"You decided? Did she go along with that?"

"Yes."

"So she wasn't in love with you?"

I looked at the mirror again. "No. I don't believe she was."

Akimoro peered at his watch, then at the tape recorder. The spools turned slowly, registering my shame in little magnetic impulses.

"Just a few more questions, Dr. Lloyd, then you can go. Did Mrs. Ehrenberger ever discuss an insurance policy on her husband?"

"No."

"Did she ever discuss finances?"

"No."

"Did she ever give you money?"

"No."

"The Bel Age is an expensive hotel. Who paid for the room?"

I avoided looking at the mirror. "She did," I answered.

"And you had no objection?"

"She preferred it that way. I didn't mind, as long as it made her happy."

"Are you in any kind of financial difficulty, Dr. Lloyd?"

He was thorough. And he had obviously done his homework. An uneasy thought began to set in, adding its chill to my present level of malaise, as if someone were treating the ache in my back by dripping ice cream down my spine. Did Akimoro have some hard evidence I didn't know about? Was there something that pointed to either of us, something Elaine had done? A frozen memory was stirring in the depths of my cortex, trying to thaw its way out of the numbness.

I wondered for the first time whether I was being foolhardy to sit there and chat so openly with the detective. Should I have asked for a lawyer after all? The only one I had ever engaged to represent me was Alice Redgood, and I had dropped her after the divorce—spat her out of my life for leaving a bitter taste in my mouth. The lawyer I had the most dealings with now was Dulles Lindstrom, but I didn't think he was appropriate for this case. He represented Rafaella in the settlement.

"You haven't answered my question, Dr. Lloyd."

"I . . . What?"

"Your financial situation?"

"No big deal. My expenses are pretty high. I pay alimony and child support. And my practice hasn't been doing that well lately. But that's not unusual. All the doctors are complaining. Competition is getting keener, and insurance companies aren't paying what they used to. I don't think I'm any worse off than anybody else."

"No special loans? No gambling debts?"

"No."

"We can issue a subpoena duces tecum on your financial records."

"That sounds like a threat. Am I a suspect in this murder?"

He rolled the dice once more, interlocked his fingers, and stared hard at me. I looked down at the table. Seven again. Must be a trick.

"We are just trying to gather as much background information as we can, Dr. Lloyd," he said.

"On the victim, I hope. Or on *me?*"

"On the case."

Fishing. When they found the motive, they would have a suspect.

"You won't see anything of interest in my financial records," I said.

"One last thing, Dr. Lloyd. Do you own a gun?"

The gun. I swallowed hard. "I did."

"You did? What happened to it?"

"I lent it out. Six months ago."

He didn't even raise an eyebrow. "Who did you lend it to?"

"Elaine Ehrenberger," I replied.

He swept up the dice and glared at me.

## CHAPTER 11

"COME DOWN OFF THAT FENCE, EMMA," I yelled.

It was the third time I had to caution her. She was balanced on the edge of a two-by-four, leaning into the paddock with only one hand for support, the other stretched toward the dappled gray mare that was nibbling the carrot she gingerly held between thumb and forefinger.

She ignored me again. Not from defiance; she was just so immersed in her magical world of equine wonder that the warning failed to penetrate her conscious mind. I sighed and picked my way across the ten yards that separated us, through a sea of mud whipped into a sawtooth pattern of peaks and troughs by dozens of curious footprints. The relentless heat of the afternoon sun had baked the crests of each little wave into a hard crust of light brown, and I could feel the crunch and squelch of my sneakers as the suction tried to pull them off.

When I reached her she was talking softly to the mare, showing no fear of the gnashing teeth, big as piano keys, only an inch from delicate fingertips. I had intended to scold her, but was so moved by the scene that I changed tactics.

"Be careful, Emma, or you're going to get hurt."

"She likes me, Daddy. Can I please ride this one?"

"I don't know, honey. I think we have to take the one they give us." I nodded toward the trailer home that served as the office to indicate the management, which in this case turned out to be a young man in dirty blue jeans and a sweat-soaked T-shirt, boots freshly dipped in muck.

"Let's go sign up and see what they have," I said.

The last remnant of carrot disappeared into the inner workings of the four-legged mulching machine, leaving Emma with nothing better to do than to obey. I picked my way back to the trailer as she followed in my footsteps.

The young man was busy sorting tack in the dark interior, rendered more obscure because of the contrast with the bright sunshine outside. He ignored me for a while, then gave a slight nod in our direction.

"*Wacca widdu feroo,*" he said, scratching the side of his head with a grimy paw.

I took it for a question and explained our desire to join the next group around the track. The source of his speech impediment was revealed when he spat a large gob of shiny brown liquid into the sawdust on the trailer floor, where it promptly disappeared. He approached and stopped short a few inches from my face, giving full benefit of his tobacco-stained teeth and breath. He looked me over, from mud-stained sneakers to starched white polo shirt, with the practiced eye of a Kentucky rancher about to bid on a tired old mare.

"She ever ride before?" he finally asked, startling me.

"Yes, a couple of times. I think she knows the basics."

"Mmm. We got a good horse for her." He gave a pointed look at my sneakers, then spat another gob of disappearing liquid at the floor. "How about you?" he added, baring his teeth in a twisted smile.

"I have, too. I can handle myself."

"Mmm. Just read these forms and fill out the blanks," he said. "You'll have to sign both waivers. There's another tour going out in about twenty minutes."

I took care of the paperwork. He asked for the fee

in advance, which might have raised my suspicions, but Emma was too thrilled for us to change our minds now.

"You'll be on Grandma and Josey," he said, handing me my change. I thanked him and carefully wiped my hands on the back of my jeans.

They called our names about a half hour later and we assembled on a wooden platform alongside the corral. There were eight of us altogether: Emma and I; our guide, Lilly; a group of four teenagers, two boys and their girlfriends; and a sullen-looking man in a shabby gray suit who kept to himself. We mounted the horses, with much laughing and kidding from the four teenagers about their form. There was a short lesson in horsemanship from Lilly, and then we set off on a well-worn trail, Lilly in the lead.

The Puente Hills stretched all around, still mantled in the green of winter's coverlet. Tall grasses waved in unison from windy canyons; laurel sumac and black sage grew thick on sunny slopes. Purple lupine and Canterbury bells vied with yellow mustard. Already the heat was on the edge of being uncomfortable. In a few more months it would be savagely hot at this time of day, and most of the shrubs would have turned as brown as the dirt beneath.

We rounded a grove of eucalyptus trees northwest of the corral. The San Gabriel Mountains were floating in the distance, above a shimmering chocolate haze of smog, peaks capped with dollops of snow like an ice-cream sundae. The horses loped along the trail as if on a giant carousel. It was soon evident that every animal might as well have been named Grandma; there wasn't so much as a canter in any of them. Our preliminary lesson in horsemanship had to be just for the record, an insurance requirement. There was no reason to touch the reins at all.

We settled into the ride in silence, each lost in our own little world. The teenagers forged ahead, bent on adventure. Lilly kept about thirty yards behind them. Emma seemed to be fascinated by this taciturn woman, with her riding boots and horsey odor, and stayed close on her tail, convinced that Lilly held the key to certain secrets of the equine world. She was right about that, and I was content to follow at a distance. The man in the gray suit trailed behind. At first, when I had seen him in the parking lot, I took him for a doting parent waiting for his child to finish a tour, having no idea what somebody like him would want out of a mundane trek around the park. But I soon lost interest in the group, as well as in the mechanics of riding. Once I was assured that Emma was managing all right, my mind drifted to other matters.

I thought about my interview with the police the day before. Actually, it was the gun that occupied my mind. Perhaps I shouldn't have told Akimoro about it. I wasn't even sure if it had ever been registered, or if it could be traced. My brother-in-law had given it to me ten years ago when he visited us in Greenfield. "You can't live in this hellhole without being prepared," Dante had said. Ever the Boy Scout, Dante's idea of being prepared was to have a weapon in every closet. I had accepted the firearm, a Beretta nine millimeter, without questioning how he had come by it. I had even gone to the outdoor range a couple of times, feeling obliged to know how to work the thing. But it had lain unused on the top shelf of the bedroom closet for the last ten years, like a dark spot in the depths of my subconscious mind.

At first I was just too busy to practice with it. Later, I began to fear it, thinking that if I gained facility in its use, it would turn me into some desperate vigilante, eager to wreak my own judgment at the slightest offense. Finally, I stopped thinking about it. My life became much too busy to concern myself with such accessories.

When Elaine and I first met, she was fund-raising for a large charity event, and she had to drive to several hospitals that were not in the best neighborhoods. It was she who had first brought up the subject of owning a gun. She had said she would feel safer with one, that she had been brought up with guns and knew how to use them, but that Jack was nervous around firearms and had forbidden them in the house. I gave her the Beretta. I had no use for it, and I had hoped my regard for her safety would impress her. By the time our liaison had become routine I stopped worrying about impressing her and gave it little more thought. I had asked her once, weeks later, what she'd done with it. She said she kept it in her car, and I had no reason to doubt her word. I had forgotten all about it until my little interview.

Our ride took the best part of an hour. We had come full circle and were approaching the corral. The horses lined up alongside the platform by the gate so we could dismount. Emma seemed to have enjoyed herself and was talking to her horse, leaning over to stroke its neck. I let the teenagers go first. The man in the gray suit held back and I went next, planning to help Emma off after me. Just as my foot touched the ground I heard a scream and a cry of pain.

Eager to prove her independence, Emma had tried to dismount by herself, before either Lilly or I could get to her. Her right leg must have caught in the stirrup—her little body spun around in a full twist. She was lying on the wooden platform, facedown on the rough two-by-fours, sobbing loudly.

I rushed to her side and gently picked her up.

"Oh, Daddy. It hurts!" she cried.

Tears flowed and I was filled with distress. Blood was running down her neck. I examined her chin. There was a gaping cut an inch long. I held her close in my arms, cradling her head.

"It's all right, love. It's all right," I kept repeating.

"Wow. That was a nasty one. Is she all right?" The voice, coming from over my shoulder, belonged to the man in the gray suit.

"No," I said sharply. Then I realized he was only trying to help, and felt ashamed. "I mean, I think so."

He knelt down beside me and examined Emma's

face intently. "Maybe you should take her to a doctor," he said.

I shook my head, distracted. "I am a doctor."

The last thing I wanted was for some well-intentioned bystander to send for an ambulance. I had no desire to spend the rest of the afternoon in an unfamiliar emergency room, waiting for Emma to be treated by some doctor I might not know. "I can take care of it," I said.

The man grinned. He had a sallow face, with gaps between his teeth, and his sandy hair was brushed back from his forehead in a long sweep. He started to rise, and as he did so the lapels bulged outward on his buttoned coat, exposing the shirt beneath. I was shocked to see the leather straps of what looked like a shoulder holster under his left arm. Nesting in there, I saw the black rubber grip of a gun butt. I figured I must have had guns on the mind. But there were other matters to tend to. I forced myself to concentrate on basic first aid.

"Daddy, it hurts." I felt Emma's arms tighten around me.

"I know, love. Don't move, I'm going to lay you down for a minute to see where you injured yourself, okay?"

The young man from the office had come running up with a blanket. I laid her down on it and felt her neck. She gave no sign of pain, and since she was moving arms and legs, I doubted a spinal fracture. I examined the rest of her as thoroughly as I could. She didn't seem to have any broken bones, but her hands were badly scraped, and the cut under her chin would need stitches.

"Shall I send for an ambulance?" asked the young man from the office.

"I'll take her myself," I said. He was relieved.

I lifted Emma carefully and carried her to the car. The others came along to help with the door. One of them laid the seat down as flat as it would go and I placed her in it. Thank heaven she was short. Her head, still shy of the headrest, snuggled firmly between the wings of the bucket seat. I strapped her in.

"You all right, love?" I asked.

She nodded, tears still filling her eyes.

I drove off to Memorial Hospital, leaving them to deal with their insurance forms and accident reports the rest of the afternoon.

Much later—after I had sutured Emma's chin, bought her an ice-cream cone from the hospital cafeteria, and cleaned her up so Rafaella wouldn't have quite so much to ramble on about when I finally took her home—I thought about that man in the gray suit.

If Akimoro had decided to have me followed, so what? I had nothing to hide. And cops carried guns: that was what they did, there was no arguing with that. But that fellow in the gray suit sure didn't act like a cop.

IT WAS TEN AFTER SEVEN WHEN I FOUND A parking spot on Melrose Avenue. Five minutes later I walked through the plate glass doors of La Luna Piena, immersed in the hustle of the evening rush.

The white-tiled walls resounded with the rattle of plates, the ringing of silverware, and the hum of conversation. The white-coifed chefs, their cotton uniforms now moist and limp and spattered with oil and tomato stains, bullied the skillets on open flames, teasing portions of fettuccini Alfredo and angel hair pasta sautéed with fresh scallops and crisp scampi. The aproned waiters, between sneaking cigarette breaks by the rest rooms, dodged around tables and chairs, their arms loaded with steaming plates of pasta, piled high like steps to a doorway. The fresh aroma of *bruschetta*, sliced bread seared in garlic oil, lingered in the air.

I nodded to the hostess and walked past the circular grill to the four hidden tables in the back. Elaine was sitting alone in the corner, an island of serenity surrounded by bustle.

It was our favorite spot. We could watch the chefs at work, marvel at their proficiency, ogle their creations, and savor the wonderful aromas that filtered back to us— all without being seen by the rest of the clientele. Moreover, there was a mirror on the hall tree down by the rest rooms in which we had a sweeping view of the whole restaurant, including the door. A most important spot, indeed. I sometimes fancied that when we were not using it, the management saved this very spot for visiting Mafia dons, movie stars out for a quiet meal, or even politicians on a tryst with their paramours.

Elaine acknowledged my presence with her usual half-smile, cheek twitching to the left.

"Hello, Gareth. You're late."

"Hi, yourself." I sat down.

"Were you followed?"

I nodded. "I think so. I didn't even bother to look this time. I've been followed by somebody or other for the last two days."

"Me, too. Since Wednesday, actually. Have you been asked to give a statement yet?"

I nodded again. "Yesterday. Akimoro gave me the third degree. How about you?"

"On Friday." She smiled. "He was quite nice about it, considering what they're thinking. What shall we do, Gareth?"

"I think we should order."

I decided on the *penne all'arrabbiato* and she went for *fettuccini ai funghi*. I asked for a bottle of Ariella to wash it down with. There was a strained moment of silence while I played with my breadstick. Then we both spoke at once.

"I'm scared, Gareth," she said.

"Where's the gun now?" I asked.

"I don't know."

"What are you scared of?"

We stopped and started again.

"You don't know what you're scared of?"

"No. I don't know where the gun is."

"What?" I became aware of eyes focused on me. Not just Elaine's, but those of a couple from the next table. I lowered my voice. "What do you mean you don't know where it is?"

She looked frightened. At another time I would have had sympathy for her, but now my own fears supervened.

"It's missing," she said. "I just found out yesterday. Akimoro asked me about the gun and I told him it was in my glove compartment. When we went to look it was gone."

"And when was the last time you saw it?"

"A month ago, when I put my new registration in the car."

I snapped my breadstick in two but didn't bother to eat it. "Don't you lock your glove compartment?" I asked.

"Yes, but somebody broke in. Two weeks ago we were at Cedars-Sinai for a hospital reception. We went in separate cars because I wanted to go shopping later. We left the cars in the doctor's lot. There was no attendant."

I wondered if she really had shopping in mind, or was there someone else in her life already?

"When we came out all the windows were smashed on both cars. We thought it was just vandalism, somebody who hated doctors. I mean, after all, two Rolls-Royces next to each other. You know how people are! We checked inside but nothing much seemed to be missing, just a couple of Jack's files. They would have been worthless to a thief. There were some scratches on my dashboard but I thought it happened when the glass broke. I'd forgotten about the gun. It must have been taken then but I didn't even notice. Jack took the cars in and had everything fixed. They wouldn't have stolen it at the shop. They're much too honest."

Likely they were. They only fiddled repair bills at Jack's garage.

"Why didn't you tell me about the break-in when we met last week?"

She gave me a sour look. "We had more important things to discuss. Didn't we?"

I nodded. Our salad arrived, garnished with red and yellow spirals, carrots and bell peppers.

"So what do we do, Gareth?" she asked.

"We eat."

The raspberry vinegar dressing tasted better than anything they served in Greenfield.

She played with her food. "Come on, Gareth, get serious. We're both suspects in Jack's murder, and we don't have an alibi except for each other. I'm sure they don't believe a word I say anymore."

"That's not enough to pin a murder on us," I said between mouthfuls. "It takes more than an affair to want to kill somebody. After all, we broke up."

I didn't want to ask her about other possible motives. I was sure Jack was well insured, but it wouldn't help to bring it up.

"I'm sure *he* doesn't think we're breaking up." Elaine nodded in the direction of the rest room.

I turned to look. I couldn't see whom she referred to at first, but then I noticed a familiar reflection in the mirror. Our young, muscular policeman from Beverly Hills was having dinner at the bar.

"Should we send him a glass of wine with our compliments?" I asked.

"Only if Pino shoves it up his ass."

The pasta arrived, mine pungent enough to sting my eyes, hers loaded with porcini mushrooms. We lathered on the grated cheese.

"What about Jack's contacts?" I asked. "He have any enemies?"

"Don't be silly, Gareth. Jack had more enemies than he had friends, you know that. But no one's killed him in all these years. Why would they want to start now?"

"Did he meet anybody unusual in the last few weeks? Did he do anything different? Isn't there anything we can go on?"

"No. I've gone over all this with the police."

"What about a gang thing? A drive-by?"

"That's ridiculous."

"No, it's not. A drive-by shooting is the easiest explanation I've heard yet. In Los Angeles, explanations don't get any easier."

"Gareth, people from Watts and South Central drive down their own streets and kill each other. They don't come up to Beverly Hills and pick off successful doctors."

She had a point. I soaked a piece of bread with sauce and stuffed it in my mouth. "Are you going to finish your pasta?"

"No. Help yourself."

She watched me attack the mushrooms.

"Do you have a lawyer?" I asked, washing down the garlic with a sip of Ariella.

"Yes. Stanley Bing. Do you?"

"No. Who's Stanley Bing?"

"He's Jack's lawyer."

"Isn't that . . . sort of conflict of interest?"

She raised her eyebrows.

"I mean, if you are accused of killing him, can his own lawyer defend you?"

"Gareth! Nobody's accusing me." Her eyes narrowed. "Or is that what you think?"

I intercepted her glare for a second, then looked at my food. I didn't know what to think.

Of course, she couldn't have actually gone out and pulled the trigger herself; she was sitting in my car when he died. But could she possibly have paid someone else to do it? Elaine had traveled in some fairly eclectic circles during her years as a model. The world of fashion was reputed to turn on a different axis from the rest of us, with a moral atmosphere that ran loose and fast. I did not doubt that there'd be plenty of opportunity for parasites, skulking around the shadows behind the floodlights, who would do anything for money. It wouldn't be hard for Elaine to revive one of her old contacts.

Back yesterday, when Akimoro was questioning me about the gun, I'd had my doubts about Elaine. But the more I thought about it, the less probable it seemed. It had to do with one of the reasons I left her.

Elaine was smart enough to know which way the wind blew. She liked men, and she understood why. She enjoyed me for my company, and she enjoyed Jack for his money, but she never confused the two of us. More than that, she understood herself. She lacked the ability to organize her life, and she had come to terms with it. She could plan for today, and she could plan for tomorrow, but she had no idea that next week even existed. I couldn't live my life one week at a time; she couldn't live it any other way. She was capable of thinking of murder, but I don't think she had the capacity to plan it through.

"Tell me, Gareth. Do you think I did it?" she demanded.

"No. I don't believe you did it, Elaine."

"Thank heaven for that," she said, with another half-smile. "You didn't, did you, Gareth?"

I looked at her. She really was beautiful. She stared straight at me with the cool power of those light blue eyes, unfeeling, reminding me of a cat, a beautiful animal to be petted and stroked, but never possessed. She had hurt me—and I wanted to hurt her back.

"Tell me, Elaine," I asked, "are you seeing another man?"

Her eyes narrowed and her nostrils flared. The color in her cheeks darkened.

"I don't think that's any of your business," she snapped.

I grinned. "You need one, Elaine. It suits you."

"I'll be just fine by myself, thank you very much." She glared at me, gathered up her bag, and strode off.

I watched her in the mirror until she was out the door. The muscular cop sitting at the bar looked confused for a moment, then he hurriedly threw some bills on the counter and followed her out.

I soaked up the last of the mushroom sauce with a big fat piece of homemade bread.

GREENFIELD BOULEVARD IS THE COMMER-
cial backbone of the city. East-west: two lanes in
each direction. It has freeway access, high visibility,
and easy parking. I cruised past car dealers, gas stations, restaurants, and fast-food pits; ignored a pet
store, a church, and a funeral home; glided by video
stores, hardware and software outlets—all of them staking
their corporate territory in multicolored signs, like giant
heraldic flags, reaching up into the smog-filled sky on mas-
sive pillars of concrete and steel.

The billboard I was looking for on that particular
Monday morning was a modest, little one by comparison,
a ten-foot board with painted white letters on weathered
pine: BEULAH'S ANTIQUE EMPORIUM.

I wasn't due in the office for another hour. I had
been thinking about Rocco's story of the airline pilot who
sold antiques. My own collection of art pottery had grown
like weeds, overflowing the bookcase in my living room
and five storage boxes in the shed. The ones I had chosen
to display were my prize finds; the rest I had grown tired
of. My tastes had changed over the years, and the idea of
selling a few of the less-treasured pieces appealed to me.
They wouldn't bring enough to make an alimony check,
but I could always use the money to buy something new
and exciting. A recirculating fund, as it were.

Beulah's was our local antique mall, a rambling
one-story building between the Midas Muffler shop and a

Ford dealership. I had passed it many times but been in only twice, and it was a year since the last time. There were half a dozen cars in the lot when I pulled in. Between the painted letters on the sign in front, you could still make out the spots where they had sandblasted the previous tenant's name away. "Harry's Unfinished Oak Furniture" was no longer in business.

The plateglass frontage was piled high with junk, squashed in, as if someone had decided to wash the floor inside and shoved all the merchandise against the windows. Opening the door tripped a photoelectric cell, and a chime sounded my entrance. The girl behind the counter looked up from a portable television set. She watched through deep-set eyes as I approached, unable to speak for the two bulges in her cheeks. Chomp, chomp, chomp, she went, lids blinking to every third bite. An enormous bread-roll sandwich was conveniently poised about four inches from her lips, clamped in position by ten pudgy little fingers, within striking distance of those fateful gnashers.

I neared the counter. She stopped chewing momentarily and, eyes smoldering with sufferance at my inconsiderate entry, swung her legs off a footstool and arose. I imagined that no matter what she was asked to do, it would invariably interrupt the act of eating, and good reason for it. Beneath her blue-and-white-patterned sundress was a figure of such proportions, it might take all her waking hours to fill.

"Excuse me," I said with some temerity, wondering if she could hear just as well with her mouth full.

She signaled me to wait, put down the sandwich, and began to wipe her fingers carefully on a paper napkin. I took advantage of the pause to look around the room.

The store seemed larger on the inside. It was subdivided into stalls by particleboard, each partition about five feet high and enclosing a space roughly twenty feet square. Most of the front stalls were chockablock with assorted merchandise. Some were neat, with items arranged in rows and by category, while others seemed to bear witness to some gale-force hurricane. One or two reminded me of Jillian's room after a weekend sleepover. The whole place smelled of furniture polish and dust.

"May I help you?" The girl's voice filtered through strands of lettuce and mounds of chewy dough.

"I was wondering about renting a space here," I replied. "I'd like to sell some of my antiques."

She swallowed the last morsel from behind her molars. "Are you a dealer?"

"No. Do I have to be? I have a fair collection of art pottery. I was wondering if there was a market for it in Greenfield."

"You'll have to speak to the owner about that," she said.

I had a fleeting image of someone even larger than she was.

"All I can tell you," she went on, "is that a space runs two-fifty a month, first month in advance. If you only want a showcase, it's one-fifty. We sell the stuff for you and pay the tax. We take ten percent commission on anything we sell. If you want to lock anything, you buy your own locks and leave a key with us." She looked at me and blinked, a little breathless after her long delivery.

"How many people do you think come in here on an average day?" I asked.

"Depends. Fifty. Maybe a hundred. More on weekends."

"And what kind of antiques do they buy?"

"Depends. Sometimes furniture. Mostly little things, I'd say. Depression glass and stuff."

I couldn't help feeling I wasn't learning much. "I'd better talk to Beulah," I said.

The little eyes went even smaller. "There's no Beulah here."

"Oh. What's the owner's name?"

"You want to talk to Rosie. She's in and out. Do you

want to leave your name? I'll tell her to call you."

I wrote out my name and phone number. She handed me a card: ROSIE MCCLANAHAN. BEULAH'S ANTIQUE EMPORIUM. APPRAISALS. PROBATE ESTATES.

I was being dismissed. She needed another three-point fixation on her sandwich—two hands and a mouth.

GREENFIELD WAS AN OLD TOWN BY CALI-
fornia standards, first settled by German Baptists at
the turn of the century. Paley Street, a broad, four-
lane avenue now lined with jacaranda trees, was one
of the original thoroughfares. In late spring and
early summer, when these trees were in bloom, with
their purple canopies framing the San Gabriel Mountains,
Greenfield was as beautiful as any place I'd seen.

At the junction of Paley and Church Streets was a
one-story bungalow built in the Craftsman era, an example
of California architecture from Greenfield's early days. I
referred to it as my corporate headquarters. The wooden
plaque outside the door bore the legend GARETH LLOYD,
M.D., INC. in large brass letters.

I drove up to the back lot and let myself in the side
door. Debbie Wolstett, high priestess of my corporate em-
pire, was sitting at her desk. She had a phone tucked under
her left ear as she scanned the computer.

"Well, Mrs. Robertson, I think we can fit you in at
five-fifteen. . . . Yes, I understand. . . . No, I can't tell you
how long it will be, but we are fully booked, so there might
be a wait. . . . And don't forget to bring your insurance
card." She hung up the receiver and rolled her eyes in despair as she caught sight of me.

"It's going to be another one of those Mondays."
She shrugged. "Just when I was hoping to get home early
for a change."

"Oh! Meeting somebody? Hot date, perhaps?" I deposited my briefcase.

"Please!" She laughed. "The last time I had a hot date he wilted like lettuce after an hour and ran home to his mother."

"Probably because you breathed all over him."

"Dr. Lloyd, if I breathe all over a man, the last thing I expect is for him to wilt," she said, winking.

I left it at that.

Debbie was my office manager, secretary, scheduler, insurance biller, coffeemaker, and bouncer. She was in her mid-thirties, divorced fifteen years earlier from a childless union with somebody she still never talked about. At first glance she presented a picture not unlike an Egyptian hieroglyph: round face with straight chestnut hair down to her neck, skinny rectangular body, flat chest with breasts no bigger than nutmegs, matchstick arms, and long skirt down to her ankles. On closer scrutiny, if you looked past the steel-rimmed reading glasses halfway down her petite nose, you could see the warmth in her light brown eyes.

Debbie had come to work for me five years ago and had soon showed such aptitude at the mechanics of running an office that I was only too happy to relinquish my control, having learned by that time I had no talent for it.

"Well, I'm glad you're in a good mood," she said. "We have a full house and we can't use the bathroom because the toilet's clogged. The plumber said he couldn't come in till Wednesday, but I persuaded him to show up tomorrow at seven, as long as we pay him time and a half. Other than that, everything's fine. Oh, there are two messages on your desk."

"Where's Lavonne? She on a toilet run?"

"Maybe. Actually, I sent her to the post office before we get swamped. We had a couple of bills overdue and they had to get out today. Don't worry about her. She'll be back before the first patient gets here."

"How's she working out, anyway?" I asked.

"Just fine. She spent half the morning on callbacks and the rest of it stocking the rooms. She's a fast learner, and she's willing. I think we got a good one here."

"It's about time. After all the bad luck we've been having."

"Tell me about it," said Debbie. "Anyway, what do you think of her? How does she work in the back with you?"

"No complaints so far. She seems to remember most of the things I show her. I think the patients like her; she's pleasant enough."

"Oh, they like her all right." Debbie pushed her glasses farther up her nose. "Charlie Perez has called three times today to ask her out. I had to tell him her boyfriend's a basketball player. I think it scared him off."

Charlie Perez was a journeyman carpenter I was treating for a minor hand injury. He always came early for his appointments and hovered at the window, keeping the girls entertained with his jokes.

"I don't think anything scares Charlie," I said, laughing. Then I changed my tone. "Seriously, Debbie, you haven't heard any comments, have you?"

"No." She filled a mug with coffee and placed it on the counter for me. "I wouldn't pay any attention to them even if I did. And I don't think you should, either, Dr. Lloyd."

"I'm not going to. I made the decision and I intend to stick by it. Mind you, I wouldn't hesitate to let her go if she messed up, but she's turning out to be the best medical assistant we've seen in years. Still, I expect I'll hear about it sooner or later from somebody. You know how people are." I picked up the coffee and walked back toward my private consultation room.

From its early days Greenfield was settled largely by Anglos and Latinos, with various Asian nationalities making up the difference. Even now, the African-American population had made little inroad into this quiet community, snuggled up against the hills away from the hustle and bustle of downtown Los Angeles. Hiring Lavonne Singleterry was like waving a red flag in the face of this middle-class suburban town.

She had been a patient of mine years ago, soon after her divorced mother had moved into a two-bedroom bungalow on the east side to serve as the first black teacher in the Greenfield school district. Mrs. Singleterry had caused quite a stir at first, although only a few of the people who talked about "that nice black lady who's teaching our little ones" could actually tell you that her subject was math and she taught at the elementary school. The buzz settled down after a few months, until the day that little Lavonne was mauled by three of her classmates in fourth grade. They had pummeled her face and slashed her cheek with the edge of a pull-tab from a soda can, which one of them, in a sadistic display of ingenuity for a fourth grader, had used as a knuckle-duster. When I arrived at the emergency room I found a very plucky nine-year-old with a three-inch gash in her chin and nail gouges all over her face. The *Greenfield Daily News* doubled its circulation over the next week as the details unfolded. The "hate crime" was investigated by the school board, but although three suspects were rooted out, and disciplinary measures imposed, formal charges were never filed because Lavonne was too scared to talk, and no one could agree on how to prosecute three nine-year-old girls from nice, middle-class families in Greenfield.

Mrs. Singleterry moved her daughter out of town shortly after and took a job as a sales clerk in Pasadena. Lavonne transferred into a more integrated school and grew up to be a very pretty teenager. The scratches on her face healed with time but the laceration left a visible scar. Twice a year they made a special journey back to my office for follow-up. Three years later I had surgically revised the scar without charge. Both the Singleterrys were eternally grateful. They still visited me periodically. Three weeks ago, when Lavonne had told me she was thinking of nursing school but first she needed some exposure to the field, I'd offered her a job. It took her ten days to think about it. In the end I'd convinced her that things had changed in Greenfield. But I hadn't yet convinced myself.

On the way to my consultation room I passed the bathroom door, with a sign saying OUT OF ORDER stuck across at eye level. I opened it and peeked inside. Thankfully the lid of the toilet bowl was down. There was a faint smell of pine-scented deodorant. If anything had spilled over, Debbie must have cleaned it up; the floor was unusually spotless. One of these days that girl deserved a raise.

I went over to my desk, shaking my head at the thought of another plumbing bill. I had bought the building eight years earlier from Dr. Painter, a general practitioner who had served Greenfield for three generations before retiring. He was known far and wide as Dr. Pain because of his disdain for anesthetics. Times like these, I was sorry I ever met him. The exterior of the building was quite lovely: stone foundation offsetting aquamarine walls, wooden front porch with stuccoed columns, shingle roof. But although the shell had been well maintained through all these years, the innards were subject to consumption, digested by the ravages of time. Every few years a major system would fail and have to be refurbished. One year it was the roof joists, next the hot-water pipes. This year the roots from the old oaks were threatening the sewer system, and it was the third time we'd sent for Ramirez's Plumbing Service.

Sometimes it felt like throwing good money after bad. This corporate headquarters, my lovely Craftsman bungalow, was not exactly designed for business, least of all a medical office.

I placed the coffee on my desk and grabbed a heap of papers from my seat. Ordinary mail was piled in the box marked "Incoming," where it sometimes yellowed before I got to it. Letters demanding immediate attention were left on my chair. Debbie figured the first thing I always did was sit down.

I checked the phone messages. One was from a doctor in an industrial clinic nearby and the other was from Rosie McClanahan. I called the doctor first. He wanted to refer a patient with carpal tunnel syndrome. I thanked him and passed the call to Debbie so she could make the appointment. Then I dialed the number for Beulah's Antique Emporium.

A woman with a clear voice answered on the third ring. I assumed it wasn't the young girl.

"Rosie McClanahan?"

"Speaking."

"Rosie, this is Dr. Lloyd. I was in your store earlier today about renting a space. I talked to your cashier about the terms."

"Yes, I know. Edna told me you'd come in. She didn't know you were a doctor, though."

"Well, does it matter if I'm not a dealer?"

"Not at all. We have a few spaces available. Did you happen to see one you liked?"

"Actually I didn't look around. But she mentioned something about showcases. That sounds more in line with what I'd like. I don't have any furniture, just art pottery."

"That's even better. We need more specialists. There's a good market for pottery nowadays. I'm sure you'll do quite well."

She quoted me some prices realized on recent sales. She said I could try it for a month or two and quit any time I wanted, there would be no long-term lease. I decided to go ahead and told her I would be in at the end of the month with a consignment.

"I'll look forward to it," she said. "By the way, what kind of doctor are you?"

"A plastic surgeon."

"Wonderful! Now I know you'll do well. I didn't realize plastic surgeons were such avid antique collectors. You're the second one I've heard of today."

"Really?" I wasn't aware of any of my colleagues with the same interest. "Who was the other one?"

"It's such a coincidence, isn't it? I was having lunch with a friend of mine this afternoon. He has a store on Melrose Avenue and he does a lot of estate appraisals, like me. He was telling me about this plastic surgeon who just died, some guy from Beverly Hills. My friend's doing the estate. Apparently, this guy had a large collection of art, some very nice pieces, from what I understood. I can't tell you much more, but my friend was pretty excited about it."

"And what was the man's name?" I asked, feeling I already knew the answer.

"Chuck Thompson," she said. "You should talk to him. The heirs might want to sell some of the collection."

"No. I meant the plastic surgeon. What was his name?"

"You ought to ask Chuck. He told me but I don't remember it now. It sounded like something to do with food."

"Ehrenberger," I said. "Was it Jack Ehrenberger?"

"Yes. That sounds like it. Did you know him?"

"Yes, I did. But I wasn't aware he was a collector."

"I've had that happen to me, Dr. Lloyd. You never can tell who's got the collector bug anymore, you meet them in the strangest places."

You do, indeed. I wondered if there was anything else Jack collected that I didn't know about.

"Can you give me Chuck's number, Rosie?"

"Sure. I have it here somewhere." She gave me a phone number and an address on Melrose. "Tell him I sent you."

"I will. Thank you, Rosie."


Lavonne returned from her errand in good time, and quietly and efficiently went about the business of moving patients in and out of examining rooms, showing that my first instinct in hiring her had paid off. We worked smoothly about two-thirds of the way through the afternoon schedule. Even the shadow of a broken toilet was losing its threat as a major catastrophe, and taking on the dimensions of a minor snafu. I was in the middle of removing sutures from a recent eyelid repair when I was interrupted by a knock on the exam room door.

It was Lavonne. "Debbie needs you at the front desk, Doctor."

"I'll be out in a minute."

I finished what I was doing, took an extra minute to discuss the benefits of various moisturizing creams with the patient, then stepped out into the hall.

"What's it about, Lavonne?"

"There's a couple of gangbangers out there, and they're giving Debbie a hard time."

"Gangbangers? What are they looking for? Free tattoo removals?"

"I don't know. They don't have an appointment and they refuse to leave."

"Let's find out."

I wasn't averse to removing a tattoo or two as a public service. Some of my colleagues had used the ploy for free publicity in the local press, and it had worked to their benefit. But gangbangers in the waiting room were apt to scare the genteel folk of Greenfield, or at least cause them to squirm in their seats and sit on their hands so they might conceal their gold bracelets and diamond rings. Gangbangers needed to be ushered in the back door, preferably for late-evening appointments.

As I approached the business office I saw two men standing just inside the doorway. They were leaning over the counter, backs toward me, watching Debbie as she argued in a slightly higher pitch than normal, stressing each syllable and using hand gestures in a way she usually reserved for patients who had trouble with English.

"But the doctor is busy now," she said. "You have to make an appointment to see him."

She was addressing the one on the right. He stood a few feet in front of the other, leaning heavily on a pair of crutches, his left leg encased in a brand-new cast. They were both wearing baggy black linen trousers and plain white short-sleeved shirts, their cropped hair slicked back with some greasy substance. The man with the crutches had his pants split up the left leg to midthigh to accommodate his cast.

"But I have to see Dr. Lloyd today," he said with a heavy Hispanic accent.

Debbie caught sight of me and shrugged her shoulders in frustration. The man she was speaking to turned around.

His face was distorted and swollen, bruised around the forehead, the left cheek, and down his short, squat neck. There were stitches around his left eye and lips, and fresh scabs of blood all over his face.

I recognized him immediately.

THE MAN FACING ME, NOW LISTING slightly as he supported most of his weight on the crutch under his left arm, was the same man whose face I had so painstakingly pieced together on Thursday night. There was absolutely no doubt. I recognized every stitch.

It was Fernando Rojas, drug dealer, career criminal, gangbanger. What could he possibly want with me?

The other man spun around, and I saw his right hand move into his trouser pocket. I could hear my pulse as I waited for his next move, but he kept his hand in his pocket and smiled. Mr. Rojas partially raised his right crutch in my direction.

"Are you Dr. Lloyd?" he asked.

I nodded. I was nervous but I didn't want to show it, at least not to Debbie and Lavonne. I had treated a few gang members recently, this one included. But they usually came to the emergency room shot or stabbed first, in a state we referred to as "acute distress." Then we strapped them into gurneys. There was always plenty of help: big, burly technicians and hospital security. We held the advantage.

In my office, however, there was just the two girls and me. If Mr. Rojas and his friend decided that they didn't like the treatment they received last week, it wasn't likely that they'd sit down and discuss it over tea. In the old days they preferred to get good and mad before they'd shoot you, but even that didn't seem to apply anymore. Was this the reason Jack Ehrenberger had met his end? Should I attempt to call the police? I could try and rush Mr. Rojas and knock him down, grab the crutch, and jab the other fellow in the neck with it. Unless he had a gun in that pocket. Wasn't that the reason they wore those baggy pants in the first place?

"Mr. Rojas," I said in a half-whisper.

He glared at me. A steady, piercing look. I tried to judge his mood, but the bloated and bruised face was unreadable. It must have been a full minute before he broke into a crooked smile.

"I'm sorry I couldn't remember you," he said. "I don't remember too much from last Thursday."

The apology put me at ease.

"I need to talk with you," he went on. "Now's a good time for me."

Just like that. I tried to figure his age. Twenty-two, maybe twenty-five: hard to tell with that battered face.

I didn't want them there one minute longer than necessary. I gestured for the two to enter a vacant exam room, and they stepped in ahead of me. I turned to Debbie and Lavonne, both staring at me wide-eyed.

"Keep your ears open," I whispered. "And call the police if you hear any trouble." I walked into the room and closed the door.

The companion was sitting in the chair that I usually used, arms folded, grim-faced, and staring straight ahead. Mr. Rojas stood next to him. I still wasn't sure what they were up to, but I knew I was the one who would be answering the questions in this interview. I sat on the exam table, in keeping with the reversal of roles.

Mr. Rojas dropped his right crutch and held out his hand.

"First, Dr. Lloyd," he said, "thank you for what you did for me on Thursday. You saved my life."

I was pleasantly surprised. "Don't mention it. I was

just doing my job. Anyway, it was Dr. Varta that saved your life. I merely stitched up your face."

"Great! I'm here now because I want you to finish the job."

"What do you mean?"

"I still have pieces of glass in my face. And up here in my hair." He ran his fingers over his scalp as he spoke. "They're stuck. You didn't take them all out."

"Oh? I tried to remove all that I could see. Some must have surfaced over the last few days."

"That's right. That's what happened. I think you need to take these out now. They won't just go away, will they?"

"Well, they might come out in time. Let me see where they are."

He leaned forward and pointed to several scabs on his forehead. I touched the skin, gently pressing the surface to feel the texture. There were three hard knots beneath the scabs that he indicated, easier to feel now that he had pointed them out.

"I'm sorry," I said. "I must have missed them when I sewed you up. I was more concerned with the gashes over your eye at the time."

"That's okay. I'm not blaming you. You did a good job already. I just want to get this over with."

"Well, those pieces need to be removed. They're too deep to come out by themselves."

"When can you do this?" he asked.

"We should wait at least a few days. There'll be some more healing by then and the job will be simpler." I was almost back to normal now. "How about Monday, a week from now?"

"Will it be all right to wait until then?"

"I can give you some antibiotics to take in the meantime. That's not the problem."

I regretted my words as soon as they were out—too late.

"Is there a problem, then?" he asked. "What is it?"

"Well." I wondered how to phrase my statement without provoking him. I had no idea what his status with the police was, but I couldn't make any plans unless I knew. "Aren't you under arrest or something? I mean, do you have any other commitments for next week?"

He smiled. "I guess you're wondering what I'm doing here."

"I am."

"I have a very good attorney. I made bail. The police didn't have anything special to charge me with. Anyway, I committed no crime. They tried to keep me as long as they could for questioning, but my attorney took care of it."

The companion nodded with each statement.

"I paid cash for my bail. And I will pay cash for your services. You don't need to worry about that." He put his hand into his pocket and pulled out a roll of hundred-dollar bills.

I was impressed. He could have put a down payment on a house with money like that.

"How much?" he asked.

"Three thousand," I answered quickly. I was already accustomed to taking payment in advance from my cosmetic surgery patients, and years of haggling over antiques had taught me how to think on my feet when money was about to change hands. "That will cover what I did last Thursday as well as the next operation."

He began to count out the bills.

"You can give it to my secretary. She'll make out a receipt."

"I don't need a receipt," he said, slowly and deliberately. "I know where to find you if anything goes wrong."

I felt a sudden chill. This was not the kind of man who would run off to a lawyer if events didn't turn out as planned. Mr. Rojas was likely to take care of any malpractice action in his own court. I wondered how many times he had acted as judge and jury. His companion, who yet remained to be introduced, seemed quite capable of carrying out any sentence that he cared to impose. In the very room where I had previously discussed risks and complications, and possible bad outcomes, to patients who were about to undergo the knife, Mr. Rojas was now reminding me of the consequences of displeasing him.

I had to tell myself this was routine. There was no chance of letting him down. It was really a simple job to take a few glass splinters out. Besides, I couldn't very well refuse. He was my patient, and I was obliged to see him through.

With resignation, I pulled a blank surgical scheduling slip out of the rack of forms on the wall and began to fill it out: "Removal of foreign bodies: Face and Scalp." I entered the patient's name and filled in the rest of the form. For anesthesia I put down "Local." I didn't want to complicate someone else's life by insisting on an anesthesiologist for the case. Mr. Rojas would tolerate a local anesthetic as well as anyone, I figured.

I opened the door to usher them out. Debbie and Lavonne were standing behind the front desk in suspended animation, two pairs of eyes on our every move. I explained to Debbie that we would be doing surgery on Mr. Rojas next Monday and handed her the scheduling slip. Then I smiled at her in triumph. "And my fee will be three thousand dollars. Cash. In advance." I was enjoying her look of disbelief. "Mr. Rojas will pay you now."

"Very smart, Dr. Lloyd. Very smart." He was following every word and seemed reassured that I insisted on being paid. I'm sure he understood those terms better than any other.

I stood and watched as Debbie entered it in the log. She took the money and tried to hand him a receipt. He waved it aside.

"You'll need this for Uncle Sam," Debbie said. "Medical expenses can be tax deductible, you know."

Mr. Rojas treated her to a tolerant glare. "I'll try and remember that," he said. Satisfied with the arrangements, he turned to me. "Seven-thirty Monday morning, Dr. Lloyd."

"Right."

"Don't be late."

"No, I'll be there."

He nodded. His companion held the door open for him as they walked out. Mr. Rojas made quite good time for a man on crutches. He never did introduce his friend. When the door shut behind them it was as if someone had just sealed the room from a cold draft.

"Now, what was that all about?" asked Debbie. "Those guys sure gave me the creeps."

I explained about the accident on Thursday night, and the transfer to University Hospital.

"My God," Lavonne said when I had finished. "You don't think he escaped from the jail ward, do you?"

"Hardly. I don't think he would have shown up here if he was on the run."

"I suppose you're right. Still, don't you think you should inform the cops or something? Maybe they would like to know what he's up to."

It seemed a good idea. I tried to think of the name of the Greenfield policeman who had spoken to me on Thursday night.

Debbie was looking at me quizzically, a hint of a smile on her lips.

"Reinholdt," I remembered. "Hank Reinholdt. Call the Greenfield precinct house and talk to Hank Reinholdt. Ask him if it's true that Mr. Rojas made bail. Tell him what's happened and ask if he thinks it's safe to go ahead and operate on him."

Debbie suddenly started to laugh.

"What's the matter?" I asked. "You seem to be in a very good mood all of a sudden."

"I am. We finally find a patient who pays his bills on time and without a whimper, and you say we should call the cops on him."

I TRIED TO SETTLE BACK INTO THE DAILY routine, but there was an excitement in the air that seemed to infuse Lavonne and Debbie with the giggles. Everything we did for the next hour was colored with anticlimax, and any complaint from a patient was met with a stifled snicker. It was while we were still in this state of lighthearted buoyancy, bathing in the afterglow of the day's highlight, that we were hit with a booster in the shape of another unexpected visitor.

We were almost through for the day. Debbie was on the phone trying to track down the adjuster for an insurance company, and Lavonne was in an exam room taking a history from a patient, when a man's face appeared in the waiting room window. I was standing by the front desk, the only one not doing anything at the moment. I walked up to the window to help.

I was startled to recognize the man in the shabby gray suit from the equestrian park. On Sunday, after seeing the gun in his jacket, I had assumed he was another of Akimoro's squad from the Beverly Hills police, perhaps assigned to follow me. It was disconcerting seeing him there in my office.

"What can I do for you?" I asked. "I hope it isn't more questions."

"Dr. Lloyd?"

"Yes? I'm afraid I'm quite busy. This is really an inconvenience."

Debbie looked up from the phone. She was on hold and waited to see if I needed help.

"I wonder if I could have a talk with you," said the man. "I can wait until you're finished with your patients."

"Well." I looked at Debbie, wishing she would bail me out. This was one time I didn't mind if she said we had to go on until midnight.

"We have two more patients," Debbie said. "They're both in the rooms already. Mrs. Robertson's the last one and she made me promise I'd get her out in time. She has to pick her daughter up from day care."

I turned to the man. "You see, Mr. . . . ."

"Plant. Bob Plant. I'm an investigator with In-fraTec Agency." He removed a card from his jacket and handed it to me. "I understand how busy you are, Doctor. I'll wait."

I looked at the plain piece of white bond: ROBERT PLANT, INFRATEC AGENCY. The address was a P.O. box in New Orleans. Nothing more than that.

"What's it about, Mr. Plant?"

He nodded toward the card. "I work for a private detective agency."

"In New Orleans?"

"That's right."

"What has this got to do with me? Aren't you a little far from home?"

He nodded. "I'd be happy to explain it to you. It should only take a half hour of your time."

I looked back at Debbie. She was still holding the phone, taking it all in with a wide-eyed expression. I could tell she was having a wonderful day, probably the only time in her life she didn't mind being on hold with an insurance company.

"Actually, Dr. Lloyd, I have a proposition for you," the man went on. "You might qualify for a reward, if you're interested."

I turned to him. He didn't seem very threatening.

In fact, a slow smile worked its way across his face and he spread his hands out in a shrug. "What have you got to lose?"

"All right, Mr. Plant, I'll be ready in thirty minutes," I said.

When I was through with Mrs. Robertson I told the girls they could go home.

"I'm going to want a full explanation in the morning," Debbie said on her way out. "This has been much too weird for one day. I may not be able to sleep tonight."

"Just make sure you're here at seven," I said. "To let that plumber in."

Debbie nodded. "By the way," she added, "I talked to Officer Reinholdt. He sure sounded nice. What's he look like? Maybe we should invite him over for a free consult or something."

I smiled. "He doesn't need my services. And you can get your dates on your own time."

"Dr. Lloyd! After all I do for you. Anyway, he said it was true that Mr. Rojas got out on bail. He said to be careful of him, he's a dangerous man."

"Thanks, Debbie. You can show Mr. Plant in now."

Bob Plant entered the consultation room and we shook hands. His suit hadn't been pressed since I last saw him, but he was wearing a fresh white shirt and striped tie. In the soft yellow glow of my desk lamp his sallow skin took on a pearly sheen, with three red pimples glowing on the left cheek, giving the impression he spent far too little time outdoors.

"I see you have an integrated office here, Dr. Lloyd," he said.

"Yes. Lavonne's just started working for me. Does very well, too."

"Lucky for you. Never can tell what you're getting nowadays."

"Right," I said, looking him in the face, feeling I

knew which side of the issue he favored. Trust the first comment to come all the way from New Orleans. And here I was wondering about attitudes in Greenfield.

"I want to thank you for your help with my daughter yesterday," I said, trying to change the subject.

"It was an unfortunate accident. I hope she's all right."

"She's fine. She didn't like the stitches, but I think she'll go riding again."

"So nice to be young."

He seemed tired. I offered him a chair.

"Well," I said, getting right into it as soon as he was seated. "What's all this about a reward?"

He looked over his shoulder, then leaned forward and lowered his voice, as if afraid my office was bugged. Something in the gesture made me want to turn on the little dictating recorder I kept on my desk, but I refrained. It was just out of perversity, and it would have been too obvious anyway.

"Let me explain," he said in a whisper. "I'm here as an agent for Gulf Insurance. We're investigating a series of art thefts in New Orleans. Several galleries and auction houses have reported substantial losses over the last six months. We've reason to believe some of the goods were moved to Los Angeles for resale. We've had certain individuals under surveillance, and the investigation is proceeding well. However, before we go any further, we need some positive identification of the stolen goods."

I wasn't sure what he was getting at. "What has this to do with me?"

"Last Saturday, you were approached by one of our suspects."

"I was?"

"The woman who spoke to you at Malbone's Auction. What name did she use?"

"Miranda Pelton?" He had my full attention now.

"Yes. That's the one."

"Miranda Pelton is a suspect in an art theft?"

"Yes. But before I begin, I'd like to emphasize that this is an ongoing investigation." He fixed me with his deep-set brown eyes. "The situation we have here is a very sensitive one. Everything I tell you is highly confidential. The police are . . ." He paused to study his fingernails. "Let's just say they are not yet involved, not here in Los Angeles, at any rate. I want you to promise me it will go no further than this room. There have been no arrests as yet, and you can seriously jeopardize the outcome by revealing any of this to the wrong people. Do I make myself perfectly clear?"

I nodded my assent. He just said the same thing about five different ways—how much clearer than that did he like to be? I half expected him to swear me in.

"Now," he said, "let me begin by asking you some questions. Did Miss Pelton make you an offer of any kind?"

"I beg your pardon?"

"I mean did she offer to sell you any works of art?"

"No."

"She didn't? Did she mention anything about art or antiques?"

"Well, yes, I suppose she did. That's sort of what we talked about."

"Aha! And you told her you were a collector?"

"Yes. I think I did."

"Good. Now, did she make any arrangements to meet with you again?"

This was beginning to take on the tones of a previous interrogation. I thought my life must be going around in circles.

"Not exactly. Why do you ask, Mr. Plant?"

"Because that's the way she operates: She sells stolen art treasures to unsuspecting collectors. She seeks them out in galleries, auction houses, museums, anywhere they tend to gather. She can't sell to the big establishments directly because they get lists and descriptions of all the stolen goods. She likes collectors. They buy art because

125

they appreciate it, then they put it on their mantelpieces and admire it for years. By the time one of the items comes on the market again, the heat is off. No one remembers the theft anymore."

"Isn't it easier for her to turn them over wholesale to some crooked dealer?"

"I don't think so. She moves around too much to establish a rapport with any of the better fences. Maybe she could sell to one of the small-timers, but only a few have what it takes to get rid of hot property. Most dealers who take stolen goods don't pay very much, and if they don't know what they're doing—say, they try to unload them at auction—they can bring the heat down in a minute. No, she sticks to collectors. She's got it all worked out with them."

"So where do I come in? I'm not exactly in the market for a Picasso or a van Gogh."

"We're not talking about high-end here, Dr. Lloyd. What I'm talking about is American twentieth century, midlevel, four- or five-figure sales. There was also a lot of porcelain: Meissen, Sèvres, Davenport, that sort of stuff. And a great deal of it was art pottery: Rookwood, Weller, Owens. You know what I'm talking about. I found out from Malbone's Auction House that you like art pottery. You're her kind of buyer, Dr. Lloyd. I thought maybe she had you singled out as her next victim. You sure she didn't show any interest in seeing you again? I think you're her man."

I stared at Mr. Plant from across my desk. His face was devoid of expression. The sweep of hair across his forehead remained frozen in place throughout his entire discourse, as if his emotions were running so cold they lacked even the spark of energy necessary to animate his features. He had come all the way from New Orleans to seek my help. There was no hint of Cajun patois in his voice. His broad tones and lazy vowels were Deep South, all right, but the accent seemed more Texan, or perhaps Alabama or Georgia—I wasn't sure. I imagined him living out of a suitcase, staying in cheap motel rooms, having to shampoo that hair each morning out of the little plastic bottles they stocked in trays by the bathroom sink. I wondered how he spent his nights. Did he hang out in bars? Did he try to pick up waitresses at the Holiday Inn? Did he end up going back to his room alone? I sincerely hoped he did. It would serve him right for implying that the woman I had put the moves on last Saturday was interested in me only as a mark.

"She did show some interest in seeing me again," I said.

"She did? Good. When? And where?"

"Malbone's. Next Saturday."

"Excellent. It's the ideal place for her to pitch her scam. If she tries to sell you anything, would you be prepared to help us?"

It seemed as if I had nothing to lose. If I was going to let anyone pitch their scam at me, as he had put it, why not let it be Miranda? "Maybe," I said.

"Great. I knew you would consider it, Dr. Lloyd."

He had one saving grace—enthusiasm. I couldn't really hate someone who liked his job so much.

"Before I agree, tell me some more. What am I supposed to do?"

"It's real simple. If she mentions anything at all about selling art works, just look interested. Go along with her. Try to see what she's got. Get descriptions. We can use everything you give us. I need for you to get into her home. Remember, that's important. What I want from you is evidence that she actually has the stuff and she's trying to sell it. I'm relying on your memory here. I want you to see and hear as much as you can and remember everything."

"Why don't you just give me one of those miniature video cameras? They make them small enough."

He forced a smile. "That's right, Doc, they do, and I'm impressed you know about that. You think you'd be willing to carry a camera? There's a bit of risk there."

I was pleased to impress him but surprised that he

would consider my health. Unless it was the risk to himself that worried him. The risk of exposing his entire operation if I goofed. I wondered what would happen to me under such circumstances.

"What exactly do you know about the risk?" I asked. "I'd like to know a little bit more about that before we get any deeper."

"I don't think you'd be in much danger. She's always worked alone. There's never been any history of violence in the past. If ever the heat was turned up, she invariably preferred to pack up her operation and get out. I just don't want her disappearing again at this point. I'd hate to have to start all over again someplace else."

It seemed as if my hunch was right: He was more concerned about his investigation than about any danger I might have to face. But I didn't like his use of the word "much" when he mentioned danger. Was there something he wasn't telling me?

"I think next Saturday we should just see how you manage by yourself," he said. "We can try a miniature video cam the next time. I want to see how you handle the situation."

That sounded reasonable to me. "How does she acquire these works of art? Who helps her? She can't be stealing them herself."

"She has a boyfriend who works for an auction house near the French Quarter in New Orleans. He's just a truck driver, but he has access to inventory lists as well as upcoming estate sales, that sort of thing. He also has access to all the appraisers' estimates of value, which means they can be very discriminating in what they take. They try not to go for anything that will muster too much attention. They seem to prefer pieces under ten thousand dollars. Easier to sell, I guess."

"Where is he now?"

"The boyfriend? Disappeared. Maybe you can find out a little about him as well."

"Is he a muscular type? Real short brown hair, like a Marine?"

He looked deeply at me. "Yes. Have you seen him?"

"Last Saturday, at Malbone's. You were there, weren't you? I mean, you had to be there to see her talking to me. How could you miss him?"

He shook his head. "I must have been concentrating on you two," he said.

I'd missed Plant, but I certainly hadn't missed the boyfriend. But maybe I was looking from a different viewpoint.

"Tell me more about the boyfriend," I asked. "What's his name? Does he have a history of violence?"

Mr. Plant pursed his lips. "I don't think I'm going to tell you his name. You might let it slip in conversation with her. The less you know, the better. As for his past, he's had a couple of minor scuffles with the law, mostly as a juvenile. But there's nothing on his present record. I've checked."

He would have, of course. It wasn't enough to reassure me, though. "That doesn't tell me that he isn't violent. Just that he hasn't been caught."

"True, but I don't think you'll have a problem. She tends to work the resale angle by herself. Prefers it that way."

He nodded in encouragement, leaned back in his chair, and crossed his legs. He had presented his case fairly well, at least enough to satisfy me. But I had one more question I was saving.

"What's in it for me?"

He gave a strained smile. "I was wondering when you would get to that. If you help us, you could be looking at a nice reward."

"Could be?"

"The insurance company has posted a reward of ten thousand dollars for any information leading to a conviction. The way I see it, it could all be yours."

He leaned forward again. "In addition, Dr. Lloyd, I made them promise ten percent of the value of any stolen goods recovered." He dropped his gaze to his hands and studied his fingernails, clicking them nervously. "It's a special arrangement between them and me, as an incentive for anybody who helps. In this case we are talking about hundreds of thousands of dollars in art and antiques. In the last heist alone, James McKilroy and Company lost two hundred and seventy-five thousand in merchandise from their art nouveau sale. And who knows how many other auction houses they hit, not to mention private homes. We're talking a lot of money here, Dr. Lloyd."

I could do the math. Figures danced before my eyes. "They're going to give me all that money just for reporting what I see?"

He lifted his gaze back to me. "That's right, Dr. Lloyd. I'm already being paid for my work, so I'm not entitled to any of the reward. It could be all yours. Are you with me?"

"Count me in," I said.

Mr. Plant was thrilled. He rose and came across the room to shake my hand.

"I knew I had the right man, Dr. Lloyd. Believe me, you won't be disappointed."

I thought it a strange choice of words.

I USUALLY STAYED AT MY DESK AN HOUR OR two each day after the office closed. Ostensibly, it was an attempt to finish my paperwork. I'd slump into my chair and fidget with one pile or another, read some correspondence, sign a few bills or letters, then leaf through *People* magazine for a half hour before I went home.

My desk was a battle zone piled high enough to cover me in the event of a mortar attack. There were stacks of patient files, journals, and review articles laid out like bricks in a solid wall around the perimeter, patched together with reams of self-stick notes. Getting through all of it was an interminable conflict in which the odds were against me, largely because I lacked the will to succeed. On certain tiresome days I found myself drifting into thoughts of arson, convinced that this was a situation in which the flamethrower would prove mightier than the pen.

On this particular night, after showing Mr. Plant to the door and taking up my customary position behind the stacks, completing the day's paperwork was furthest from my mind. I had in my hand three sheets of paper, photocopies of a list that Mr. Plant had produced before his departure. He'd told me it was an inventory of the stolen items from his client's warehouse. I was to memorize as much as I could, then attempt to match the goods with anything Miranda should show me.

I studied the list carefully. The letterhead read

"James McKilroy and Company, Fine Arts, Auctioneers and Appraisers," with an address in New Orleans. It was divided into sections: Paintings, Sculpture, Ceramics, and Glass. Each was subdivided by era: 19th Century, Art Nouveau, Art Deco, and Contemporary. The items were listed by an auction number, followed by an abbreviated description, as if excerpted from a catalog. There were no notations as to marks or condition and no estimates of value. Still, there was enough there to make an easy identification in most cases.

I tried to imagine the upcoming rendezvous with Miranda on Saturday. I would have to go from "Hi. Remember me?" to "Let's go to your place and check out the merchandise" in the course of an afternoon's idle chatter. But if Plant was right, I probably wouldn't have to work very hard at setting it up. She would be calling the tune herself. All I had to do was watch my back. I'd have to make sure that her young friend was out of the picture. I hoped that Mr. Plant's analysis of him was accurate.

I pulled a clean sheet of letter paper out of the top drawer of my desk and wrote the name "Miranda Pelton" on it. I circled it, stared at it for a moment, then wrote the words "Art thief" alongside. As an afterthought I added a slash and then "Fence." In a lighter, more hesitant script, I wrote Jack Ehrenberger's name. She had been at his funeral, and I really didn't believe her story about being his patient. I stared at the paper for another minute, my thoughts churning. Then I rummaged around my desk for the day's messages. I had to lift a pile of charts to find what I was looking for, a square piece of yellow paper with "Rosie McClanahan" written on it. Beneath her name was another with a telephone number.

I dialed. It rang once, twice. I looked at my watch. It was seven-thirty. I had no idea where the time had gone. A third ring. I was beginning to think I would get an answering machine, when the fourth ring was interrupted by a soft "Hello." I couldn't tell if it was a man or a woman.

"I'm looking for Chuck Thompson."

"Who wants to know, dear?"

"My name is Gareth Lloyd. I was given this number by Rosie McClanahan."

"Oh, Rosie! She's a sweetheart, isn't she? I just had lunch with the little darling today. What can I do for you, dear?" He seemed to have a penchant for drawing out certain words, giving them an extra syllable as if he were singing a refrain.

"Mr. Thompson, Rosie told me about an estate you were working on. Somebody who just died—a plastic surgeon, I believe. I was hoping you might have something interesting for sale."

"Well, Mr. . . . . whatever your name is, dear. Everything I have is interesting, and it's all for sale. But it *is* very late, and I was just closing, and do you know I just haven't got around to that estate yet, sweetheart? Now why don't you give me a chance to work on it, and toddle down to the old shop later this week? We can have a nice little chat."

"Much obliged, Mr. Thompson. How's Wednesday afternoon sound?"

"Just fine, dear. Well, toodle-oo, then."

I managed to squeeze in a request for directions before he hung up. His shop was on Melrose Avenue, toward La Cienega. I knew the area vaguely.

I added Chuck Thompson's name to my little work sheet, alongside Jack's, and put a question mark next to it. I was eager to find out a little more about Jack's art collection, and I wasn't sure I could trust Elaine to tell me all, especially not after the little scene at the restaurant. Maybe there were even some things she didn't know about him. If Jack collected antiques, he might have bought one of Miranda's stolen pieces. Why else would she be at his funeral? I couldn't see a patient going to her plastic surgeon's funeral, especially not a patient who had canceled the surgery.

There could be a connection there, if only I could

see it clearly. Maybe Jack had discovered that the goods were stolen, perhaps after he'd bought a few. Had there been a confrontation? Would Miranda kill Jack for that? I couldn't imagine that and didn't want to try. What about the young man I had seen with her? He looked capable of anything.

I put down "Boyfriend" next to Miranda's name and added another question mark. Stare at them as much as I did, the names failed to tell a story.

I tried to focus myself by doing some paperwork. I had completed just two charts when my mind began to wander again. Miranda's image floated past my eyes. This was the way it always was, like trying to read a textbook in bed. Five minutes and my thoughts would start drifting. I decided to do something more mechanical and sift through the day's mail. I threw all the envelopes marked "Personal and Confidential" in the trash, and followed suit with everything from the American Medical Association. The magazines were next. Most were unsolicited journals on various themes, paid for by advertising from pharmaceutical firms. They went in the trash, too. There was one on antiques that I put in my briefcase to take home. The last of the bunch was the monthly news journal from the Plastic Surgery Society.

I skimmed through it. The feature article was on the latest study of breast implants, a never-ending struggle between lawyers and manufacturers. There was too much money at stake for the truth to even matter. I read through the key points but there was nothing new. I glanced at the classifieds. Most of the ads were from young graduates looking for jobs. My gaze fell on an item marked "Obituary." It was unusual to find one in there and it caught my attention.

**Epstein**—George Epstein was shot and killed in Huntsville, Texas, on January 15. He had just finished his weekly racquetball game at the Health and Sports Club, and was killed in the parking lot about ten feet from his car. There were no witnesses. Police believe the motive to be robbery. Dr. Epstein's wallet and watch were missing. There have been no arrests so far.

Dr. Epstein had been in solo practice for twenty-five years. He is survived by his wife, Connie, and three sons: Ivan, Peter, and Daniel.

The hairs on the back of my neck began to rise as I read it through. The scene was too damn familiar. Was this the man Peter Heering had mentioned at Jack's funeral? Couldn't be. January 15 was just two months ago, and Peter had talked of somebody who was shot six months back. Also, the guy Peter mentioned was a member of the board. He would have had a much bigger write-up than this. Could there have been two plastic surgeons shot within the last year? Three—counting Jack?

I dialed Peter Heering's number. Cindy answered.

"Hello, Gareth. You coming down with something? You don't sound so good."

"I'm fine, Cindy. Peter there?"

"No. He got called down to University Hospital for a case."

"Can you have him call me at home as soon as he gets back?"

She sensed my urgency. "What's wrong, Gareth? You're not in any kind of trouble, are you?"

One thing worse than knowing a busybody is knowing a busybody with insight.

"No, Cindy. It's nothing like that. I just wanted to talk to him about a surgeon he used to know."

"Who was it? Maybe I can help."

Just like Cindy, hated to be left out.

"He mentioned someone he worked with on the board, someone who was killed last year. You don't remember who that was, do you?"

"In Los Angeles?"

"No. I think it was Texas."

"No, I don't remember." She sounded as disappointed as I was.

"Well, just have him call me."

"It maybe late, Gareth. He said it was a long case."

"That's okay, Cindy. I'll be up."

I replaced the receiver. Then I put George Epstein's name next to Miranda's on my work sheet, with "Huntsville, Texas," beneath it. The paper was starting to look quite crowded.

I was tired. Bits of the day's events kept repeating themselves in my mind, like anchovies after a pizza. I thought of Fernando Rojas and Mr. Plant. I thought of Elaine and Akimoro. I thought of Miranda Pelton. It was well after dark and my office was not in the safest of neighborhoods. There had been several shootings within a few blocks. For the first time in years, I missed my gun. I wondered if it wasn't time to go out and buy another one.

Then I did what I always did when the willies began to strike. I replaced the charts on their respective piles, locked up the office, and went home.

IT WAS WEDNESDAY AFTERNOON. GOLF DAY for some. Wednesday afternoon off is a tradition in the world of medicine, perhaps because it perfectly divides a stressful week into two manageable halves. Not being a golfer myself, I usually kept the afternoon free for unforeseen events, like completing my hospital charts if the Medical Records Department was on my back, doing a semi-urgent case when someone was in too much of a hurry to wait for the regular schedule, or going shopping for a birthday present for which I was already a week late.

On this particular Wednesday I found myself parking the Alfa on a side street off Melrose Avenue and walking up to the thoroughfare as it curved gently east, looking for a sign that would say C. W. THOMPSON, ART APPRAISALS.

This far west on Melrose some of the storefronts were unlit and barred; others bore signs that proclaimed them open "to the trade only." There were a couple of restaurants, an electronics store, and a store that specialized in lamps, but most of the signs, when they were present, had something or other to do with antiques.

I finally saw Mr. Thompson's shingle on a small brick building across the street. There were very few pedestrians to be seen, and not a single double-parked car, which meant the traffic on Melrose moved swiftly and smoothly. I waited for the light to change before I could cross.

The door to Mr. Thompson's establishment was of some age, a heavy weathered oak, painted brown at least twenty years ago, by the look of it. There were two small beveled-glass peepholes set at eye level—that is, eye level if I were on the inside. From the street I would have to get up to the second step on my tiptoes to see in. Fortunately, this wasn't necessary, because of the large storefront windows on either flank. There were security bars across them, and the window cleaners had been unable to do them justice. The view to the interior was darkened by years of grime that had built up over the windowpanes, like a cataract growing on a lens.

The wooden floor was varnished oak, partially covered by a faded Aubusson. Several paintings near the windows were set on easels at right angles to the street. They did not show very well from where I stood. I figured they were placed that way to catch the light but were meant to be viewed to full advantage from inside. There were more paintings hanging on the walls around the room. In the back I could make out a magnificent Eastlake rolltop desk, piled high with books and papers. There was a pair of large, fur-covered slippers next to the chair, with nobody in them.

From the street where I stood, my eye was more or less level with the desktop inside. I looked hard for a pair of stockinged feet to go with those slippers. Nothing moved. I walked up the steps and rang the large brass bell a couple of times. I could hear the chimes but no human sound. I had thought we had agreed on Wednesday afternoon, but I hadn't pinned Mr. Thompson to the hour. I looked at his sign. In small letters on the bottom it said HOURS BY APPOINTMENT.

After ten minutes of this I gave up and walked west across La Cienega to a small café I had noticed earlier. It was one of those trendy cappuccino bars with wire twist chairs and the comfortable aroma of coffee grounds and chocolate, where everybody knows one another and they don't go out of their way to serve tourists, meaning anybody from east of Fairfax. I dialed Mr. Thompson from the pay phone, but there was no answer. I ordered a cup of espresso and sat down.

I took out a small square of paper from my pocket and unfolded it. The work sheet I had started on Monday had another name on it now—Jed Neifosh. He was the ex-member of the Plastic Surgery Board who had been killed outside a theater in Houston. Peter Heering had given me some of the details when I finally managed to track him down on Tuesday afternoon. When he was through telling me about Dr. Neifosh, I had asked him if he knew George Epstein as well, or any details about his death. He didn't and wasn't all that excited to hear that he'd been killed.

"There's over four thousand plastic surgeons, Gareth. And there's a lot of guns in the world. People get shot every day. I think you're making a big case out of nothing."

I should spend my energy cutting skin grafts to cover burn wounds was what he meant.

"Get some sleep, Peter," I had replied. "You sound tired."

After talking to Peter I went straight to my atlas and looked up Texas. I saw that Huntsville, where George Epstein was killed, was only about an hour from Houston.

My curiosity about Jack's art collection was mounting by the hour, but it looked as though I would get no satisfaction from Chuck Thompson. I would just have to ask Elaine. I wondered what the Beverly Hills police would think if I met with her again, but I didn't really care. If they thought I was guilty, they would have arrested me by now, and I hadn't heard anything further from them since my interview. I recalled my cold panic last Saturday, thinking that Akimoro must have known something that pointed the finger at Elaine. Maybe it had to do with the art collection.

It was time to pay her a visit. Knowing her, by now she would be a little less mad at me for what I'd said on Sunday, but she would still want to make me squirm. That's why I couldn't call first; she might tell me to go to hell. I would just have to show up unannounced.

My espresso arrived. I tossed the lemon rind, stirred some brown sugar into my cup, and took a sip. In a single gulp, I drank it down, tilting the bottom up so the sugar dregs slid down my tongue.

I watched the young couples around me, the men proud and self-assured, the girls firm and healthy. They were trying to impress one another with what they knew about this strange brew, so foreign in its many variations. I was sure none of them had ever spent any time at the Fontana di Trevi, or the Piazza Navona, watching Italians at the ritual and learning to do it right. Those were memories of Rafaella and me, reminders of uncomplicated days in an endless summer, when our passion for each other simmered in the streets and fountains of the Eternal City and came to a boil in a small shuttered bedroom off the Via Parioli. I had spent a year calling it home, doing research in the Policlinic at the Università di Roma. Those carefree days were gone now. So was Rafaella. One of them I didn't particularly want back—but the memories were priceless.

I paid for the coffee and left. The way back to my car led me past Mr. Thompson's storefront. Just as I neared it I noticed a man walking briskly up the steps. He was very nattily dressed in a green plaid double-breasted suit, an olive loden peaked cap with a long feather tucked in the band, and brown alligator shoes.

"Excuse me," I yelled up to him. "Do you know when Mr. Thompson will be back?"

"Who wants to know, sweetheart?" he replied.

Mr. Thompson unlocked the door and let me in ahead of him. The first thing I noticed were the colors of the interior; they were brighter and cleaner than they appeared from outside. The second thing I noticed was that the furry slippers developed four legs and a tail, and transformed themselves into a cat, which promptly strutted over to its master for a scratch behind the ears.

"Endora, my little precious," he said, picking her up deftly with one hand. "Did you miss me, sweetheart?"

He tucked the cat under his arm and took his cap off, eyeing me carefully up and down.

"So, Mr. Lloyd. You're the man who called me the other night."

He was a few inches taller than I, his thinning hair darkened with some greasy substance and combed straight back to his collar. Around his neck and tucked into the broad striped gray shirt was a flowing silk cravat, patterned with a small blue fleur-de-lis. A marcasite brooch, pinned to his lapel, bore the crouching figure of a jaguar.

"Endora, this is a friend of Rosie's." He introduced me to the marmalade furball under his arm. "Gareth Lloyd." He rolled it on his tongue. "Sounds like one of those English painters."

A large dewlap under his chin, reminiscent of a water buffalo, lolled gently as he spoke. I gathered the cravat was worn to camouflage this bovine attribute. It seemed to me as if it served to accentuate it instead.

"The name's Welsh, actually," I corrected him.

"Oh! How nice for you, sweetheart. Tom Jones is my favorite. He's such a doll, isn't he?"

"Yes."

I was cautious, having some trepidation about this visit, based on his idiom and manner of dress. Not that I minded one bit what somebody did in the privacy of his bedroom, but Mr. Thompson had an air of aggressive hunger in his gaze that gave me to infer he might have wanted to do some of those things to me. I figured I should get to the point and get out of there.

"I was wondering if I could have a look at some of the antiques in that estate Rosie McClanahan was telling me about," I said.

"And which estate would that be, dear?"

"The one belonging to a plastic surgeon."

"My, my! Rosie has been a naughty little girl! I told her it was all very hush-hush."

He leaned closer. He smelled of lavender and cat piss.

"They want to keep that estate quiet from all those nasty wagging tongues on the circuit. That's why they gave it to me and not to those dull old farts at Butterfield's. I do hope Rosie knows you very well, dear boy."

"Oh, absolutely," I lied. "We're old friends. My lips are sealed."

"But you thought you'd just sneak in and have first crack at the best pieces, sweetheart. Well, isn't that just typical? I must say I like a bit of spunk myself. I think it shows character, don't you? I mean, wouldn't this world be just so terribly boring without a teensy-weensy bit of naughtiness?"

I had not considered that there might be a breach of confidentiality involved in my quest to discover more about Jack's art holdings. It was a good thing that I was worming my way into Mr. Thompson's confidence, by dint of nothing more than some lecherous fantasy on his part. It seemed as though in their efforts to keep the contents of his estate private, Jack's lawyers had chosen the one dealer who was the antithesis of the very quality they most desired.

"And what makes this particular estate so interesting, Mr. Lloyd?"

"I read about him in the newspapers," I said quickly. "I feel somebody like that must have a few really nice pieces. You know how difficult it is for us collectors to find something really unusual anymore."

"Well, I don't know about that, dear boy," he said, holding his head up with pride. "I can usually satisfy all my clients' needs." He gave a little toss of his head. "Funny thing! You know, I've been in this business forty-five years. I know everybody in the circuit. Some of them I wish I'd never met—you know how that goes, don't you, sweetheart? Yet I'd never heard of this chap Ehrenberger until now. I wonder what stone he's been hiding under?"

The whetstone, I thought to myself. He'd have heard of Jack Ehrenberger in a minute if he'd considered getting rid of that dewlap flapping in the breeze. It was starting to distract me.

"As a matter of fact," he added, stroking the purring cat at his chest, "that's what I was thinking about you as well. I'm wondering how your name hasn't come to my attention, either. What kind of art do you collect, dear?"

It appeared that my self-congratulations were a little premature. Mr. Thompson had lost his affable tone, shed it like a mantle, as if he had cheerfully entered a gay bar and found, instead, a convention of income tax agents.

I had prepared an excerpt of Mr. Plant's inventory of stolen items in my head, memorizing a few pieces of high value from each category. I recited the list now, trying to sound as casual as I could. He listened intently. When I finished, he carefully let the cat down.

"You run along and play, Endora, while I finish talking to this nice man."

He brushed a few invisible hairs off his immaculate suit.

"That's not much of a collection, Mr. Lloyd. You shouldn't be wasting my time looking for items like that. You'd do better at one of those antique malls, or you could try Malbone's Auction."

I hadn't expected this reaction. The items I'd picked to memorize were desirable pieces, averaging a couple of thousand dollars each, some of them as high as five. I would have been happy to own any one of them. He must have seen the disappointment on my face, for he softened a bit. An antique appraiser deals with disillusion more often than a judge at a beauty pageant. Mr. Thompson had the moves down pat. He reached over and touched me on the arm.

"Don't be too upset, dear boy. There are several reasons why I can't help you with the doctor's estate. First, it's not for sale yet; I've just been given the commission to catalog and appraise it. Second, there are some highly unusual items in it—shall we say, irregular?—and I doubt most of it will ever be for sale. Third . . ."

He smiled at me, a friendly, persuasive kind of smile that came from as deep as the first layer of muscles on his face, and not much deeper. I shuddered.

"Thirdly," he said, "I think you're barking up the wrong tree. You and the doctor were not quite in the same league. From the sound of your list, you could sell your entire collection and still not be able to afford just one of his paintings."

CHAPTER 19

DRIVING DOWN SUNSET TOWARD BEVERLY Hills in the evening traffic, I considered making a quick detour to avoid being followed but shelved the idea. If the police were watching me, they would be watching Elaine as well, and there didn't seem any point to losing one tail and picking up another as soon as I got to my destination.

After talking to Mr. Thompson, I was even more determined to find out about Jack's art collection. It weighed on me like an obsession, driving away all fear of coming under further suspicion by the police. . . . *there are some highly unusual items in it—shall we say, irregular?* What had he meant by that? He had obviously considered the paintings very expensive. Could Jack have owned such a collection without Elaine even giving me a hint of it in all these months? She must have known I'd be interested. I had told her all about my passion for antiques.

I made a right turn up to the hills where Elaine lived. The rush of traffic stayed below on Sunset Boulevard. The tree-lined streets around me were wide open, beckoning me on as if I were entering another time zone.

I pulled up at the gate of the Ehrenberger residence and pressed the buzzer on the intercom. A blue Ford van was parked across the street. I couldn't see anybody through the blackened windows, but I was tempted to give it the finger.

"Yes. May I help you?" a woman's voice answered in a gruff Mexican accent.

"Yolanda, can you open the gate? I want to see Mrs. Ehrenberger."

I had never met the maid, but I knew a good deal about her from Elaine, and figured if I sounded familiar, she might let me in without question. I figured wrong.

"Who is this, sir?"

"It's Dr. Lloyd."

"You have an appointment?"

"No," I answered, wondering if the occupants of the blue van were registering the conversation with a boom mike.

"I will have to ask the lady."

There was a five-minute hiatus that seemed more like twenty while I tapped my fingers on the wheel and raised the volume on the radio, hoping to blow the eardrums off the guys in the van, in case they happened to be listening.

"Dr. Lloyd," the intercom crackled.

"Yes?"

"She's not home right now. Can you leave a message?"

It was time for the hard sell. "Yolanda, if you don't open the gate right now, I'm going straight to the INS and tell them you're working here without a permit."

There was another interminable pause.

"What the hell do you want, Gareth?" came Elaine's familiar voice.

"Elaine, would you *please* open the gate? I have to talk to you."

"I don't want to talk to you."

"Do you want me to get into it right here, Elaine? There's two guys in a blue van taking down everything I'm saying."

Silence. The gate swung open slowly. I pulled up the short drive and parked beside a silver Rolls-Royce.

I had never been inside Jack's house before. The two-story stucco, with its steeply sloping slate roof and gray stone trim, seemed much too big for the lot. A half a dozen gable windows gave it an expensive air. The landscaped front garden was immaculate, the stone pathway leading to the front door flanked by oversized terra-cotta tubs flowing with geraniums.

Elaine opened the door herself. She had on no makeup, and there were rings around her eyes. She was wearing blue jeans and a T-shirt, which I found disconcerting, considering I had never seen her in anything less expensive than the designer dresses from Neiman Marcus that she favored. Except, of course, when she wasn't wearing anything at all.

"Well," she said. "What do you want?"

She seemed upset. Newly upset, not a sham anger held over from Sunday. I had an impression it wasn't entirely my doing.

"You've no business scaring Yolanda like that. Is that all you came here to do?"

I walked into the room without answering. I was struck by how plain her face looked. The features were familiar, but with the makeup gone some of her glamour had faded, too. She had always taken great pains to look her best whenever we met. I wondered if part of her anger was because I had called unannounced, because she hadn't had time to prepare herself, as if the web she had so carefully spun for my benefit had unraveled before me.

"I'm sorry to barge in on you like this," I said, realizing too late that it was not the best opener. "I mean—"

"What is it, Gareth?"

"I want to talk to you about Jack."

"About Jack?"

"In a way, yes. Can we sit down somewhere?"

She led me from the hallway to the living room. The decor was the same plush marble and chintz that Jack had in his office. The furniture was classic French, dark painted woods with parquet tops and ormolu fittings. I paid particular attention to the paneled walls. There were a couple of ornate framed mirrors. Nothing else, not a canvas or a print, even though the furnishings seemed to cry out for them. Above the sideboard, I thought the lighting was deliberately aimed to highlight the entire wall, but there was no sign of an art collection.

She sat at the edge of the couch, without inviting me to do the same, leaving me uncomfortable in that large, cold room.

"Well!" she said.

"I've just come from Chuck Thompson's art gallery."

The anger slipped slowly from her face, her features softening like an animated cartoon changing before my eyes. I waited for her to say something. Looking closer at the wall, I thought I could make out several clean patches on the paneling, as if frames that had hung there for years had recently been removed. She must have taken everything to Mr. Thompson.

"It's not something that concerns you," she finally said.

There was another pause. I wondered if she was going to sell the art. Did she need the money? That must be it. The way Jack's office was done up, he probably owed a fortune.

"You've no business poking your nose where it doesn't belong, Gareth. What the hell were you doing at Mr. Thompson's, anyway? And what did he tell you? He's got no business talking about private matters to anybody who walks in there."

"Slow down, Elaine. He didn't tell me very much of anything; that's why I'm here. I wanted to hear it from you."

"Well, you can go talk to Stanley Bing."

"Who's he?"

"He's my lawyer."

I remembered; it was the name she had given me at the restaurant.

"Listen, Elaine, I'm not just a stranger in this. You know damn well that we're both suspects in Jack's murder, and it doesn't help a bit that the gun I gave you is missing. Christ's sake, there's even a cop parked outside your driveway. For all we know, they're listening to us right now."

"Then you shouldn't have come."

"No, you're right. I shouldn't have come, but I want to do all that I can to get out of this mess. Last Monday I found out something that maybe even the cops don't know yet."

"Really?" She had a sarcastic tone. "And what is that?"

I sat down. It probably wasn't going to make much sense, not with what little I had to go on, but I had to sound it off to someone, and Elaine was as good a start as anybody else.

"There's been an art theft, a fairly big one, in New Orleans. It's some kind of ring."

I watched Elaine turn pale and her eyes widen.

"One of the members—a girl—has been seen selling the stolen goods to people—"

"How do you know about this, Gareth?" she interrupted.

"It's true. I was approached by a detective on the case."

"The cops approached you?" Her voice quivered.

"No, not a cop, a private detective. He wants me to find out some more about her. He's been working on it for months. I don't think anybody has tied it in with Jack's murder yet, but the funny thing about it is . . ." I hesitated before dropping the bombshell. "I saw her at Jack's funeral."

She stared at me. "You *know* the person who's been selling the stolen art?"

"Yes. Well, what I mean . . . I don't know her, I've just talked to her."

"You talked to her? How did you get involved in this, Gareth?"

"I recognized her at the auction."

"You recognized her? You're losing me, Gareth. You're in this deeper than I thought."

She got up suddenly, strode across the room to the paneled wall, then turned abruptly and walked back to me. "Look at me, Gareth. Just look into my eyes and tell me one thing."

I was looking at her already, but now I stared into her eyes. The blue was deeper than I remembered, pupils wide. I saw a little lost soul, burning with fear.

"Just tell me you had nothing to do with Jack's murder," she said.

I felt sorry for her. "Listen to me, Elaine. I didn't kill Jack and you know that, but we've both been sucked into this because of our affair. I don't know what the cops have, but it can't be much, because they're still on our tails instead of the person who really pulled that trigger. Maybe it was a random killing, and maybe it wasn't. I think I have something that may lead to the truth. But before I go any further, I need to know as much as I can about Jack's art collection. Why didn't you tell me he collected paintings?"

She didn't say a word. She just looked at me and her face melted into tears. She began to shake. I got up and put my arms around her, holding tight. It was a reflex action; I felt no more emotion than if I had been comforting a child. She must have sensed it. Her arms came up behind me for a minute, then pushed me away. She walked over to the sideboard and opened the top drawer. Then she did something I'd never seen her do in the six months I'd known her. She took out a pack of cigarettes and lit one with shaking fingers.

I watched her slowly exhale. The trembling stopped.

"I had no idea about the art," she said.

I waited for the rest.

"We own a small condo in Santa Monica, near the

beach. Jack told me he had it rented for the last year. He collected the checks. He told me the family was very private, that they didn't want any intrusions, so I never interfered. Last week, before the funeral, Stanley Bing came over to settle details of the will. One of the things he offered to do was to check the condo. He found out it had never been rented. It was furnished, and apparently Jack had used it from time to time."

She took another puff before continuing.

"At first, I thought Jack must have taken women up there. I figured he was screwing somebody on Monday nights. Isn't it ironic? But the strange thing is, when I got up there, it wasn't furnished like a love nest at all. More like some sort of gallery. There were paintings hanging on the walls, and one room was a storage area, with stacks of paintings still in delivery crates."

"Jack's collection? And you had no idea it existed?"

She stared at me through a veil of smoke, shaking her head.

"No. There were no records of any kind. No sales receipts. No inventory. Stanley said he would have them appraised. He said he would pick somebody discreet. He found Mr. Thompson somewhere, maybe a recommendation from a friend. I don't know. Lord knows I didn't have too much confidence in him at first, but he had all the right credentials. We had the shipment delivered Monday. Stanley called me with the news this morning."

She broke into tears again.

"Gareth, I have no idea what to do."

"What did he tell you, Elaine?"

"Apparently, I'm in possession of ten million dollars' worth of stolen paintings."

I LET OUT A SOFT WHISTLE. "TEN MILLION dollars' worth of stolen paintings?"

She nodded sullenly.

I began to laugh. Slowly, a smile spread across her face, too. My laughter had always succeeded in infecting her with the giggles. This time, however, she was determined not to be happy.

"It's not funny, Gareth."

"No, I don't suppose it is. You sure they're stolen?"

"Mr. Thompson is. He has these lists they send around after a major theft. They were stolen from auction houses all over the country; most from New York, some from Boston, and I think Chicago. All in the last two years."

"They were all from different places?"

"That's right. Jack was running a warehouse for stolen art works right there in our condo."

"You sure Jack was involved in this?"

She picked up the ashtray and slowly crushed her cigarette, as if pulverizing some bitter pill in a mortar and pestle.

"Well, what do you think, Gareth? Of course Jack was involved in this. How else would they be stored in our condo?"

"Has Mr. Thompson gone to the police?"

"Yes, he's gone to the police. He's a legitimate art dealer. He has to report it."

I wouldn't have used the word "legitimate," but I knew she was right. She was treating me like a schoolboy, impatient that my reasoning was so far behind hers. I didn't mind. She'd had more time to work things out.

"And what did they say?" I asked.

"Who?"

"The cops."

"They questioned me for four hours this afternoon. I'm exhausted, Gareth. And I'm a nervous wreck. Why the hell do you think I started smoking again?"

"I hadn't noticed," I said.

She gave me a look that sizzled. "They went on and on about finances and lifestyles. They wanted to know every trip we've ever been on, what clubs we belong to, what museums we go to, what restaurants, who our friends are. They even wanted employment records on all my maids. I've never been so embarrassed in my life."

"Did they search the house?"

"They cleaned out Jack's desk in the library, and in his office. They went through the rest of the house, but they didn't exactly turn it upside down, thank heaven. They took every painting off the walls. There was a hell of a mess, but Yolanda helped me clean it all up after they'd gone."

I was impressed. She was holding up fairly well for all she'd been through, both physically and mentally. It was hard enough for her having to find out Jack was a thief, barely a week after he had been murdered, without having to put up with the police, be suspected in his murder, be questioned over and over, then have her home searched.

"Tell me, Elaine," I asked, "do you really suppose Jack could have done all this without you knowing it?"

She looked at me with a wild look in her eyes that lasted a fleeting moment.

"I guess he was capable of it. Jack was capable of anything. He would go after everything he wanted and get it. It was scary, sometimes, how intense he could get. He told me a long time ago never to pry too far into his business."

The gangster's moll, I thought. A classic pair.

"Jack had some old-fashioned ideas, and I respected them. He was a provider, and he was damn good at it. He made more money than anybody else. He shared it with me, gave me everything I wanted; why the hell should I upset him by questioning how he did it? Even you, Gareth. You were something he gave me. Surprised? Oh yes, he knew about you, but he never mentioned it. There were some things we never talked about. It was only because we understood each other so well."

I was amazed. After having stifled my loathing for Jack all these months, out of a sense of guilt for what I was doing with his wife, I was having trouble coming to grips with what I was hearing.

"I don't suppose you have any idea who his accomplices were?" I asked.

She shook her head. "Harry? Ivan? Pierre? It could have been any one of his friends. He told me they dropped by the office after the patients had gone, to sit and talk, have a drink, play backgammon. Whatever. He never brought them home."

"Well, that's a start," I said. "Do you know anything more about these people? What business were they in? What about last names? Did you tell all that to the police?"

"There wasn't much to tell. He never told me any last names. I never even met them. They were just names he gave me when he'd come home late."

"You never saw any of these people?"

"No."

"Well, what about his staff? Somebody must have seen these guys."

"If they existed," she said.

"You mean they might have just been names he invented as an excuse against coming in late?"

"It seems that way, doesn't it?"

I was gaining a new perspective into her approach to life in the fast lane.

"Didn't you ever check up on him?" I asked. "You must have had reason to call him sometimes, just to say dinner was ready or something."

"If I wanted to talk to him, I always used his pager. The office phone switched over to the exchange at six every day."

"So you've no idea if one of these people he was meeting was a woman?"

"If it was, he gave me no reason to be jealous. He always treated me well."

"You mean in the off moments you were together?"

"Don't patronize me, Gareth. You know how we lived. After all, you were able to take advantage of it."

"I wasn't the only one taking advantage, Elaine."

"Okay, okay. Let's not argue. I'm much too tired for it."

I sensed a dismissal and got up to leave. "I guess you've gone over all this with the police today."

"Yes," she said, her tone telling me that the stress was catching up with her.

"And did they believe you?"

She sighed. "I think they did. They said it opened up a new angle on the investigation. I guess that means they're going to start looking a little bit further."

I was relieved. "That's good. At least they'll have a few more suspects now. Maybe they'll stop concentrating on us."

She shook her head. "I wish I could feel the same. I was never that worried about them. I knew I had nothing to hide, and I always thought Stanley Bing would protect me. Now I'm not so sure." A tremble crept into her voice, a glint of moisture in her eyes. "I'm scared, Gareth. I could lose everything."

I stood in silence for a moment. "I'd better go," I said.

She walked me to the door. We stood awkwardly at the threshold. I decided on one last try.

"Are you sure you've never seen Jack with a young blonde?" I asked, searching for ways to describe Miranda that would jog her memory. "Slim, average height, dresses sort of mod."

Elaine looked at me with pity. "You've got to do better than that, Gareth. Half his patients were young blondes."

"I know. She wears a ring, a silver skull and cross-bones with emeralds for eyes."

Elaine was interested. "I've seen something like that recently," she said. "Is that the girl you met at the funeral?"

"Yes. Do you know her?"

"I can't remember where I've seen that ring. So she's the one selling the paintings. Is she pretty?"

"Yes."

She looked at me sharply. "I've got it. The gallery."

"What gallery?"

"Down on Melrose. Pacific Studio, I think. We went there for an opening. Some art show."

"Come on, Elaine. Close your eyes and go back. What else do you remember?" I was prompting her with my hands.

"She asked for a double Stolly, neat. That's what got my attention. I remember thinking it was too much drink for a girl like that. I stopped to watch her sip it. I wanted to see if it was really for her."

"And . . . "

"The ring was on her hand, the one that held the glass."

Bingo. "So Jack knew her?"

Elaine shook her head. "No. It was the boyfriend who introduced her. Jack knew him."

"What was his name? What did he look like?"

"I don't remember. I think he was from back East.

He looked young for an art dealer. It was the first time I'd seen him."

"How did Jack know him?"

"They didn't say. It wasn't a big deal. We stood there a minute and that was it."

She held on to the doorknob. The lines on her face seemed etched a little deeper than usual.

"What about the paintings?" I asked. "Did Mr. Thompson say any of them were from an auction house in New Orleans?"

"I don't think so. I can't remember."

"Try, Elaine."

"I'm too tired, Gareth."

"I'd better go."

I gave her a hug. It felt comfortable playing a fatherly role. "Get some sleep. You'll need your rest when the papers come out tomorrow."

"It's not going to be in the papers for a few days, thank heaven. The police want it quiet so they can check on the art thefts."

"How do they expect to keep something like this quiet? There's too many people involved. All those auction companies, for instance. If I found out about it, the newspapers can, too."

She shrugged. "They think the auction houses will cooperate. And Mr. Thompson's been sworn to secrecy. How did you find out about Jack, anyway?"

"I have my sources, Elaine," I said.

I WAS RIGHT. THE STORY WAS IN THE PAPERS the next day, not the front page, but the "Home" section:

### Silicone Empire Linked to Art Thefts

There was more biography on Jack Ehrenberger, stating that his legacy included a "cache of stolen paintings from East Coast auction houses." Someone had dredged up a picture of Jack in a tuxedo, Elaine next to him in Dior splendor, handing over a check to the curator of a local museum in some ancient fund-raiser. The implication was, while he generously gave with one hand, the other was in the cookie jar replenishing his funds.

I read the article Thursday morning in the doctors' lounge of Memorial Hospital while I was on my rounds. One thing was certain, if Miranda Pelton had anything to do with all this, the story would drive her underground. I figured if I waited until Saturday for her to show up at Malbone's, I'd be left cracking my knuckles. Not that I was still so sure I wanted to get involved. This thing was certainly bigger than I had first imagined.

The questions haunted me all morning: Should I pursue the plan that Plant and I had formulated? Was the reward enough incentive to put myself in jeopardy? Ten million dollars' worth of stolen paintings had already been recovered and was sitting out of circulation in some police lockup. Ten percent of that would have looked good in my bank account, but it was now out of my hands. Could there be any more out there?

I made it to my office early and found the business card Plant had left me. He had warned that he'd be moving around quite a bit, but had scribbled a phone number where I could leave a message. It was a prefix I didn't recognize.

"Rosemead Lodge," came the answer.

"Is Mr. Plant there?"

"Nobody's here but me."

"I'm looking for Bob Plant. He said I could call him here."

"Oh, yeah. He comes in from time to time. Any message?"

I left my name and phone number. The anonymous man didn't sound too hopeful about when I could expect a reply.

I took out the work sheet that I'd started Monday night. I circled Jack Ehrenberger's name and wrote "Art thief" next to it. Now I had two names with that designation: Jack and Miranda. On impulse I crossed out the names of the two plastic surgeons who had been killed. It was too much of a coincidence to expect them to be involved in this art theft business. "People get shot every day," Peter Heering had said. Jed Neifosh and George Epstein must have been no more than unfortunate statistics.

I pondered all afternoon about my next step, coming back to my work sheet between patients and staring at it for inspiration. In the end it wasn't the reward or the desire to clear my name that decided me. It was that inexplicable thrill I was beginning to feel about being involved in this whole affair, that fluttering deep inside my chest whenever I found out something new about the case. I had felt it on the night after Mr. Plant had left my office, and again as I was walking back to my car after talking to Mr. Thompson, and yet again standing in the hallway at Elaine's house, when she told me about having seen Miranda at the art gallery. I had become enamored with the excitement of discovery, and I wanted more.

Once I decided how to proceed, I knew I had to act fast. Miranda was sure to have seen the newspaper article. I couldn't count on her being at Malbone's on Saturday. I dialed a number and impatiently waited for the pick-up.

"Malbone's Auction. This is Peggy. How can I help you?"

My lucky day! Peggy liked me. She would smile and flirt every time I approached her counter to make a transaction. The attraction wasn't mutual, but I wasn't about to let that get in the way now. After the usual pleasantries I got down to business.

"Peggy, I wonder if you would do me a favor."

"Shoot."

"Well, I promised to take a vase over to somebody I met there last week, but I've forgotten her address. Think you can find it for me?"

"Give me a name."

"Pelton." I spelled it for her. "Miranda Pelton."

"It's not showing up on the computer. Maybe she registered under a DBA. Do you know the name of her shop?"

"I don't think she has a shop."

"No? Well, sometimes they don't actually have a shop but they use some catchy name or other to get their resale license. Wait a minute. Here it is . . . on the add-on list. Miranda Pelton. She must have registered for the first time last week. They haven't got around to entering those names yet."

Peggy gave me an address in Los Feliz. "Do you want the phone number, too?"

"I was just going to ask you for it. I hope this doesn't get you into trouble or anything."

"Trouble? Not me. I hope it doesn't get you into trouble, Dr. Lloyd. It doesn't say if they're married or single. What does she look like?"

I laughed. "Single. And ravishing. But not as good as you."

"Oh, yeah? I don't see you coming around asking for my number." She paused to let it sink in, but I wasn't biting. "Anyway, I do this all the time for customers. The boss sells our mailing list to anybody who asks, so I figure it's no sweat to give out an address once in a while. Come to think of it, just last week somebody wanted information on you."

"Really? And who was that?"

"Some guy in a business suit."

"Middle-aged? Sandy hair?"

"That's right. I hope it was okay?"

"No problem. He came to see me already. Thanks for the information, Peggy."

Soon as I hung up I dialed Miranda's phone number. No answer. I dialed again three times during the next few hours. Still no reply. I was becoming edgy. The afternoon schedule seemed to drag on interminably.

After work, I looked up my street atlas for directions to Miranda's house. Evening traffic was piled thick on the other side of the median, but I made good time down the freeway to Los Feliz. Her house was south off the boulevard, not far from a one-block strip that claimed to be the historic, old-town district. It seemed to be a neighborhood of two minds: partly upscale, reclaimed two-story homes with tended gardens and new roofs, and partly run-down rentals and apartment complexes. Miranda's house turned out to be one of the latter, a single-story white stucco in need of a paint job. I pulled up a few doors away just as it was getting dark.

A man walked his dog past my car as I got out. Opposite, I saw the head and shoulders of a white-haired lady in a lighted window, but the shutters slammed shut the moment she realized I was looking. The man and his dog rounded the corner and I was alone.

I approached the door to the darkened house. Not even the porch light was on. I knew before I rang the bell there would be no answer. I waited a healthy minute and tried again. I looked around, half expecting the dog walker to return. The little strip of lawn in front was neatly trimmed, the flower beds lining the house sporting a thick growth of ferns and miscellaneous subtropical palms, standard features in the low-maintenance gardening scheme of most Los Angeles houses. She could be around the block at the supermarket, or she could be a thousand miles away. I walked down the side to a latch gate in the picket fence, opened it, and slid through to the cover of an arbor heavy with trumpet vine. Around the back was another small lawn, an avocado tree loaded with fruit, a rusting barbecue grill, and a redwood trestle table with two chairs. A black cat slunk cautiously away from under the shade of the tree, but there was no human sound; not there or from either of the adjacent properties.

The back door was locked, as expected. I wiped the dust from one of the kitchen windowpanes with my fingers and peered through. I couldn't make out a thing inside. I had a miniature flashlight on my key chain, no bigger than a Ritz cracker and with just enough candlepower to find a door lock in the dark. It was an advertising promotion the trim shop had given me after I had my convertible roof fixed. I tried it now but the light was too poor to penetrate the dark of the kitchen.

I had reached the point where I normally would have turned around and gone back to my car, driven home, and settled down to a book the rest of the evening, figuring I had done my best. But something in me had changed. I had made a decision that afternoon, just before I picked up the phone to call Malbone's looking for Miranda's address. I had tasted the thrill of the hunt, and it was back this very minute, flitting around inside me like a bat under my rib cage. I pushed up on the casement window to check the fit of the catch, then tested each of the panes of glass by knocking on them. I grinned as I heard what I wanted.

I walked over to the trestle table looking for a suitable instrument, but there was nothing there. I tried the barbecue grill. This time I was in luck. On the wooden shelf I found a rusty scraper, once used to clean the top. I was about to return with it to the house when I spotted a grimy kitchen rag hanging from one of the hooks. I picked that up, too, and carefully wiped all the surfaces I had touched.

Going back to the window, I scrubbed my fingerprints off the panes. The loose one was in the bottom left-hand corner. I pressed the scraper blade between the wood and the glass and began to work my way round. The thumping in my chest seemed to weaken my grip, and my hands began to shake. I dropped the scraper on my foot. Cursing silently, I retrieved it and looked around to see if I was being observed. There was no one. Satisfied, I gripped the instrument in both hands and resumed my efforts. The dried putty came away easily on the inside, and in a few minutes I was able to knock the pane inward, onto the windowsill. I reached in and released the latch, pushing the window open. I felt a blast of hot air wash over me, like a surge of adrenaline.

I wiped my prints off the scraper and returned it to the barbecue grill, taking a minute to collect myself. If pressed, I could have rationalized all I had done so far. If a police officer had come bursting round the side of the house and pinned me in the glare of his flashlight, my fertile mind would have invented an excuse for every action. "I'm just cleaning her windows, Officer," or "I thought I'd repair the loose pane while I was in the neighborhood." But stepping into the house through a forced window was clearly breaking and entering, and I seemed to recall this was a punishable offense. Was it a misdemeanor or a felony? I could lose my rights to practice at Greenfield

Memorial Hospital for a felony conviction. Maybe even my license! What on earth was I doing to myself?

My brain was screaming at me: *Run, run, run!* All the lessons gleaned from past experience told me it was better to take to my heels. The going was getting rough, and there was nothing to be gained by acting tough about it. But my heart wasn't willing to accept failure again. I was on the trail of a thief, and possibly a murderer. I stood to clear my reputation. The excitement circulating inside me was like a drug. More powerful than an aphrodisiac, it accepted no remorse.

I made another thorough check of the perimeter. Still no sign of life around me, except the cat, which had returned to watch from behind the avocado tree. I placed my hands on the windowsill and hoisted my weight. In a matter of minutes I was inside. I wiped all the areas I had touched, closed the window, and carefully replaced the pane. I pushed some of the dried putty back in place to hold it there, hoping the break-in wouldn't be too noticeable, at least not from the outside.

The air inside was musty and still warm from the baking heat of the sun, and I soon began to sweat. The light from the bulb on my key chain had about a two-foot radius, just enough to avoid the obstacles. I tossed the grimy rag into the waste bin under the sink and found a clean one for any interior surfaces I would touch. Then I began my reconnaissance.

The kitchen was a small room, tidy by my standards. It seemed as if someone had taken the time to clean up before leaving, as if they might be gone a long time. There was a breakfast table and four folding chairs in white enameled metal, a small refrigerator, and, in one corner by the door to the front room, an old oak rolltop desk with the curved tambour top closed. All the dishes had been put away, and the kitchen counter and tabletop had a thin film of dust. I opened the refrigerator. The sudden flood of light cast a huge shadow against the wall and window. It startled me, and I quickly shut the door. The temporary rush of cool air felt good against my sweat-damp skin.

Growing accustomed to the darkness again, I tiptoed to the desk. The top rolled back easily. Using my flashlight, I rummaged through a couple of cookbooks, a collection of *Sunset* magazines, and two large piles of glossy art journals covering the last two years. I checked the drawers. Pencils, pens, and old receipts in one, utility bills in another, addressed to M. Pelton and going back almost a year. Nothing of any interest. In the last drawer I found three spiral-bound exercise books. They appeared to be filled with notes and research on art and artists: names, prices, dates. I put them aside and shut the desk.

The front room was just as neat as the kitchen, with the same film of dust. The curtains were drawn over the bay windows. I walked over and pulled one aside far enough to peek out. The neighborhood was still deserted, in full darkness now, the lone streetlamp some fifty yards away. I saw the outline of my Alfa parked by the curb.

I tested the fabric on the curtains; it seemed heavy enough to cloak the light I was using. I saw a couple of worn armchairs, two beanbag seats, a coffee table, and a lamp table. Against one wall was a fireplace, with a pile of white ashes swept into a neat heap in the middle. Next to it was an entertainment center with open shelves. The largest one held a television with a rabbit-ear antenna, but the rest of the shelves displayed a collection of pottery. My heart began to race as I went down each row with my little light source, occasionally picking one up with the kitchen rag to examine it. It was a mixed bag—some of it art pottery, but there were also some European figurines and some English porcelain. There were more on the mantelpiece, one of them the little geisha doll for which I had unsuccessfully bid last Saturday.

I could almost feel Miranda's presence in the room, a ghostly aura that mingled with the warm, stale air. How many of these little treasures had she stolen—pirated from rightful owners? Did she think that pilfering from the stacked shelves of an auction warehouse was somehow less heinous than snatching cherished mementos from a collector's hand, like robbing from the rich instead of looting the poor? How would she like it if I slipped one of these pieces into my pocket right now? Perhaps the little geisha doll? She might feel the loss of that one; I had watched her paying good money for it. Could she be out there even now, rounding up more little treasures to drag back to this lair of hers? And if she was, would it be by purchase or plunder? It was still hard for me to imagine her playing the role of thief, let alone accessory to murder. She seemed so fresh and wholesome to me . . . just like that little doll on her mantelpiece.

I made a cursory check of the rest of the house. There were two bedrooms, only one of them furnished, with a made-up twin bed and oak headboard. There were a few more antiques there: two dusty, reverse-painted bedside lamps, a Chippendale mahogany vanity mirror, and a beautiful cut-glass dressing table set. The closet was only half full, mostly skirts and jackets. In the hall I found a large walk-in storage space, with some folded blankets and a few cardboard cartons. By the time I had foraged through the cartons and discovered nothing but old clothes, I was hot and sticky, sweating profusely. The nervous tension was burning up calories faster than a jog around the park. I was tired of being on tenterhooks.

I was startled by the sound of a passing car. Was it Miranda returning? Or perhaps her boyfriend? I switched off the flashlight and listened. Nothing. With mounting anxiety, I decided it was time to leave. I picked up the three spiral-bound notebooks from the kitchen, wiped the last of my prints off the desk, and walked out through the back door.

The air outside smelled cool and fresh, and I savored it. I deposited the notebooks in the trunk of my car, checking the street once more for signs of life. On impulse,

I walked up to the house where I had seen the white-haired lady in the window and rang the bell.

I heard the sound of a chain sliding across a safety lock.

"Who is it?" The question floated softly through the door.

"Excuse me, ma'am. I was wondering if you knew anything about your neighbor across the street. I've got some urgent news about her sick mother but there's no answer over there."

The door opened a crack to the limit of the safety chain. One eye peered at me through a thicket of white hair.

"You talking about that young girl lives over there?" she asked.

"That's right. Miss Pelton. Do you know her?"

"She ain't been here too long. She keeps to herself."

The bills in Miranda's desk went back a year. I wondered how long one had to live in this neighborhood before they accepted you.

"You don't know where I can find her?" I asked hopefully.

"What's the matter with her mother?"

"She's in the hospital," I replied, warming to the story. "She asked to see her daughter. You know, just in case . . ."

"That's a shame," the old lady said, eyeing me up and down suspiciously. "These young folks today just don't care."

"You ever speak to her?"

"Hardly. She was a strange one. Had a fire going last Saturday. Can you figure that? Three cold, wet days and never does a thing, then stokes a fire when the sun's out and it's eighty degrees. Drugs! I tell you, they're all on drugs."

I remembered the pile of ashes in the fireplace.

They were fine and powdery, no charred bits of wood or unburned logs. "When was the last time you saw her?"

"She packed up and left last Sunday. Boyfriend helped her. I ain't seen her since. The house been deserted all this time."

"Boyfriend? Maybe that's where she is. Can you tell me anything about him?"

"Nope. I wouldn't let *my* granddaughter anywhere near him. Showing off his tattoos, no shirt on all the time he was loading that pickup. You with the police?"

"No, ma'am. Just a friend of the family."

"Too bad. I was hoping they'd finally come by. Been calling all week about that other man hanging round here, but they don't pay me no mind."

"Somebody's been hanging around?"

"Ever since she left. Don't like the looks of him much, neither."

"What does he look like?"

"Wears a suit. Just sits there in his car and stares at the door. Gives me the creeps. Don't know what this world's coming to."

The crack in the door half closed as she inched it shut.

"Well, thank you, ma'am. Could I ask you to call me if she returns?"

I searched for a piece of paper to write my number on. I felt a card in my jacket. Extracting it, I saw Rocco Gambella's address from last Saturday. I didn't want to relinquish that, so I took out my wallet and removed one of my business cards. I wrote my home number on the back and handed it to her.

She read it carefully, then turned it over. I saw her read my name and profession.

"This your card?"

"Yes."

"You must think I was born yesterday."

She slammed the door in my face.

As I made the right turn back on Los Feliz Boulevard, I was almost rammed by a police cruiser taking a short left down the street I had come. He was moving awfully fast, although he didn't have his siren on.

I ARRIVED AT MY OFFICE AN HOUR EARLY ON Friday morning, planning to finish off some of the mounting paperwork on my desk. There were two cars already in the lot, only one of which I recognized. I let myself in the back entrance and dropped my briefcase on the cluttered surface of my old oak leathertop.

Debbie came in clutching a hot cup of fresh brew. "Morning, Dr. Lloyd. I think you're going to need this."

"Thanks, Debbie. Who owns the Suburban in the parking lot?" I was referring to the expensive black wagon taking up the space next to her car.

She rolled her eyes. "Your first patient, Mr. Al Capone from the drug cartel."

"Mr. who?"

"Fernando Rojas. Complete with personal trainer."

"I thought I didn't see patients until ten. Change of schedule?"

"They were here when I got here." She shrugged. "No appointment. I told him you weren't expected until later, but he said he'd wait."

"What's the matter? They want the three thousand back?"

"He wouldn't say; just that he had to see you."

"You should have called me at home."

Her look was defiant. "If he wants to see you without an appointment, he can wait just like anybody else."

"It's not that. I don't like you being alone with them all this time." I didn't want to say what I was really afraid of, in case I scared her.

She grinned, brown eyes shining behind her glasses, and pointed to a little yellow canister on her desk. "I thought of that, too. I'm ready for him."

"What *is* that thing?"

"Pepper spray. I keep it in my bag."

It was my turn to roll my eyes. If Mr. Rojas had tried anything, I might have found an ambulance in the parking lot beside the two cars. "Put him in a room," I said, thinking that the room he really belonged in was a few miles away in the county jail.

Mr. Rojas rose on his crutches as I entered. His face was a smile of mock politeness.

"Dr. Lloyd, I'm sorry to bother you." He was wearing a crisply starched shirt with a bolo tie in silver and onyx, and the baggy new black jeans barely hid the bulk of the cast on his left leg. His unnamed companion was similarly dressed, white shirt and black jeans, but without the bolo tie. Instead he sported a black Napa leather vest.

"Is everything all right?" I asked.

"Everything's fine, Doc." Fernando Rojas was almost apologetic. "I just wanted to be sure you still need to operate. You know, everything seems to be healing now."

He was steadier on his legs this time. Having less reliance on his crutches, he laid them down and was gesturing in a peculiar way, as if he were shadowboxing but with fingers fully extended.

I examined his wounds. The bruises and swelling had subsided, the healing lacerations leaving raised, reddened welts across his forehead and eyelid. The smaller abrasions had healed completely. He looked almost handsome with his dark curly hair and piercing black eyes to match his bolo tie.

"Looks pretty good to me," I said. "Seems as if everything's healing normally."

"That's what I mean, Doc. It looks much better than it did last week. Are you sure you want to be cutting me open next Monday?"

I dodged his gesturing hands, then closed in again to run my fingers over his forehead.

"I can feel a couple of lumps under there. I think the glass is still inside. The rest of it may heal but that glass will turn into thick scar and bother you. I think we should get it out."

"Shit!"

"Of course, you're entitled to another opinion."

"No, no. You're the man. I trust you, Doc. But I don't want to have another surgery unless it's necessary. I was hoping maybe the glass would just be rejected, you know."

"It could, but chances are it might get infected and then the scar will look worse."

I was beginning to understand. This macho male who had chosen to live beyond the law, a life that at times must certainly have involved cold-blooded violence, was himself deathly afraid of the needle and the knife.

"Well, Doc, if you say so, then that's what I have to do. My little *chavalas* need to see me at my best. But I really don't want to feel nothing, you understand? You have to promise me that."

I wondered how he would react to the sting of the lidocaine syringe.

"I was planning to do it under local anesthetic, like a dentist. But maybe you'd be better off asleep," I said. He'd certainly be less trouble, and we'd all be better off, was what I thought.

"No, Doc. No sleep. I heard too many things about what happens when they sleep. I'm gonna be awake. You just make it numb, that's all."

"If that's what you want."

"That's what I want. I see you Monday. Shake on it." He held out his right hand in a street handshake, intertwining my fingers with his. Then he thumped me on the back and hobbled out, his silent partner close at heel.

I made a notation in the chart. "Discussed alternatives to surgery—refused option of second opinion." Defensive medicine. Cover your ass, they called it. With Mr. Rojas, I was going to cover my ass with a chastity belt.

This little interruption took up most of the hour I was counting on to do my paperwork. It was that way all the time. I would sit at my desk with the best of intentions, and then some distraction would intervene. I fiddled with a few charts as my mind kept returning to more important matters.

My thoughts raced around in circles. I pined for action, like a thoroughbred at the gate. Plant hadn't called me back yet. I had three notebooks to show him, pilfered from Miranda's house, and hopefully a reward to claim. Not that I had learned much from them myself, but I was sure he would. I had pored over them the night before, checking and cross-referencing with the lists he left me. Nothing matched. Most of Miranda's notes had to do with paintings, and I didn't know that much about them. I wished I could get hold of Mr. Thompson's report on Jack Ehrenberger's collection. Maybe Elaine could help there.

I studied my work sheet again. Perhaps it was premature of me to cross off the two doctors, Neifosh and Epstein, from the list without following up in some way or other. I decided to try and be a little more thorough, and pulled a dusty spiral-bound book off one of my shelves. It was the roster of the American Society of Plastic and Reconstructive Surgeons. Distribution was limited to members, and inside was certain information not available to the general public.

I found the two names easily enough. Dr. Epstein attended Downstate Medical College in New York and did his residency in Philadelphia. Dr. Neifosh went to Harvard Medical School and was trained at Northwestern, in Chicago. There was an office address and phone number listed for each, but I wasn't sure if they would still be staffed, and I didn't want to be talking to any partners who might recognize me. Instead, I copied down the home address, home phone number, and the wife's first name for each entry.

I had saved the obituary on Dr. Epstein and I dialed his number first.

"Mrs. Connie Epstein?" I asked the woman who answered.

"Yes."

"Mrs. Epstein, my name is Gareth Lloyd. I'm a plastic surgeon in Los Angeles and I knew your husband back in New York, when he was in Downstate."

"George was killed on January fifteenth." She delivered the line in a flat, emotionless voice, from somewhere a lot farther away than Huntsville, Texas. I figured if there was any news there, I'd better go carefully, or I might lose her. She seemed to be teetering on the brink, and I didn't want to be the one to shove her over the edge.

"I've just heard, Mrs. Epstein. I read about it in our newsletter. I'm terribly sorry; George was a really great guy."

"How did you know him, Dr. Lloyd?"

"I was a resident there about the same time," I said, scrambling through the entry in the directory to find out exactly what time that was.

"You were a resident at Downstate? George was only a medical student when he was there."

"That's right, yes. But he made such a great impression. We all liked him. That's why it was such a shock to hear. How did it happen, Mrs. Epstein?"

"That's funny. George never had that many friends."

"Perhaps he was too busy with his career. He didn't seem the type to make enemies, though. What do you think the motive was?"

"He was shot." Her voice finally broke. "It was a

terrible, terrible thing. We moved here to get away from all the violence. . . ." She trailed off into silence.

I was suddenly sorry I'd called, stirring old ashes when the fire wasn't yet out. "Yes. Well, I don't want to impose. I didn't mean to cause you pain."

"No. No. I'm glad you called. It was very nice of you to think of him."

Now she sounded upbeat. I summoned the courage to continue. "I was wondering if they caught the killer."

"No. There were no witnesses and the police say he may never be caught."

"It's a shame. There is one question I had, Mrs. Epstein, although you may think it rather strange."

There was silence.

"Hello! Are you still there?" I asked.

"Yes. What's your question?" She sounded irritated.

"I was wondering if George collected anything. Paintings or antiques of any kind."

"I . . . Well! Why did you say you were calling?"

She sounded mad now. I started to explain, but she hung up on me. Embarrassed, I wondered what a rapist might feel after he's had his way.

The Neifosh number was next. This time, I decided to use a less personal approach.

"Is this Mrs. Dana Neifosh?"

"No, this is Darcy. Mom's at the store."

"Hi, Darcy. My name is Gareth Lloyd and I'm calling from Los Angeles. I wonder if you could have your mom call me when she gets back?"

"I'll give her the message. What's it about?"

I hesitated, then plunged in. "I'm a reporter, Darcy, and I'm doing a story about violence against plastic surgeons. I thought maybe she could help me out if she wanted to talk . . . you know, about your father."

I could hear her breathing. "I don't think Mom would want to talk about that," she said.

"I understand. I'm not going to mention any names. It's just that there have only been two or three incidents, and it would be so important to learn why this thing happens."

More breathing. "Why don't you ask me?"

"You? Oh, I don't know . . . How old are you, Darcy?"

"Fifteen."

Fifteen! Two years older than Jillian.

"I was there," she whispered.

"Were you? That must have been awful."

"We were standing in line to go to the movies: Mom, Dad, and me. We were going to see *Schindler's List*. Dad moved away to see how long the line was, and someone came up from behind and shot him three times."

I could sense she'd told the story a few times already, whittled it down to the essentials so she could get it all out in one breath. As if it would hurt less that way, like a quick jab with a syringe. I was ashamed to be the one extracting more blood. "I'm terribly sorry, Darcy."

"He didn't die right away. Mom held his head in her lap and he kind of talked to us for a while. He said he loved us, and that we shouldn't blame ourselves for anything. Then he talked about our summer vacation. Then he just drifted away."

Her voice was soft, barely above a whisper, but her delivery was calm and even—not a choke or a sob. It would have been less distressing had she cried. It had been only six months. I was glad I wasn't a real newspaperman, having to earn a living at this kind of thing.

"I don't suppose they have any idea why this happened?"

"No. Nobody knows. It wasn't like a gang or anything."

"Did you see the man?"

"He was white. I couldn't see his face because he was wearing a hat, but his arms were covered in tattoos."

"Tattoos? What kind of tattoos?"

"I don't know. It was too dark to see what they were."

"But you're certain he was white?"

"I know a black man when I see one."

"Oh, sure. But you said it was dark. Could he possibly have been Hispanic? I mean, brown skin and white skin could look the same on a dark street."

"Well . . . I suppose you're right. I guess he could have been Mexican."

"Do you know what kind of gun he used?"

"I don't know about guns," she replied quickly. I thought for a second there'd be more, but there wasn't.

"The police didn't say?" I asked, wondering if they'd be called Rangers in Texas.

"Have you talked to the cops?" she shot back.

"No, I haven't."

"They don't know what they're talking about."

Now the grief was coming out as rage, I thought; blaming the police for the whole affair. Perhaps they hadn't responded in time. "What do you mean, Darcy?"

"Nobody believes me. You say he wasn't white. The cops say there must have been two killers. I was there and I saw it. There was only one." Her voice trembled with emotion.

"I was only curious about what you saw," I explained. "I didn't mean to doubt your word. I know what you must be going through and I think you've been really brave. I have a daughter about your age."

"I'm not a child."

"Neither is my daughter. But why do the cops think there were two killers?"

"They say there were two different kinds of bullets."

"I see. Well, they must have analyzed them."

"I don't know anything about that. I know what I saw."

"Maybe I can talk to them. Do you know who the investigating officer was?"

"I forgot. He hasn't called us in a month. Wait a minute, we have it written down somewhere. Here it is, on the refrigerator." She gave me a name and number.

"Thank you, Darcy. I'm very sorry about what happened. I'm sure that while he was alive your father was truly proud of you."

"Are you going to use Dad's story?"

"I don't know. Not if it upsets your mother."

"Okay. But if you do, be sure and send me a copy. I'm collecting a scrapbook."

"I will." I knew what she had done with her grief. She had buried it between the pages of some album, on little pieces of newsprint, to be exhumed at some future date when the demons called.

"Speaking of collecting, Darcy, did your Dad like to collect anything? Any paintings? Or antiques, perhaps?"

"He had a lot of baseball cards. Is that what you mean?"

"Is that all?" I wondered if Miranda Pelton's taste ran to baseball cards. "Were any of them valuable?"

"He thought they were. But Mom sold them to a dealer and I don't think she got much for them. Why?"

"Just curious." I thanked her and put the receiver down.

I played with my work sheet, nervously flicking the edge of the paper with my fingertips long after it had ceased to be crisp. Next to Jed Neifosh's name I wrote "killer" and then "hat" and "tattoos." After a while I added the word "two" in front of "killer," and an "s" after it, changing it to "two killers."

WHEN I FIRST START A NEW PROJECT I HAVE nothing but enthusiasm for it. I plunge in whole-heartedly, immersing myself as if jumping into the water chute at an amusement park, trusting blindly that no matter in which direction it will spin me, in the end I will emerge on terra firma, whole and un-scathed. I had undertaken this mission with much the same outlook. It was an adventure: not without risk, of course, but I was working parallel with a professional, if not actu-ally by his side. I trusted Plant would not lead me into dan-ger. After all, he knew what I did for a living. I was a man of healing, not a martial arts expert.

If only he would call and give me some direction.

But he didn't. The call I got instead, as my office hours were winding down for the morning—and in fact for the week, having no regular duties scheduled for Friday afternoon—was from Detective Akimoro. I had all but written him off after my talk with Elaine.

While I thought of Plant as an ally, a man with whom I had a working commitment borne of a common goal, there was more to it than that. He was, in a sense, my mentor in this maiden voyage I was taking into the under-world. I held his image in my mind's eye, the seasoned pilot who would guide me into port. Even though I had not spo-ken to him since that short visit to my office, every deci-sion I made, every time I picked up the phone or wrote an entry on my work sheet, it would have to meet with his imaginary approval. Would Mr. Plant do it that way?

Not so with Detective Akimoro. He represented the forces of distraction, circling around me like a great white shark, ready to sap my concentration and my energy from the task ahead. He had not started with the best of credentials. Being a policeman, I felt his efforts would be mired in protocol and show a lack of enterprise and ingenuity, so essential to the job at hand. True to this stereotype, he had wasted valuable time at the outset by pursuing his suspicions of Elaine and me. Only now we had shown him the error of his ways. There was undeniable evidence that Jack Ehrenberger was involved in a million-dollar art heist. Did Akimoro need more motive than that? I was still having trouble assimilating the magnitude of Jack's secret role. It must have taken an inordinate amount of planning and manipulation to orchestrate the clandestine movement of so many valuable works of art from so many different sources—all funneled into an apartment in Santa Monica. Detective Akimoro should have his hands full following up leads. I couldn't believe that he still persisted in harassing me.

The call that he placed through to me that morning was an official summons to a lineup—an identification parade, as they called it back in Wales. Akimoro wanted to put me in some dog-and-pony show for the benefit of an eyewitness who had stepped forward. He wouldn't say who it was. He gave me to understand that I had the power to refuse, and he advised me to retain a lawyer.

I was indignant. I felt humiliated. I couldn't believe he was so far off track. But I went. If there was one way to get Akimoro off my back, this had to be it. I would prove that he was gnawing at the wrong bait.

Two o'clock Friday afternoon I found myself in a large room in the Beverly Hills police headquarters, playing chorus line on a well-lit stage with four other men. A darkened glass partition ran down the width, behind which no light was visible at all.

My memory of the event is purely visceral. My ears were burning with embarrassment, and my throat was parched, but I cannot remember the color of the wall, nor the faces that were lined up along it. I can recall the pounding resentment in my heart, and that my nostrils were flared, each breath pungent with the odor of sweat oozing from my armpits, but I forget the instructions they gave me, or even who it was that gave them. I do remember Detective Akimoro and several uniformed police, as well as a grim-faced, dark-suited man introduced as the district attorney. All I wanted was for it to be over, so I could go home and shower, wash the smell of anger from my pores.

Who was behind that partition? Was it one witness or more? Perhaps the parking attendant from Jack's office building. Who else? I hated whoever it was behind there, one and all—hated that they had been so vague in their original descriptions of the killer, that Akimoro had seen fit to drag me here so they could have a second look.

When they told me I was free to leave, I walked out into the dry heat of the bright afternoon sun and stood against the wrought-iron railings, taking great gulps of air until my breathing slowed. It wasn't until I was back in the parking lot, sitting in the familiar surroundings of my Alfa, that I finally began to calm down. I punched the gas and felt the shudder of the starter kicking in, smelled the fumes as the engine roared to life, and just sat there, steeping my bruised ego in the comforting resonance of the idling motor. I don't know how long I waited, drowning my rage in the gentle vibrations, soothing as a hot tub, while a single thought kept repeating in my mind.

I would get my own revenge at Akimoro and the unseen witness. I would show them for what they were, a bunch of confused and inefficient flatfeet. I would find the killer myself.

I needed someone to talk to, and the natural choice was Peter Heering. For one thing, University Hospital was directly on my way home, and I could avoid the Friday traffic if I spent an hour or so with him. Peter would be winding down his afternoon clinic and wrapping up his teaching duties for the week, and this was the most likely time to catch him when he wasn't rushing somewhere. Besides, Cindy wouldn't be around and I could have him to myself.

I parked in the visitors' lot and walked across the complex to the main building, up the wide stairway to the impressive facade, and into a vast hallway. I saw immediately that nothing much had changed since I was last there, except for a few more security guards and a bulletproof barrier from Reception through to the emergency room. The same dejected mass of people thronged the hallways and the waiting rooms, filling every chair, sprawling on every inch of available bench space, and spilling over into sundry groups scattered around the perimeter of the floor. They sat in stoic silence: the destitute and uninsured, the sick and injured castoffs from every private hospital within miles. Their faces and their anima were drained, more by the inhumanity of having to wait hours than by their ailments.

I followed one of several colored lines down the center of the corridor to the elevator banks and caught a car up to the seventh floor. The door to Peter's office suite was open. His secretary recognized my face but registered surprise at my presence, as she cast into her rusty memory for a name.

"It's Dr. Lloyd," I said brusquely. "Is Peter in?"

"Yes, Dr. Lloyd."

I walked through without invitation.

Peter was sitting at his desk reading a journal, ignoring the lovely panorama of downtown Los Angeles beyond his window.

"Professor Heering," I said. "Got a few minutes for an old friend?"

He looked pleased to see me. "Hello, Gareth. What brings you down here on a Friday afternoon?"

"It's a long story, Peter."

"Sit down. Too bad you couldn't be here a couple of hours ago; you might have played visiting consultant at clinic. The residents can always use another opinion."

He leaned back and stuck his hands deep in his pockets. "Sometimes I wonder if they fully trust my judgment. I think they feel that I've been in academic practice too long and I've lost a sense of what one would do in the real world."

Peter was always enthusiastic about work, and I'd forgotten how much I enjoyed his company. We didn't spend much time together anymore. For a year or more I had seen him only at social gatherings, when he was with Cindy, and he never said much in her presence.

"Is that what they think, or what you think?" I asked. I sat back in a lumpy old leather sofa and put my legs on his coffee table. "So you're starting to feel like a tired, old fart, too. I think it's because we're both reaching the wrong side of forty."

He grinned. "I've got three years left. How about you?"

"I'm afraid I reach that milestone this Sunday."

"No kidding? Hey, we have to do something. You got any plans? Why don't you come over for that dinner we've been promising you?"

"No thanks, Peter. No offense, but maybe some other time. I feel like a quiet evening alone. I want it to slip by without too much fanfare. I was going to take the kids out to lunch somewhere exciting and then just sit back with a movie or a good book."

"Are you sure? It's really no trouble, you know. You sound sort of down. I think you need a good night out."

My idea of a good night out was not dinner with Cindy. "I'll be fine," I said.

"It's this thing with Elaine, isn't it?"

Peter had never been so direct before.

"I was breaking up with her, anyway," I said. "It's

just a little sticky because he was murdered before the breakup became common knowledge. So I guess it puts me right in the middle when it comes to suspects."

"Whew!" He gave a little whistle. "I hadn't realized that before. You *are* a suspect, aren't you? Hey, have you been questioned or anything? Wait until Cindy finds out, she'll hit the roof. You know, she's over there right now on some lineup or other, doing her thing as a citizen."

If I turned another color, he didn't seem to notice.

"Cindy is doing what?" I asked, trying to keep my voice on an even pitch.

"She was asked to join a couple of other witnesses at the Beverly Hills P.D. and pick somebody out of a lineup. I guess they've finally hauled in some guy they can pin this thing on. Which means that you can breathe easier, old buddy. Consider yourself off the hook."

"Yes." I felt the rage returning. "You mean out of the frying pan."

The possibility that I could be in the fire was lost on him. "You know she saw the whole thing last week," he said. "She was sitting across the street having dinner with Rafaella."

"Yes." I nodded. "I'd forgotten she told me that."

My mind was flaming over Cindy Heering being on the other side of that reflective glass partition, holding my fate in her meddlesome little hands. Obviously she must have cleared my name, or they wouldn't have let me go. And she couldn't have known that I was going to be in the lineup. If she had, the whole charade would have been unnecessary. She would have just told Akimoro that I wasn't the man she'd seen in the car. But she must have enjoyed herself watching me squirm. I could just imagine the conversation she would have with Rafaella, laughing about it.

"It's funny, though," Peter said. "She didn't see the other guy."

"What other guy?"

"The second killer. She swears there was only one."

"The second killer? Why do you think there was someone else?"

"There had to be. That's what Von Mueller said."

"Fawn Moler?"

"Arnie von Mueller in Pathology. He moonlights for the coroner's office. He had something to do with the postmortem on Jack Ehrenberger. He told me there had to be two guys involved. I mean, this is on the Q.T. Don't you go blabbing it to anybody."

Blabbing? Not me. But Plant might be interested in this. Peter had my full attention now; the rage in my head was starting to clear. Maybe it was the vindication that when it came to a choice between Cindy's word and that of Von Mueller, Peter favored Von Mueller's.

"Why does this pathologist think there were two killers?" I asked.

"Something about the bullets. It sounded a bit technical."

The rage faded further, and the skin on the back of my neck began to crawl. This was the second time that day I'd heard of a dead man relinquishing two kinds of bullets, and both victims were plastic surgeons on *my* work sheet. "Can I talk to Von Mueller?"

"He's not going to be happy I told you."

"Please, Peter."

He looked at me and nodded. "I guess so. Let's see if he's still downstairs." He picked up his phone and dialed an extension.

I walked over to the window, taking in the view from the Hollywood Hills all the way down to Palos Verdes. How many bullet-ridden corpses were left sprawled on the sidewalks of a city this size every year? How many in Houston? I wondered what the odds were on having two assailants for each victim.

"He's still there," Peter said. "I'll take you."

I followed him back to the elevators and down to Pathology. Arnie von Mueller's office was a cubicle much smaller than Peter's, and I gathered it said something about the pecking order that he had no secretary. Peter made the introductions and explained the purpose of our visit.

"This isn't supposed to get around," the pathologist said. "What's your interest in the case?"

"Jack Ehrenberger was a friend of mine." I looked meaningfully at Peter to keep him from saying anything. "I'm pretty close to his wife, and I just wondered if there were any leads."

"How's she taking it? I suppose she's still in shock. Anyway, I don't know anything about leads."

"She's holding up pretty well," I said.

"Well, I did help with the autopsy. The guy was in good shape, too—arteries were clean—must have had good genes. Too bad. He might have lived to be a hundred."

"Tell me about the bullets."

"You know we don't do any ballistics. We just hand them to the investigating officer. They take over from there."

"Why do you think there were two killers?"

"We took four bullets out of his chest. Two were full metal jackets and two were silvertips. Had to be two guns."

"Were they the same caliber?"

"Looked like it to me. Nine millimeter."

"And you couldn't tell anything about the markings?"

"The silvertips were exploded—couldn't tell much. But that's not really my bag. You'd have to ask the cops. I have the name of the detective in charge somewhere." He started to open a desk drawer.

"Thanks, but I have that," I interrupted. "You think they could have been fired from the same gun?"

Arnie von Mueller looked over at Peter. His eyes told me he'd said too much already. Then his gaze fixed back on his desktop, as if further eye contact with me was dangerous.

"Why would somebody put two different bullets in the same gun?" he asked.

I WAS IMPATIENT ALL THE WAY HOME. I KEPT thinking about the case, so much that I almost crunched my rear fender on a lane change, then missed my exit off the freeway. I considered calling Texas from the car phone, but the work sheet with the numbers I needed was still in my office. Houston was two hours ahead, and I wasn't even sure I'd get any answers this late on the weekend.

It was after six when I pulled into the office lot. I let myself in and rushed over to my desk. I found the number Darcy Neifosh gave me and dialed the Houston police.

"Homicide," a voice answered.

"I'm looking for Detective Heintz."

"Sorry, he's gone for the day."

*Damn!* "When will he be back?"

"I don't think he's on again till Monday. Is there anyone else who can help you?"

"No. I need to talk to him."

"Care to leave a message?"

"It's about the Jed Neifosh murder. I heard he's got the file."

"I think you'd better talk to someone else. Hang on."

I waited a couple of minutes, listening to the beep of the recording device at the other end.

Another voice came on. "Officer Dooley. Can I help you?"

I told him who I was. "I need to know about the bullets that they took out of Dr. Neifosh. His daughter said there were two kinds."

"Dr. Lloyd, are you giving us information or looking for it?"

"Officer, there's been a similar murder here in L.A. There could be a link between the two. I'm just trying to find out as much as I can." I went over some of the details about Jack's death, leaving out the bit about the stolen art. I didn't want him to think I was raving.

"Why don't you give me your name and number, and I'll have Heintz call you," he said.

I did, then hung up, disappointed.

Next, I placed a call to directory assistance in Huntsville and asked for the main police station. I dialed through and introduced myself to the woman who replied, saying I was following up a lead on Dr. Epstein's murder. "He was killed outside a health club on January fifteenth."

"I know," she said. "We remember it well."

I asked for the investigator on the case.

"That will be Syllovitz. I'll put you through."

I felt lucky; the grin on my face reflected from the framed photo of Jillian and Emma on my desk.

"Detective Syllovitz." His deep, bass tone had a slight rasp.

I introduced myself again and repeated my purpose in calling. "Is there anyway you can help me with a few details?"

"Dr. Lloyd." He took his time, as if it hurt his throat to speak too fast. "You a private investigator or a private citizen?"

"I'm doing a study on violence against surgeons. It's a project for the Plastic Surgery Foundation." I figured there was no way he could check on that until next Monday.

He was silent for a moment. "Look, Dr. Lloyd. It's

Friday night and I should be home with my wife. We already got two homicides this week and now there's reports of gunfire over by the bus depot. I got police work to do, if you don't mind."

I thought he was about to hang up. "Wait a minute, Detective. A plastic surgeon was killed here in Los Angeles last week, in almost similar circumstances to Dr. Epstein. All I'm saying is there could be a connection. I think it's worth looking into."

"You telling me the guy who killed Epstein made it all the way to Los Angeles to look for another plastic surgeon?"

"I . . . I'm not sure."

"What are you sure of, Dr. Lloyd?"

I felt as if I had gone off half-cocked, without taking the time to sit down and work it out. Did I think the doctors had been silenced because they had stumbled into a ring of thieves? Or was there a pair of crazy assassins roaming half the continent just looking for plastic surgeons to knock off?

"What about Houston?" I said. "The first murder was in Houston six months ago. That's close to Huntsville, isn't it?"

"We've already checked Houston, Dr. Lloyd. We've cross-checked the whole goddamn state for armed robbery, going back two years."

"I'm not talking about armed robbery. Neither of the other two surgeons was robbed."

"Then what are we talking about, Dr. Lloyd? You think this is some kind of conspiracy? You saying we need the FBI in on this?"

He waited for my answer. I began to suspect that he wasn't in a hurry at all. He was just playing with me, volleying the ball back to my side of the net to see how I would react. I tried to organize my thoughts. "I don't know," I replied. "I'm looking at a bunch of murdered plastic surgeons, that's all. Trying to make some sense out of it."

Syllovitz was silent. Occasionally, I could hear the intrusive beep of a recording device, but I was accustomed to that now. I had no secrets to conceal, just some thoughts that I desperately wanted to share with someone—someone who would tell me I wasn't going bananas. I could almost see the detective, scratching the stubble on a sun-baked neck, trying to do the same thing I was. Make some sense of it. "Tell me what you know," he finally said.

I told him all about Jack's death—the two types of bullets that Von Mueller identified. I told him what I'd heard about Neifosh from his daughter. I gave him Detective Heintz's number in Houston. "You might want to call him up."

"I will."

I was relieved. He had taken the time to listen and I thought he'd believe me. "Will you tell me what I want to know about Epstein's murder now?" I asked.

"Why would I want to do that?"

"Because I've helped you by telling you something. And . . . " I hesitated, stifling the thought that was slowly creeping into my mind.

"And what?"

"And because I could be the next victim." It was numbing to hear my words, but it was a possibility I had to face. I had spent the last few days abandoning myself to a process I didn't fully understand. The whirlwind of events had carried me to a point where I was scarcely in control. It was exciting, but I hoped I hadn't raised my level of exposure to the degree that my life was in danger. What scared me was that I didn't really want to stop.

My thoughts were interrupted by a vibration from my pager. I reached down automatically to shut it off.

"You think your life is in danger, Dr. Lloyd?" Syllovitz asked.

"I don't know. I've been poking my nose around,

asking questions. Somebody's bound to have noticed."

"And why would you want to do that? Why don't you just go to the police?"

I hesitated. "That's not easy. They have me as a suspect."

There was another pause. I wondered if Texans ever had time to finish what they had to say. I checked the number displayed on my pager. It was the emergency room at Memorial Hospital.

"Why do you think you're a suspect?" asked Syllovitz.

"Because I knew Jack Ehrenberger. Actually, I knew his wife."

"I see. Well, depending on how friendly you were with his wife, I might consider you a suspect, too."

Policemen were the same all over the world, I thought. "Look, Detective Syllovitz! If it's any help to you, I didn't do it. But I'd like to find out who did before my reputation's ruined."

"I think you should leave that to the police, Dr. Lloyd, and go back to practicing medicine. You've given me a lot of information, and I'm obliged. I'll get on it with Heintz and the guy in Beverly Hills you told me about. Can you spell his name for me?"

"*A-k-i-m-o-r-o.*"

"Thanks. But if you want my opinion, unless you've got some secret you're not telling me, I don't think you should be in any danger."

"And why do you say that?"

"The guy who killed Epstein is no crazy amateur. The way he shot him—the slugs, the ambush, the whole MO—he had to know what he was doing."

"Did he have two different bullets, too?"

"Yup. Two full metal jackets, two silvertips. Four shots to the chest."

"Same as Jack Ehrenberger," I said in a whisper. "But how can you be sure it was only one man?"

"Just one gun, Dr. Lloyd. Thirty-eight. The markings match."

"And the choice of bullets tells you he was a professional?"

"It appears that way."

"Thank you, Detective Syllovitz."

"You're welcome," he said.

I hung up, then dialed the hospital emergency room. Apparently, Huntsville wasn't the only place where guns were being fired. They had a victim with a gunshot wound to the forearm they wanted me to see. I locked up the office and headed for my car.

I FINISHED ROUNDS EARLY ON SATURDAY morning. The shooting victim from the night before was doing fine after surgery, although he'd lost the use of a sensory nerve to his hand. Could have been a lot worse. I wondered if he'd been in any way responsible for provoking his injury, or had truly been minding his own business, the way he recounted. You tend to get quite skeptical, treating victims of violence. I figured if I were a cop, I probably wouldn't believe a word I was told.

I called Rafaella so I could arrange to pick up Jillian and Emma for Sunday lunch. I liked taking the kids somewhere on weekends, even if we could manage only a few hours together. This time, I was especially looking forward to it. I would be turning forty on Sunday, and there was no one else to celebrate the day with.

She was less than cooperative.

"I don't think it's a good idea, Gareth," she said.

I became annoyed. "You have other plans?"

"Yes, I have other plans. I have plans to cut off your visitation rights altogether. I've talked to Dulles Lindstrom and he's going to draw up the papers next week. I don't want you seeing the girls anymore."

Dulles was her lawyer, a flaxen-haired, smooth-talking Swede who wore the most lurid ties, and who was spending altogether too much time with my ex-wife.

"What's this all about, Rafaella? Who the hell's

going to act as their father if I don't take them out once a week?"

"You should have thought of that before, Gareth."

She had the infuriating quality, thoroughly Italian, of raising her voice in exact measure to that of her opposition, whether she was confronting a butcher over the price of hot sausage, negotiating a discount at the crafts fair, or arguing with me.

"Should have thought of what?" I asked hotly.

"Should have thought of your children before you became involved."

I exploded inside. Cindy Heering had to be behind this; she would have told Rafaella the story of the lineup by now. I took a deep breath and tried to calm down. "What have you been telling the kids?"

"I haven't told the kids anything. You think I would tell them that their father was a suspect in a murder?"

"I am not a murderer, Rafaella."

"There's no need to shout."

"Shout! Damn it! You want to take my kids away and there's no need to shout?" I could barely hold the phone to my ear. "Listen! The only person I would consider murdering is Cindy. She's been feeding you a bunch of garbage, hasn't she?"

"See, that. I knew you had it in you, Gareth. Listen to that temper."

I took a deep breath and counted to ten. I tried pleading with her. "It's my birthday, Rafaella. You can't deny me seeing them on my birthday."

"I don't care what day it is. I won't have my children put in danger."

"Danger! What are you talking about? You know me better than that. You're just doing this out of spite. Cindy has no right to put you up to this."

"It's got nothing to do with Cindy, and it's got nothing to do with spite. I discussed it with Dulles and I agree with him."

"Oh! You agree with *him?* What exactly does he say?" That damned Dulles was second on my murder list.

"He says knowing you're a suspect in a murder makes him liable if any harm comes to the kids. He says he has an obligation to keep them out of danger. He says any social worker would cut your visitation in the same circumstances."

"Social worker! Circumstances!" I was livid. "Where the hell are we? China? What the hell is going on between you and Dulles, anyway?"

"I don't know what you mean by that. And there's no need to shout." There was a click, and I was left staring at a dead receiver.

I had every need to shout. I wanted to let out a bloodcurdling yell. But I could scream all I wanted, to no avail. The specter of child abuse had been raised, and, the system being what it was, I knew that every family court in the country would be happy to sign any document that Dulles cared to draw up.

Short of kidnapping Jillian and Emma, I was going to spend my birthday alone.

I was in a sour mood as I donned my jeans, T-shirt, and denim jacket in preparation for Malbone's that afternoon. Rafaella had robbed me of some of the pleasure of going. I couldn't even look forward to seeing Miranda Pelton. She had vanished without a trace. Not that I had any desire to abandon my trip to the auction house. In my frame of mind it would have been unthinkable. I would have brooded all evening at home. It was now incumbent on Malbone's to get me out of the doldrums. Maybe I would find some sleeper, some rare and hidden treasure, to make amends for my pain.

With the eternal optimism of a poker player wending his way to the gaming tables, I was ready for my royal flush. After all, it was almost my birthday. I had endured forty years and somebody owed me for that. Malbone's owed me. If ever I was going to hit the jackpot, this had to be the day.

After a quick lunch, in a slightly better mood, I started up the Alfa. It came to life in a puff of blue haze, a lifelong smoker clearing its throat. That phlegm-filled roar topped me with satisfaction. There was no mistaking the characteristic sound. In any other car I would be looking for a hole in the muffler, but in an Alfa that throaty warble means all systems are go and she is ready for action. I headed for the freeway.

The weather gurus had promised rain, and I could see why. Cold gray clouds hung to the north and west, and an even darker sky peeked over the San Gabriel Mountains, as if it was already raining up there.

Malbone's lot was jammed. I parked and walked the back stairs to the warehouse deck. Once inside, the familiar musty odor of buried treasure and the amplified drone of the auctioneer's voice enveloped me. I felt better for it.

I saw Rocco Gambella pawing through some old frames, scraping the gilt finish and testing the wood.

"How's it going, Rocco?"

"All right. Finding anything today?"

"Just got here, Rocco. How about you?"

"I'm having a good day." He was poker-faced. I could see excitement glowing in his eyes, his pupils exploding with some hidden secret he was trying to keep from the world.

"Let's have it, Rocco. Come on. What's the dirt?"

He bent his neck in a conspiratorial whisper. "You don't go for paintings, do you?"

I shook my head. "Strictly pottery."

"See these here." He indicated the frames he was gripping. "Eighteenth century. I don't know how they fell into this lot. I'd love to have the paintings that went in them."

"Frames worth something?"

"Can't say for sure." He had a sly grin. "Let's wait and see if there are any experts here today."

I let him have his game. "You know a lot about paintings, Rocco?"

"Been studying them for years, Doc."

"Tell me, what would you think if you discovered a hidden stash of stolen art?"

"Discovered?" He looked straight at me, and his eyes lost some of their sparkle. "I'd say not interested. Legit only."

I wondered if there might have been a time he would have answered differently. "No, Rocco. I'm just talking hypothetically. What would someone be doing with a stash like that? What kind of people would they be dealing with?"

"I'd say they were asking for trouble and get the hell out of there." He looked over to the podium, as if the conversation was officially over. I guessed he might have had his share of problems from similar situations.

We watched a heated struggle for possession of an old brass fireplace set. After it was over he turned to me. "I'd say it sounds a lot like that story in the papers Thursday. That guy was a plastic surgeon, too. He some friend of yours?"

"I knew him."

"They shot him, didn't they?"

"You think it was over the paintings?"

"Why else? Ten million dollars—that's big-time." He turned his attention back to the frames. I didn't push him, not wanting to tread on his toes. It wasn't long before he looked back up at me. "Say, Doc, you wouldn't be in any of that, would you?"

I smiled. "Would I be here if I did?"

He seemed as if he was trying to work out what I meant.

"You read the article. Any ideas who shot him?" I asked.

He shrugged. "Anybody who dealt with him. His partner . . . the competition . . . Sometimes they're one and the same."

"Who's the competition? Organized crime?"

Rocco scratched his head under his ponytail. The crowd was milling all around us, but nobody appeared interested in a little tête-à-tête between an art dealer and a collector of art pottery, and there didn't seem much risk of being overheard.

"I don't know," he said. "Everything's different now. In the old days, when they didn't keep track of everything with computers, it was a lot simpler to find a willing buyer. Now the market's closing down. There's only a few people left with a taste for the really hot stuff. Nobody has the budget to handle secret viewing rooms and everything else it takes."

He rolled his tongue over his front teeth. "Maybe the mob has taken over. Who knows? Maybe it's the drug cartels. Nowadays, everything's so damn organized. They got CPA's working out the projections, and lawyers drawing up the fine print." He lowered his voice and leaned in toward me. "You aren't thinking of getting into this business, are you?"

I thought about what he said for a moment, watching Easton the auctioneer hammer down a Limoges fish set for seven hundred.

"Where would I start, Rocco?"

He looked me up and down, then broke into a grin. "You know what it's like dealing with those drug dealers? Totally unpredictable. It takes an iron gut to put up with that crap. You think you have the stomach for that, Doc?"

I certainly didn't. I didn't think Jack did, either. Knowing Elaine, she wouldn't have stayed with him all those years unless some shred of sensitivity, some common decency, ran in his veins. He didn't even like guns, or so she said. I saw him more as the gentleman crook.

"Isn't there another market somewhere? Some

place a guy could quietly deal this stuff to millionaire collectors without having to worry about machine guns, midnight drop-offs, bodyguards, all that subterfuge?"

He shrugged. "You can't make any money without some risk. Of course, there's always the Far East."

"The Far East?"

"Those Asians are really getting big on Western art. They know the value of it, and they got the money for it. The bigger corporations are stockpiling originals by the busload. Most of them can afford to buy at auction, except from countries where there's an exportation ban on local art. Then they go underground. The Japs used to have the corner on it, but now the Taiwanese and Hong Kong Chinese are getting in on the game. There's big money coming out of Thailand, too."

We had to move out of the way while three wiry men wearing abdominal binders helped move a large bedroom set into the center of the crowd. The ugly back belts around their waists might have done little to prevent injury, but every employee had one on—another victory for the personal-injury lawyers who plied the fertile field of workers' compensation fraud.

Rocco walked over to a collection of old lithographs propped against a couch, and surreptitiously slid his antique frames into the bunch. He rubbed his hands in anticipation as he returned to my side. "Let's see if anybody can spot them now."

"You think the Far East is wide open, Rocco?"

I saw his mind change gears, as though he had already moved off the subject. "Yeah, I suppose it is. But it's not easy, either. You've got to have some real good contacts, somebody who knows the language and the customs—when to deal, when to hold your ground. It's a big circus. Those brokers come in all businesslike, polite and bowing and all, and they watch you to see do you have the right moves. They don't trust us round-eyes. If you spook 'em, you're out of a deal."

He laughed as if he'd made a joke, shaking his head. "No way. I got no head for that stuff anymore. There's enough money in resale, if you know what you're doing. And a lot less hassles, too."

His attention wandered back to the podium, and I let him chase his antique frames.

I thought about what Rocco had said. Somehow, it all made sense: Jack Ehrenberger's office, his house, the Rolls-Royces, the trips to Paris. Even with the best practice in the world, there was a lot of competition in plastic surgery, and Jack would have had to work real hard trying to juggle that. But not if he had tapped into some underground source for his funds. A pipeline across the Pacific. I wondered if Jack had been any good at bowing from the waist.

Elaine fit the puzzle, too. She was the perfect companion for such a career. As long as Jack kept her content she wouldn't have bothered to pry into his books, wouldn't have questioned her life in the fast lane. To Elaine, mathematics was the art of figuring how many pieces of jewelry made an ensemble.

Rocco came back to shake me from my thoughts, the biggest grin I ever saw across his silver-capped teeth. He was clutching both frames in his left hand.

"All mine," he said. "And for only three-fifty. I'm having a very good day, Doc."

I WAS IN A REFLECTIVE MOOD, PULLING OUT drawers from an old pine dresser, when I saw her. I was inspecting the dovetailing, hoping to learn something new, anticipating that the boards would somehow reveal their age. She was sitting on an oak desk with her back against the wall, hugging her legs, chin resting on bony knees protruding through her tattered jeans.

I caught her silently watching me, blond hair a shade darker today, wet with gel. Those hazel eyes were taunting me, with a glint of a smile on rosy lips. I pushed the drawer back, keeping my gaze fixed on her, waiting for some word of recognition. She rocked her body from side to side, saying nothing.

I walked up to the oak desk. "Hello, Miranda."

"So you remembered my name?"

"You made an impression on me."

She gave a look as if she'd heard the line before. Then the smile was back. "And how are you, Gareth?" There were bells in her voice.

"Fine, thanks. I didn't expect to see you here."

"Why not?"

"I . . . I don't know."

She ran her forefinger around the lip of a cut-glass vase within her reach. "You can't keep me away from an auction," she said.

"Me, too."

"Then we have something in common."

She was dressed more casually today: a lacy half-sleeved top that fell short of her belt, faded blue jeans with strategic rips, and black boots with yellow laces. The ring was still on her left hand. I had taken her for mid-twenties, and now I wondered if I had misjudged her age.

"But we've already established that, haven't we?" she said.

"What's that?"

"That we have something in common. Antiques!" She emphasized the last word in answer to my quizzical look.

"Oh yes." I was remembering Plant.

"Buying anything today?" she asked, picking up the vase and inspecting the bottom.

"No. Nothing yet."

"Me neither." She put it down quickly, as if her inspection revealed nothing of merit.

"Do you . . . " I hesitated. It was difficult for me to get to the point.

She waited.

"Do you have anything to sell?" I blurted out.

"I hope that doesn't mean what it sounds like." She raised her head.

I smiled. "No. I'm sorry. I didn't mean that. I just wondered if you sold antiques. I thought you might be a dealer."

"Why did you think that?"

"No particular reason. I just wondered what you do, that's all."

"Sometimes I wonder that myself." She looked away, then back at me. "What do you do, Gareth? Tell me about yourself."

She caught me unawares. I was not prepared to tell her the truth, but I had no confidence in my acting, so I couldn't afford to be too inventive. "I take care of people."

She laughed. A little snicker. "I know a lot of people who do that. Could you be a little more vague?"

"I work in a hospital. University Hospital. I'm in the operating room, helping with surgery."

"A nurse? No, a surgical tech." She made the conclusion I was hoping for. "Is that why you were at Jack Ehrenberger's funeral?"

I nodded, wondering where she had learned about operating room technicians. I noted she had said "Jack," not "Dr. Ehrenberger."

"I thought he worked at Cedars-Sinai," she said.

"How did you know that?"

Another snicker. "I told you, I was a candidate for surgery."

If she was making all this up, she certainly remembered her story line from week to week. I hoped I would do as well.

"He did," I replied. "He worked at Cedars-Sinai when he wasn't using his own operating suite. But he used to come to University Hospital at one time. That's where I met him."

We were both silent for a while, watching Easton do his thing up on the podium.

"Well, we're not going to buy anything from back here," I remarked.

She shrugged. "I'm not really interested today."

"Tell you what," I suggested, "let's go around and check out the merchandise. It could be fun. You teach me what you know, and I'll do the same."

She agreed.

We spent the next two happy hours romping through five-hundred-odd lots of mostly junk, with enough antiques scattered among them to deepen our acquaintance. She knew an awful lot about porcelain and pottery, somewhat more than I, and when it came to paintings and silver, she was way ahead. She didn't seem to mind my ignorance, explaining ardently, with what I took to be a genuine love of history and all things old. By the time we were through I was thoroughly captivated by her, and I didn't care if it took another day or two to find out if she traded in stolen goods.

I wanted her to like me back, and noticed two things that gave me hope. The first was that she was no longer nervously looking over her shoulder, in a hurry to go somewhere, as she had been the week before. The second was that her young, muscular companion was nowhere in sight.

"What shall we do next?" I asked as the hammer was going down on the last few lots.

"We? Don't you have somebody to go home to?"

"No. Do you?"

She ignored my question. "I've got a long drive home. I think I'd better be on my way."

"But I thought you told me you lived close by."

"Did I? I don't remember saying that. Anyway, I've moved."

"Really? Where?"

"Oh, it's quite far. Over two hours. So I really shouldn't stay much longer."

"Could you be a little more vague?" I said.

She laughed. She had a musical laugh, like a chiming bell. In spite of her words she made no move to leave, which gave me more hope.

"I don't suppose you'd be interested in a meal or a drink someplace. I guess not if you have to drive that far. What about a coffee—a cappuccino?"

She might have seen my desperation. A smile spread across rose lips. "I'll let you walk me to my car."

Outside the light was fading fast. Gray clouds had rolled down off the mountains, and the air was cool with the smell of rain. I followed Miranda down the steps and through the back lot. There were two dealers loading up their trucks at the bay, but after we passed the Dumpster the lot was deserted. She kept on going until she reached a battered olive Datsun Z in the back row. She couldn't have chosen a more sequestered parking spot. No wonder she wanted company on the way there. I looked around, half expecting to see her muscular friend, but there was no one.

She opened the car door, then turned to me, leaning against the frame, one leg hitched up against the paintwork. It was not the stance of someone in a hurry to leave. I felt a large drop hit my nose. She laughed, then leaned closer and gently kissed me where the skin was still wet.

"Thanks for a wonderful day," she said in a whisper.

I looked into her eyes and saw she meant it. "Do you really want it to end?"

"No."

"Then why don't you stay with me for dinner. You could wait until it stops raining before you make that drive."

She smiled. "Or I could leave now before it gets real bad."

She was teasing me. The drops began to fall harder. I saw splashes on her arms and little wet spots on her lace top. With a little bit of luck, in a few more minutes that top would be soaking wet.

"Shit! I could use a drink." She informed me of this change of mind with a toss of her head. "Do you know a place?"

I did, but I couldn't suggest it. My home was not appropriate for what Plant had in mind, although what *I* had in mind was beginning to outweigh that.

"Do you?" I asked.

"How about Rosarita's? It's not far."

I knew the spot. On a backstreet near the freeway. I passed it every Saturday on my way to and from Malbone's. I had never been inside. "Sounds good; I'll follow you."

She climbed into the Datsun and cranked the motor as I started through the rain to the other end of the lot. I heard her pull out behind me, then her headlamps were illuminating my path, raindrops gleaming in their arcs. It was a warm rain and felt good on my forearms.

She waited until I was safely in the Alfa with the motor running, then raced ahead. I peeled off after her, jouncing over the curb on a tight turn into the street, and thanked Malbone's for my birthday present.

I DROVE THE TWO BLOCKS TO ROSARITA's close on Miranda's taillights, noticing that they were of different shades, one red and the other rose, as though she had replaced one with an off-brand spare.

She was really quite an enigma. Last week she had struck me as being suave and sophisticated; now she looked more like something out of the pages of *Modern Teen*. There was nothing inherently wrong with that, of course; on Miranda the mode seemed to fit. I would have been happy to stroll with her, arm in arm, up Rodeo Drive, Knightsbridge, or the Via Condotti. I was comfortable in her presence. Funny what a kiss on the nose will do.

We reached our destination and she pulled into the small lot next to the brightly lit neon sign. The place had taken on an aura quite different from the simple cinderblock building I was used to passing in the daylight hours, an atmosphere of ultramodern techno-glitz, in concert with the green-uniformed valet with phosphorescent hair and neon cap who silently handed me my parking ticket. Miranda was waiting in the rain, and as we walked up the lush green carpet to the canopied door, she took my arm. I loved the gesture.

An impassive doorman let us in. The blast of music was loud, fast, and strange, a synthesized beat with a short, repetitive melody. The interior was fairly well lit, but with a pink-orange glow emanating from several neon sculptures along one wall. Inside, the cinderblock had been replaced by unpainted brick, and the tables and chairs were of tubular steel and blond maple. I was impressed with the decorator's budget, but not his taste, and felt instinctively that comfort had never been a consideration.

Fortunately, it was not very crowded. Perhaps because of the early hour or the rain, there were a few empty tables. We picked one farthest from the jukebox and sat down while I glanced around. It was an older crowd by Miranda's standards, more in keeping with my age, but dressed in Saturday evening best: loose plaid jackets, string ties, lace and linen and ruffles on every torso. I was sadly out of place in my denim jacket, but it didn't bother me one bit. I had more interesting things on my mind than running with the hounds.

She smiled at me. "What do you think?"

I shrugged. "You like it here?"

"It's safe."

Not understanding what she meant, I smiled vacuously.

We were approached by a perky redhead in shorts and a pink gingham apron. Her hips twitched rhythmically to the music as she held pen and pad at the ready.

"Can I get you anything from the bar?"

Miranda ordered a double Stolly and I an old-fashioned.

"An old-fashioned what?" the waitress asked.

"A plain old-fashioned drink," I replied. "Bourbon, a pinch of sugar, Angostura bitters. Ask your bartender to look it up in his *Funk & Wagnalls.*"

"He cain't find his fuckin' Wagnalls," she said, breaking into hysterical laughter. She gave me a thump on the shoulder.

"What'll it be, really?" she asked, winking.

"Just bring me a double Stolly like the lady here, Dwan," I said, wondering if her name tag was really a misprint. "Got anything to eat?"

She pointed to the printed menu on the table with its short list of appetizers. "You find anything on that?"

Miranda leaned over to read it with me.

"Can we share?" she asked. "I'm not too hungry."

We settled on a plate of assorted cheese and fruit and I watched the waitress hop from table to table. I was more relaxed and the music seemed to take on a new dimension. I nodded in time to her hips as she twitched her way around the room filling her page with orders.

There was a small dance floor beside the tables, but it wasn't getting much action at that hour. Most of the life in the place was concentrated against the far wall with the jukebox and neon sculptures. There was a pool table there and a foursome was laughing around it, occasionally hitting the ball in a very loosely structured game.

"Like to dance?" I asked Miranda.

She declined. She had moved in closer to read the menu with me and I could feel her warmth radiating across the gap between us, and picked up a charge from her like some photoelectric cell. I turned to face her and found her eyeing me intently.

"Tell me about yourself," she asked.

"I already did. It's you I want to know about."

"You're no OR tech."

"Why do you say that?"

"You don't behave like one. And you wouldn't be collecting art pottery on an OR tech's salary."

I looked into a pair of steady hazel eyes. She was no modern teen after all. She had a keen mind, a knowledge of antiques that implied at least ten years' experience in the trade, and the composure and self assurance to go with it.

"Actually I'm sort of in charge down there," I said. "And I have a patent on two instruments that brings me a nice royalty check every quarter." I revealed this news with such glibness that I almost believed myself. But I wasn't sure if she did.

The food and drinks arrived. Between mouthfuls of

cheese and fruit washed down with Stolichnaya vodka, we exchanged life stories. I must confess mine was more than a little bit altered—edited to fit the circumstances—and I dare say hers was, too. All the same, what she revealed made very interesting listening, and I suppose that some of it was an approximation of the truth.

She was born in Maryland but spent the first part of her childhood on Long Island. Her father had something or other to do with the United Nations, and they were transferred to Tokyo when she was seven. She attended an American school, along with most of the offspring of the diplomatic community and the various military personnel stationed there, and some of her classmates had even been Japanese children being groomed for a career in the world at large.

"How did you get along with them?" I asked.

"I hated the American kids. Brats, all of them."

"I meant the Japanese." I was thinking of the little geisha doll she kept on her mantelpiece. They seemed to have something in common, she and the doll. Perhaps it was the way they stood apart from their surroundings.

"Well, actually my two best friends were Japanese. My father encouraged it. He thought it was good for us to integrate. Of course, that made the American kids hate me even more."

"How'd you manage with the language?"

"Oh, they all spoke English very well. I picked up a lot of Japanese, though. By the time I was in high school I hung out more with Miko and Reiki than with my family. We used to do everything together."

As with most children of American expatriates, she had returned to the States for her college education. She became increasingly distanced from her family, she said, dropping out of Wellesley in her sophomore year and taking up with a drummer in a rock and roll band—Black Cat Voodoo. It was a group I'd never heard of, and no wonder.

It sounded as if they were into heavy-metal music, heavy drugs, and the occult—in whichever order they could lay their hands on. She drifted up and down the East Coast with her drummer for a while, putting up with his beatings because she was scared to go back home. She finally found religion and came West with a health food and herbal medicine guru, settling near Flagstaff, in Arizona. She got tired of that, too; couldn't stand all the peace, love, and hugging anymore. She ran away to Hollywood and paid the rent waitressing on Sunset Boulevard. She'd had several odd jobs since then, but the story became increasingly vague as it ambled into the present. I gathered her latest was as some sort of receptionist in a gallery, which seemed to coincide with what Elaine had said, and gave me reason to believe that she was steering close to the truth.

Dwan, if that was her name, returned with offers of more vodka. Miranda accepted, but I was becoming cautious with my intake. After she had been served, Miranda took a long draft and sighed.

"Now I've got to start all over again."

"You mentioned moving," I said. "What happened to your job at the gallery?"

"It fizzled out. It closed."

Odd, I thought. Elaine might have mentioned that to me. "How did you get interested in antiques?"

"My father used to collect. He was an art pottery freak, like you." She smiled and played with the hairs on my wrist. My whole body began to tingle, and not because she was comparing me with her father.

"He used to collect Rookwood and Weller and Owens pottery long before anyone knew what it was. When we were in Japan he got into Nabeshima and Sumida Gawa. He taught me how to judge a quality piece without ever turning it over to see the mark. My favorite is Staffordshire. I just naturally love it. I can spot the real thing from twenty feet."

She developed a faraway look in her eyes. "It was the only time we ever really talked, the only time he chilled out enough to pay me any attention."

I wondered if her present passion for antiques had anything to do with trying to reach back to her father. "Where are they now?" I asked.

"Who?"

"Your parents."

"Hilton Head. He's retired, writes occasionally for collector magazines."

"Did he give you any pieces to start you off?"

She pursed her lips and took another long sip. "He wouldn't give me the time of day. I haven't seen or spoken to him in ten years."

"I'm sorry to hear that."

"I'm not." She forced a smile. "He never got over it after I dropped out. He wanted me to be a lawyer." She tossed her head. "He can bury himself in Arita, for all I care. I've bought and sold more antiques by now than he's seen all his life."

This astonishing revelation brought me right back to the business at hand. James McKilroy and Company, Auctioneers and Appraisers, had a reward posted on some stolen goods they wanted back.

"Have you ever been to New Orleans?" I asked.

"Sure. Why?"

"I like New Orleans. They have a lot of nice antique stores down there."

"I guess so. What made you bring that up?"

"Nothing. Talking about antiques just reminded me of New Orleans. That's all."

"I was in New Orleans four years ago. It was all right, I guess, if you like that sort of stuff. Too many geeks. I prefer Mexico."

"Oh, really? You've been to Mexico as well?"

"I've been to Mexico lots of times," she said

proudly. "Never got sick once. I think Mexico agrees with me."

"That's nice." I was losing control of the conversation, if I ever had it in the first place. I began to wonder whether another drink wouldn't help oil things along—her libido, at least, if nothing else. "Would you like another Stolly?"

"Are you trying to get me drunk?"

I wondered how much vodka it would take. "Not really. What would you like to do? Are you ready to drive home? You said it was a long way."

"You want me to leave?"

"No. I'm enjoying your company."

"And I'm enjoying yours. I feel safe here with you."

"That's the second time you've used the word 'safe.' Is there something you're scared of?"

She looked at me for what seemed like an eternity, while I stared at my empty glass, trying to look as unassuming as I could. She should be scared of me, I was thinking. I was there to trip her up, acting nice as you please to get under her skin, and then, *wham*, a baseball bat to the side of the head as I left her to Plant's clutches and stalked off to count my reward money. You can't trust anybody anymore.

I ventured my gaze up to her face, half expecting a fiery blast from those penetrating eyes. Instead, they were like dull, beige orbs . . . lifeless, as though I were looking at Niagara and the water had suddenly turned off, rocks drying in the noonday sun. She was lost in deep reflection.

"Penny for your thoughts," I said.

She swallowed. And then, with pent-up force, the words came tumbling out. She might have been waiting all week for someone to listen.

"I just want to get out of L.A. I'd like to go far away and start again. Maybe New York; maybe Boston; maybe even Montreal. I don't know! I feel the world is closing in, and I don't know where to turn anymore. I'm tired of looking behind me, and I'm tired of looking ahead of myself, having to watch every step I take. I know you don't understand what I'm talking about."

She stopped to look at me, eyes brimming now. "I know you're just looking for a good time on a Saturday night, but you've been nicer to me than anyone else in the last week and I'm glad you're here."

I took her hand and squeezed it gently. She pulled away, wiping her eyes.

"Look at me," she went on. "See me sitting here in this stupid outfit, dressed as if I were a sixteen-year-old going to the mall. This isn't me. I'm too old for this shit. I've had to keep up this show all week just so I'd have a place to stay, a place that I thought was reasonably safe. But it wasn't. Not anymore. There's no place I can turn. I wish I could go to the airport and take off somewhere."

She drained her glass, set it down heavily, and looked around the room, as if to order another. I held back from raising my hand to help, deciding she didn't need one more.

"I'm sorry," she said, forcing a laugh. "I didn't mean to scare you. I'll be all right. Just give me a minute."

I sat still, wondering about the demons that were in her head.

"I don't suppose I could go home with you?" she asked, then shook her head. "No. I'm sorry, forget I said that."

Yeah! Right! Just forget that an enchanting beauty was practically sitting on my lap, entreating me to whisk her away under my protection. And on the eve of my birthday, no less. Not a chance! Plant and his harebrained schemes disappeared in a puff of smoke, as lust fanned the flames inside me. It's a wonder my eyeballs weren't glowing.

"No problem. My place is yours. We can leave anytime you're ready."

"No. It wouldn't be fair to drag you into this."

"Into what?"

"Never mind." She composed herself. Then, pulling her shoulders back and sitting up straight, she went on. "I have a place. It's not too far. And I'll probably be safe there tonight."

"You can stay with me. Really." Please!

"No. Your life would never be the same." She laughed at the expression on my face. "Trust me. I'd better go back to my old place tonight. There's just one thing."

"What's that?" I was a genie emerging from a bottle. Her wish was my command.

"I don't want to go there alone. Will you come with me? Will you follow me there and stay with me a little longer? Just make sure I'm safe before you leave."

I smiled. "Would you like me to tuck you into bed? I'll stay with you all night if you wish."

"You might have to." She laughed impishly. "I'll know how I feel about that when I get there."

I TOOK MIRANDA'S HAND AND WE WALKED out into the rain. She had insisted on driving her own car and wanted me to follow. I was a bit hesitant on this. Not so much because of the double vodkas—she assured me that she had only scratched the surface of her capacity there, and I saw no reason to disbelieve her—but because I didn't relish the thought of trying to stay on her tail on wet asphalt. Fortunately, I thought I knew where she was heading. Then I remembered her dual-colored rear lights; they would make her easier to follow.

I gave our tickets to the valet and we waited in the rain, with Miranda snuggling up to my side, resting her head on my shoulder. Her moist hair clung with the fragrance of strawberries and lime. I inhaled deeply, wondering about other aromas that lay waiting to be discovered.

Her Datsun arrived first. She climbed in and gunned the motor with a roar that caught the attention of everybody in the lot. She gave me a wink and a thumbs up, then a screech of rubber and she was gone. I cinched the lap belt on my Alfa. If there ever was a time for a crash helmet, this was it. I was no longer on the brink of my fortieth birthday, but eighteen, and I felt like the first man ever fascinated by a woman.

I followed her spray out of the parking lot, catching up to her mismatched taillights a hundred yards up the road. She gunned the Datsun again. I could hear her tires queal as she took the on-ramp to the Pasadena freeway. I resigned myself to the chase and she weaved in and out of the fast lane, leaving a trail of mist behind. We went straight east toward Glendale, a long sweep with no on-ramps or distractions to slow us down, while the throaty whine of my four cylinders sang an aria of contentment. Even my car was enjoying itself.

We were at the peak of a long curve when a shadow flitted into my line of vision, jarring me. I thought I saw the outline of a highway patrol car ahead. My foot leapt off the gas pedal. Too late I realized it was only the roof rack on somebody's car. The Alfa went into oversteer and the hood dived toward the center rail. I jerked the wheel back to compensate, pumping the brakes frantically as I braced for a crunch.

I could feel the skid starting as the *thump, thump, thump* of the lane marker buttons jerked the front end round even more. The tail went out ahead of me and I prayed for life, promising my guardian angel I would buy a crash helmet first thing in the morning, if there was to be a morning. The sheet metal shuddered and bumped as gravel hit the undercarriage. I closed my eyes and felt my neck snap and my nose crunch against the steering wheel as I jolted to a stop.

A sharp pain flashed across my face to the roots of my teeth. I opened my eyes but moisture blurred my vision. I was still vertical and I could hear the wipers flopping back and forth. My face was wet. I glanced up to see if the roof had been damaged, but the new ragtop was still in place. Tears of pain filled my eyes and were sliding down my cheeks. They tasted funny, both salty and sweet. *Blood!* It was blood mixed with tears. I tried to wipe my mouth but my hands wouldn't move. Looking down at the steering wheel, I could see that they were tightly twined around it, stuck fast, like frosty fingers to dry ice.

I took a deep breath to compose myself. My heart was pounding. The Alfa was way off the edge of the shoulder, out of danger from passing cars. My right rear wheel must have been half in the gutter, judging by the angle the car was listing. The engine had stalled. I pried my fingers off the steering wheel in slow motion and wiped my face. My hands felt sticky. I reached in the console for a tissue and the flimsy white paper turned dark. I couldn't make out the color but I didn't have to. I held the tissue firmly against my nose and felt pain again.

A few cars slowed down as they zipped past me but no one seemed interested enough to investigate. Not that I expected it. After all, this was Los Angeles and people had much more important things to do on a rainy night than to stop and see if some fool skidding off the road required assistance. It was exactly as it should have been. If anyone had bothered to come to my rescue, his motives might have been suspect.

I wasn't sure how many minutes I'd lost, but Miranda must have been at least two miles down the road by now, probably on the way to her rented house. My nose was throbbing, waves of pain rising and then receding from under the tissue in my hand. There was no time to pay it any heed. I started the motor. The engine coughed and spit erratically for a minute, then settled into a reassuring purr. I eased the clutch down and felt the rear tires bite. Gradually, the car moved up the shoulder and righted itself. With a sigh of relief, I pulled off the gravel up to the asphalt, ready to accelerate back onto the freeway. I looked back to see if the coast was clear.

It was then that I noticed the other car. About a hundred and fifty yards behind was a medium-sized sedan, parked by the shoulder. Its flashers were on, and I could easily see the silhouette in the glare of passing headlights. As I watched I thought I saw movement from the driver's seat. If there was someone inside, he made no effort to come any closer. Thank heaven for that, I thought; I had no desire to waste time on explanations. Obviously, I was no longer in need of his assistance, if that was what he had stopped for. It was time to catch up with Miranda again, or risk giving myself away when she realized I knew the road to her house.

I pounded my foot on the accelerator with enough force to kick it through the fire wall. Spinning tires spewed gravel into the wheel wells. Suddenly, I was hurled onto the freeway, faster than I ever suspected my little Alfa could go—as if she'd been holding out on me. The gear changes came automatically and my seat pushed me forward into the wet night. I had one eye on the rearview mirror and the other scanning the freeway ahead for the pattern of Miranda's taillights. There was no time to watch the speedometer, which was just as well. Sane and safe motorists around me veered away as I cut a track through the fast lane.

I finally saw the Datsun as I neared the Glendale intersection. She had slowed to a crawl in the right lane, signaling she was about to take the exit. She must have been watching for my headlights. I flashed my brights and she speeded up, while I changed lanes to follow. We merged onto the Glendale freeway and headed south. By now I was certain of her destination and following was less of a strain. She went north up the Golden State and made the exit at Los Feliz Boulevard. We finally coasted to a stop outside the little house that I had scouted out two days before. She turned into the driveway and parked in front of the garage, while I pulled over to the curb about twenty yards beyond, waiting inside my car as she walked up to the porch and stood at the door.

I cut the engine and listened. My desire for Miranda was tempered by my instinct for self-preservation. If this was a setup of some kind, I didn't want to be caught off guard. Detective Syllovitz in Huntsville had personally assured me that I was in no danger, but I thought a little caution might still be in order. I watched her open the door with a key. There were no lights on inside, and no signs of life stirred as she turned on the porch light. The street was deserted, except for a dozen parked cars. I looked at the house opposite and saw slats of light through the half-drawn blinds of the front window. I thought I saw them move. My friend the watch-lady was entertaining herself again.

I figured it was safe and stepped out of my car. Miranda was standing by the doorway, her hair illuminated with a pale yellow glow, as if on fire, her slim figure moving rhythmically to some inner music, tapping her fingers on the doorpost by her side. Impatiently, she beckoned me to join her.

As I walked up the path, a car turned onto the street two blocks away and headed in our direction. It slowed down suddenly and pulled over to the curb a block from where we were standing. I fought an overwhelming desire to jump back in the Alfa and make for home.

I QUICKENED MY PACE TOWARD THE HOUSE. Miranda's figure looked alluring in the soft backlight from the lone bulb under the eaves, her hair glowing like a lighthouse beacon, enticing me like a lost ship to her side. The sudden appearance of another vehicle up the street was more than an omen, it was a distraction that needed to be addressed, more so because of its erratic dash for cover at the side of the road and because I hadn't seen anybody alight from it. I remembered the car I had seen waiting by the side of the freeway. The idea that someone might have been following us was like a lead weight in my shoes, holding me back. But the pull I felt toward Miranda was more overwhelming, and I was convinced that safe harbor lay under her roof. I swept her in and shut the door.

She turned on the living room light. Her first reaction was to recoil in horror. "What happened to you?"

Her expression changed to one of sympathy as she moved closer to touch my face. "Your nose is all bent and swollen. It looks a mess. And you're bleeding." She pulled her hand back to examine her fingertips.

"I skidded off the road and hit my head. It's nothing." I was surprised by the nasal quality in my voice.

"So that's where you disappeared. I thought you'd changed your mind and turned back. My God, it looks terrible. I'd say you need a plastic surgeon. Come into the kitchen and I'll wash you down."

I followed her through to the kitchen while she ran water in the sink and motioned me to stand over it. Traces of red soon mingled with the clear, cool water as she sponged my face. A wave of pain returned. I realized then that my nose was completely stuffed. I had been breathing through my mouth for the last half hour.

"Jesus, it looks bad. I think I should take you to an emergency room." She walked over to the refrigerator and took some ice out of the top compartment.

"Do you have a mirror anywhere?" I asked.

She guided me into the bathroom, leading me by the hand. This was the one room I hadn't checked out before. It was a small space: white linoleum floor, blue and white tile from there to eye level, peeling blue and gold wallpaper the rest of the way up, little angelfish swimming in and out of the stripes, bubbles rising from their mouths. There were no antiques of any kind. A mildewed sliding door enclosed the tub. She stood me in front of the half-length mirror above the sink and I stared at myself in disbelief.

It was more a patient who stood before me: hair wet and flattened down, nose swollen in brilliant hues of blue and red and veering to the left, dried streaks of blood like caked wax on my upper lip. I was not surprised at the pain I had felt.

"What do you think?" Miranda asked.

"I'd say it's broken."

"Wonderful! What do we do now?"

"You can fix it for me."

"Me!" She acted as if I had gone quite mad.

"Well, I don't think I could do it. But I can tell you what to do. It's easy enough." It was making me out of breath to put more than two sentences together.

"Do what? Fix it? You're crazy! We're going to the emergency room."

"Nonsense. It's just like working Play-Doh. You put your thumbs against it and shove it back in the middle."

"You're kidding. What if it doesn't turn out right?" I saw her becoming intrigued at the prospect of fixing it, in spite of her initial reluctance.

"It will turn out just fine. It wants to go back where it belongs, anyway. You're just going to help it along."

"Will it hurt?"

"Probably. Got any anesthetic?"

"There's a bottle of Stolly in the freezer."

"Perfect."

We went back into the kitchen and I sat down on one of the metal folding chairs in front of the kitchen table. She handed me the ice pack she had taken from the freezer and went rummaging for some glasses. While she fixed a large vodka for me, and an equally large one for herself, I pushed on the base of my nose with moderate force. I wanted to test the pain factor and see if I was up to it. My thumb slipped and I broke into a cold sweat. I couldn't do it myself. Inflicting pain on others was one thing, but the minute I felt the first twinge my hands would start trembling and I would be reduced to a quivering mass of jelly. I hoped for my sake she would be up to it.

This was no time for sympathy. What I needed now was someone with purpose, someone who could do the necessary with a sense of detachment, the faster the better. These are the qualities all good surgeons learn—sometimes to their detriment, at the risk of being labeled cold and callous, a distinction they carry with melancholic pride.

"Drink this," she said, plunking down an absurdly full glass of clear iced liquid in front of me. From her authoritative manner I knew I was in good hands. "It's special. Stolly Cristall. Eighty proof and clear as Baccarat. It's better than two Valiums." Again she spoke with the conviction of experience and I reassured myself that I was in the control of a seasoned anesthetist.

I took a large sip, letting it slide down my parched throat, dry from too much mouth breathing. She did the same, smacking her lips with her tongue, an image that warmed me deep down inside just as much as the vodka had seconds earlier. Watching her thus, in preparation to do battle with my fractured nose, and probably to inflict intense pain on my person at the same time, was not having the predicted effect of subduing me. Rather, I was experiencing a paradoxical surge of strange pleasure, a wondrous sense of sharing my pain with her, and exposing an emotion that I normally would keep bottled up within. It made me want to share more. It seemed odd, and I wondered if I might have been some closet masochist, but I was starting to become distinctly aroused by the situation.

"What do I do now?" she asked.

I pushed the chair I was sitting on away from the table and turned it around. "You sit on my lap." I motioned her forward. "Facing me."

She advanced with legs apart and straddled my knees.

"Sit down and get comfortable."

She wriggled. "You have bony knees," she said. "They're poking my ass."

I parted them slightly to oblige and felt her weight as she relaxed.

"Now, you hold my face in your hands like this, fingers resting on my temples, and put your thumbs one on each side of my nose." I demonstrated, holding her face in my palms.

She burst into excited laughter. "This is so weird."

"Go ahead."

She tried it. Either from trepidation, or because her hands were much smaller than mine, her thumbs failed to reach their target.

"Slide your hands forward on my face. It doesn't matter if you're covering my eyes. It's more important that your thumbs have enough slack to push."

"Wait. I think I need another drink." She swallowed several more fluid ounces from her glass, then held it to my lips, ordering me to do the same. "Anesthetic for the surgeon and the patient," she said.

She held my face again, this time correctly. "Are you going to sue me if it doesn't turn out right?"

I didn't answer. I couldn't have her thinking that way; I was busy figuring it out for myself. I would give her one try, perhaps two, and then, if I hadn't passed out from too much pain, we would have to go to an emergency room. I didn't relish the thought of spending half the night in some antiseptic hospital cubicle. I made a silent prayer for her success.

"Relax your elbows," I said. "Now hold my nose between your thumbs, squeeze tight, and push it over to the middle."

"Just like that?"

"Just like that."

There was an agonizing click of snapping bone, as if my nose were being wrenched off. The pain radiated to the roots of my hair, bringing a flood of tears.

"Oh! Did you hear that?" she asked timidly. "Did I do something wrong?"

I took a deep breath, feeling air suddenly coursing through my nostrils again.

"Hey!" she yelled. "It's back. It's in the middle now."

A fresh river of blood poured down my lip onto my shirt. She handed me a couple of paper towels from the dispenser above the sink. I held them tightly under my nose, throwing my head back and marveling at how the pain had suddenly eased.

"This is great," she said, doing a little dance, and then sitting back down on my thighs as naturally as if they were the only available seat in the room. "I've found a new career. I'm going to hire myself out as a nose fixer."

In order to see her with my head bent back I had to look down past my fractured nose, which seemed to be radiating little curlicues of heat straight up toward the ceiling, like shimmering, hot asphalt on an Arizona highway. She had two beautiful rows of pearly white teeth and full pink lips I would have loved to caress with my own. If only she wouldn't mind kissing a man with a bleeding nose.

"Stick with me, babe," I said. "I'll teach you how to do face-lifts next."

There was a silence. She held the smile while I realized I might have given too much away . . . wondered if she suspected I was more than just an OR tech.

"What else did you learn from watching the surgeons?" she asked innocently.

"How to make a pass at the nurses."

I dropped the paper towels and began to caress her waist with both hands, working them over the skin where her top fell short of her belt. My right hand snaked its way around her back, feeling her bony spine all the way up to her bra strap. She wriggled in mock distaste, the look on her face telling me she was really enjoying it.

She said, "Why don't we go back to the sink and get that blood off your face?"

"All right." I waited for her to get off my knees. "I'm going to take a look at the results first." I walked into the living room and headed for the mirror above the mantelpiece.

"No confidence in your doctor?" she asked.

I was about to congratulate her on the result when we heard a sudden sound from outside: a thud, followed by the crack of a twig.

"What was that?" I asked.

"I don't know."

"You heard it, too?"

"Yes."

I walked over to the front window. "Turn off the light for a minute."

She did as I asked and came up to join me. I drew the curtain aside. The scene was much the same as we'd left it. The blinds in the house opposite were drawn shut and the old lady was nowhere to be seen. I looked back up the street but the car I was searching for was out of sight.

"Do you have a pair of binoculars?"

"No. What would you want them for?"

"To look at a car."

"Which one?" She leaned closer to see down the road, brushing her cheek next to mine.

In spite of my recent olfactory trauma, I could still detect the faint aroma of strawberries and lime. "You can't see it from here."

"Oh, shit!"

"What?"

"It's George." She drew back quickly and let the curtain fall. "Damn! He's staring right at us."

CHAPTER

30

I MOVED BACK QUICKLY FROM THE WINDOW to a safer position by one of the beanbag chairs. "Who the hell is George?" I asked.

"George Kershen. He's got this thing for me. Like he's my protector. He probably followed me here. You know, I wouldn't be surprised if he's kind of upset that I'm in here with you."

"Marvelous! You could have told me about him." I was half torn between sitting down and listening to her story, and wanting to get going while the getting was good. I recalled the concerns I had when talking to Plant about the boyfriend and his affinity for violence. He'd had some minor scuffles with the law, was what I'd been told.

"I had no idea he'd be here."

"That's not what I mean. You told me there was no one else."

"You mean me and George? It's not like that at all. I don't want to have anything to do with him anymore."

"Anymore? I see. Does he know that?"

She was quiet for a moment. "I haven't told him yet."

"Brilliant!" Things were not looking good at all. A jealous lover was dangerous enough, but a spurned and jealous lover could be as unpredictable as a rhinoceros, a superhuman pain in the ass. What the hell was she doing, encouraging me in the kitchen with this animal lurking about?

I pulled the curtain open a crack to size him up again. I remembered him as having at least thirty pounds on me. I still couldn't see his car all the way down the block. "Where do you see him?"

"Across the street, about two houses down. He's in the pickup."

"Oh! There." It was a dark-colored pickup with an extended cab. This was not the car I had seen back on the freeway. A small part of me was hoping it would be someone other than the short-haired Marine type who had been at the auction house a week ago, but when my eyes adjusted to the streetlight, and I could barely make out a figure in the driver's seat, he appeared to be the same size and build.

"How upset does he get?" I asked, wondering if there was a chance reason could prevail, or whether I needed to get a head start now.

"You don't want to know," Miranda replied with a toss of her head.

I did want to know, though, very much, even though I suspected I wouldn't like hearing it. "Tell me anyway. How long do we have before he decides to break in and sort me out?"

"I don't know. He's very weird. I knew he was a little strange but I didn't realize how much until I moved out to his place this Sunday. When I read about Jack in the newspaper I just had to get out of here. George said I could stay with him, but it didn't turn out to be a good move. He's into guns and—well, I just got the creeps out there. His friends are all wackos. They scare me half to death."

She paused for a breath. I didn't like the word "guns," and I didn't like the word "wackos," but what stood out most was her familiar use of "Jack" instead of "Dr. Ehrenberger." I kept quiet and let her talk.

"Today," she went on, "I couldn't stand it anymore. I figured even a couple of hours away would do me good. I told them I had left some clothes here in L.A. and I had to drive down and pick them up. I waited until George had gone to the store before I said anything. I knew if he was around, he would insist on coming with me. I just can't tell him to his face, Gareth. He'd go nuts. I don't know what he'd do."

The word "nuts" didn't exactly fill me with confidence, either. "He's probably sitting there right now wondering what we are doing in here," I said. "I can't imagine what must be going through his mind."

"It's not like him. George doesn't usually sit still for more than five minutes at a time."

"He's probably confused."

"George doesn't think enough to get confused."

"You know, it's bad enough when you tell a guy to his face that you don't like him anymore. It's a nightmare when he has to figure it out for himself. It could make him real upset."

I felt her warm breath on my cheek as she exhaled sharply. "I wonder what he's going to do now."

I wondered, too. "I guess he must have driven out here and waited for you; figured you'd show up sooner or later."

"I'm sorry if I've dragged you into this mess."

Sorry! What mess? Just a broken nose, that's all, and an imbroglio with a jealous boyfriend. A young, muscular, jealous boyfriend, against whom I wouldn't even last a single round. A "wacko," waiting outside with possible mayhem on his mind. And all for what?

I went back to the window and took a second look down the road. Everything was the same, the outline of the driver still visible against the rear window of the cab in the pickup. I tried to figure what the best escape would be. Any attempt at getting back in my car would have to be carried out under his nose.

"Maybe you should go out there and see what he wants," I suggested.

"Me? No way. You do it."

"Uh-uh. I'm the last person he wants to see right

now. No, Miranda, it's your mess. I think you're the only one who can straighten it out."

The seeds of a plan were starting to germinate inside my mind, a plan that did not include Miranda. If I could only get her to go out and talk to him, maybe I could sneak into my car unseen and take off while they sorted out their differences.

"One of us has to make a move," I said. "We can't sit here all night wondering what he's going to do next."

"I suppose you're right. You think it will be okay if I just go out there for five minutes? He wouldn't do anything stupid, would he?"

Likely he would. He didn't strike me as the smartest guy in the world. "He's your friend. If he feels that strongly about you, I'm sure he'll at least listen to what you have to say."

She thought about it. "Okay." She took three steps toward the door and stopped. "What shall I tell him?"

"Tell him you want him to leave. Tell him you just need some time alone. Promise him you'll go back there tomorrow. I don't know. Tell him whatever he wants to hear."

She started off down the path on her way to the truck. I stood and watched her just short of the threshold, not wanting to reveal my presence by the light on the porch. She crossed the street to the driver's side of the pickup. I half expected George to step out of the cab and come toward her, but his silhouette didn't move an inch in the shadows. Miranda leaned in through the open window. I saw her raise both hands through the opening and shove the figure of the driver.

Something was wrong. His head flopped forward like a nodding marionette's onto the steering wheel. The horn began to sound . . . loud as a tugboat on a foggy night down in San Pedro. Miranda started to scream, adding to the raucous din of the horn with her own eerie contribution as she raised both hands to her head and came running back down the street.

"He's dead. My God, he's dead!" she howled.

"What?" I shook her by the shoulders and said, as firmly as I could, "Calm down, Miranda. He can't be." More for my benefit than for hers.

Suddenly, from somewhere behind us came the crash of breaking glass.

"My God, what's that?" she asked.

"I don't know."

Just then the lights went on in the house across the street. Meanwhile, over by the pickup, the horn was braying incessantly as George's head pressed down upon the steering wheel. I had no time to think. I had to do something quickly or the entire neighborhood would soon be out there with us.

I sprinted over to the pickup, with Miranda following close at heel.

"He's dead, Gareth," she cried. "He's been shot."

There was enough light from the streetlamp to see the red on her hands. I grabbed George by the shoulders and pulled him back. The horn ceased abruptly, giving way to Miranda's sobbing as she clutched my left arm tightly. George's head was heavy and matted with blood. It swayed gently to the right, then his weight pulled away from me as he slipped through my sticky fingers to slide down the front seat to the passenger footwell. Fortunately, his chances of sounding the horn again were now quite remote.

I glanced down at my own hands. They were covered in blood. My adrenaline began pumping and I was conscious of a pulsation in my fingers, which seemed to swell before my eyes. Ever since the spread of the AIDS virus I had learned to treat human blood as the deadliest form of toxic waste. Fighting back my acquired loathing for this body fluid, I wiped my palms on the seat back and tried desperately to take stock of the situation.

George was very dead indeed; some form of missile through his skull had seen to that. Miranda had stopped yelling and was now shaking uncontrollably, tears streaming down her face. A few more lights came on down the street as curious neighbors awoke to that singular Los Angeles nightmare: the sounds of turmoil outside their front doors.

While I was standing there casting around for inspiration, the figure of a man popped out of the house we had just vacated and rushed to the curb, looking frantically right and left. In his right hand was the unmistakable outline of a gun barrel, glinting in the ever-increasingly ambient light along the street. It was an extremely long and phallic protuberance, several inches larger than any other gun barrel I'd ever seen, and I recognized this immediately as some form of silencer.

"Quick." I pulled the truck door open and shoved Miranda firmly. "Hop in."

She grabbed hold of the door frame and resisted, pushing back with both legs. "Gareth," she howled, "what are you doing? I'm not going in there. He's dead."

"Get in," I screamed. "I don't want to be dead, too."

"What?" She turned and saw the shadowy figure the minute he spotted us. Her body went limp for an instant and I seized her by the waist and lifted her into the cab, just as the man dropped to one knee and aimed.

I saw a flare of white and yellow erupt from his hand and felt a whistle by my ear. Another flare: I heard the shrill twang of metal on metal, while a shower of paint chips splashed my forehead. Miranda scrambled over to the passenger seat, trampling on George's body in her rush to safety. I followed her into the pickup and slammed the door shut, just as a third slug crashed into the window pillar. In a single movement we dropped down to the floor of the cab, neither of us hesitating for a second at the prospect of having to share the crowded space with good old George. He certainly wasn't complaining.

It didn't take a rocket scientist to figure we hadn't long before we'd be sharing more than just space with

George. What we needed now was wings, but not the kind that angels wear. I was sure that this was going to be the end. I looked around desperately for a shield, some piece of metal we could use as protection when that enormous gun barrel came poking its way through the open window, ready to blow us into the hereafter with a silent *whoosh* as silvertips tore through our gray cells. Nothing in the cab seemed up to the task.

My head was inches away from the steering column. The solution to our predicament was almost poking me in the eye. George's keys were still in the ignition. I turned the switch and the engine roared to life. My Alfa could not have done me as proud. Daring to raise my head above the wheel, I jammed the gearshift into drive. A rain of glass washed over me, stinging my right ear. I kicked my foot down on the accelerator pedal and wrenched the steering wheel sharply left, away from the curb.

The pickup lurched forward with a jolt. There was an immediate crunch, but it was only the rear bumper of the car ahead of us. I was ready for it. Another wrench to the steering wheel, a further thrust to the accelerator, a fresh grinding, searing jolt, and we were away, careening down the street.

"Where are you going?" screamed Miranda as my foot pushed hard down on the pedal, knees wobbling with the pressure, or perhaps with fright. "Back up. Back up, damn it!"

But I had no intention of backing up and craning my head around to see the road, just so I could take a bullet through the occiput. No way. I was quite comfortable with my eyes scarcely an inch above the steering wheel, lips pursed tight. In forward gear it wasn't that imperative to see where I was going. I was ready for the Braille School of Driving. The wheels would keep a straight course down the road by themselves, until they found an impassable object.

There was another explosion through the windshield, and a second rain of splinters was upon us. I reached for the headlight switch and turned it on. What I saw, through the maze of cracks that radiated across the glass, seemed fantastic in the extreme. The man had marched out into the middle of the street and was now standing firm directly in the path of the pickup, the gun aimed straight at us, grasped in both hands. His body was turned sideways as if to present a smaller target, a professional stance that might have inspired me to think twice about taking him on, except that I was sitting in the driver's seat of a pickup truck, with at least six and a half feet of front bumper at my disposal, and I couldn't figure how he intended to sidestep that.

Did he know something I didn't? Did he really hope to stop me in my tracks with his elongated weapon? How many bullets did he have left? He had already used five that I could recall, more if you counted those in George's head. How many bullets did George have in his head? Maybe I could ask Miranda to count them: *See how many times your finger sinks into his skull, my dear.*

What difference did it make? He had probably reloaded by now, anyway. Perhaps he had some sort of armor-piercing bullet; perhaps the truck was about to explode in a searing flash of gasoline the minute he pulled his trigger. Even as these thoughts raced through my mind, they failed to slow me down. I was completely taken with the game. It was him or me, and there was no question where my loyalties lay. With a surge of aggression, I floored the accelerator pedal. I was going to get first blood and mow the bastard down.

I ducked beneath the steering wheel again. I heard two bullets slam into the radiator grille, heard two more crashes through the windshield, felt the rain of splinters on my hair and neck, and then a dull thud and a cry of pain above the roar of the engine. I stayed down for what seemed like another minute, then looked up.

We were well past the house, but a maze of finely

spread cracks hampered my view. I tried the windshield wipers. The screech of glass felt like chalk on a blackboard. The windshield smeared and visibility became worse. I turned them off. I looked for the rearview mirror but it was gone, blown away by a silvertip, no doubt. I craned my neck to see behind. The street was empty. I let out a sigh of relief.

Then I remembered the cry of pain. I seemed to have come out unscathed, but Miranda . . . I looked down at the passenger footwell and saw her hunched down, clutching her knees, eyes popping like two fried eggs.

"Did you get him?" she asked.

"Yes."

"Damn! That was close. Is he dead?"

"I bloody well hope so."

"Are you going to stop and find out?"

"No way in hell."

"Thank God."

I slowed to an acceptable fifty miles an hour and took the next left, turning onto Los Feliz Boulevard. There was a fair amount of vehicular traffic, but if we presented an odd sight, no one braked to raise an eyebrow. No big deal, really; just another pickup on a Saturday night, with two bullet holes in the radiator, four in the windshield, and a dead body in the passenger footwell.

I might have carried on forever in spite of the impaired vision, having no particular desire to stop, but fairly soon the engine failed to respond to any pressure on the gas pedal, and smoke began to issue from the hood. We wound to a halt in another twenty yards, and I pulled over to the curb with the last vestige of momentum.

"Where are we?" Miranda asked.

"Somewhere in L.A." was all I could say.

I looked around. There were no pedestrians in sight, and the cars whizzing by seemed oblivious to our plight. Cautiously, I opened the door and got out. We were at the corner of Los Feliz and some residential side street, and there was even a phone box conveniently located on the opposite corner. Miranda stepped out on the passenger side and shivered in the damp air.

"What do we do now?" she asked.

I noticed the goose bumps on her arms. I walked back to the driver's side and pulled a worn red-and-black-plaid hunter's jacket off the back of the seat, throwing it over her shoulders. She pulled it around her and fondled the soft fabric.

"It was George's," she said.

"He won't be needing it."

"There's a phone over there. I think we should call 911."

"In a minute." I walked up to the hedge beside the pavement and stood for a moment, contemplating the oleander, glistening with damp.

"You know, I got a look at him when you turned the headlights on."

"Really!"

"Yes. I raised my head for a second and looked right at him. I'm sure I know who it was."

"You do?" I was preoccupied with something else. With the tension of the moment suddenly withdrawn, I was feeling a stinging pain from my bladder. "And who was it?"

"It was Broder. I'd swear on it. He's fucking crazy."

I unbuttoned my fly and relieved myself on the hedge, savoring the relief washing over me, and thanking my guardian angel for keeping my sphincter tone intact over the past fifteen minutes.

"Do you know anybody who's normal?" I asked her.

I CROSSED THE STREET TO THE PHONE booth, dialed 911, and gave a brief summary of events to the operator, who seemed much too slow on the uptake, and altogether too inquisitive, to be very efficient at her job. When it came to the address, I could only give her an approximate location. For some reason, she wanted me to stay on the phone and talk, but I thought that a waste of time. I told her we weren't in any immediate danger, and she should go back to work and save a few lives.

Miranda and I sat down on the grassy curb, neither of us wanting to return to the pickup and deal with George, or rather, what was left of George. Miranda squatted with knees drawn up and tucked under the flaps of the oversize red and black jacket, while I hugged myself in bare T-shirt and dealt with the cold.

"Who was Broder?" I asked.

"One of the creeps who hung around George."

"Why would he want to kill George?"

"I don't know." She acted annoyed. "I told you they were crazy, didn't I? What I want to know is why he wanted to kill us."

"Well, I suppose he didn't want any witnesses, once he had killed George."

"Then he could have just disappeared, couldn't he? I mean, we never saw him kill George. He could have just taken off quietly and we'd never have known he was even around." She sounded offended that he had dared to stay and take potshots at us—or perhaps just at her. Was there some bond between them?

She was right, though. He could have bolted, unnoticed, after killing George. Or was it Miranda he was after? She was hiding something from me. I felt sure of it. Was it something Broder didn't want revealed?

"Perhaps he didn't kill George at all," I suggested. "We're only assuming he did because we saw him with a gun. What if he came by the pickup, saw that George was dead, and thought we did it? That might give him a reason to want to kill us."

It didn't make sense inventing another person whom neither of us had seen or heard to explain how George met his death. I felt I was just dredging up more questions instead of providing answers. There was, of course, yet another possibility—that he was really after me. I began to realize it was high time I stopped worrying about Plant and his silly little antiques, and started working on who was trying to kill whom before I ended up on the slab myself.

I didn't think I could leave it up to the police; they didn't appear to have the slightest notion where to begin. By then I was beginning to feel much more at ease in my new role as sleuth, and it was the most natural thing in the world to slide from one investigation to another—from a ring of thieves to a multiple murder—especially when they appeared to go hand in hand.

"How did you meet George?" I asked her.

"He drove a delivery truck. He carried a load for us once and we got talking about furniture and stuff. He seemed kind of nice at first."

"For us? You mean the gallery you worked for?"

"Yes."

"What did you sell?"

"Paintings." She spoke in a tired monotone, her mind miles away.

"What about pottery? And porcelains? Did you ever deal with those?"

"No."

"And were any of these paintings stolen, by chance?" I asked, coolly and deliberately, as if I were the man standing in the road aiming a bullet at her.

It struck. Her eyes refocused from the glaze and came to rest on my face.

"How did you know?" she whispered.

I wasn't prepared to disclose that yet. I tried to frame a reply that would draw some more information from her without divulging my sources. It turned out I didn't have to.

"So that's what you were doing at the funeral. Did you work for Jack, too?"

I tried to hide my reaction, realizing I was not so accustomed to this cloak-and-dagger routine, after all. I had to think fast. "Yes. And what did you do for him?"

"He never told me about you. Did you have something to do with the buying?"

"I guess you could call it that. What about you? The selling?"

"Yes. He needed me because I spoke the language. I helped him make all his contacts in Tokyo. I helped with delivery, too. I'd go down to Acapulco with the truck and help them get through Mexican customs." She looked at me and grinned. "All I had to do was show them a nice smile and a handful of dollar bills. Those Japanese would get so uptight about it. They never trusted the Mexicans, even after they'd been bribed."

"You mean especially after they'd been bribed."

She laughed, then leaned closer and touched me on the shoulder. "You have to tell me about your end. I've always wondered how Jack snagged all those great paintings, and nobody suspected a thing. Every time I asked him he told me someday I'd find out." She snuggled up beside me. "Maybe today's the day, Gareth."

I was silent.

"All that travel," she went on. "It was a wonderful job and I had a ball. I miss him. I've been scared to death ever since he was killed. I was thinking of going back East. Maybe now there's a reason to stay here after all. Jesus, it's a real coincidence, meeting up with you. Think we could keep it going?"

My head was reeling, as little bits of information fell into place like pieces in a puzzle. *A pipeline across the Pacific*. It was all making sense now. Jack Ehrenberger was selling stolen paintings to the Japanese with Miranda's help, shipping them out of Acapulco. I wondered if Neifosh and Epstein had anything to do with that. More likely they were involved at the supply end.

"Speaking of Jack," I said, "who do you think killed him?"

Before we could discuss it further the patrol car arrived, and two uniformed officers stepped out to hear our version of events. They checked George out, then sealed off the pickup. One of the officers called it in to headquarters, while the other stayed with us, perhaps to dissuade escape. I had done all the running I cared to for the night, and was glad of his protection, but I watched Miranda closely to see how she'd react. Whatever apprehensions she might have had she kept well hidden.

We waited on the curbside by the boulevard. Where previously not a soul had bothered to stop and make an offer of assistance, there was now an endless line of vehicles slowing down to speculate on the nature of our plight, the occupants rubbernecking their way past. It was the patrol car with its blinking light bar that did it. Los Angelenos, jaded by Hollywood, never sit up and take notice unless you bring out the flashing lights.

Soon, we were joined by two more patrol cars. A solemn-looking officer with a scar down his cheek and GARCIA on his name tag came by to announce he was removing us from the scene. We were to be escorted back to

Miranda's rental to give our statement to the field sergeant. I was disappointed by this news, thinking that a quick statement back at headquarters would see us done much sooner. Apparently, an investigation of sorts was already under way back at the house, after a neighbor had sent for the police. I could very well guess which neighbor it was.

Garcia drove us back to the rental, where there were more patrol cars with flashing lights and another gaggle of spectators, this time nearly all of them on foot, held at bay with yellow tape strung across the porch and down the driveway. I noted the conspicuous absence of an ambulance or coroner's van, and wondered what they had done with Broder's body. Oddly, I had no regrets. The onlookers gave the scene a carnival atmosphere, and I half expected a hot-dog cart to appear, with offers of boiled franks, churros, and popcorn. I wouldn't have turned down some nourishment myself at that point—liquid and strong, of course. I was feeling the need of a little internal combustion to replace the warmth, and the courage, that had drained from me.

We were ushered up the driveway, where two patrol cars formed an effective barrier against the throng, and where a policeman about my age and with a very flustered manner had cordoned off some form of mobile headquarters. The tag on his shirt said LARSON. I was glad they all had name tags; it was getting to be the only way I could tell them apart. Larson seemed in charge.

I recognized the neighbor lady from across the street. She was standing on the small strip of green that substituted for a lawn, scolding an elderly gentleman dressed in chinos and a frayed cardigan. By the one-sidedness of the discourse I took him to be her husband.

Garcia, the officer with the scar, went up to Larson and reported on the state of events back on Los Feliz Boulevard. "They're waiting for a coroner's van," Garcia said, after giving his account. "What's happening here?"

"Place's been trashed," replied Larson. "Looks like

the perpetrator broke in through a back window and went berserk. I don't know how they're going to tell what's missing."

Miranda stiffened and shot forward like a coiled spring. "My antiques!" she yelled. "The bastard! I'll kill that son of a bitch."

She pushed her way to the front door but they wouldn't let her inside; those yellow tapes were sacrosanct. I rushed up to join her and saw what Larson was talking about. The contents of the living room had been turned upside down. The entertainment center was lying on the floor amid broken bits of glass and pottery. The mantelpiece was bare. I wondered when Broder had had the time to do that.

"Oh no!" Miranda beat the doorjamb with both fists. She buried her face in her hands and went limp.

"Easy there, lady," said Larson, catching up to us. "I can't let you in there just yet. You got to stay outside."

I pulled her away from the door and led her to a wooden seat at the far end of the porch. She sat down as if in a trance, the pain of her loss showing clearly in her expression. I had no words to console her. I wanted to tell her not to worry, the son of a bitch was already dead, but all the evidence around me pointed to the contrary. The only vehicle large enough to hold a body was a white van, but it lacked the emblem of the Los Angeles County coroner. The only crime scene they had roped off was the interior of the house, and Broder would have died in the street. Either the crowd beyond the driveway was trampling on bits of flesh and bone, unbeknownst to Larson and his squad, or something was seriously wrong.

I felt somebody pinching me on the shoulder. "Ain't you the young man that was around here the other night, asking about this lady and her boyfriend?"

The old woman from across the street had apparently decided to ease up on her husband and start in on me.

Garcia's ears pricked up, and Miranda's mouth opened wide.

"You've been here before?" Miranda asked loudly. I didn't like this at all.

"He sure has," the neighbor exclaimed. "He was asking all about you and how long you been gone. Some kind of doctor, ain't you?"

She turned to me, snapping her fingers in recollection. "Plastic surgeon, you said. I still have that card up by my fridge." She gave a wide, satisfied grin, showing a stained set of choppers, while two little dimples lit up her cheeks.

I threw her husband an agonized look, wondering if he was capable of coming to my rescue. His eyes told me he had no such intention; he was enjoying himself. I glanced at Garcia and saw that his jaw muscles were clenching and unclenching rhythmically, as if working up to a line of questioning all his own. I realized that I might soon be the focus of an inquisition, possibly even to the point of replacing Broder as the villain of the night. Like vigilantes, they were hungry for blood, and mine was warm and within their grasp.

I desperately cast around for some red herring to throw them off the spoor.

"I thought you said you were an OR tech," Miranda said, the accusation in her voice unmistakable.

"Yes," I replied, faltering. "Same thing."

And then, I was inspired. Turning to the neighbor lady, I said, "And you were very good, told me everything I wanted to know. I knew I could count on you, you're a natural observer. Tonight, for instance, you probably saw everything from across the street, didn't you? Why don't you tell us what you saw?"

My instinct was correct. "Well," she commenced, with an innocent grin, and the dimples made their appearance once more. "It was like this."

She had been craving to tell her story ever since she'd first laid eyes on the scene across the street from her house. Her call to 911 was just a cry for an audience, but Larson had placed a gag order on her until he was ready for a statement, and by now she had reached the boiling point. She was so pent up with her need to talk that it was bursting through the gaps in her gnashers. She went on to recount the details from her particular perspective, starting with the moment Miranda and I arrived in separate cars. I hadn't realized she'd been watching all that time, and I marveled anew at her dedication to the art of prying.

Garcia momentarily abandoned his interest in me, eager as we all were to hear her story. Even Miranda, after first glaring at me with sullen distaste, began to soften and pay attention once the old lady reached the point at which we had entered the pickup, and aimed it at the spot where Broder held his last stand.

"He just jumped out the way," she said. "Like this."

She gave a nimble little sidestep, almost landing on her husband's toes.

"I think he hurt hisself. He rolled on the lawn and he was grabbing his leg. I thought his trousers was torn. Right here." She pointed to her right knee.

"Then he got up and limped into the house. Pretty soon I heard this crashing sound. He turned the lights on inside, but the curtain was open only a crack, so I couldn't see much. That's when I left to call the police." She wagged a finger at Garcia. "I know how long you boys take to come by. Fifteen, twenty minutes at least. Like the other night when I called 'cause *he* was snooping round." She wagged the same finger at me this time.

I glanced at Miranda; she was glaring daggers at me again.

"When I got back," the old lady continued, "he come out the door—limping still. He starts beating on the bushes near the porch and thumping on the lawn. Like he lost something small. I never saw him find nothing. Then he starts for his car down the block there. Takes a while, too. I kept thinking you boys gonna make it in time." She shook her head sadly at Garcia.

"What kind of car?" I asked.

"I already discussed that with the first policeman. A car don't mean much more to me than something you sit in to go to the store. It was small, and it could have been blue or it could have been green, I couldn't tell on account of the light being so poor. I certainly couldn't see his tag number from where I was sitting. But there was something familiar about it, and danged if I can't place my finger on it."

She stopped, savoring the attention, scanning our faces one by one, showing off those false teeth again in a satisfied grin. I would have asked another question, ready to do anything to keep the attention off me, but there was a sudden commotion over by the neighboring yard. One of the onlookers rushed over to Garcia to inform him they had found a gun. The scar-faced officer signaled to one of his colleagues to fetch Larson, and together they cleared a path through the jostling crowd. Our little party wedged behind. On the way there the annoying neighbor lady pinched me on the shoulder again.

"I know what it is," she said excitedly.

I tried to be polite. "It's probably the gun that the killer lost on the lawn."

"No, no. I mean the car. I know what was bugging me about the car."

"And what was that?" I feigned interest.

"It was exactly like the rental car my daughter had last summer. She flew in from Johnson City with Jolene, my granddaughter. We drove around in it for a week. Dang, I can't remember what it was called."

We had come to a stop at the fence that separated the neighboring yard from the next one farther along. The object we were after was lying at the base of a podocarpus tree. Garcia extracted a plastic bag from his pocket, carefully enveloping the weapon before picking it up. He held it to the light, close to my face, and asked if it looked like the gun the perpetrator had used.

It was then that I realized I was in for a very long night. Far from being almost over, the endless rounds of questions and answers had only just begun. I looked at my watch and saw that it was surprisingly early—only ten-thirty. I could go on pretending that I was an innocent party, surprised by an intruder in the ordinary act of taking a girlfriend home; make whatever statements such casual involvement required; then go home and nurse my nose, waiting for the phone to ring once their investigation was under way. Or . . . I could admit to my complicity on a much greater scale, in a scheme that encompassed murder, ten million dollars in stolen art, and whatever else remained to be discovered. Better to put them on the right track now, before they stumbled on it of their own accord. Innocent as I was, they would not be so convinced of it if they discovered that I had obscured the truth.

I made a decision to take the hard way, hoping it would prove to be the shortcut in the end.

"This thing ties into a crime that's already under investigation," I said to Garcia. "Detective Kenneth Akimoro at the Beverly Hills Police Department needs to be informed."

The reason, of course, was the gun. The long, gleaming silencer was familiar from the events of barely two hours ago. But the weapon it was attached to was an old friend from much farther back. It was my Beretta 92, the one I had lent Elaine months ago, and that had been stolen from her Rolls-Royce when it was at Cedars-Sinai.

THE COPS ALLOWED US TO WAIT FOR AKI-moro on the porch, and we made ourselves as comfortable as we could on the wooden seat. After hearing of the Beverly Hills police investigation from me, Larson had seemed relieved that the whole complex affair would soon be taken off his hands. Perhaps he was still a little green about the ears; perhaps he yearned for an ordinary drive-by shooting. I was simply grateful he had permitted me to retrieve my jacket from the living room, although even that had been a struggle.

"It could be evidence," Larson had shilly-shallied.

I was short with him. "It's only evidence that I've been here, and you know that already. Why would anyone else want to touch the damn thing? Besides, it's cold outside."

He had finally conceded and Garcia had fetched the jacket for me, after a quick search of the garment to make sure I wasn't hiding anything. Really!

Miranda asked for a bag of ice from the freezer. "It's for his nose," she explained.

I was touched. I thought by now she'd be ready to murder me herself.

"What's the matter with his nose?" Larson inquired, as if I usually walked around with a turgid, mauve proboscis, twice the size of Gerard Depardeau's.

"It's broken," I said. "Didn't you notice?"

"I didn't like to say," he replied, embarrassed.

"Thanks."

"Would you like to see a doctor?"

"No, thanks. I've already seen one."

They fetched the ice. At that point I tried to suggest that the frozen bottle of Stolichnaya might perform better as a cold compress, but Larson bristled and stalked off, convinced by now I was possibly dangerous.

We sat there in sullen silence, huddled on the porch seat: I in my denim jacket, ice pack pressed to the root of my nose; Miranda in her borrowed red-and-black-plaid hunter's coat. The crowd gradually dispersed. The neighbor lady gave a formal statement to the officers, promised to make herself available to Akimoro the next day if he had more questions for her, then went back to her house with her husband in tow, no doubt to resume her window perch. Garcia was left in charge of us, and he soon slipped back into his patrol car to busy himself with paperwork, stopping every now and then to glare at us with disapproval through the windshield.

When I was convinced the coast was clear and all potential eavesdroppers were otherwise occupied—that Garcia, not fifteen yards away in the driver's seat of his car, probably couldn't hear us over the crackle of the police scanner coming from his dashboard—I made my first conciliatory advance.

"Thanks for getting the ice for me, Miranda."

"You're welcome," she spat through clenched teeth. "I just wanted you to be in good health for when I cut your throat."

"You mad at me?"

She pounced. "You lied to me, you son of a bitch. You pretended to like me, when all you really wanted to do was check up on me." She stared off into the middle distance, eyes flashing.

"Partly true," I said. "I did lie to you, but that doesn't mean I don't like you."

She began to bounce her knees up and down nervously. "You didn't have the decency to trust me. After all I've done for Jack. I never crossed him once. Didn't he tell you that?"

I was taken aback. "No, he didn't." I shifted the ice pack slightly on my nose.

"Figures. Well, I'm sorry about the paintings. They're gone, and there was nothing I could do. You should have told me who you were at the funeral. Or at the auction the day after."

"I should've?"

"Yeah. Maybe we could have figured out something together. Somewhere to stash them. The better ones, at least. But no, you tried to be so smart." She was rocking her body side to side with pent-up rage. "You waited to check me out first, and see what happened. It's all your goddamn fault."

"It is?" I moved the ice pack again.

She turned to face me, eyes wide and accusing. "We lost the whole goddamn lot. Ten million dollars' worth. What the hell was I supposed to do with them by myself?"

"I haven't a clue."' I wondered if it was time I told her the truth about me. "Miranda, who do you think I am?"

"I know exactly who you are."

"Good. Tell me."

"Don't worry. All your secrets are safe." The words were reassuring, but the tone was mocking. "When I found out Jack was shot, first thing I did was go over to the apartment and collect all the records. Then later I burned them. That's why I'm not too worried about these bozos here." She nodded her head at Garcia and the cops in the house. "The way I figure, all our buyers are in Japan. They've got nobody to question."

"Really?"

"Yes. So you had no reason not to trust me, except that you lost your paintings. It's your fault for not showing up sooner. I thought of burning them, too, but I just couldn't—not the paintings. Besides, what was I going to do? Set fire to the apartment? No way."

I had wondered what she had burned in the grate that Saturday. I was really quite taken with this little waif of a girl, and her passion for beautiful things, no matter how they were acquired. I could see myself, in different circumstances, spending a lot more time with her.

"So you just destroyed the paper trail," I said.

"That's right. The way I see it, the paintings have been missing for a year now, some of them two years, and the FBI haven't been able to trace them to us. They're going to find the trail pretty cold now. It's going to take them a while. If you've done your job well, and I think you have, it may take them forever."

"I see."

She stopped rocking and turned to stare at me. "You know, I had no idea you even existed. Jack never told me. If it hadn't been for that old lady, and what you said to me before, I never would have put two and two together."

Thank heaven for modern math, I thought. I decided not to tell her the truth right now; she probably trusted me more thinking the way she did.

The arrival of Akimoro ended our discussion. He was wearing the identical suit he had on the Saturday before, although the shirt looked washed and starched, as did his face. There was no hint of fatigue or frazzle. The detective spent a half hour inspecting the house and its environs, then instructed that we be driven to the Beverly Hills police headquarters for our statements, while he made a short detour to examine the pickup truck, still parked on Los Feliz Boulevard.

When Miranda and I reached our destination we were escorted to separate rooms. I ended up in the familiar shoe box with the one-way mirror and the tape recorder, Miranda presumably in a similar cubicle on the same floor. An officer I didn't recognize came in to set up the preliminaries, and Akimoro followed some fifteen minutes later. This time I was not cautioned about the need for a lawyer. I was bolstered by this, and, coupled with the newly gained assurance in my own investigative abilities, found myself approaching the examination on a more equal footing.

Akimoro began. "I understand you have a confession to make, Dr. Lloyd."

"I do?"

"Yes. Isn't that why we're here?"

"I thought I was here to give a statement on what happened tonight."

"What happened tonight is being investigated by the county police. I thought you were here to explain how your gun appeared in such a strange manner."

"So you don't think this was the same guy who killed Jack Ehrenberger?"

He wrinkled his forehead, bringing those gray bristles on his scalp even closer to his eyebrows. "The man who killed Jack Ehrenberger?"

"That's right."

He stuck his left hand in his pocket as before and brought it out closed in a fist. I waited for the familiar grinding sound.

"The only connection I can see, Dr. Lloyd, is you."

I was mad. "Look, Akimoro! I don't have to take this abuse. If you keep insisting on holding me suspect, I'm going to refuse to talk. I thought you'd be interested in the truth."

He leaned back and began to crunch his dice. "Tell me, then."

I did. I told him about George Epstein and Jed Neifosh, about silvertips and full metal jackets. I gave him Detective Heintz in Houston and Syllovitz in Huntsville. He listened with mouth slightly agape.

"How do you figure those deaths are related to Ehrenberger?" he asked when I had finished. "Just because they're plastic surgeons? That's pretty slim."

"Damned if I know the connection. That's your job. Think about it, Akimoro. Three plastic surgeons killed within a year, all in the same way. Those are significant statistics for my profession. That kind of malice is usually reserved for abortionists. We generally just get sued."

"What about tonight?" he asked.

"Maybe it was my turn." I put it that way to avoid implicating Miranda. I didn't want to tie her in just yet. She might have been in the very next room, spewing beans on the table, absolving her conscience, but I doubted it. I tried to make it seem as though I'd picked her up at the auction house and Broder had followed us to get at me. It was chilling to realize I could have hit on the truth.

"Why would he be after you?"

"I told you, I don't understand the motive. There's a lot I don't understand."

"Well, that's a relief," he said.

"Tell me about bullets," I asked. "This thing with silvertips and full metal jackets intrigues me. Why would somebody use two different bullets in the same gun?"

Akimoro shrugged, and rolled his hand. Seven again.

"It's unusual," he said, "but not unheard of. People choose an ammunition according to their needs. A full metal jacket prevents the lead from spreading. It has more penetrating power. A silvertip, on the other hand, is only partially coated. It's designed to spread once inside the target. It causes a lot more destruction. You use one or the other, depending on what you intend to shoot at. A combination of the two may be the killer's way of covering all bases."

"How many times have you seen this combination used?"

"Not often." He picked the ivory cubes off the table.

"So it may be considered a sort of signature, in a way? A special calling card?"

"Now you're starting to sound like a reporter," Akimoro said.

I winced. "You checked the gun. What kind of bullets were left in the magazine?"

"It was empty."

"Then compare the slugs in the pickup with those in Jack's body."

Akimoro stared at the spools on the recorder. "Why would he steal your own gun to use against you?"

"I can't understand that. But he wouldn't have known it was my gun. He would have thought it was Ehrenberger's. He took it from his Rolls."

The detective nodded. "Did you ever collaborate with the other three doctors in your work?"

"No. I've never worked with Jack, and I didn't even know the other two."

"Do you have any enemies?"

"No one who'd want to murder me. Unless you count my ex-wife."

He turned the recorder off and rose to his feet. "Thank you, Dr. Lloyd. It seems as though you've done some checking up on your own. I would like to remind you that it is *our* job, and you'll be a lot safer if you go home and leave the rest to us."

We shook hands.

"Those dice are loaded, aren't they?" I asked.

He shrugged. "A souvenir from my first case."

"By the way," I said before leaving the room. "You should talk to Miranda's neighbor. Call her daughter in Johnson City, wherever that is, and ask what kind of car she rented last summer."

"Miss Pelton's neighbor?"

"The one who lives across the street. She's a gold mine."

I WAS ESCORTED BACK TO A WAITING ROOM, to pace the floors with a rancid cup of coffee while I waited for Miranda. I was beginning to fear that she had told them everything and that she would be marched downstairs in irons for her complicity in the art thefts. She suddenly appeared round the corner, somewhat harrowed but unfettered. When she saw me, she gave a tired smile and I glimpsed a note of triumph on her face.

"You survived, too," she said.

"Let's go home."

"Home?"

"To my place."

The police offered us a ride back to the house, where the evidence men were still busy doing their collecting. Miranda went straight to the Alfa and waited for me to open the door.

"Don't you need to pack a bag or something?" I asked.

"What with? There's nothing in there I'd want to wear. I moved out last week, remember?" She shrugged. "We can come back tomorrow and pick up my car. The cops should be done by then, and I'll go through what's left and see if I can salvage anything."

"You can borrow some of mine." I let her in the Alfa.

The freeway was damp only in patches as we drove

back to Greenfield. At four in the morning, traffic was as thin as it ever gets in Los Angeles, which can still beat rush hour in a place like Huntsville. I turned the radio on low, to my preselected station. Somebody was soulfully blowing his horn; sounded like Miles Dewey Davis.

"What did you tell them?" I asked, eyes on the road.

"Nothing."

"You were in there a long time."

"That's because of the police artist. They made me wait while they sent for him. I helped him draw a sketch of Broder. Came out real nice, too. I must admit he knew his business."

"And when they found out you knew him . . . how did you explain that?"

"I didn't tell them. I pretended this was the first time I saw him. I told them I had a good look at him when the headlights lit up his face." She paused. "You should have hit him a lot harder. They'd be picking bits of him off the front fender of that truck by now."

"I suppose you're right." The gravity of what I'd tried to do to Broder was sinking in, and I was still a little bewildered at my lack of remorse. I tried to keep my mind on the road, straining to see the lane markings as we merged from one freeway to the next. "Wouldn't it help them find him if you tell them everything you know?"

"Are you kidding? They'd be all over me. I'd still be in there answering their questions. I don't know that much about him, anyway. I don't know what he does, and I don't know where he lives. I can't help them find him." She turned to me suddenly. "You didn't tell them, did you?"

"No. I told them the same thing you did."

"Good."

"What *do* you know about him?"

"George introduced us. I don't know how they knew each other. Maybe from some past job. I got the impression George didn't think much of Broder."

"What did George say about him?"

"Not a lot. Actually, it wasn't me that Broder was interested in."

"You mean he was that way—wanted a piece of George?"

"No." She slapped me playfully on the knee. "It was nothing like that. He wanted to get to know Jack. He was interested in dealing art. That's what he said."

"Did he have a gallery, too?"

"I don't think so. He didn't strike me as knowing the least thing about it. I don't know. Maybe I was wrong about him. Maybe he *was* that way. Maybe he just didn't open up to women."

His loss, my gain, I thought. I sneaked a sideways glance at my companion, to gloat over the prize I was actually bringing home. If only Rafaella could see me now.

Miranda was staring straight ahead, looking somewhat forlorn, tousled blond hair capping the oversize red and black jacket we had borrowed earlier. I wondered if I was doing the right thing. Then my eyes traveled down her jeans to where the bony skin of her knees protruded through the torn fabric, and I was reassured.

"Did Broder ever get to meet Jack?" I asked, forcing myself to look back at the road.

"Yeah, a couple of times. Jack didn't like him, but when I tried to find out why, he wouldn't tell me. I just assumed Broder was looking for a job. Maybe to muscle in on the sales."

"And George never talked about how they knew each other?"

"No."

"But you said maybe it was from a past job. I gather you meant something illegal."

"No shit, Sherlock! After what he tried tonight, do you have any doubts?"

We were off the freeway, and the streets of Greenfield were peaceful and deserted at that hour of night.

"This looks like a neat place," she said. "I've never been here before."

"We try to keep it a secret from the rest of L.A. We roll up the sidewalks at nine every night, so there's no earthly reason to come here unless you live here. It's a nice, safe place to bring up kids."

"You sound as if you might have some experience with that," she said.

"I do. Two girls: thirteen and ten. That's a lot of experience, if you add it up."

"And how does your wife feel about you bringing home strange women at four in the morning?"

"She doesn't mind at all . . . as long as they don't set their sights on her share of the money. She has her claws in me for half of everything I make. The rest, I can do as I please with."

"And where does she live?"

"A couple of blocks away from me."

"So you can spy on each other?"

I smiled. "So we don't disrupt the children's lives too much. It's the closest thing to family life, without being a family."

She placed her hand on my knee. "How many women do you bring home? Let's say in a typical month."

I turned into the driveway. "Is this a leap year? I bring one home every February twenty-ninth."

"You're a little late."

"No matter. Next one's not due for a while."

"Are you shy?"

"I'm cautious."

"I'm not," she said, and smiled at me.

THE DARK HOUSE SEEMED MUCH TOO QUIET after what we'd been through. It was almost ominous not to see a patrol car in the driveway. I was wary as I let Miranda in the door, but there was no sign of any intrusion and the alarm had not been tampered with.

"It's pretty," she said. More or less out of obligation, I thought. Over the last two years the house had taken on a dark and masculine look, as I gradually replaced the trinkets and paintings that Rafaella had usurped with those of my own taste. I was never so conscious of it until now.

"You tired?" I wondered how I should approach the subject of sleeping arrangements. The spare room was fully furnished and the bed made, but even though the maid came once a week to clean up after me, she often skipped the areas I never used, and there was probably a fine layer of dust coating everything up there. Of course, I had hoped it wouldn't be necessary to use the spare room, but I was prepared to make it my first offer.

Miranda walked into the kitchen and started opening cupboards, sniffing around as if I had asked her to prepare a meal or something.

"I'm exhausted," she said. "But I can't sleep yet. Got anything to drink?"

"Yes." I was glad that she had also avoided the prospect of going to bed. "In there." I indicated the cupboard I used for alcohol.

"Mmm." She swung the door back and forth as she scanned the shelf. "Where's the Stolly?"

I went over to her side. "Should be . . . there it is." I extracted the bottle with a flourish, to find it had only an inch of clear liquid sitting in its base.

She looked at me with mock reproach. Silently she took the bottle from my hands, unscrewed the lid, then tilted it up to the ceiling and emptied it in one gulp. She rolled her tongue around her moist lips seductively, then handed me the empty, while her eyes transfixed me in her gaze, never wavering.

"If you want to get me into bed," she said, "you'll have to do better than that."

I stared back, considering the challenge.

Her lips pulled outward in the faintest of smiles. "Don't you have another?" she prompted helpfully. "Where's your spare?"

"There's maybe twenty bottles in there. Why don't you try something different?"

She let go of the cupboard door and collapsed against the counter, feigning despair. I stared at the back of her head, longing to touch her blond hair, to tousle it more; an inch away from grabbing her by the shoulders and twisting her around, aching to kiss the vodka from those lips and take her right there on the kitchen floor. While I was still thinking about it, she rose and began to browse through the shelves.

She finally settled on a bottle of Havana Club and poured a generous helping over ice. "You having one, too?" she asked, pulling down a second glass at my nod. She wrinkled her nose. "Not as good as Stolly. But it'll do."

I thought it might slow down her intake. We moved to the den and sat on opposite ends of the long sofa. She undid her laces and kicked her shoes off, then her socks, raising her legs and placing her feet on my lap. She held her glass up to me. "Cheers."

"Tell me about Jack," I said.

"Why?"

"I want to know."

She lowered her glass suspiciously. "I thought you worked with him."

"Yes, but I want to know about *you* and Jack. How did the two of you meet?"

"He never told you?"

"I want to hear it from you."

She put the glass down on the coffee table. "I get it. Damage control. The debriefing. You want to find out where everybody stands so you can make your plans. Maybe disband the gang and dissipate the heat. Or fire it up again."

"Something like that." I had another attribute to add to her credits: a vivid imagination.

"Okay. I was working at a gallery on La Cienega and he walked in, asking about American Impressionists. I think he was doing research for a sale. He invited me to dinner and I went. That's how it started."

"You had an affair?"

"Don't be so corny. We had a good time. We liked each other. He knew what I needed, and he knew when to leave me alone."

I had heard this before. From Elaine. "So you didn't go to bed with him?"

She tossed her head. "Of course I went to bed with him. What do you think I'm saying?"

I wasn't sure. It seemed that, nowadays, the measure of a man was the knowledge of when to leave women alone. In Rafaella's case, I had measured up the minute I was making enough to hand over a decent alimony check.

"Go on," I said. "How did you start working for him?"

"When he found out I could speak Japanese he asked me to do him a favor. He sent me to Tokyo to meet some dealers. I took his catalog: photographs of Impressionist works of art he wanted to sell. He gave me a price and a margin, and I negotiated the sales. It was the easiest money I ever made."

"You sold them all?"

"Not the first time. But the second time I sold them all. Those dealers soaked them up like sponges. It was like bargaining didn't even occur to them. I got a salary plus commission and had a great time."

She tossed the last of her rum and ice cubes down her throat, as if in celebration of those hedonistic days. "You'd put me on the same terms again if I worked for you, wouldn't you?"

The idea was tempting. I wondered how she would fare showing patients to their rooms, taking histories, and arranging bandages. Bankrupt me in a minute, no doubt.

"How many times did you go to Tokyo?" I asked.

"Just twice. After that they came here. We bought the apartment in Santa Monica and set it up as a gallery. Jack would fly them in, book them into the Nikko in Beverly Hills. Just like a regular business trip. We gave them everything they wanted: visits to the County Museum of Art, weekends at Pebble Beach for golf."

"And you shipped the paintings back to Japan via Acapulco?"

"You know that part."

"How did he acquire them?"

"You're asking me?"

My mistake. In her mind that was my end of the deal. "I just wanted to know if you'd heard."

"You said you'd tell me. Remember?"

"That's right, I did. But first tell me about George."

She swung her feet down to the floor and sat up. "First I need another drink. How about you?"

"I'm fine." I watched her as she left the room; not a trace of wobble in those lissome thighs. I wondered if her capacity for alcohol was acquired or hereditary.

I heard the clinking of ice cubes heralding her return from the kitchen. She glided in softly on the balls of her feet. She was pinching two glasses full of ice between the fingers of her right hand, while she swung the bottle of Havana Club with the other. I thought for a minute she might break into the Charleston.

"I brought you one anyway, just in case you change your mind." She plopped the whole ensemble down on the coffee table and poured two generous helpings, almost to the brim. She sat down, a little closer this time, so that when she raised her limbs again her knees were on my lap, while her feet hung suspended over the edge. She propped a pillow behind her back for ballast, swallowed a few ounces, and looked at me solemnly. "Where were we?"

"You were going to tell me about George?"

"Ah, yes. George worked for Jack. Not at first; he came in later, about six months ago. He was real intense."

"Intense?"

"Yeah. You know—passionate. Not with women, with his philosophy."

"He was a philosopher?"

She gave me one of those condescending smiles one might reserve for people of lesser intelligence or social standing; a semaphore of congeniality across an impassable chasm. "He was a white supremacist."

"Oh! And Jack still employed him?"

"I don't know if Jack ever knew. George was just the deliveryman. They didn't have much social contact. And he didn't exactly wear a swastika on his sleeve."

I remembered there was a time and place when they did. "What did George think of Jack? Some of them don't like Jews or Catholics, either."

She paused while it sank in, took another sip to help the brain cells. She sat up suddenly. "Do you think George could have killed Jack?"

"I was wondering. How serious was he about all that supremacy thing?"

"Very serious. I didn't find out until last week.

George had a thing for me and I . . . I liked him. We were sort of thrown together on the trips to Mexico."

"How did Jack feel about that?"

"Oh, Jack and I cooled off a long time ago. Soon after we bought the Santa Monica apartment. He said it interfered with business. I think there was someone else. I didn't mind. He was still nice to me. I used to joke about it sometimes when he paid me—called it hush money. I was very expensive when it came to hush money. . . ." She trailed off, her mind retracting into the treasures of her past, while her face acquired a self-satisfied grin.

"You were saying?"

"Huh!"

"George the supremacist," I prompted.

"Well, when Jack died I was in a panic. I didn't know what to do at first. I cleaned out the apartment in Santa Monica and took all our notes home. On Saturday, the day I met you at Malbone's, George was there, too. He told me it was best to get out of L.A. until the heat cooled off. He offered me a place to stay, said he had a cabin up by Lake Isabella. I went home, burned all the paperwork, packed up, and moved out the next day.

"Hah!" She raised her glass for another sip. "A safe haven, he called it. Turned out to be more of a loony bin. It was some sort of motel out in the woods. Probably went bankrupt, a bunch of cabins around a cookhouse. I stayed in one with George. There was Timmy, Bo, Eileen and Mickey, Samson, and Purdy." She counted off the names on her fingertips.

"They were a bunch of kids, really. They came from all over the place. They called themselves the White Aryan Resistance. Their emblem was a skull and crossbones, with a black eyepatch over the skull. The letters spelled 'WAR.' "

"WAR?"

"Yeah. White Aryan Resistance. Get it? Very weird. I think I preferred all the peace, love, and hugging from my Flagstaff days."

I remembered the health food guru she had stayed with before coming to L.A. It seemed months since I'd heard her life story, but that was less than twelve hours ago, at Rosarita's. "Were they armed?" I asked.

I intercepted another patronizing smile.

"Does a bear shit in the woods? They had a cellar that was stocked. Not wines, either: Uzi's, M-16's, shotguns, handguns; I don't even know what half those things were called. They also had a generator, a computer system, and enough food and water to last through Armageddon."

And well beyond, by the sounds of it. George would have had plenty of access to silvertips and full metal jackets. But why would he need to steal the gun from Elaine's car?

"George was gone most of the day," she continued. "They would practice shooting down in a gorge in back of the property. I stayed in the cabin, reading. He tried to convince me that if I left the cabin, I'd be in danger. He'd bring me books back from the store in town. He liked Anne Rice. Yeech! I was desperate, though. I went through one, sometimes two a day. I felt like a prisoner. George became possessive and demanding. He wanted me to dress like Purdy. She turned him on. Christ's sake, she couldn't have been more than fifteen."

"How did you get away?"

"Whenever George left he had Bo guard the keys. This morning—I mean Saturday morning—he left early for Bakersfield. He was all excited about something big, some kind of ceremony they were having. Timmy and Bo stayed to watch the camp. Purdy stayed because they never took her anywhere. About ten o'clock I heard this tremendous fight outside. I found Bo lying in the dirt. He had a busted knee and his face was bleeding. Timmy took off and left him."

"What was that about?"

"Who cares? It was my big chance. Purdy tried to get Bo in the car but he was in too much pain. They wanted to wait for George. I convinced him to give me the keys so I could go to town and get some pills. I went into Lake Isabella, sent an ambulance out to the camp, then called Purdy and told her I just had to go on to L.A. for some clothes. All the way to Bakersfield I kept thinking I'd run into George coming back from his meeting."

I was troubled by what I'd heard, and felt constrained to say so. "Miranda, the police need to know about all this. The camp, the guns, the White Aryan Resistance—didn't you tell them any of it?"

She shook her head stubbornly. "George is dead now, so what difference does it make?"

"It might help them find Broder."

She shrugged. "They can find Broder on their own; I've given them a description. Who cares about him, anyway? If they want to kill each other off, that's their problem. It was the same with Mickey and Bo. Half the time they're blood brothers, and the other half they're at each other's throat. At least we're out of the limelight. I don't want to end up in jail because of those paintings. Believe me, I did a very thorough job of burning the evidence. If you've covered your tracks half as well, there's no way the cops can find out."

I took a large sip from the spare drink she had poured, and sighed. "Miranda, it's not the paintings. I haven't figured it out yet, but I think they're after me."

"After you? The cops?"

"No. Broder. George. I don't know who. They've already killed three plastic surgeons: Jack, and two others in Texas."

She sat up, bringing her face within inches of mine, eyes wide pools of curiosity. "Why?"

I told her what I knew. I had the story down to the essentials by now, having repeated it twice already. She listened to the end.

"What have those other surgeons got to do with the paintings?" she asked.

"Not a thing. *I've* got nothing to do with the paintings."

She jumped back as the realization struck her. "You weren't working with Jack?"

"No." I felt dismal, thinking she'd be mad that I'd deceived her all this time.

She stayed calm. There was a long silence. I thought she may have been counting to ten under her breath. "Why did you let me think you were?" she finally asked.

"It was easier," I admitted. "I thought the truth was too complex."

"And what's the truth? Why were you snooping around my house? How'd you find out about me and Jack, anyway?"

I shrugged. "A lucky break. I was investigating Jack's murder."

"Because you felt you'd be the next target?"

I took another sip of my drink. "No. Because I was a suspect."

"You? A suspect?"

"That's right. I was . . . I was having an affair with Elaine."

A smile spread slowly across her mouth. Her lips were pale, with only traces of lipstick now, the rest gracing the rim of her glass. She began to laugh.

"You? And Elaine?"

I nodded, grinning.

She smacked her thigh. "That's the silliest thing I've heard all night."

My grin faded. "There's no need to be quite so rambunctious."

She giggled. "I'm sorry. I just can't see it. She wouldn't fit in here."

"She never came here. I guess you're right. It was destined for the rocks."

She stopped laughing. "It's over?"

I raised my right arm. "I swear."

She took my hand gently in her own. "Let's go up-stairs," she said.

THERE WAS A PERSISTENT RINGING IN MY ears. I stirred and with the dawning of consciousness realized it was the phone. Why wouldn't it stop? Was there something wrong with my answering machine again? I let it ring until it was tired of annoying me.

There were other things annoying me, anyway. My mouth was parched as a canyon in Death Valley; my tongue a jumping cholla cactus; and my head as heavy and as turgid as a prize pumpkin, and possibly just as useful. I tried to shake the sleep away, half expecting to hear the rattle of seeds. Each movement was accompanied by a flash of white light and a sharp twinge down to the base of my neck. It was entirely appropriate that, on my fortieth birthday, I should wake up with a hangover.

I lay there, staring at the ceiling, wondering what time it was, much too wary to invite further stabs of pain by tilting my head to look at the clock. From the intensity of sunlight pouring in through the open window I figured it must be late morning. Eleven, maybe twelve hours into my birthday, and it had already proved to be so eventful that it was almost like a condensed version of the entire preceding year. Not much happened from year to year in Greenfield, although this last one, starting with Elaine and ending with Miranda, was turning into quite an exception. Perhaps it was a portent of much bigger things to come. Who could tell what the next year would bring? Maybe it was time I had another look at that little red Ferrari down in Newport Beach. Maybe I should go out and buy a lottery ticket. There was a catch, though. If I was to do anything, I would have to get out of bed, and my body was no longer responding as it used to.

I sidled my hand crablike along the bedcovers, taking great care not to move my neck and hoping thus to avoid any further punishment from my throbbing head. The rumpled sheets beside me were cold. I searched with sensitive fingertips for the impression Miranda's supple body must have left on the mattress, like Braille to a blind man. Was it just a dream after all? Up by my chest was where her shoulders should have left their mark, the strong curve of her back a little lower down. Surely the deeper form of those taut buttocks would still be present. There was nothing. The mattress, with its tempered coil springs, was as flat and unreadable as a sheet of rolled steel.

I opened my eyes. The pillow next to me still held the outline of a head pressed into it. I pulled it closer and inhaled. There was a sharp pain in my nose as the soft, downy surface made contact, just another reminder that the night had been all too real. My sense of smell was still alive, though. A faint trace of strawberries and lime lingered on the cotton slipcase.

I shut my eyes again and listened. The ringing of the telephone had been replaced by a faint buzzing, as if my tympanic membranes had been tightened to a higher acuity, like the parchment of a drum. My body had been transformed into an inert blob of jelly, but my senses were trying to compensate for it. I heard the sharp whistle of a mockingbird nesting in the elm outside my window, followed by a shrill series of warning chirps. The neighbor's cat had probably come too close. I heard the sounds of water running in the kitchen downstairs. She was humming a tune. Was it "Strangers in the Night" or something by Pearl Jam?

Last night we had floated up the stairs like two

young lovers in a fairy tale, she leading me wordlessly by the hand, as if to a secret hiding place. Tenderly, we had peeled the clothes from each other, stopping every now and then to steal soft, succulent kisses, but holding back the rest, as though the rapture of seeing our naked bodies was the pinnacle of every desire we had shared that night.

It was a dance. A tango without music.

I think I choreographed it, but she followed perfectly in step, a willing second to my lead. We stood there by the bedside full erect, I in my own way and she in hers, as we reveled in each other's form—touching, absorbing the bare pleasure of our intimacy.

And then lust had erupted in an exothermic flash, and we plunged into each other's bodies, writhing, twisting, fused to one another like copper on silver, congealing with a hiss of steam and a shower of sparks. It was a different species of dance now—a tribal boogaloo, a melodrama of sweat and passion. Each sensual organ was alert, pressed into action, and in due time we were consumed by ecstasy.

My pleasure achieved an altitude it had not known in years. It seemed as if my mind was working at a heightened level, potentiating the experience until it doubled. Perhaps it was my newly gained landmark; perhaps forty is the blending point between healthy sexual appetite and dirty old man. My poor nose got the worst of it, though. Now and again, a sharp pang had reminded me of the punishment it had already served. I think I even bled once or twice. No matter, it would give the maid something to think about.

"Gareth," Miranda's voice came softly up the landing. "Wakey, wakey. Breakfast time."

Her invitation was like a mating call. Minutes later I clattered down the stairs feeling like Marley's ghost in irons, following the aroma of fresh-brewed coffee and warm buttered toast into the kitchen. She was wearing one of my old flannel shirts and watched me enter with an amused look.

"Save it," I said, trying to squash the obvious comment about my appearance. "You, on the other hand, look very nice this morning."

She walked up close and studied my face. "Thank you. In that case, I won't say anything about your nose." She kissed me and handed me a wine flute, half filled with a rich, golden nectar. "What you need is the hair of the dog. This will snap you out of it."

I tasted. She had found the Château d'Yquem I was saving in the back of the refrigerator.

"It's sweet, but much better than that rum you force-fed me last night."

"It should be. Nectar of the gods. The Russian czars drank nothing else but this. They ordered it by the case in crystal decanters lettered in gold." I reached in through the shirt flaps, intending to grab her by the waistband of her panties and draw her to me. She wasn't wearing any.

"And by the way," I added, "I didn't force you to do anything you didn't want to last night."

"Oh?" Her eyes betrayed her mock severity. "I thought you were an animal."

My joy was complete.

"Have something to eat," she said.

I took another sip of Sauternes. "With this, it should be baked Alaska."

Instead, we munched on toast and marmalade.

"The phone's been ringing off the hook," she said. "I didn't know if you'd want me to answer. I've been listening to the messages. I think your machine is full. The last one was from your exchange. It sounded kind of urgent; that's when I decided to wake you."

I pretended to look concerned. "Hope nobody's died of a leaking breast implant."

She ignored my sarcasm. "Akimoro's been trying to reach you, and two were from other cops. Sounds like you've been real busy working on this case."

I walked over to the answering machine. There were seven calls registered. I sighed. It seemed the life of an investigator was busier than that of a surgeon, especially on Sunday mornings.

I went over to the liquor cabinet, where I also kept a small first-aid kit, and extracted two aspirins. Popping them in my mouth, I washed them down with a little Sauternes, then retrieved a pad and pen and sat down at the phone desk.

I hit the play button. The first call was logged in at 8:00 A.M. and was from the exchange. A Dr. Kapoor from Riverside wanted to talk to me, but it wasn't urgent. They would call back later. The next was at 9:05. It was a long and endearing message from Jillian and Emma, wishing me a very happy birthday and saying that they had two special presents for me. I was touched. I knew Rafaella wouldn't have been awake to prompt them at that hour.

Miranda waited for the next beep before coming over to sit on my knee. "I didn't know it was your birthday."

"It's a secret."

The third message was from the exchange again, saying they were still trying to reach me. The remaining four had come within the past hour. There was Detective Heintz in Houston, who said he was returning my call from Friday, and that he'd heard I had something important to tell him. Next was Akimoro; he wanted me to call him back as soon as I could. Then there was Syllovitz from Huntsville, informing me that he had checked with Forensics in Houston, and thanking me for my help. I assumed by this that the bullets in the two Texas murders were a match. The last call was from my exchange, in a more urgent tone this time. They were wondering where I was, and could I please call them.

"See what I mean?" Miranda said. "What's it like when you're actually working?"

"It's murder," I replied. "I'm sorry. It looks as if I have business to take care of."

She shrugged. "Do you want me to leave?"

"Not at all. But do you think you could shift your weight a little?"

She smiled and rose, then went behind me and began to soothe my neck with her soft hands. "Go ahead," she said, craning her head forward to listen.

I called the exchange first, and they recounted my message. Dr. Kapoor from Little Sisters Hospital in Riverside wanted to talk to me about a patient named Gambella. I didn't have a patient named Gambella, but then I made the connection. It was Rocco. What on earth had happened to Rocco? Could it be his prostate again? If it was, surely I couldn't help; it was out of my specialty. I dialed the hospital number and asked them to page the doctor, but he didn't answer. I left my home number and they promised to keep trying.

Then I called Rafaella and asked to speak to Jillian and Emma. She was aloof but she obliged. I thanked the kids for their thoughtfulness and made all kinds of promises about where I was going to take them the next time we met, knowing Rafaella would be listening on the other phone. Let her explain the new restrictions to them, I figured.

I tried Houston next. Detective Heintz had the amiable voice of a native Texan, a weathered, soothing drawl that conjured up the image of mud-caked boots and blue jeans.

"I got a call on an old case this morning," he said. "It's been on the back burner far too long. Seems like they got a murder in Huntsville that matches one of mine. I had a talk with the detective and he told me he got it all from you. Sure enough, there's a message on my desk for me to call you. Mind telling me what this is all about?"

I tried, hoping that repeating the story might reveal some new clue. I wasn't sure if his part in the investigation might not be over. I told him George had been killed, and I didn't know the extent of Broder's involvement. "You can call the Beverly Hills police and ask for Detective Akimoro. He'll fill you in."

He asked a few questions of his own, but I couldn't answer most of them. He thanked me and said he'd be in touch. As I was hanging up, the phone rang in my hand. It was the doctor from Little Sisters Hospital, with a pronounced Indian accent.

"Do you know Rocco Gambella?" he asked.

"Yes."

"He was admitted to our hospital this morning. He was assaulted at home and he's taken quite a beating; four broken ribs and a laceration of his spleen. We had to do a splenectomy."

"My God, that's terrible."

"Yes. He also took a bad blow to the right eye. There's some retinal damage. Dr. Hamill, our ophthalmologist, has done his best but the prognosis for return of vision is poor."

"Oh no. How's he taking it?"

"He's quite desperate. I wanted to sedate him but he insists on seeing you. I promised I would call. I got your number from the Los Angeles medical directory."

"But I don't have privileges at your hospital," I said, indicating that I couldn't help in any way unless he was transferred to Greenfield.

"No. Not to do surgery. He wants you to visit him."

"To visit him?"

"If you could. I think it would cheer him up."

"What's his condition?" I wondered how I was expected to cheer up Rocco Gambella.

"Stable. He'll be in Intensive for a few days. We're watching for a coagulopathy. We had to give him six units of blood."

"I'll leave now." I asked for the address and wrote it down.

Miranda sat down on my knee again. She looked worried. "What's wrong?"

I looked at her with a glum face. The sight of her wearing my flannel shirt was appealing in a rather androgynous way, and the weight of her body rocking on my knee gave me a feeling of strength. The knowledge that there was nothing more between my knee and her buttocks save for a thin layer of woven cotton gave me a feeling of a slightly different nature. I had been anticipating a leisurely morning, perhaps another tribal ritual with Miranda in the bargain, and I thought she'd be inclined to agree. Now it appeared as if my plans would have to go on hold.

"Damn!" I said.

"What's going on? Is it something to do with work?"

"It's a friend. He's been admitted to the hospital. I'm afraid I have to go to Riverside. I'll only be a few hours."

"I'm not waiting here. I'm coming with you."

MIRANDA WATCHED ME WITH AMUSEMENT as I recorked the bottle of Sauternes and put the breakfast dishes in the sink.

"Domesticated, aren't you?"

I shrugged. "Habit. Inside me there's a slob waiting to express himself."

We went upstairs to change. Miranda stayed in my flannel shirt and pulled on her jeans from the night before. I wondered what the nurses at the hospital would think when they saw us.

She went out the front door first while I set the alarm. When I joined her on the brick pathway she was studying the flower beds to the right of the entrance.

"Someone's knocked your sign down," she said.

"What sign?"

"This thing here." She bent down in the dirt to pick up a one-by-two-foot metal sign attached to a spike. It was the warning for the alarm company. THIS PROPERTY PRO-TECTED BY ULTRATEC, it said. They had advised me its presence would deter predators. Someone had shown his disrespect by trampling all over it.

"I think we'd better have a look," I said.

We walked around the perimeter of the house, checking the flower beds and window screens. Practically every window had footprints leading up to it in the wet mud. There was no sign of forced entry—the screens were all intact. Besides, the flashing green when I had checked the alarm had reassured me of that. But it seemed as if some curious, booted animal had spent a lot of time peering into my house since it had rained last night. There was only one likely candidate I could think of.

Broder.

How in hell would he know where I lived?

"He's been here." Miranda reinforced my suspicions. "It couldn't be anybody else."

"Maybe we shouldn't jump to conclusions," I said, trying to ease my own concerns. "It could have been just a burglar. They do exist, you know."

"A burglar wouldn't have left this." She pointed to a mark on the stucco wall under the den window.

I looked closely. She was referring to a blob of chocolate brown, with a few smears next to it. We walked over to the next window and saw a similar Rorschach pattern.

"Didn't that lady tell us that Broder's knee was injured?" Miranda said, driving home her point.

"You think that's blood?"

"What do you think, Gareth?"

"I think we better get out of here fast" was all I could say.

There was no thought to lowering the ragtop as we jumped into the Alfa, even though it was turning out to be quite a gorgeous day. I pumped the clutch and floored it, leaving a trail of burned rubber halfway up the drive.

We sped east down the freeway.

"I've been thinking," Miranda said.

"What about?"

"I could handle the paintings. But people are dying now. I've got to get out of here."

I sighed, changed lanes, and slowed down. "Broder's a maniac, isn't he?"

"Yes. I can't figure it out. What do you think he was looking for last night?"

"You mean at my place, or at yours?"

"Mine. You saw the mess. You heard that lady describe how he went from room to room."

"You have something he wants?"

"Obviously. But what?"

I couldn't help her there. I was upset. She had something *I* wanted. I hadn't finished playing with my birthday present yet, and it was going to walk out of my life. Maybe Broder wanted the same thing from her. Maybe he had fired at us in a jealous rage, then trashed her place out of vengeance.

"Maybe he thought I kept Jack's records," she said.

"Or his cash."

She was silent.

"Miranda, what happened to all his cash? He must have kept a fair amount on hand. He couldn't very well write checks to cover expenses."

She didn't answer. I sped up to keep pace with traffic again.

"So you're going to run away and leave me in Broder's clutches," I said.

"You can come, too."

"Thanks." Somehow, that didn't appeal to me all that much. "Where will you go?"

"I'm not sure. Back East. I'd like to start a little gallery somewhere."

I smiled. "I suppose it gets in your blood. Sounds like it will take some capital."

"I have a little stashed away from what I earned."

I knew her hush money wouldn't have been enough to start an antique gallery, no matter what Jack had paid her. I wondered just how much of Jack's bankroll she had managed to stash; perhaps she got a few of the smaller paintings in the bargain.

We continued down the freeway, each lost in our own thoughts, chased by the demons that had so rudely interrupted the leisurely morning I had planned. We passed the slag heaps of the old Kaiser Permanente foundries and the railroad yards. The land around us used to be an agricultural haven; now the farmers had all sold out and moved away, the tractors and livestock long since gone. They were replaced by new bedroom communities, as middle-class families moved farther and farther down the corridor east into Riverside County. They were trying to get away from the angst and violence of inner-city life, chased by demons of their own. Sooner or later, those hellhounds seem to catch up with the lot of us.

"Riverside seems a long way," Miranda said.

"We're almost there."

"Who's your friend?"

"We're going to see Rocco, some guy I know from the auction circuit. He was beaten up this morning and went through surgery. He's asked to see me."

"Who beat him up?"

"No idea."

"Is he involved in this?"

The inevitable question. "No," I answered, not wanting to admit the role Rocco had played in working out Jack's little scheme. But I did wonder. *Was* Rocco involved in this? Why was it he had to see me so urgently? I hardly knew the man, except for swapping a few pleasantries with him at Malbone's every Saturday.

"That reminds me," I said, "we forgot to call Akimoro back. Do you still have his card?"

"I think I do." She fished in her bag for a minute, then emptied its contents onto her lap. Lipstick, keys, a couple of pencils, and various other paraphernalia tumbled out, until she found what she was looking for.

"Here it is. I'll dial it." She pushed the numbers on the car phone, leaving it on speaker mode. When Akimoro got on the line I quickly explained about our visitor during the night.

"Did you hear anything?" he asked.

"No." I looked at Miranda. She hadn't, either.

"Did you go straight to bed?"

I glanced back at Miranda. She returned with a glare, as if to say one word from me and she would ram one of those pencils straight through my heart.

"No," I replied. "We sat up talking for an hour."

"And there was no disturbance? No loud noises, no police sirens going by your street?"

"No. None that I recall."

"So you think this visitor, this Peeping Tom, just hung around for a while, then left?"

Miranda colored visibly. I dodged a kamikaze Sunday driver and looked in vain for the highway patrol car that should have been on his tail.

"Maybe he didn't see us and thought nobody was home," I suggested.

"Where did you park your car?" Akimoro asked.

"In the driveway."

"In plain view?"

"Yes."

"So he would have known someone was home."

"Maybe he came by before we got there. After all, we didn't get home until well past four. Maybe he got tired of waiting for us and left, and we just didn't notice the trampled sign because it was dark."

I braked for another loose cannon, skijet in tow, while I waited for Akimoro to assimilate my theory. For myself, I realized this would mean Broder knew exactly where I lived, without needing to follow me.

"Where are you now?" Akimoro asked.

"On our way to Little Sisters Hospital in Riverside. An art dealer I know from the auction has been mugged, and he's asked to see me."

"An art dealer? Is there any connection with Ehrenberger?"

Again, that little incubus of doubt reared its ugly head. Was Rocco involved in this? Did Akimoro see it clearly, as well as Miranda? Was I the only one slow on the uptake?

"Not that I know," I replied.

"Are you being followed?" Akimoro asked.

"I don't think so. I've been watching my mirror, slowing down and speeding up, and none of the cars behind me have followed all the way."

"That's good. I'll assign an officer to protect you. When you get to the Little Sisters Hospital, wait there. I'll send someone. Call me back in half an hour and I'll tell you when and where to meet him."

"Okay," I said. I liked that idea. "By the way, what was the reason you called this morning?"

"The gun. It was registered to a Mr. Dante Felice from Hackettstown, New Jersey. How do you explain that?"

"He was my brother-in-law. Dante gave me that gun ten years ago."

"It's also the one that killed Jack Ehrenberger. We matched the slugs."

"You did? Great! That takes me off your list of suspects."

"We're still investigating, Dr. Lloyd. We have some new evidence now, and it might throw a different light on the case. You can tell Miss Pelton I'd like to talk to her again. I have a few more questions for her."

Miranda punched the "End Transmission" button with a jab, almost causing me to swerve onto the shoulder.

"What did you do that for?" I howled, jerking the wheel with one hand while the other shot instinctively up to cover my nose.

"I don't want to hear him. Can we get out of here?"

I steadied the Alfa. "Let's hear what he has to say. You've got a head start on him. You're in Riverside County already." I pressed the redial button. "Akimoro? You there?"

"What happened?"

"We got cut off. What did you want to speak to Miranda about?"

"There's a lot more about Broder we need to know. He's had her apartment under surveillance all week. I had a talk with Mrs. Goodman this morning."

"Mrs. Goodman?"

"The old lady across the street. She identified the car. It was a blue Ford Taurus."

THE LITTLE SISTERS HOSPITAL OF RIVER-
side was a small, two-story gray-and-white building
on a quiet block east of University Avenue. It had an
aura of sleepy restfulness, in contrast to our own
monstrosity back in Greenfield. I pulled into the
visitors' lot and found a shady spot for the Alfa. I was
reminded of siesta time back in Italy, or even south of the
border. There was hardly any activity visible from the
grounds: no ambulances, no security patrols, no construction projects, no detours, and no patients. I was not surprised.

Once, these small community hospitals were sacred
cash cows, serving the gainfully employed suburbanite and
dispensing adequate and competent health care, from the
initial, winsome greeting of the ward nurse to the bright ef-
ficiency of the medical staff—a benign crop of Marcus
Welbys—who would spare no effort, and no expense, in
testing and X-raying, ultrasounding and scanning, scoping
and graphing, and generally probing and jabbing until
they, and their patients, were completely satisfied that a
headache was, in fact, only a headache, and an irritable
bowel was nothing more than a bowl of chili eaten in haste
at Jose's Burrito Barn.

All of this lasted just fine as long as somebody was
willing to pay for it. Then, when the winds and whimsies of
the insurance industry began to blow the other way, and

patients began to shift their allegiance to the HMO's, it was as if Moses had come down from the mountain and broken his tablets. The orgy was over. Nurses, once pleasant, turned dour with the burden of paperwork, while bedpans were ignored and left to cut red rings in sore buttocks. Call bells pealed unanswered, the food grew cold, and curtains faded. Amid all this jaded splendor, doctors would sneak in and out with such dispatch, as if they were ashamed of the general state of deterioration all around them. The ailing were bundled off home before they even learned to pronounce their ailments, get-well cards would have to be forwarded, and a new industry would thrive as visiting nurses scrambled to minister to patients recovering at home. Hospital occupancy rates plummeted, and hospital incomes with them. Little wonder so many small suburban hospitals had to fold. Lucky for Rocco Gambella, this one was still chugging along.

We walked into Reception and asked the volunteer for the Intensive Care Unit. She looked up from her book. She gave us visitors passes like name tags at a Christmas party, and with a smile she waved us to the elevators. Upstairs and to the right, the corridor was deserted. I found a door marked ICU and it swung open as we approached.

The air inside was fetid with the odor of senescence and human waste. The large room was unusually quiet, the fluorescent lighting almost unnecessary, illuminating every inch of a workstation where no work was being done, at least not to my standards. There were no charts or clipboards cluttering the desk; no pharmacists, therapists, or technicians traversed the faded blue carpet. The three nurses on duty, rather than drawing up medications into little vials, or measuring fluids in graduated flasks, or scanning monitors, or even exchanging complaints about the doctors and the patients, were tranquilly reading from glossy magazines, as if they themselves were in some doctor's waiting room.

"Can I help you?" one of them asked, looking us up and down.

"I'm Dr. Lloyd. I'm here to see Mr. Gambella."

"Oh." She glanced at the others. "Excuse me, Doctor. What did you say your name was?"

"Lloyd. Gareth Lloyd."

"Are you on staff here?"

"No, I'm not. I'm just here to visit him."

"Oh." She turned to her colleagues for a whispered discussion.

I stepped back to rejoin Miranda and study the layout. There were five open beds in bays and two isolation rooms. Two of the beds were empty, and the remaining three had occupants neatly tucked up to their necks in clean blue blankets, heads propped up on pillows. Their stringy hair, pale hanging jowls, and hooded, unblinking eyes reminded me of buzzards waiting for death, in this case possibly their own. The rows of monitors, with flickering red and green warning lights, seemed more animated.

The nurse rose to speak, this time less timidly. "I'm sorry, Doctor, but I will have to get permission to let you see him."

"Why don't you call Dr. Kapoor?" I suggested. "He asked me to come in."

She picked up the phone to dial. "Who is the lady with you?" she whispered.

"A friend."

The nurse drummed her fingers on the desktop while the call went through. The other two watched with some concern, stiffly holding their magazines, as if ready to swat me if I proved hostile. The doctor answered within minutes and she explained the situation. She listened, nodded twice, and then hung up.

"May I see your ID?" she asked.

I showed her my driver's license.

"Okay. He's in number five—over there."

She pointed to one of the isolation rooms, then went back to her reading. Miranda and I walked over to number five and rolled back the door.

The patient lying in bed was not immediately recognizable. A turban of gauze covered most of his head and the right side of his face. The left cheek was bruised and shapeless, the eye red and straining through swollen lids as it watched our entry.

"What do you want?" A deep, bass voice issued from behind us in the darkened corner of the room. I froze in midstep. A swarthy figure stepped forward, a startling genie of a man: head shaved, eyebrows bushy, enormous upper body clad only in a tank top, with tattoos swimming on rippling fat along both shoulders.

"It's okay, Liston," Rocco said in a hoarse voice. "It's Dr. Lloyd."

Liston grunted and went back into the shadow like an obedient Rottweiler.

I introduced Miranda and advanced to the bedside. "How are you, Rocco?"

His neck bent slightly forward as he strained to speak. He worked his mouth, silently at first, and then the words came, out of synch with the lip movements, as if he were speaking from light-years away. "So this is Miranda."

"That's right. She was at the auction. Remember? She bid on the little geisha doll."

The mouth moved again. It was like watching a badly dubbed foreign movie. "Listen, Doc." His hoarseness made the words barely intelligible. "You owe me. You owe me big time."

I started to feel the *thump, thump* in my chest. "Slow down, Rocco. You want some water?" I looked around for a carafe but there wasn't any. "Are you allowed water?"

"I get my water through that tube," he said.

"I'm sorry, Rocco. I'm really sorry. Can you tell me what happened?"

He did, with much difficulty, while watchdog Liston sat in his corner, quiet except for his panting.

"Seven-thirty this morning," Rocco said. "I was in the kitchen making a pot of coffee. Liston was gone . . . out to buy the paper. Doorbell rang. There was this bastard standing there, blood all down his leg."

"Broder!" I interrupted. "What did he want?"

Rocco groaned and paused to catch his breath. I saw him trying to swallow, and a strange rattle came from his throat.

"Go on," I said. It seemed an effort for him to work up steam, and I wondered if he resented the interruption.

"He was swinging a baseball bat. First thing he did was shove it hard in my gut. Took the wind out of me. I fell . . . backwards. Then he came in and shut the door."

The voice was a low monotone, as if he had already distanced himself from the event and was recounting it like a dream.

"He started working on me. Hit me in the chest a couple of times. Then in the face. All I remember for sure is the pain. It was like he was possessed."

His sentences came out in short bursts. Four broken ribs can do that to a man. In spite of the pathos of the scene my guilt was fading fast. In its stead was another emotion—the *thump, thump* in my chest reminding me of the need for self-preservation.

"What did he want?" I asked. "What did you tell him?"

"He asked me if I was Rocco Gambella. He had my card. Kept shoving it in my face."

The card. So that was it. I reached in the top pocket of my denim jacket, where I had stuffed Rocco's business card. It was gone. Broder must have found it when he went back in the house.

"Did you give him my card?" Rocco asked.

"I didn't give it to him, Rocco. It was in my jacket."

A little gurgle arose from Rocco's chest and erupted

from his mouth with a popping sound. It resembled a distorted chuckle.

"So that's what happened," he said. "You left your jacket for him to find."

I started to defend the accusation, then thought better of it.

"I hope . . . " Rocco shifted painfully in bed. "I hope at least you had your pants on when you ran."

"I'm sorry, Rocco."

His left eye swiveled slowly toward Miranda. "You're very pretty. That man must love you very much. He was madder than a hornet." He coughed and winced. The bandages shook violently. "He kept asking me if I knew where you were, the two of you. He thought I was hiding you in the house."

"Did you tell him where I lived?" I asked, trying to remember if I had ever given Rocco my address.

He treated me to a contorted grin, one tooth missing, the rest stained brown. "He said he'd just come from your house."

So Broder did know where I lived.

"I would have told him anything, just to get him to stop." Rocco raised his arm, stretching it beyond me, fingers grasping. Liston came silently to his side and took the arm in two enormous hands.

"Easy, Rocco," he said, tenderly stroking his swollen cheek. "Take it easy, now."

The bandages shook violently again, while Rocco's chest gurgled. "He would have killed me if Liston hadn't come in just then."

Liston nodded solemnly, fondling Rocco's shoulder. "It's over now. You get some rest, Rocco."

I was amazed at how gentle this giant of a man could be. "What happened then?" I asked. "I suppose he got away."

Liston took over the tale at that point, laying Rocco gently back on the pillow to rest. "He took a swing at me as I walked in." He shrugged. "I just brushed it away. I would have torn his arms off. I think he realized that. He left the baseball bat and ran. I couldn't chase him; I was too worried about Rocco. I called the paramedics and we brought him here. I've been here ever since."

I nodded. "I'm really sorry about all this, Liston. We had no idea how crazy this guy was. I sure hate to see Rocco like that."

"*See Rocco!*" Liston's voice broke. "At least you can see him. What about my Rocco? He might lose his fucking eye on account of you. Did you know that?"

I stepped back, alarmed. Part of me felt that perhaps Liston was right. There was an awkward silence while I searched for something to say. "The cops are looking for Broder now. They've got a sketch of him. I'm sure they'll find him before long."

Liston composed himself and sat down, rocking slowly on the bed, swaying his bulk from side to side between us and Rocco's head, as if challenging anybody to threaten his lover. "I haven't told them who it was," he said. "We gave them a description when it happened, but I didn't see the police sketch of this guy Broder until I read the paper in the hospital. They don't know he did this. I never called them back."

"You mean Rocco hasn't identified Broder as the assailant?" Miranda asked from behind me.

"No," Liston replied. "And neither did I. We refuse to talk to the police again. I don't want those bastards here. You should have seen them, with their attitude, as if people like us should expect to get beat up every once in a while. We only decided to tell you because you might be in danger. I got the paper hidden under my chair there." He pointed to the corner where he had been waiting.

So that was why Akimoro didn't know about the assault on Rocco.

"Liston," I said, "the police don't have to bother you anymore. I've told the detective in charge about the mugging, and I'll call him now to let him know it was Broder. You're sure it was him, though, aren't you, now you've seen the police sketch?"

Liston nodded, then changed his tone slightly. "I guess I should've told them, but I'm scared. I don't want that lunatic coming back to get us. You understand?"

I understood perfectly. I was curious about the picture, though. I hadn't seen the sketch yet myself. I went to the corner and reached under the chair. "Do you mind?" I asked Liston. "I'd like to see what he looks like up close."

"Help yourself."

I pulled the newspaper out and stared in disbelief at the grainy picture on the front page. The face, expressionless in black and white, was that of my old friend, the insurance investigator from New Orleans. Bob Plant was staring back at me from under the caption: HAVE YOU SEEN THIS MAN?

"EXPLAIN IT TO ME AGAIN. WHY DID
Broder call himself Bob Plant?" Miranda asked.

We were down in the reception lobby of the
Little Sisters Hospital, in a small, wooden telephone
booth, having left Rocco upstairs in Liston's safekeeping.

"Because he didn't want to give me his real name."

"I know that. But why was he pretending to be an
insurance investigator?"

"Because he's a dick."

She got it wrong. "You mean a detective?"

"No. I mean a prick. He was trying to get me involved for some reason. He wanted me to meet with you
this weekend." I explained about the visit to my office and
Broder's promise of a reward if I was to help him in his so-
called investigation.

Miranda's lower jaw dropped, and her eyes went
dark with fire. "So that's why you asked me out," she said
softly. "This is all about money, isn't it? You thought you
were in for a reward?"

I was mortified. "No, Miranda. That's not it at all.
I was curious, but if you remember, I asked you out last Saturday, before I ever met Broder."

She didn't seem entirely convinced. This was not,
however, the moment for justifications. Another fear was
tearing at my rib cage, fast building up into a blinding rage.
Broder had visited me in my office, and before that he had

been in the park when I went riding with Emma. It had to have been him, in the blue Ford Taurus, who had followed Jillian and me last Saturday. How long had this psychopath been on my tail? If Broder knew where I worked, and where I lived, he must know where Rafaella lived, too.

My fingers flew across the numbers as I punched them in a panic. It took forever for the tone. Furiously, I entered my billing code.

"Your call cannot go through as dialed."

Damn! If that bastard harmed one hair on my family, I would kill him myself. I forced my fingers to slow down and redialed. This time I connected. Rafaella picked up on the second ring.

"Rafe, are you all right?" I hadn't called her that in years.

"Gareth? Yes, I'm all right. What's the matter with you?"

"No time to explain. Jillian and Emma . . . they with you?"

"I already told you. You can't have them this weekend."

I kicked the side of the phone booth. "No, Rafe. I'm not talking about that. Has anybody come by—a stranger, late thirties, white male?"

"Why? What's going on?"

"Listen to me. You could be in danger, and the kids, too. Have you seen the paper today?"

"Yes."

"You've seen the picture on the front page? The guy who's wanted for Jack's murder?"

"I saw the picture. But it's not going to make me change my mind, Gareth."

She could be so frustrating. "Rafaella, he's after me, and he may know where you live. I want you to take the kids and go somewhere. Can you stay with Peter and Cindy tonight?"

"Gareth, what have you been up to? Cindy was

right; you're in some kind of trouble. Now I'm glad I listened to Dulles."

She had more to say. I listened to it for a minute, holding the receiver away from my ear and making a face at Miranda next to me. Useless to interrupt Rafaella when she was this way. It's a hard life, being married to a surgeon, and she had a long list of gripes that still needed venting.

When she was through with her tirade she said, "Gareth, there was a strange van parked up by the driveway."

"A van? What kind?"

"A dirty old white van. I thought it was funny. Nobody got out."

"Is it still there?"

"No. It stayed a half hour and then drove off."

"What time was that?"

"A little after midday."

"Shit! On second thought, don't leave the house. Are the kids inside?"

There was silence. I could hear her breathing heavily.

"Rafaella! Where are the kids? Will you answer me?"

"Jillian's watching television."

"And Emma? Where's Emma? Rafaella, will you answer me, goddamn it?"

"Emma went to the park on her bicycle."

"No!" I beat the side of the phone booth with my hand.

"She's done it a hundred times before, Gareth. She's always been fine. She calls me collect if she's going to be late."

"Did she call you?"

"Yes."

"When?"

"Half an hour ago. She said she was going to her friend Jessica's house. Gareth, what's wrong?"

"Nothing." I felt a flush of relief. "I'm just worried about you, that's all." I tried to collect myself. "Rafaella, why don't you call Emma's friend Jessica and see if they're all right. Meanwhile, I want you and Jillian to stay inside. Lock all the windows and doors. I'll phone the police and ask them to check on you. Don't let anybody in unless you're sure he's a police officer. You don't have a weapon, do you?"

"A weapon! What are you talking about? Gareth, you're scaring me."

I was scaring myself. I wished I had given her a gun, something, anything to defend herself with, even a baseball bat. Maybe I should have asked her to boil some water.

"I'm sure everything will be fine," I said. "I'll get the police to help. You stay in the house and don't move, you hear?"

"You'd better get over here, Gareth. If you've got us into any kind of trouble, I'll murder you myself."

I hung up, wondering how Broder would fare if he meddled with her while she was good and truly mad. It might have made an interesting match.

"He's been to your house," Miranda guessed. "Is anybody hurt?"

"No. Everybody's fine, but Emma's not home. She went to the park on her bike."

"Oh, Lord. I hope she's all right."

I dialed Akimoro in Beverly Hills and explained the situation, telling him how Rocco had been visited by Broder and that I was now afraid for my own family and wanted them protected.

"My wife said there was a strange white van parked in front of her house this morning," I told him. "I don't like the sound of it, Akimoro."

"I don't see why your family would be in danger, unless there's something you're not telling me about your involvement in this."

"Look, I've told you everything I know, but there's a lot I don't understand. All I know is this guy Broder's a maniac. You should see what he did to Rocco Gambella. And he's been following me all week. I didn't realize it until I saw the sketch in the paper this morning."

"I'll send somebody over. Meanwhile, tell your wife to lock herself in the house."

"I did."

"Good. Now, what about you? Are you still at the hospital? I've sent an officer out to meet you. Hilton Collins. He's a good man."

"How soon before he gets here?" I looked at my watch.

"Depends on traffic. He's only been gone fifteen minutes."

"Could take him another hour. I don't know, Akimoro, I feel like a high-tension wire."

"You'd better try and calm down. Your imagination is getting away with you."

"It is. I need a tranquilizer. I wish there was something I could do."

I looked around the empty lobby, trying to think if any white vans had trailed me down the freeway. The elderly lady in the red-and-white-striped apron was still sitting at the reception desk, engrossed in her paperback. Through the glass doors I could see the hospital parking lot, and the street beyond.

"I don't think I could hang around here for an hour," I said into the receiver. "There's a diner across the street, the Cluckburger. We'll wait in there. I expect Miranda's hungry, and I can use a drink. Will you radio Collins and let him know?"

"Cluckburger. I'll let him know, but you be careful."

I grabbed Miranda by the hand and led her over to the reception desk.

"I'm Dr. Lloyd," I said to the elderly lady.

"Yes, Doctor." She showed the automatic deference of most hospital volunteers to the title.

"If a police officer named Collins comes in here looking for me, will you tell him I'm in the diner across the street? Only if he's a police officer, mind you. Do not tell anybody else who asks. Can you do that, please?"

She nodded, eyes bright with awe. I knew she would do the right thing by me. The novel she was reading was an Elmore Leonard.

WE DROVE FROM THE HOSPITAL PARKING lot to the diner across the street. A short distance, it's true, but I took advantage by looking in the mirror to see if a white van was following. Sitting outside the Cluckburger with the engine running for a minute, I tried to clear my thoughts. All I could do was hope Emma was safe.

"Strange name for a restaurant," Miranda said.

"Sounds like one of those fad places. Chicken burgers instead of beef. Low cholesterol. The latest thing in dining."

"Spare me."

I agreed with the sentiment, but I had already told Akimoro we'd be there, and I didn't feel like driving back across the street and amending my instructions to the lady volunteer.

"Let's do it," I said. "Aren't you hungry?"

"Starved."

I watched her get out of the car. Before joining her, I reached over to the glove compartment for the *Antiques* magazine that I had stashed there Monday when I left the office.

"What's that for?" she asked.

"Just following up a hunch." I locked the car door and we went inside.

Cluckburger's interior decoration was a little bizarre, especially for Riverside. Geometric shapes abounded: Formica-covered tables and vinyl chairs in sub-dued pastel colors, accented by chrome. The fifties decor would have been quite chic, had it not clashed with the scattered images of poultry in assorted media. Posters and paintings of chickens from several different schools of art were displayed on every available surface. Classic Flemish and Dutch scenes of farmyard bliss hung serenely against one wall, while naïf images competed with the surreal on another, and Abstract Impressionist with neon art on a third. Everything had a chicken on it.

We were led to a corner booth and seated. The glossy illustrated menu proved my surmise to be correct. Every item was a sandwich based on a chicken patty. Even our waitress, Suzy, sported a T-shirt with a rooster embla-zoned over her 44 double-D's.

She was poised with pad and pencil. "Something to drink first?"

"Anything with a head on it."

She looked at me suspiciously. "What?"

"What kind of beer do you serve?"

Suspicion turned to disdain. "We don't serve liquid poisons here."

Only solid ones, I thought. "I'll have a coffee."

Miranda ordered iced tea. "We haven't been here before, Suzy," she remarked. "What do you recommend?"

Suzy looked as though she would remember very well if we had been there before. "The Andalusian's kind of popular. That's with avocado, bacon bits, and mayonnaise. Or the Philly. That's with cream cheese."

Neither of them sounded very low cholesterol to me. I settled on an apple pie à la mode, while Miranda chose an Oriental chicken salad.

Suzy departed for the kitchen. I was still worried about Emma and tried to diffuse the tension. "That's the first time I've been called a liquid poison," I quipped.

She didn't get it. Rafaella would have appreciated it, even without translation.

"You going to read?" Miranda indicated the magazine I was holding.

I opened it. "When Broder pretended to be Plant, he gave me a list. They were supposed to be items stolen from an auction house in New Orleans. I recognized the name of the auction house; I think I've seen it in this magazine." I scanned the index of advertisers. "Here it is. James McKilroy and Company, New Orleans: page ninety-seven."

It was in the section pertaining to upcoming auctions, a full page describing several estates with selected photographs of Georgian furniture. There was a listing of phone numbers and the auction date.

"Hey, we're in luck. It's today." Seeing my birthdate in print still brought out the child in me, as if everything that happened on that day carried the magic promise of a happy event. "They're having an auction today at one." I glanced at my watch. "Three o'clock. They're two hours ahead, but they might still be there. I think I'll try it."

"Go ahead," Miranda said with a wry smile. "Maybe they'll give you his address."

I left her playing with her straw while I found the phone booth. It was back near the entrance next to the rest rooms.

"James McKilroy," said a bright young female voice at the other end of the phone.

I decided on a hard-line approach. "This is Detective Lloyd with the LAPD. Can you give me the person in charge of your porcelain department?"

"That would be Hans Leiter. He's tied up at the moment."

"This is a police matter, miss. It's urgent."

"Well, sir, he's on the floor taking phone bids. May I ask what this is about?"

"It's about the theft of some of your merchandise. It can't wait."

"I could get someone to relieve him. Please hold."

I held and, while I waited, grabbed a paper napkin with a red and brown cockerel printed on the corner and began to scribble down all the stolen items I had memorized from Broder's list. I tried to make it as extensive as I could.

"Leiter here," someone said in a Teutonic accent approaching soprano. "Can I help you?"

"Mr. Leiter, I have a suspect here with some items we've traced to your establishment. I would like to know when they were stolen and if you know anything more about the circumstances." I read from the list, trying hard to sound as businesslike as I could. His silence gave me the impression he wasn't buying it.

"Mr. Leiter, are you still there?"

"How did you trace them? We have no such items stolen."

"Are you sure?"

"Detective, we are a reputable auction house. We are quite sure when it comes to theft."

"I see."

"As a matter of fact, those sound like some of the lots stolen from the Houston Galleries. They had a problem with that last year. Why don't you ask Jeffrey Arnold? He's the owner. He's right here attending our auction today. I'll get him for you."

"Thank you, Mr. Leiter, much obliged."

I was happy to wait. Reading that list was a good idea, after all.

"Yes, sir. Jeffrey Arnold," came a deeper voice with a cozy drawl.

I retold my story and read the list again, playing the part of an overworked burglary investigator, deliberately mispronouncing several names of German porcelain companies for emphasis.

"Yes," he said. "We had some losses at the end of last year, the November and December sales. We reported it to the Houston police. They were given the itemized list.

Sounds like you've found some of them. May I ask the prisoner's name?"

"It's a . . . Bob Plant."

"Well, it's not the person we figured. But the items you mentioned match our missing lots."

"You suspected someone else?"

"Yes. We hired a private investigator to find the goods. He pretty much had the thing solved. He thought it was James Page, one of our drivers. I was certain he was right. Mr. Page was with us only a few days and we had to let him go. A very strange man, indeed. The thefts started a few weeks after we fired him."

I was disappointed. "Are you sure? Maybe I could talk to this investigator. Can you give me his name?"

"I'm afraid he's dead. He was shot to death in a hotel room downtown. He was actually pretty close to nailing Page when it happened. Awful thing. In a way I felt responsible. We gave the details to the police, but then Page disappeared and they didn't seem too interested in following up, based on what little we had."

The skin on the back of my neck began to crawl. "Can you describe Page?" I asked.

"Late thirties, skinny, straight blond hair. No real distinguishing features, unless you want to mention acne. He was some sort of right-wing fanatic. He hadn't the slightest appreciation for art or antiques. He had no regard for our business, and even less for our customers."

I sighed. Broder was turning out to have more names than a Spanish archduke.

"Thank you, Mr. Arnold, you've been very helpful. Where can I call you if I need more information?"

He gave me the number of his gallery in Houston. "Excuse me, sir," he said, "when can we expect those items you've recovered? I'm anxious to get them back, you know."

I'll bet you are, I thought. "We'll have to hold them for evidence," I said stiffly. "I'll be in touch with the Houston police when we're done. Of course, we'll also have to report this to your insurance company, in case they've already reimbursed you."

"Oh, yes. Absolutely." He sounded indignant.

"There is one more thing," I said. "When are you returning to Houston?"

"Tonight. I'm flying back as soon as this auction's over."

"Then I would appreciate very much if you could go straight to your office and fax me all of Mr. Page's employment records." I gave him my home fax number.

I hung up, satisfied that my jab about his insurance reimbursement had hit home, and that he would probably do as I asked. I was about to call Rafaella back and see if she'd heard from Emma when I looked out the window and was horrified to see a dirty white van pull into the restaurant parking lot.

I had gory visions of the old lady volunteer at the hospital reception desk lying supine in a pool of blood, while Broder extracted our location from her with sadistic malice. I rushed to the table and found Miranda crunching on a mouthful of lettuce.

"Quick! I think he's here."

"Who?"

"Broder. I saw a white van come in the lot."

"A white van? What happened to the blue Ford?"

"He switched. Rafaella told me. Look, there's no time to discuss it. Get back there in the ladies' room, quick."

We scurried to the rest rooms, she to the ladies' and I to the men's, trying desperately to hold back from running in order not to draw too much attention to ourselves. I bolted my door, trusting Miranda would do the same on her side.

After several minutes I realized we couldn't stay that way forever. Somebody would presently come knocking on the door, even if it was only Suzy the waitress, looking to see why we hadn't touched our food, or if we intended to pay for it. And Broder, if he was out there searching for us, would soon eliminate all the other hiding places. The flimsy plywood door was not an effective barrier against a well-planted foot, or a full metal jacket. I wondered what a silvertip felt like as it tore through sinew and crashed against bone. Hopefully, death would be instantaneous. I looked around for a weapon of my own. Luckily there was one, right next to the toilet bowl.

Clutching the plunger tightly in my right hand, I slid the bolt back and pulled the door open a crack. I peeped through, half expecting a bullet between the eyes. I could see most of the main room from my vantage point, but not the exit. None of the customers seemed to register anything unusual. I figured the coast was clear.

With a bold sweep, I opened the door and stepped out. Five quick strides and I was by the telephone. I could now see through the door out to the parking lot. The white van was nowhere in sight. I thought of dialing Emergency, then decided against it. If Broder came in while I was on the phone, they might as well put me in one of their cluckburgers. I started for the swinging doors through to the kitchen.

Suzy caught sight of me and took a step in my direction, then saw the plunger and changed her mind. Maybe she would call 911, I hoped. I stepped through the kitchen door, fully prepared to duck.

The atmosphere inside was like a sweatshop. Fluorescent light filtered through air thick with grease and hung with wisps of steam. Pots and pans were scattered around, and blobs of red and brown sauce littered the countertops as though a giant tomato had exploded in there. Every working surface was covered with a thin film, as if all the cholesterol extracted from the food before it passed through the swinging doors was released into the kitchen, to settle where it may.

There was no sign of Broder, but two Hispanic men

313

in stained white uniforms melted into the shadows when they saw me, obviously reluctant to confront anyone crazy enough to be wielding an upraised toilet plunger. I strode through to the back door and walked out to the bright sunlight. There was no crash of gunfire, no searing pain. I was alone.

Across a narrow strip of asphalt I faced the property boundary, an eight-foot block wall with blue sky above it. I measured the distance. There were no footholds on the wall, but I figured with the right velocity I could conquer it, pulling with my arms and vaulting my feet horizontally over the side. I might escape. Broder would be hard-pressed to follow suit with a gun in his hands.

It wasn't the thought of leaving Miranda behind that made me change my mind. It was the unknown. What if I landed on all fours on a pile of junked cars or a sea of broken glass? Or worse? A kennel of pit bulls?

I sidled along the wall to the cover of the Dumpster and looked beyond. There was the white van, pulled head in, facing the restaurant. I peered through the driver's window. It seemed empty. Slowly, I worked my way along the wall until I was within a few feet of the front bumper. Still no sign of life inside. My heart was thumping wildly as I braced for flight. I heard the sound of footsteps coming round the corner.

A young man in jeans, boots, and a cowboy hat strode into view. He was carrying a brown paper bag, holding it carefully in both hands, as if it contained some species of chicken soufflé that would collapse at the slightest tremor. He walked toward the white van, spotted me, then made a detour round the back, keeping his eyes fixed on me at all times. He came up the driver's side still staring at me, and balanced the bag precariously in one hand while he fished for his keys. He gave me a dubious smile and said, "Howdy."

Quickly, he opened the door. He threw the bag in, jumped in after it, and slammed the door shut, locking it.

The engine fired up and he gunned it. He jolted into re-verse in a screech of tires. I stood transfixed, upraised hand still clenching the plunger, and watched the van out to the street.

"Dr. Lloyd?"

"Huh!" My hand jerked violently, ready to strike.

"Easy now," said a voice to my left.

I turned to face a young black man in uniform, pleasant-faced and slightly heavy in the waist. He wore a startled expression.

"You want to put that plunger down, Dr. Lloyd? I'm Hilton Collins, with the Beverly Hills PD. Detective Akimoro sent me." He waited to be sure I understood.

"Your girlfriend told me you'd be out here," he said, pointing to the window and then smiling broadly at me, as if he wasn't yet sure what language I spoke.

I nodded. "It's good to see you, Hilton."

His face showed relief. "You had me fooled for a minute, Doc."

He wiped his brow and thrust out his right arm. I transferred the plunger to my left and shook his out-stretched hand.

"Akimoro says you'd better call home right away," he said, wiping his hand on his shirt front. "Your daughter seems to be missing."

IT WASN'T THE SMARTEST IDEA, LETTING ME drive alone, but I had insisted on it, even though Officer Collins offered to escort me. I knew that, as fast as he might be willing to drive, I would have ridden impatiently on his bumper all the way home. Not that I was looking to break the sound barrier, but in my state of mind I needed to make my own pace, and it would have been too distracting to keep adjusting to his speed. I suggested that he take Miranda to her house and pick up her car, then over to headquarters to answer Akimoro's questions. They could join me in Greenfield later.

Miranda looked at me with anguish. Was she feeling for me, and for Emma? Or for herself, upset that I was throwing her to the police?

"You'll be all right," I said, kissing her cheek. She hugged me close.

Hilton Collins leaned against the Alfa and shook my hand. "Take care, Doc."

"I'll be fine. The Greenfield police will be there to look after me until you get back."

"That's not what I mean. Drive safe."

"I promise I will."

I didn't, of course. I raced east on the freeway in a blind trance. I could have been followed by a white van, a dozen highway patrol cars, or even a helicopter, and I wouldn't have stopped or deviated for any one of them. I wouldn't have seen them in my rage. I don't remember seeing anything. I did get on the phone to Rafaella. She was falling to pieces.

"Gareth, they found Emma's bike near the park in the alley next to Mrs. Watson's house and her change purse was still in the carrier and I know she would never leave that and she doesn't have any friends in the alley and I've called all her schoolmates and nobody's seen her and I don't know what's going to happen—"

"Slow down, Rafaella."

"Oh, Gareth, I'm so worried."

"What are the police doing?"

"They've looked all over and they're here now getting some of her clothing and they're going to get the K-nine unit and put the dogs out but I don't know how that's going to help if she's in somebody's van . . ." She broke out sobbing.

When I couldn't stand to listen to any more I begged off and told her I'd be there soon. My guts were churning. In silence, I drove alone with my thoughts, sucked into a vortex of fear. If Rafaella had left the kids with me—if only Dulles Lindstrom hadn't interfered—Emma would be safe right now. I searched my memory for the times I'd talked to Emma about child molesters and kidnappers.

*"Don't talk to strangers. Don't accept rides or gifts from anybody without our permission, even if you know them from school."*

Why hadn't I discussed it more thoroughly? Why hadn't I sat down and rehearsed it with her, played out the scene so she'd know what to do? I had avoided the details, never wanting to face the situation. But she would need those details now.

*"Scream! Bite! Kick him in the balls."*

*Oh, God! Be brave, Emma. We're coming to get you.*

I screeched to a stop in Rafaella's driveway, next to a Greenfield police car with K-9 UNIT on the doors. I ran up to the house. The door was open and the front room was busy with people, an atmosphere charged with tension. Rafaella rushed up from the sofa to hug me. It felt good. I held on a minute longer than usual.

"Oh, Gareth," she said.

There were two uniformed police officers around the coffee table, waiting to take a statement. A neighbor had come by to help and she strolled in from the kitchen carrying a tray with coffee and cookies. Sitting next to the fireplace, in my favorite old armchair, was Cindy Heering, watching me with eyes narrowed. She didn't get up. I had the impression she was accusing me of staging the whole affair.

I listened with an aching heart as Rafaella gave the police a rundown of Emma's daily habits and a list of her friends. They asked me if I had been contacted. I said not yet. They asked me if I had any ideas. I said I knew exactly who it was. They jumped on me for a statement and I told them about Broder and the Beverly Hills police investigation.

Cindy came over to hug Rafaella and looked at me with lightning bolts in her eyes. Then she turned on the police officers.

"Shouldn't you be bugging the phone lines here? And at his house, too?" She jabbed her thumb in my direction. They took a step backward.

"What about TV?" she pursued. "Shouldn't Dr. and Mrs. Lloyd go on the news tonight and make a plea to the public? Ask for help? Somebody must have seen something."

I warmed to her, although I didn't relish the thought of showing my grief in public. They said they'd talk to their sergeant about a phone tap. I wondered if Cindy had ever considered entering law school.

The officers departed, telling us they would call if there were any developments. They left us with a guard at the door and nothing to do but wait. The neighbor excused herself with apology. The atmosphere in the room slowly began to congeal as four of us gathered gloomily around the coffee table.

Rafaella and Jillian sat on the couch, silent and withdrawn. I was on the ottoman next to the sideboard, awkward and out of place, uneasy at our being drawn together this way after two years apart. Cindy was in my old armchair, grating on my bruised nerves. We were each in our own little orbits, tied only by the centripetal force of our common anguish. I felt paralyzed with inertia. I desperately wanted to do something, if I only knew what.

The shrill ring of the telephone startled us. It was Dulles, asking if we'd heard anything. He promised to come right over.

"What does he have to come here for?" I snapped.

"He's her lawyer," Cindy explained. "He has a right to be here."

"Oh, yes? What's he going to do? Negotiate with Broder? I bet he sends me a statement for the visit. Probably be higher than the ransom note."

"Don't you have something to do?" Cindy asked.

"What!"

"Cindy!" Rafaella chided.

"No, really." Cindy turned to Rafaella. "Shouldn't he be at home or something, sitting by the phone? He's the one they're after." She turned back to me. "They're going to call *you* when they want to talk."

"My phone's not listed. If they get it from Emma, she'll give them this number."

I knew Cindy was right. I should be doing something.

All my life I had shown a tendency to pick up and run away in the face of adversity. But over the past few days I had surprised myself by taking the initiative. Jillian and Emma were going to grow up here in Greenfield, and I was going to make sure they did. No one was going to interrupt that plan by throwing me in jail, or shooting me, or kidnapping an innocent child. I was going to give my kids something my father hadn't given me—a sense of continuity, a sense of place. And the only way to do that was to get off my behind and kick some ass.

Except that Broder's ass was nowhere in sight. Still, if I was going to wait around, I could do more good by waiting at home. An unlisted number couldn't be much of an obstacle to a resourceful animal like Broder. Cindy was right. If he did want to make an overture, it would only be to me.

I embraced Rafaella and Jillian in turn and glared at Cindy on my way out. With her as a friend, Rafaella didn't need Dulles Lindstrom.

LATE SUNDAY EVENING, MIRANDA, HILTON Collins, and I were in my kitchen. I paced the floor nervously, Miranda played with her pasta and salad, while Hilton dished up seconds for himself. I looked at my watch for the umpteenth time.

It was only eight-thirty. We had dissected every angle on the case, trying to figure where Broder could be, and if he would call. I had given Hilton the number to the Rosemead Lodge—the one Broder had left in my office. There was no news yet. I began to think that Cindy had struck on a great idea about getting on the local TV stations.

I watched Hilton slurp the last strand of pasta off his fork before he attacked the leftover sauce with a piece of bread. I was glad Akimoro had sent him, and not one of his other muscle-bound henchmen from headquarters. Not that Hilton was particularly awe inspiring, or even physically threatening. If I had been asked to conjure up a bodyguard, I would hardly have imagined a round-faced African-American male, soft at the waist and heavy in the neck, with a prematurely balding dome some two inches below my eye level. He had the build of a Samoan, but the sparkling white glint from his perpetual smile eradicated all hint of threat.

Despite his proportions, Hilton measured up just fine in my book. He was easy on the nerves, and if I had to have a representative of the police spend the night in my house while I was distraught and on edge, it was far smoother putting up with him than some of the others I had encountered. His attentiveness and his manner gave me the impression that in this hour of need his loyalties were with me. This, too, was reassuring. Since coming home that evening, I had tried to work out every possible outcome to the kidnapping. Rightly or wrongly, I imagined that sometime, in the course of events, the interests of the police and those of the family might be at odds. If that were true, it was comforting to have Hilton at least pretending to be on my side. Besides, when it came to physical presence, what he lacked in height he made up for in spirit. He seemed capable enough, and he certainly wasn't timid.

"We ain't gonna take no bullshit from the bad guys tonight, are we, Doc?" he asked as he went from room to room, checking doors and windows with a professional air.

"No, we aren't."

"That's right. Let somebody try to bust in here. Li'l Martha and me'll blow the bejesus out of him." He patted his sidearm lovingly. "Tell me about the alarm system."

I explained the workings to him.

"Right. My guess is you and the missus'll be sleeping upstairs."

Miranda shot me a glance.

"I don't think I'll be doing much sleeping," I said.

"You do as you must, Doc. But I'll be staying awake for both of us. Think I'll park myself up there." He indicated the landing at the top of the stairs. "Nice view of anybody busting in from there. You got a chair or something I can use?"

"There's an armchair in the spare bedroom. It's old but it's comfortable. You think he's actually going to bust in here?"

He stuck his thumbs into his belt and looked at me. "I doubt it, Doc. But since I'm here for your protection, I might as well do my job."

The arrangements were to his satisfaction. I offered to brew him a pot of coffee for his sojourn.

"Good thinking, Doc. I'm going to need it."

We returned to the kitchen. I ground some beans, plugged in the percolator, and soon the vapors were filling the small room.

My nerves were winding tighter by the minute. I kept thinking about Emma. Was she hurt? Was she in pain? Was she dead? No! Not that. Broder had nothing to gain by killing her. Why hadn't he called?

I thought I saw a shadow cross the kitchen window. I jumped, not knowing whether to drop to the floor or run out.

"What's the matter, Doc?" Hilton asked. "Getting a little jittery, are we?"

"I saw something out there."

"Where?" The gun was in his hand in an instant. I pointed to the windowpane. "Get down," he said.

He went out to investigate. I peeked through the window to watch him. He disappeared around the front of the house for a while, then he was back, wiping his boots on the kitchen mat.

"There's no one out there. But we'll be seeing a lot more shadows before tomorrow. We're in luck, though. There's a full moon and a clear sky. We'll see him before he sees us." He sat down at the table. "That's when the kooks come out, isn't it, Doc? Full moon."

"Ask anyone who works in an emergency room and they'll bear you out."

"Ask a cop and he'll tell you the same thing," Hilton said.

There was a sudden whirring and clicking from the den, as if by collectively dwelling on the pull of the moon, we had summoned a poltergeist from another world. Miranda jumped, and Hilton's gun appeared in his hand again.

"It's my fax machine," I said, running in to take a

look at what had come through. My heart began to flip-flop as I approached the curled paper lying on the desktop. Could it be a ransom demand from Broder? I was sure Emma didn't know my fax number.

There were four pages. The cover sheet explained that it was a transmission from Jeffrey Arnold at the Houston Galleries. The second and third pages were copies of an employment application form, neatly filled in by hand with a small, slanting script. The name, Jim Page. The address, an apartment somewhere in Houston. The date of birth was 3/4/55. Education was listed as Sequoia High School, graduation date 1973. "Military Service" was checked yes, with Fort Dix, New Jersey, scribbled in. The service branch was not entered; dates were listed only as "1974." The section for "Special Education and Training" was one big blank. Under "Special Interests" the first entry was heavily scratched out, then he had written "hunting" and "history."

I scanned the next page for his employment record. There were only two entries. A checker at a Wal-Mart for three years from 1987 to 1989; reason for leaving—"store closed." And a Houston cab company from 1990 to 1993; reason for leaving—"didn't like it." There were three names listed under "References." One of them, I noticed, was "Major Frank Musgrave," whose address was given as the West Houston Boys Club. The other two seemed like acquaintances. All together, it was not an inspiring submission, but there appeared to be nothing sinister in it, either, unless you wondered about all the items left blank.

The last page was a work sheet with the Houston Galleries address. It contained notes Mr. Arnold might have taken at the employment interview, if there had been such a thing. "Seems nervous but polite" and "Appearance neat, clothing clean and conservative" was followed by "Salary—asking $9, start at $7 if refs. check out." Then, in another pen, "Major Musgrave remembers—quiet most of the time, needs encouragement, loner," and "Starts Monday 8/4." The final entry was "Dismissed 8/20—Unable to tolerate customers, disruptive, prejudiced."

Cover your ass, I thought. Everybody was doing it.

I told Hilton what the document represented, and summed up with everything I knew about Neifosh and Epstein.

"The chief needs to have a look at that," Hilton said. "Can we fax it to him from here?"

I took care of it, while Hilton called Akimoro on the second line to explain our newest discovery and to let him know the document was on its way.

"I wonder what that military service bit means," I asked Miranda.

"Probably got a dishonorable discharge."

"Did he ever talk about it?"

"Not to me, he didn't."

"What about 'prejudiced'?"

"He hated blacks, hated immigrants, hated Jews, you name it. Hated anybody that wasn't white. They all did."

"All?"

"Broder. George. Everybody up at the ranch house. That's why I left."

"I suppose it could be rather embarrassing to an auction house if your employees are like that," I said.

"It's embarrassing anywhere," she replied simply.

Hilton and I sat down with our coffees, trying to analyze the application form for something we might have missed. Miranda decided to do some laundry.

"I've been in these jeans for two days now and they're sticking to me. You got anything you want to throw in with the load?"

I found a set of operating room greens for her to wear and gave her some of my clothes to wash with her own.

"Wait a minute," I said, "you probably shouldn't do that one. The police might consider it evidence." I extracted George's red-and-black-check jacket from her pile of washing. "We found this in the pickup, remember?"

She nodded. "It's filthy, though. He couldn't have washed it for months."

"Even so. It was taken from a crime scene and they might want to claim it."

She shrugged. "If you think so. I won't be wearing it again." She started to throw it to one side and stopped. "There's something in the pocket here." She removed a small brown manila envelope, about four inches square.

I studied it. There were only two words written on the side: "George Kershen." Inside was a computer disk and a small handwritten note: "George, Congratulations on your election. These records are yours for safekeeping. Guard them with your life, Ed."

"I guess he took his responsibility seriously," I said.

WE WERE HUDDLED AROUND MY COM-
puter, I in the desk chair, Miranda seated on a stool
to my right, and Hilton breathing over our necks. I
booted up and inserted the disk we had just found.
The directory listed six files of varying length. I tried
the first one.

The screen filled with a database of names and addresses. It looked like a mailing list of sorts, with a few
columns of additional information, which included "Member since," "Previous activity," "Position," and "Status." It
seemed innocuous enough, but as I scrolled through to the
second page, I noticed some strange roles listed in the "Position" column.

"Look at this. 'Nighthawk.' There's a 'Cyclops.'
Here's another one. 'Kleagle.' What the heck is this?"

"Kluckers," said Hilton.

"Who?"

"A Klavern. A Klan cell—the Ku Klux Klan. Believe me, I know."

"I thought they were ancient history."

He shook his head. "They're everywhere, very
much alive. The numbers went down a lot, and many of the
Klaverns branched off and went underground, but they
still surface every now and then. Skinheads, Aryan Nation,
the Brotherhood; it's all the same."

"So George was a member of the Klan." I looked at
Miranda.

"White Aryan Resistance," she said.

"Same thing," Hilton added.

I hit the "Page Down" button again. The addresses issued from all over the state, with a predominance in Los Angeles, Riverside, and Kern Counties. We came across a "Grand Goblin," an "Imperial Kleagle," and a "Grand Wizard."

"Too many fairy tales," I said.

"This is no fairy tale," Hilton replied. "We got ourselves a master list of Klan activity in Southern California. The antiterrorist squad would love to get their hands on this."

"You think this is what Broder was looking for?" Miranda asked.

"I bet you're right," Hilton said. "He must have known George had it with him when he died."

"This is what's going to get Emma back," I said.

They both turned to look at me.

"Simple. He knows we have it. He wants to trade."

"So why hasn't he called?" Miranda asked.

"He's waiting. Maybe he feels I'm too well protected."

"Darn right," Hilton said.

"Maybe he'd make a move if I was alone."

"You want to be the bait?" Hilton asked.

"I want Emma back. Let's see if he's in here," I said, turning back to the computer.

We scrolled through the list again. "Nothing under Broder. Nothing under Page or Plant, either. Maybe he has another alias."

"Could be," Hilton said. "Let's check out the other files."

I found the directory and keyed in the rest, one by one. There was a record of rules and regulations, a procedure manual, an oath of inauguration, and a list marked "Activities." This last category turned out to be particularly distressing. There were a number of places and dates:

a synagogue in San Francisco, 1988, followed by the word "Bomb"; a pawnshop in Portland, 1989—"Fire"; the call letters to a television station in Salem, 1990—"Bomb"; a Roman Catholic church in Sacramento, 1987—"Bomb"; a foreign-sounding name, Portland, 1988. I remembered the incident, an African student who was dragged out of his car and beaten to death because he was in the wrong place.

I wondered about Hilton and the reason he knew so much about the Klan. I thought of Lavonne Singleterry and the gash on her chin when she was in fourth grade. I thought of the three classmates who had disfigured her. What were they doing now?

"A lot of people would like to see this list," I said. "Maybe close the files on some unsolved crimes. Do you think they could get indictments on the strength of this evidence?"

"Probably not," Hilton replied. "But I'm sure it will help. Looks like we got a real windfall. I'd better call the chief and let him know what we found."

"Look, there's more," Miranda said, taking over the keyboard.

She scrolled through the activities for 1991 and 1992. One grouping in particular stood out among the others: three addresses in Los Angeles—Crenshaw Boulevard, Vermont Avenue, and Ninth Street. One was dated 4-30-92 and the other two 5-1-92. The names were listed only as "black male."

"Shit!" Hilton said. "The L.A. riots. Over forty people killed, most of them still unsolved. Looks like some Kluckers came down to join the party."

"Why wouldn't they record all forty?" Miranda asked.

"They would only list the hits they were responsible for," he replied. "I guess they must have kept a low profile. Too many brothers running around with guns, if you ask me. Too dangerous for them to make a big show."

Miranda punched the keys and the last file appeared, this one titled "Candidates for membership." It was a short list, and Thomas Broder was the first name on it.

"Got him," I said, bringing my fist down on the desktop. The address listed was the one we knew, the Rosemead Lodge in Arcadia. There was a previous address, which matched the one on his work application. "There! Broder and Page were definitely one and the same."

"Looks like he came to California and tried to join the Klan," Miranda said. "That's how he must have met up with George. George was a member from way back. But then, why would Broder want to kill him?"

"Look at this," Hilton added. " 'Previous activity: Neifosh, Houston, Texas; Epstein, Huntsville, Texas—To be verified.' Our man Broder was one little killing machine."

"Do they all have to murder somebody before they can join?" Miranda asked.

"No," Hilton replied. "They wouldn't have that many members if that were true. Most Klansmen don't have the gumption to take on somebody one to one; that's why they join the group and hide behind those sheets. If they wanted to verify Broder, looks to me like they just didn't trust him. My guess is he's been shooting off his mouth about what he's done and they want to find out is he a liar. You got to realize there's all kinds of people trying to infiltrate a Klavern—FBI, newspaper reporters, book writers, you name it."

"You think they're investigating him?" I asked.

"That's right. Say Broder comes down and starts talking big about who he killed back in Texas. Now that's a long ways away. Who knows if it's true? Could be he's FBI. Could be he's just blowing wind. So what do they do? They check up on him. Put him on hold until they're sure. May take a while, but it's worth it to them."

He looked knowingly at us and nodded his head. "That's the way I see it," he said.

"You think Broder might have been acting on his own back in Texas?"

"Maybe he was part of a Klavern there, and maybe he wasn't. If he was, and doing well, why would he want to leave? Maybe he got kicked out for taking his own initiative. Kluckers put a lot of weight on playing the game; that's how you work your way up in a Klavern. There's a lot of politics, believe me. In spite of what you see on those lists, most times there's more talk than action. There's a bunch of rival factions and sometimes they don't get along. It's a national organization with no master plan."

I was impressed. "How do you know so much about the Klan, Hilton?"

"Yeah, Hilton," Miranda teased. "Have you been working undercover?"

He laughed. "I got a few white sheets at home. My wife thinks I do my best work under those covers." The smile faded. "I grew up in Alabama. Plantersville, not far from Selma. We got a Huntsville down there, too, in the north. We had a few Kluckers in my hometown. Everybody knew who they were, but they weren't so active as nowadays. Mostly, they just sat around, drank beer, and complained a lot."

"Sounds no different from some people I know," Miranda said.

But it didn't sound like Broder to me. He had gone through a lot of trouble to set me up. If only he'd just sit around, drink beer, and complain a lot.

I thought about his victims: Neifosh, Epstein, and Ehrenberger. And his other potential victim: me. It didn't fit. What was the connection with the stolen paintings? I didn't collect paintings and, according to his daughter, neither did Neifosh.

I turned to Miranda. "You ever hear of Epstein or Neifosh before?" I asked.

She shook her head, reluctant to speak in front of Hilton. I didn't think it made any difference.

"Jack ever do business in Texas?" I asked.

"All our paintings came through New York City. And they went to Japan. I don't know anything about Texas."

"So it appears there was no connection between Jack and the other two surgeons."

"Not paintings, at any rate," Miranda said.

"What you getting at?" Hilton interjected.

"Trying to figure out why Broder picked those three doctors," I replied. "You think just because they're plastic surgeons?"

"Maybe he got a bad result from a nose job." Hilton laughed. "You see that ugly old schnozz in the police sketch?"

"Whatever the reason," Miranda said, "it had nothing to do with Jack's paintings."

"You don't think so?" I asked.

"No. If Broder killed for them, he would have made sure he got the paintings, wouldn't he?"

"Good point. Did he know where they were kept?"

"Sure."

I began to pace the floor. The more I thought about it, she was right. "It couldn't have been the paintings. What about the disk? Maybe Jack was killed for the disk."

"No," Miranda said. "Couldn't be that, either."

"Why not?" asked Hilton.

"If Jack found the disk, he would have come to me about it," she replied. "And he didn't."

"Besides," I added, "if Broder even thought Jack had the disk, he would have gone looking for it at the apartment. And we know he didn't, or he would have left it a mess. We've all seen how he left Miranda's place after he searched it."

"I agree," Miranda said. "Anyway, Broder never passed up an opportunity. If he had entered Jack's apartment, for whatever reason, those paintings would have been long gone."

"Which takes us back to where we started," I said. "If not the paintings, or the disk, what was the connection? Why plastic surgeons?"

"I don't know how this thing got so complicated in the first place," Hilton said. "I always figured it was because they were Jewish."

"Then why me? I'm not Jewish," I said, thinking mostly, Why Emma?

AKIMORO WANTED US TO DOWNLOAD THE entire disk to headquarters. I wasn't sure that I knew how. I had paid some kid to install the equipment, but had used my modem only to access patient records from the office. Miranda offered to help. I watched with mixed feelings as she worked the mouse and transmitted the data to Beverly Hills.

I knew that Akimoro would act immediately, using the information to draw the net even tighter around Broder. But how long would that take? If Broder were to call now, I had lost my exclusive bargaining chip. The trade-in value of that disk was depreciating as fast as Miranda's index finger was clicking the files through the phone lines. Would it put Emma in any more danger? Why hadn't he called yet?

Miranda announced that she was ready to go upstairs and read herself to sleep. She pleaded with me to accompany her, saying I needed the rest. I declined. I was tired but far from sleepy, and I feared that I would not be up to the physical performance implied in accepting her invitation. Hilton tactfully decided to remove himself from the discussion by taking another snoop around the yard. I stayed downstairs and called Rafaella for something to do.

"I haven't heard anything from the Greenfield police, Gareth."

"Akimoro's working on it. He has Broder's address

now. I'm sure it's only a matter of time. How are you holding up?"

"I'm okay. Cindy's spending the night. Do you think he'll hurt her, Gareth?"

"No. I think . . . I know he won't. When I talked to him he didn't seem like the kind who'd hurt children. He even rushed up to see if she was all right when she fell off the horse."

"You took him horse riding? With Emma?"

"No, Rafe. He was there. He must have been following us. I had no idea who he was."

"Gareth . . ." She started talking about the things Emma did when she was little. I couldn't stand to hear and made some excuse to hang up. But I somehow felt better after that conversation.

Around eleven the phone rang and it was Akimoro with an update. He was impressed with the disk. He had taken it to his chief and they had every available man on the job. They were checking out the Rosemead Lodge in Arcadia, as well as some of the other addresses. The Greenfield police would keep an eye on my house throughout the night. He asked to speak to Hilton Collins. I handed the phone over.

"Looks like there won't be any negotiating tonight," I said, dejected.

While Hilton talked to Akimoro, I considered the night ahead. I was exhausted but still couldn't think of sleep. Yet I needed repose. Monday morning, bright and early, I had a surgical date with a drug dealer, a man who probably identified more with Broder than with me, and who might not excuse a lackluster performance under any circumstances. He had paid in advance for my services, and he would expect me to carry them through. I told Hilton I was going to try to get some rest.

"I won't take my post on the landing just yet, Doc," he said, giving me a wink. "I'll stay down here for a while, give you two a chance to fall asleep before I come up."

I nodded. "Anyway you want it, Hilton."

"I think that's best. But before you go, I have something for you."

He went out to his car and returned to the kitchen with a shiny chromed revolver in his hand. It was a thirty-eight with a short barrel and wooden grip, all bulges and curves like a cartoon gun, shorter than my old Beretta. He handed it to me butt first.

"I know you're not going to need this up there," he said. "I want you to hang on to it anyway—for security. You know how to use one, don't you?"

I shook my head. "Not that I don't know how to use it. I'm not comfortable holding one anymore."

He pressed it forward. "I know how you doctors feel about guns, but this guy's a psycho. You've seen what he can do."

"Have you ever killed anybody, Hilton?"

"No." He placed the gun on the kitchen table and kept his eyes down, looking at it instead of at me. "It doesn't happen as often as people believe."

"How would you feel about pulling the trigger, if the situation arose?"

He raised his glance now, looking at me. "I've been around guns ever since I was a kid. Talk about second nature; when I get mad, or scared, li'l Martha's in my hand. You've seen that. If I ever feel someone needs to die—if it's him or me—I'd do it. I'd have to be pretty clear on it, though, in my mind. The gun, that's just the instrument. I never been trapped into that situation yet."

I nodded.

"How about you, Doc? You deal with life and death all the time. Ever come close to shutting down the power, just because you thought they'd be better off dead?"

I had the answer rehearsed, thinking about the question all day. "There's only one time in my life I really wanted to kill someone. It was very strange, not the way I thought it would be. At first there was anger, then there was fear; but once I made the decision it sort of calmed me down. I don't think I would have had any regrets."

"What happened?"

"He got away. It was last night, and the man was Broder."

"Take the gun," Hilton said.

I had no doubt the world would be a better place with Broder in the morgue. He had killed four or five people already, likely more, and could be weighing the scales of my daughter's life this very minute. Not that locking him up and throwing away the key wasn't an acceptable alternative; whatever means they used to stop him were fine with me. But if they failed to neutralize him, and I had a chance, I would be his last vision on the way to Hades.

I leaned forward and picked up the weapon. It was much lighter than I had anticipated. "A Smith and Wesson. Funny-looking thing. Where's the hammer?"

"It's what they call a Bodyguard. The hammer's concealed so it doesn't snag." He showed me how to work the hidden lever. "The body's aluminum, that's why it's so light. And it only takes five rounds. I trust that's enough."

"I was hoping for an M-60."

He laughed. "I loaned mine out to a schoolkid in Watts. You'll just have to make every shot count."

"I'll be very careful."

"I know you will, Doc." He shook my hand, holding it warmly for a minute. "I may not be here when you get up in the morning. I'm pulling a double shift, anyway, and I may get out early. Don't worry about the gun; I'll pick it up from you later."

"Thanks for everything, Hilton. Hope you have a quiet night."

"Me, too, Doc. And don't worry about Emma; the chief will find her."

I climbed the stairs slowly and deliberately, as if my ankles were shackled together on a short chain. Had I not been thinking about Emma, I might have bounded up them two at a time. But in my state of mind even the prospect of Miranda waiting upstairs in bed brought no pleasure.

She was lying on top of the covers, reading a magazine by the light of the bedside lamp. Her long, slender legs were crossed at the knees, the left one uppermost and bouncing slowly to some inner music, toes twitching. The fresh shirt she was wearing had ridden up to her waist as she slouched down in bed, showing the smooth skin of her thighs from beneath the strategically held magazine.

"You look very comfortable there," I said, shutting the door and putting the gun on the dresser.

"Going to shoot me?" she asked, laying the pages across her hip and smiling.

I smiled back. "You feeling guilty of something?"

"Only of making myself at home. If you'd seen where I spent the last week, you'd know why."

I walked up to the bed and looked down at her, taking in every inch. She patted the bedcovers, inviting me to sit down, and made room by shifting her long legs slightly, knocking the magazine away as she did so. I was drawn down as if by a magnet.

She started to unbutton my shirt as I watched her face. She had a relaxed, almost contented expression; at peace with the world. Her eyes looked green by the lamp on the bedside table, inviting, shimmering like the surface of a whirlpool under the lights. When she reached the last button above my belt she stopped, then lifted my hand and placed it gently on her thigh.

"I don't think I can tonight," I said.

"Let me help you forget."

I stroked her thigh, looking into her eyes to avoid staring at the patch of downy pale skin that I was about to renounce. "I appreciate the offer, but I wouldn't be any good."

She touched my cheek. "You're so different from Jack."

"How do you mean?" I asked, curious.

She laughed. "Jack wouldn't have refused, for a start."

I shrugged. "They never had any kids. If they had, he might have felt differently."

She was shaking her head. "Jack never had any kids because he couldn't feel anything. He never gave himself; he couldn't stand to be attached. He had a wonderful life: great job, beautiful wife, and a gorgeous house full of art and antiques. But it was all show, an image that he thought was expected of him."

She took my hand in hers, playing with my fingertips. "He always wanted more. That's why he started selling the paintings. It became an obsession—like a competition that he had to win. The sad thing is, I think he was competing with himself. It never occurred to him that one life would eventually destroy the other."

"Did Elaine know?" I asked.

"I don't think so. If she did, she pretended not to. She never came near the apartment. She was too busy spending as fast as he could make it. You know about that."

"Did Jack ever talk about her?"

"Not really."

"Never said a word? That he was jealous of her, afraid she would go out with other men, things like that?"

"No. Never." She looked at me. "Were you worried about that?"

"Not about physical harm," I said. "But she recently told me that he knew and never stopped it. Do you think that's possible?"

"I suppose. I don't think he cared enough to be jealous of her. It would only have mattered if he lost face."

"Why did you keep working with him?" I asked, meaning to say something different but changing the words as the question came out.

"You mean what did I see in him?" She put her

hand inside my open shirt and played with the hairs on my chest. "He was exciting."

I watched her face again, so serene and peaceful. She had succeeded in what she set out to do: drawing my thoughts away from Emma, even if only for an instant. She seemed to have an insight, an understanding of people. She was a curious thing, so youthful, yet so wise. And no wonder; she had probably seen more in her short life than most do in twice the time. In forty years, perhaps.

"And me?" I asked.

"You're solid. A rock."

"Now you're teasing."

"No."

"I think you just like older men. The father figure."

"You wouldn't say that if you knew my daddy."

"Tell me about him," I asked.

"He was a hard one to please. He believed that people should behave like grown-ups from the day they were born. If they didn't, they had to be beaten into it."

"Did he beat you?"

"Often," she said, as if she were telling me how many times she changed clothes or took a shower. "It was different growing up in Japan. I think the boys there were scared of me. A few of them tried to date me, but I swear they only did it on a dare. I never had any interest in them, anyway. When I came here to college I went wild; left school like I told you and partied from night till dawn with the band. It was all in rebellion."

She brought her knees up to her chin and was hugging her bare legs, either shamelessly unaware of the effect she was having on me, or else still trying to seduce me.

"Jack was different." She stared at me with those hazel-green eyes. "At first I thought him debonair. Such a gentleman. He could be so charming while he went about getting everything he wanted."

"When did you find out he was married?"

"From the start. I didn't give a damn about that. Why should I care if he didn't? Besides, she had a boyfriend tucked away somewhere, didn't she?" Miranda gave me a sardonic smile.

"She did," I said, swallowing.

"Yeah, well." Miranda began to undo my belt buckle. I didn't stop her.

"Jack knew my moods. I felt safe with him. Perhaps we were two of a kind. Maybe it was the mystery of sharing him, maybe I can't stand to be smothered. All I know is, we worked well together. Even after he cooled off, it was still more exciting than anything else I've ever done."

"You like excitement?"

"Who doesn't?"

She had my belt and fly undone by then.

"And me? What's so good about a rock?" Perhaps the wrong moment for profound questions.

"Security. You know how to get what you want in life, just like Jack. But what sets you apart is that you have boundaries, a sense of values. You've surrounded yourself with the things you love: this house, your family, the antiques. You couldn't just get up and leave it all. You don't need to let anyone in that door who could possibly destroy what you have."

She sat up and pulled me closer, kissing me gently on the mouth. Her lips were warm and dry. She kissed me again, on the chin, on my chest, working down now, her hands fondling my waist. When her mouth reached the soft hairs beneath my waist I held her face in my hands and pulled her back upright. She resisted.

"I want you, Gareth."

"I won't be any good."

"You don't have to do anything. Just let me."

"Maybe tomorrow."

"I'm leaving tomorrow."

I'd expected it; knew it was time. But I had to ask. "Why? What happened with Akimoro?"

She shook her head. "Nothing. It's not that. We just talked about Broder, and George's camp. I don't think he cares about me and the paintings, as long as he finds the killer."

"Then why?" I had to see if she felt the same way I did.

"I have to, Gareth. I don't belong here. You have a life, a family, a career. I need to make one of my own."

I knew she was right. "Then why make love to me?"

She drew me toward her. "I want something to remember you by."

"You've forgotten yesterday? Already?"

"Yesterday I made love to a man who I thought was going to open new doors in my life. Yesterday you were a blank check. Tonight . . ." She sighed. "Tonight you're a house with a chimney and a picket fence. I want to see what you feel like tonight. I need some of your strength." She laughed and pushed me back on the bed, straddling me as I fell. "Anyway, I was drunk yesterday, and I'm sober tonight. Don't you want to know how good I really am?"

She started kissing me again. Why was I hesitating? I was concerned for Emma, but there was something else. For the first time in a long while I was starting to feel my roots again; I was not just a career man with part-time kids, but a man with a family. And Rafaella's face was beginning to creep into the background. Damn! I became mad at myself for letting her haunt me so.

I let Miranda slide my trousers down. When she attacked me, I could tell that she was burning with desire. I felt the tension ease out of me. I aroused to her passion, and abandoned my body to her clutches. She was every bit as nimble as the night before, and possibly more resourceful. I imagined it had something to do with growing up in Japan.

I WOKE WITH A START FROM A NIGHTMARE and looked at the clock. It was 3:15 A.M. Miranda was curled by my side, legs drawn up, sheet pulled tightly around her neck. She was snoring lightly.

I must have dozed off, exhausted after our session, and been asleep all of two hours. I thanked her silently for that. But it was futile to lie there, eyes closed, hoping for more sleep. I tossed and turned for a bit, then, rather than stay and wake Miranda, I decided to go downstairs.

When I opened the bedroom door, Hilton was not at his post on the landing. By the light of the night lamp I could see that the cushion seat on the old armchair was smooth and plump, and I figured it had never borne his weight. I felt the familiar *thump, thump, thump* in my chest. I went back in the bedroom and lifted the gun from the dresser top. Mouth dry, I went back on the landing and listened.

Not a sound. I tiptoed down the stairs. There was a creak and I started, gun coming up. Nothing moved. I listened again. Silence. Damn! This was the reason I had tossed my Beretta on the top shelf of my closet and left it there almost ten years. I never wanted to be coming down my stairs with it, ready to shoot holes in the ceiling for every shadow that flitted across my sight.

I adjusted my grip on the Smith & Wesson in my hand and continued down, pulse racing. There were no strange shadows in the hallway. The door to the kitchen was shut, but a bar of light shone through underneath. Getting a firm grip on my weapon, I poised my index finger near the trigger, opened the door, and strode through, gun held high in front of me.

Hilton was slouched forward on a chair, head and arms sprawled across the kitchen table, eyes shut fast. I approached cautiously, listening for sounds in the den beyond the kitchen, and studying the floor for telltale rivulets of blood. I saw none. I did see him stir and realized he was still breathing. I gave him a shove.

"What?" He awoke with a start. "Who's there?" He glimpsed the gun in my right hand and immediately reached for his own. "What's happening?"

"Take it easy, Hilton. I think we're alone. You fell asleep." I considered telling him the whole place had been burgled in the interim, but that would have been cruel. He was embarrassed, anyway.

"What time is it?" he asked.

"About three-thirty."

Hilton shook himself awake. "Got anything to eat?"

"Help yourself." I pointed to the refrigerator.

He tossed his head. "No, Doc. I mean the good stuff. Where's your munchies? If I don't get some sugar quick, I'm having a meltdown."

"Like what? You diabetic or something?"

"Come on, Doc. You don't have to be diabetic to appreciate candy bars."

I never ate them, and hadn't the prescience to know I'd be entertaining when I last went shopping. Between his comments on the state of my larder, and Miranda's on my liquor cabinet, I was beginning to feel like a miserable host.

We settled for two bowls of dry cereal, his submerged in granulated sugar, and moved into the den to watch late-night movies. Perhaps befuddled from lack of rest, we lost all pretext of quietly lying in wait for Broder. We sat there spooning sugared flakes, high as teenagers after a night on the prowl. We each had a pistol, and if Broder dared to show his face, he would be all the sorrier.

We watched Lon Chaney, and then Betty Grable and Don Ameche, and during the breaks Hilton told me what it was like to grow up in Alabama. He had spent four years in the army, then quit when the childhood sweetheart he married wanted to move to L.A. to get into the movies. She had settled for bit parts in commercials, and he had joined the Beverly Hills police.

We moved back into the kitchen at the first light of dawn. Hilton tried another bowl of cereal and I was just brewing a pot of coffee when the call came. It was Akimoro himself.

"We found Emma, Dr. Lloyd."

"You have?" There was a flush of relief so great that my knees went weak and I had to sit down. I was much too tired to show elation. "Is she all right? Where was she?"

"She's fine, but she's had a terrible fright, poor thing. She's starving and I guess a little dehydrated. She was locked in one of the rooms at the Rosemead Lodge. It's a run-down old boarding home up in the hills. We had a hell of a time finding it."

"Did he touch her?" I was shaking.

"No. He left soon after taking her there. We haven't found him yet. There was only an old caretaker, and he didn't know much. The place is used as a safe house by some of the supremacist groups. The owner was on your list of Klan members."

"Can I talk to her?"

I heard some muffled instructions, then Akimoro was back. "She's coming. We need to take her to the hospital for a checkup. It's routine, you understand. She has a cut on her chin, but I don't think it's from last night. Here she is."

"Emma! Emma, how are you, honey?" There was no answer. It was a minute before she came to the phone, and I watched Hilton do a little victory dance around the kitchen table while I waited.

"Daddy? Is that you?" She sounded distant and weak. "Daddy, I'm scared."

It was wonderful just to hear her voice. "Emma, it's me. I love you very much, honey. And I missed you. Are you all right?"

"I want to see Mommy."

I told her she could, and that we would both be with her very soon. Over the phone it was hard for me to tell if my words had any effect.

Akimoro came back on the line. "We're taking her to the Huntington Hospital. You can speed things up by calling them, give your consent to check her out. That might cut through a lot of red tape."

"I'll do it now. Do you want me to meet you there?"

"I think it may be better if you don't, Dr. Lloyd. What's your schedule like this morning?"

I felt a rush of panic. "Why? What's wrong? Are you lying to me, Akimoro? Is there something you're not telling me?"

"Relax, Dr. Lloyd. Your daughter is fine, but it's Broder I'm worried about. We've had the lodge under surveillance and the phone's tapped and there haven't been any calls in or out. He's still out there somewhere and he doesn't know we have her yet. He wants something from you. My bet it's the disk. He's working on a trade and it's my hunch he'll make his move sometime today. I'd like to keep this quiet until he does. I don't want him following you to the hospital and finding out she's safe. Fortunately, we didn't take it to the media, so there's little risk one of the nurses will call a reporter."

I calmed down. "I understand," I said. "But you can't expect me to let some doctor examine Emma without one of us there. I have to call her mother. Broder wouldn't be watching her. She's the one who should be present at the examination, anyway."

"Fair enough. But can you stick to your regular schedule this morning? You should be someplace he knows how to reach you."

"You want me to be the decoy?"

"If you're willing. It's no different from what you've been doing all night. We'll have you covered at all times."

Hilton poured me a coffee and brought it over. I studied his uniform. "Akimoro, if he sees your men around me, he'll never show his face."

"I'll deal with that," he said. "Where are you heading first?"

"I'm due at the outpatient surgery center in an hour. Broder doesn't know where that is."

"It's unlikely he'd do anything there, anyway. What about afterwards?"

"My office from nine-thirty to noon. He's been there before. Then lunch, I could come home for that. After that I'm back in the office until six."

"Most likely he'll pick your office. Is Collins still there? I'd like to talk to him."

I handed the phone to Hilton and went in the den to call Rafaella on the other line. She was so happy she was speechless. I gave her directions and told her to be careful because it was rush hour. When I went upstairs to change, Hilton was still on the phone. I left the gun on the kitchen table.

Miranda was sleeping soundly. I got dressed as quietly as I could and wrote her a note: *They've found Emma. She's fine. Send me an invitation to the opening of your gallery. And thanks for a wonderful birthday.*

I signed it and left it on the dresser where she would see it. I gave her one last look and shut the door. Hilton was waiting for me in the hall.

"It's all arranged," he said as we left the house. "My relief will be here any minute. This is the plan. Our boys will stay visible, but not too close. We don't want him to get suspicious by dropping out of sight, but we want him to have plenty of chance to slip through. We're going to make it easy for him, and while he's congratulating himself on what a smart dude he is, we'll have a plainclothesman right at your side. We'll box the bastard in before he knows what hit him."

"I hope it works, Hilton." I started walking toward the Alfa and he kept pace with me. "I don't look forward to confronting Broder. You've got to figure he'll have fire-power."

"We will, too; don't worry about it. We'll count the surgery center as a dry run, and you'll see just how smoothly this thing goes. By the time you get to your office, you'll feel like a pro."

"You sure, Hilton?"

I heard a car draw up. We turned at once and saw it was the relief unit he had told me about. He waved to the driver, then thrust his hand out to me.

"Good to meet you, Dr. Lloyd. You're all right. I'll stop in and see you again sometime—might need some liposuction or something."

We laughed and shook hands. "Thanks, Hilton. You're a good man, too. Stop by anytime you want. I'll give you two for the price of one."

I entered the Alfa and started her up. Hilton leaned through the window, gave a quick look at the patrol car across the street, and dropped something heavy in my lap. It was the Smith & Wesson.

"Why don't you hang on to it for a bit, Doc?" he said in a whisper. "I'm in no hurry to get it back."

I had to raise my voice through the sound of the engine. "Hilton, you're not making me feel very safe."

His look hardened as he signaled me to lower my voice. "You'll be safe. I know. I saw you handle yourself yesterday. But it's going to take more than a plunger to get Broder. I want you to promise me something, Doc. You carry this under your belt all day today. All day, you understand?"

"I don't have a license for that, Hilton."

"I know that, and if anyone asks, do me a favor and tell them you picked it up from your kitchen table, and I knew nothing about it. But this is one day you don't want to be worrying about a license, Doc. Believe me. Just do as I say."

He had changed from the optimist of a minute ago. I looked over at the young officer in the driver's seat of the relief car. We were back to the muscle-bound type today.

"Hilton," I said, "I take it you don't think much of this plan, either."

"It's the official plan, Doc, and it sounds like a good one, but I don't trust Broder one bit. Personally, I'm all for blowing the bastard away. Problem is, some of the suits are interested in Broder. There's a lot we don't know about the white armed-resistance movement, and a few folks at Parker Center would like a chance to talk with him, one on one. So we come up with this plan. I tell you something, Doc. Nobody's going to know you have that gun unless you need to use it. And when that happens, a license don't mean shit."

THE OUTPATIENT SURGERY CENTER WAS situated in a dusky-gray building on Paley Street, not two blocks from my office. It was a streamlined structure with wide expanses of blue glass, a private venture started several years ago by a group of local businessmen. Like the building, services were kept simple and therefore efficient. The center was not affiliated with any hospital and was unencumbered by the morass of equipment and staff necessary to provide a full spectrum of basic medical care. If minor surgery was what you needed, and the procedure didn't promise to take so much out of you that you couldn't hop in a taxi and go home right afterward, the Surgery Center was the place to be. The employees pampered the surgeons and coddled the patients equally. Usually, it was a pleasure to work there.

We turned in to the parking lot as a team, the Alfa leading the black-and-white patrol car. I would have preferred a high-speed escort, but they didn't go for it. I pulled into a spot near the back service entrance, and they stationed themselves around the side. I joined them to explain the lay of the land, showing them the three entrances: front, side, and back.

"Where's the plainclothes guy?" I asked.

"Probably inside already."

I went in to find him in the employees lounge, another young, muscular type. He was in jeans and a linen jacket, with too many creases to disclose any metallic bulges under the armpits. His name was Perry Maclean.

"How do you want to work this, Maclean?" I asked. "You want to come into the operating suite with me? We might have to clear it with the head nurse. You understand they have some rules about observers, and you'd also have to wear a scrub suit."

"I've already scoped it out with Nurse Overman. I think I'll stay right here; I'd be too conspicuous wearing greens. I'll just pretend I'm waiting for a job interview." He took out a copy of the police sketch of Broder as if to memorize that face one last time.

"There won't be much traffic coming through here," I said. "You can familiarize yourself with the staff now. The only new faces will be the surgeons coming in to do their cases. Just make sure you don't mistake one of them for Broder."

He smiled, showing a row of perfect teeth, and clicked some buttons on his radio. "I'll be careful, Doc. Where are the boys in uniform?"

"Around the side."

"Good. I see only two ways into the operating room: the side through the patients' waiting room, and this one here. If our boys stay where they are, he'll come this way." The radio crackled loudly and he picked it up to explain the situation to the men outside.

Nicki Overman strode in through the connecting door. "You'll have to keep that thing turned down," she said. "It's scaring the patient."

"I guess she's right," I said. "We have someone who's sort of . . . allergic to police."

Maclean seemed annoyed. "We'll try and keep radio silence unless it's necessary."

Nicki rolled her eyes and turned to me. "Morning, Dr. Lloyd. My goodness! What happened to your nose? You been playing racquetball with Dr. Elliot again?"

"No, Nicki. Just a little accident in my car."

"Good Lord!" She came up close to examine the

bruised flesh. "Looks like you could use a good plastic surgeon." She smiled. "Does it hurt?"

"No, Nicki. It's fine. Really."

"How many times have I told you to get rid of that silly little car and get yourself a nice sedan?"

Nicki Overman had been in this business longer than I'd been alive. She had worked with some of my old mentors when they were as young as I was now. They were long gone, and Nicki was all that was left of the old era, carrying the history of forty years of surgery in her encyclopedic head. She had seen all there was to see—felt the heat from temperamental surgeons accustomed to having their own way, witnessed their fear when they were in over their heads, experienced their elation when a life was saved, and burned with their sadness when one was lost. She could anticipate trouble before it was there. If she offered a certain instrument, and I was using another, I did better to take the one she suggested. We affectionately knew her as "Mother," but only behind her back.

"Are you having one of those days, Nicki?"

"Not until I saw your patient. I can't imagine where you find these people, Dr. Lloyd."

"Has Mr. Rojas been causing any trouble?" I asked innocently.

"Nothing we can't handle. He didn't want Stacy to start an IV, says he doesn't need it. He didn't want any sedation, says he doesn't want anybody messing with his head. He just gives me the creeps, that's all."

She eyed Detective Maclean again as if to underscore her point. "What's this bozo done, anyway? You think he's going to try something?"

"I'm sure he won't. The detective is here on some other business. Mr. Rojas knows he needs this operation and I'm sure he'll cooperate. I think he's just nervous."

"Nervous I can deal with," she said. "I'd better put him in the room while you get ready."

I ducked in the side door to change. I pulled the

gun out of my belt and laid it on the locker bench, staring at its chrome finish. I knew I couldn't mention it to Maclean; likely he wouldn't approve. Should I leave it in the locker? I remembered the insistence in Hilton's voice. *"It's going to take more than a plunger to get Broder."* I put on a scrub suit and tucked the gun under my waistband, pulling the shirt over it. It held snug against my waist, but I was a little worried about where it was pointing.

When I stepped into the operating room, Fernando Rojas was already on the table, covered with a thin white blanket up to his neck. Nicki was scrubbed and gowned, busying herself getting the instruments ready. Stacy, tall and skinny and with wisps of blond hair showing under her paper cap, was attaching the monitor leads. She was the circulating nurse and it was her job to keep an eye on the patient, making sure we had everything we needed.

"Morning, Fernando. You ready for this?" I asked.

"Yes, I am, Doctor. You got a good night's sleep, I hope?"

I walked over to his side. "I slept as well as I could, thanks. How about you? I trust you weren't out all night getting into trouble."

"I never get into trouble, Doctor. I'm just a home-boy, minding my own business."

"That's good. And you'll stay that way for at least the next three days, so your stitches have a chance to heal."

"Whatever you say."

"I'm going to inject a little Lidocaine under your skin to numb the scalp. I can give you some sedation if you're nervous; it will make you a little drowsy."

Rojas raised his head off the table to look at me. "When you make it numb I won't feel it anymore, right?"

"Correct."

"Then why you want to make me sleepy as well? The only place I sleep is at my home. I don't want to sleep here, okay?"

"Fine with me."

I looked at Nicki and shrugged. Things were always a little more difficult with patients awake. Often, when they heard the snipping of the scissors and felt the blood trickling down, they would tense. Sometimes their blood pressure would rise uncontrollably, and we'd have to calm them down before we could continue. At the very least, we always had to watch what we said. It's not uncommon during surgery to have some member of the staff walk in and make a comment about the proceedings, assuming that the patient cannot hear. There were days when the nurse would have to write the words PATIENT AWAKE in big letters on a placard, and stick it on the operating room door, as a warning to the staff. You always knew, when you saw that sign, some loudmouth must have ambled in and shot off his mouth.

I touched Rojas's forehead and scalp. The little knots under his skin were easy to feel. I marked them with indelible ink, as they would be impossible to distinguish once the anesthetic was injected and the tissues swollen.

"Here it comes, Fernando." I pierced the skin with the tip of the needle and pushed. Rojas winced but said nothing as his skin rose like an inflating balloon. I turned the radio to my favorite station and adjusted the volume. Then I left to scrub my hands while the numbness set in.

Rules for the surgical scrub are posted over every operating room sink. A universal cleansing ritual, the scrub was meant to cut the infection rate. I thought of Semmelweis, poor bastard. He was the first surgeon to advocate scrubbing, to protect the pregnant women in his Viennese clinic. They were dying of infections because medical students were examining them after an autopsy class without washing their hands. Today's lawyers would have had a field day with that one. Even so, the local doctors resisted his innovation and kicked him out of Vienna. Perhaps because he was a foreigner, a bloody Hungarian. I figured medical politics hadn't changed much in a century and a half.

In the mirror over the scrub sink I could see Maclean sitting in the lounge. The digital clock timer showed 7:42 A.M. I realized Debbie would be opening my office in a few minutes. I walked over to the lounge door, dripping Betadine soap in a brown trail along the linoleum floor.

"Maclean," I said. "What about sending a man up to my office? Broder's been there before, and it's the first place he's going to look for me this morning. My office manager will be there in a few minutes, and she's going to be alone."

"Give me the address." He took a pad and pencil from his pocket to write it down. "I'll call it in to headquarters. Might take a while to get a man down there, though."

I thought of Miranda. "What about the officer who's watching my house?" I asked.

"Your girlfriend's still there, isn't she?"

"My office manager is in more danger than she is. Why can't they go over to my office instead? It's not far from here. I think they'll be wasted at my house; Broder must know I won't be there anymore."

I was taking a risk pulling the cops off Miranda's back, but she needed a clean field to get away. What if Broder did decide to go to my house and look for the disk himself, instead of making a trade with me? It was possible, but I wouldn't have played it that way; it could take too long to find. I had to take the chance.

Satisfied with my arrangements, I rinsed off and went back to the operating room. Stacy had prepped Rojas's forehead and scalp with Betadine. Nicki placed sterile towels around his face, leaving the mouth and nose free so he could breathe. She helped me into a surgical gown and gloves, and I took my position at the head of the table.

"Can you feel this?" I touched Rojas's forehead with the scalpel.

"Go ahead, Doctor. It's numb."

The glass fragments were no longer palpable. I made the incisions to follow my pen marks, adjusting finger pressure so I wouldn't go too deep.

"Scissors."

Gold-plated handles thudded into my palm with a flick of Nicki's wrist. Tungsten-carbide blades honed to a keen edge all the way to their pointed tips, they snapped shut with the clear ring of metal on metal. I snipped and prodded, exposing the pink dermis beneath the skin. Two small bleeders began to spurt.

"Bovie."

A pencil-like instrument landed in my hand. I zapped the bleeding arteries until they withered, each in turn, with a small charge of direct current. I was reminded of an arcade game I played with Emma. Little gophers would pop their heads out of a box at random. You had to bop them over the head with a plastic mallet before they disappeared. The faster you beat one down, the faster the next one would pop up. You never knew from which quarter it would spring.

I mopped the wound and ran my fingertips under the skin. I could feel something sharp. Carefully, I extracted a small sliver of glass. I repeated the process at the other two sites.

The phone rang and Stacy answered it.

"Dr. Lloyd, it's Debbie."

I moved closer so she could hold the receiver to my ear. "What is it, Debbie? Everything all right?"

"Ready for another Monday, aren't we?" Her voice was as cheerful as usual.

"I guess you haven't had a visit from the police, then."

"The police! No, Dr. Lloyd. It was a pretty dull weekend."

"Debbie, we may have a visitor this morning, the same guy who showed up last Monday. The police are anxious to talk to him. They're sending a couple of men over now."

Mr. Rojas began to stir uncomfortably. He was only loosely strapped around the waist and I thought he might try to get up and see what this was about. Patient awake, I thought to myself. He had heard what I said to Debbie.

"It's all right, Fernando. This has nothing to do with you. Just relax now, and we'll be done in a minute."

"What's that?" Debbie's voice came through the receiver.

"I was saying if a couple of cops come by, do whatever they say. I'll be there right after this case. Maybe forty-five minutes."

"Great. I was calling to find out how long you'd be. I just got a call from Memorial Hospital maintenance department. The foreman said one of his men cut his hand during the night shift. He insisted on bringing him to see you."

"Why doesn't he go to Emergency like everybody else?"

"I suggested that, but he said he didn't trust the doctors there. He said you did a great job suturing him a few years ago and he wouldn't let anyone else near him after that."

"I did? What's his name?"

"John Bonham. I don't remember him. Do you?"

"I'm not sure. Sounds familiar. What did you tell him?"

"I told him you were at the Surgery Center and wouldn't be available until later, but he kept insisting. I said I would talk to you and call him back."

"Tell him if he can wait an hour I'll see him in the office."

"Sure thing, Dr. Lloyd."

Stacy placed the receiver back on its hook and I returned to Rojas.

"Suture."

It was a wisp of blue nylon, attached to a small, curved needle. I wove it in and out of the skin on each side of the wound, deftly bringing the edges together, tying knots with my Webster needle holder and holding the ends up for Nicki to cut. It was mechanical work, and my attention wandered to the radio station. They had just started playing "Stairway to Heaven," an old favorite from medical school days. I listened to the fluid blending of flute and electric guitar, and began mouthing the words to the plaintive ballad by Led Zeppelin.

And then it clicked. Bob Plant, James Page, and John Bonham. Broder must have been a fan of Led Zeppelin; he was picking his aliases from the band members' names.

"Stacy," I said, a sudden dryness in my throat. "Run and get Detective Maclean. Now."

Stacy left for the lounge. I placed the last two sutures quickly, sacrificing accuracy for speed. Stacy came rushing back, out of breath, pupils dilated, and a tremble in her voice.

"He's not there. There's a trail of blood leading from the lounge."

"Are you sure, Stacy? That's the Betadine I dripped when I went in to talk to him."

"No. It's not Betadine. It's blood—and it's fresh."

A FIGURE APPEARED IN THE DOORWAY, A man wearing greens, booties, paper cap, mask, the works. He was of medium height and carried himself hunched slightly forward, shoulders down. An unassuming stance. He might have been rather inconspicuous in that clinical setting were it not for the gun held firmly in both hands. The nickel-plated finish of the automatic was almost hidden in his double grip, but the bulky outline of the silencer was in plain sight, a cold reminder from two nights ago.

Although the gun wasn't the most striking thing about him. That honor was reserved for his tattoos, dozens of black-and-white and colored images that coiled and snaked up his arms to disappear under the short sleeves and emerge again, in tantalizing animation, at the V neck of his shirt.

Broder reached for the mask and tore it off his face. He broke into a snarl as he transfixed me with those wide, deep-set brown eyes. The lines around his mouth, which only one week earlier when he was in my office I had attributed to wisdom and experience, now resembled more the contortions of an insane mind.

"Your turn, Lloyd," he said, advancing slowly into the room.

My gut tied itself into knots. Fear oozed out of my pores and stuck my feet to the ground. My heart contracted into a solid rubber ball that bounced around my chest with every quivering beat. I heard the chart Stacy was holding drop to the floor.

"Excuse me, young man," Nicki said. "This is an operating room. You can't just walk in here like that."

"Shut up, bitch!" Broder snapped. "You two, get in the corner." He moved his intertwined hands to indicate he meant Stacy and Nicki. He seemed to have other plans for me.

Fernando Rojas, perhaps the most experienced of the lot of us in situations like this, went limp and pretended to be asleep, and I wished I could take my cue from him.

The two nurses shuffled into a corner, Stacy whimpering and Nicki trying to comfort her, while Broder checked the layout of the room. I thought of the two policemen waiting round the side. They could be having coffee and doughnuts this very minute, oblivious to our fate. Thanks to the radio silence on which we had insisted, they would not be inclined to call in and check on us. I wished I could summon them telepathically. Perhaps one of them would have to use the bathroom. I prayed that the coffee would be plentiful and strong.

I figured Maclean was dead. He would have been at the disadvantage when Broder made his entrance in surgical scrubs, tattoos notwithstanding. The gun I was carrying might as well have been in my locker for all the good it was doing, buried under the drawstring of my greens. The surgical gown was actually the biggest obstacle, tying in the back, with no access down the front. There wasn't a hope in hell of outgunning him, even if I could somehow summon up the courage to try.

"What's here?" Broder asked, pointing to a solid metal door at the side of the room.

"The sterilizer," Nicki said.

"Where's it go?" He aimed the question at her.

"Nowhere. That's the back of it, for maintenance. It's nothing but a closet."

"Open it."

Nicki held the door wide for his inspection. Broder slid along the wall up close to it, then thrust his gun into the darkened bay with both hands, ready to shoot the slightest wisp of steam that issued forth. He checked it up and down carefully, making sure there was no way out.

"Does it lock?"

"None of the doors here lock," Nicki replied.

He thought about that for a minute. "You two," he said, "get in and stay there. Poke your head out and I'll shoot it off. Understood?"

Nicki led Stacy inside and the door closed slowly behind them.

I marveled at Rojas's form. He must have had lots of practice at playing possum. He would have realized the minute Broder came in the door that this was a situation he didn't need to be part of. His imitation of a dead man was remarkable: both eyes firmly shut, his freshly closed wound oozing a small trickle of blood that pooled in the left eyelid before slipping down his cheek. It must have taken great concentration not to instinctively wipe it away. His breathing was barely perceptible under the sterile sheets. Broder stood beyond him, back to the wall not ten feet away, gun still leveled at my chest.

"Want to see your daughter again, Lloyd?" He removed one hand from his grip on the weapon and held it out, palm up. "The disk."

Beads of sweat started on my brow. My brain had turned to water and was filtering out. Drops ran down my nose behind the mask onto dry lips.

"I don't have it."

He smiled triumphantly. I could have bitten straight through my tongue. I should have said, "What disk?"

"So you found it!" He was thrilled. He'd caught up with the Holy Grail.

"It's not here."

He resumed his two-handed pistol grip. "Where is it?"

"In my office."

"Don't mess with me, Lloyd," he snapped. "I hold all the aces here. I have your daughter, and I have the gun." He looked down at his hands, as if bewitched by the weapon that he held. I followed his gaze, obsessed, in my turn, by his tattoos.

"You haven't been to your office all weekend," he said. "So where is it?"

His eyes were wildly dilated. Had he been up all night, too, or was he high on something?

"I . . . I went to the office on Saturday night. Before returning home. I put it on my desk."

He thought about what I'd said for a moment. "Then you haven't seen what's in it?"

"No. I didn't have time."

He smiled, the lines around his mouth splaying out. "Is it on the desk with all the other crap—files and shit?"

I nodded fiercely. He had a good grasp of the way I felt about my desk.

"Then they'll throw it out with all the other garbage when you're dead."

His reference to my imminent demise was most unsettling. He shifted the gun in his hands.

"Maybe I'll blow up the whole damn office. That would be a nice statement. Just think of it, Lloyd. Your death will make Klan history. It's going to be a turning point, and all down to me."

I was still in shock. I wondered what the headlines would say—SKINHEAD DOWNS SKIN DOC? I noticed that his speech was becoming less tense, his sentences less abrupt. He was feeling more comfortable in his role as executioner. I thought I might gain some time. Where the hell were those cops, anyway?

"You're not really a member of the Klan, are you, Broder?"

He lost his smile and lowered his hands about six inches from his line of sight. "Who told you that? George tell you that? No, he must have told the girl. She told you that."

Sweat poured down my neck. It was a close call; he might have realized I'd read it from the disk.

"Where is she?" he asked. "Still at your house?"

"She's gone. Left this morning."

"Gone? They let her go? I don't believe it. What about the money? They let her take that with her?" His hands came down even farther.

I was calculating, gauging the distance. But rushing him was out of the question; my feet were still cemented to the floor. "So you killed Ehrenberger for the money?" I asked, stalling.

He straightened up to his full height, bringing the gun up to his line of sight again. "I killed Ehrenberger for the Klan," he said proudly. "Same reason I killed the other two."

"Why?"

He sneered. "You want to know? You're a dead man, Lloyd. You give a shit about why?"

He came forward off the wall and listened out the door. I couldn't hear a sound. Rojas was still lying motionless on the table.

Broder looked at me and nodded. "When you're gone the whole world is going to know. I've got my statement ready—twenty thousand words. Tells the whole story. They'll listen to me then. Even the Klan. I'm going to be somebody."

He leaned back against the wall again, eager to explain himself now. My hands slid slowly behind me to the knot on my gown.

"They don't trust me," he said, viciously. "Me! I've

dedicated my life to the cause, and they put an asshole like George Kershen in charge. They're no different from the bastards I left behind in Houston."

He shook his head from side to side and the gun went down another six inches. "I could've joined anyone—the National Alliance, the Nazi Party, you name it—they would've taken me in a minute. But it had to be the original. The Ku Klux Klan. You know they go back over a hundred years, all the way to Nathan Bedford Forrest. He was my great-great-grandfather."

I didn't question his lineage. Nathan Bedford Forrest featured in the Civil War, and it seemed as if there should have been a few more generations in there somewhere. But as he talked, my hands were moving slowly. If I could just get the ties on my gown undone, I might have a chance. At what? If I could just keep him talking.

"What do I have to do with all this, Broder?"

He smiled. "You're going to do it for me, Lloyd. You're the icing on the cake. You're going to get me on national television, maybe an interview with Barbara Walters."

That was news. I had an interest in staying alive just to watch that one.

"The first one—Neifosh—he wasn't big enough. They put him on the third page. I thought the second one—Epstein—would do it. He was easy, but they couldn't make the connection. I knew I had to go somewhere you guys are big news. Where else but Beverly Hills? I was right. Ehrenberger sure made a splash." He sneered. " 'Plastic surgeon to the stars.' Nice touch, killing him with his own gun, don't you think?"

Nice try, Broder. Problem was, it was my gun. I had the ends of the knot in my fingers now. I began to pull.

"Get your hands where I can see them, Lloyd. You want to hear this? I can kill you now."

I jerked my arms out to midair. "No. Please! Tell me. Why do you want me?"

I was ready to do anything to get myself out of this. What were the two girls in the front office doing? They usually wore street clothes in the reception area, and they never came back to the operating suite, considering it out of their bailiwick. Couldn't they break with tradition just this once?

"You're a plastic surgeon, aren't you? I miscalculated with Ehrenberger. He was big but he didn't go national. They thought it was a drive-by—just an L.A. thing. So I figured it would take more. I saw you at the funeral, talking to the girl; made me suspicious. I checked you out. Perfect for number four. I chased you all the way down the coast, but you got away. Then I found you at the auction talking to her again. That was when I hit on my plan."

Everybody had a plan; if only Akimoro's hadn't gone awry. I had my hands up in the air and was waiting now. I was out of options.

Broder was starting to enjoy himself. "I had to get you together with the girl; kill you all with Ehrenberger's gun in the house where she had his money. When the cops found all that they couldn't close the case in a hurry. They would have to start sniffing everywhere. It had the makings of a great story. I could just see it on *Current Affair.*"

I could, too. They could satisfy everybody's craving for publicity on *Current Affair.*

"Everything was falling into place," Broder said. "Ehrenberger made the papers again Thursday and the story was ready to blow. I had my statement prepared. I could see those reporters sharpening their pencils."

He looked at me with disgust. "Snagging you was easy. All I had to do was cook up a scheme with pottery— they told me at Malbone's you were a sucker for it. You should have seen your face when I mentioned that reward."

Broder grinned and adjusted his grip on the gun.

"Why did you follow me into the equestrian park?" I asked.

He shrugged, still grinning. "Get to know you better. How else would I have found out about Emma? Anyway, you don't seem that concerned about her, Lloyd. Don't you want her back? What kind of fucking parent are you?"

"Never mind about my daughter," I said, gaining strength from what I knew about Emma. "Why did you want me and Miranda together? You arranged that deliberately, didn't you? Was it just so you could kill us both?"

"You're pretty smart, Lloyd. You're going to go far." He laughed. "In the next two minutes, that is." His grin faded and he shook his head. "George had to get in my way. Fucking asshole! He brought Miranda up to the lake. I was sweating on that one. How the hell was I going to get her down here in time for your meeting?"

He straightened up again, pointing the gun back at my chest. "Lucky for me, those two dickheads he left guarding the camp hated each other. Just goes to show the White Aryan Resistance don't have what it takes."

He smiled again, a wide grin, showing the dull gray tips of his incisors. "That was a touch of genius on my part. I put a few rumors out, and they went at each other like mad dogs. They were ready to cut each other's throats. No class. Not like the Klan. We're something else." He stood tall, the gun steady at my chest. "The Klan has a sense of history, Lloyd, and you and I are going to be part of it. Don't that make you proud?"

Broder paused and pointed a finger in the air. "Don't you agree it's a good idea to dynamite your office?"

It would only be a good idea if he was in it, I thought. I still didn't feel enlightened. He had bared the workings of his deranged mind but hadn't answered my key question. Or maybe I'd missed it.

"Why do you want plastic surgeons, Broder?"

He came away from the wall to peer at the operating table. Rojas was still submerged in his role as Rip Van Winkle. Broder sneered when he saw his face, then stepped back and glared at me.

"You want to know why? It's what you're doing right now. Look at that lowlife on the table. What are you changing today? His nose? His lips? The color of his skin? You guys are all the same—plastic surgeons, hairdressers, makeup artists. Trying to imitate Aryan beauty. It's a conspiracy to integrate. You're mixing up the gene pool. It's getting so bad you can't recognize the Jews and the niggers anymore."

I got it. Fernando Rojas got it, too. He must have figured then that he was part of the equation. No matter if Broder considered him anesthetized, he had been named in the suit. He was as much a symbol of what the man hated as I was, and it was a toss-up whether he would be sentenced along with me. Rojas's right hand was next to me, on Broder's blind side. I saw it slowly groping for the edge of the sheet, lifting it gently away. In slow motion, he undid the latch on the table strap that held him down.

PATIENT AWAKE. I was grateful no one had put a placard up to warn Broder. He was apparently still under the impression that Rojas was floating on Pentothal.

"You're a race traitor," Broder went on. "We have to stop the scum mixing it up with the chosen race. You're contaminating us, Lloyd, altering their noses, bleaching their skin, changing their hair. It'll be a lot better when we go back to making them wear a badge on their arms. Tattoo on their forehead, is more like it."

I couldn't believe this final unveiling. He didn't really mean tattoo; he wanted to brand them like cattle. I thought of Lavonne Singleterry and the scar on her cheek. Something inside me snapped. Maybe it was just my gut uncoiling. I had to do something now.

Fernando Rojas's right hand was reaching out, the tattoo of the marijuana leaf on his shoulder sliding out from under the sterile drapes. He touched my thigh and I risked a glance downward. The Mayo stand with all the instruments on it was next to me, about six inches from his grasp. I realized what he was trying to do. I pushed the stand by inches with my right foot, closer and closer to his outstretched fingers.

Broder leveled the gun one last time, and I saw his brows come together with concentration. My heart was in my mouth. I thought the end had come.

"Now you know, Lloyd. The whole world will be reading about this pretty soon."

I braced myself for the bullet, wondering which one it would be: a silvertip or a full metal jacket? I was about to duck beneath the table when Rojas turned, his head facing Broder, and opened his eyes.

I saw the momentary confusion as Broder's hand dropped a fraction of an inch. Rojas sat bolt upright, and, with a slight roll of his hips, his right hand shot across his body, from the Mayo stand toward Broder, making an arc that brought it within inches of my chin. For a split second something shiny gleamed in front of my eyes.

Broder was unprepared for this raising of the dead. His hands came up again, too far, then recoiled. A rush of compressed air whizzed past my ears; a white flame and a puff of smoke came from his gun. Another flame; Rojas's hip jarred backward into my waist. There was a cry of pain.

I saw the shiny gleam of silver curling through the air from Rojas's hand. A scintillating line of magic light arced ten feet across the room to Broder's head. I was looking straight at Broder's face when his right eye exploded, globs of currant jelly splattering across his cheek. Six inches of shiny metal, the back end of a Universal blade holder, was sticking straight out in the air where his right eye had been. The number-ten scalpel blade was completely embedded in his eye socket.

The gun recoiled again; another rush of compressed air, a puff of smoke. The spotlight above my head shattered, dripping shards of broken glass down on the sterile drapes. Another cry of pain and Broder's face contorted in agony. He dropped the gun in his left hand, his right reaching for his face. He fell back against the wall, the gun going off repeatedly. Plaster rained down from the ceiling.

I tore at my gown and ripped the ties open, wrenching it off in one sweep. I pulled my shirt up and dove into my pants for the wooden handle of the thirty-eight. It came up fluttering. I grabbed with both hands to steady it.

Broder's left hand moved, the business end of the silencer revealing its deadly bore. I squeezed my index finger and heard the loudest noise I ever heard in my life. My hand recoiled and a red hole appeared in Broder's shirt. Maybe it was the impact, but I thought I saw his hand thrust forward again. I squeezed a second time. Another deafening roar and another red hole, this one ripping off a chunk of tattoo on his neck. His head twisted into an unnatural angle. He twitched, and slumped down to the floor.

The little room reverberated with sound as the acrid smell of cordite and gunpowder mixed with a fine mist of broken plaster. My eyes stung and my ears were ringing like church bells pealing benediction. I looked down at Rojas. He was groaning and holding his side. The sterile drape had been ripped and splattered with blood, plaster, and splinters of glass. I pulled off the sheet to assess the damage.

He had taken a bullet through his right flank. Part of his ilium was shattered, and the muscle torn, but that was all. I stemmed the bleeding with a sponge.

"Is he dead, Doctor?" I read his lips, my ears still ringing from the shots.

I nodded. "He's dead, Fernando." My voice came from far away. "Thanks for saving my life."

His lips moved again. "You saved my life before, Doctor. Now we are even. Am I hurt bad?"

"No. A flesh wound."

He smiled at me through clenched teeth. "Can you fix it, Doc?"

I grinned reassuringly. "You bet. We're in the right place. Just lie back."

He nodded. "Tell me something, Doc? How much you gonna charge?"